THE
TIGRESS
AND THE
YOGI

BOOK ONE OF THE SADHANA TRILOGY

A NOVEL

SHELLEY SCHANFIELD

THE TIGRESS AND THE YOGI

LAKE
HOUSE
BOOKS

Lake House Books,
Ann Arbor, Michigan

(The Sadhana trilogy ; book 1)
LCCN 2015916485
ISBN 978-0-9968491-0-4
ISBN 0996849106
ISBN 978-0-9968491-1-1
ISBN 978-0-9968491-2-8

1. Women heroes--Fiction. 2. Aṅgulimāla--Fiction.
3. Yogis--Fiction. 4. Yoga--Fiction. 5. India--
Fiction. 6. Epic fiction. 7. Religious fiction.
I. Title. II. Series: Schanfield, Shelley. Sadhana trilogy ; bk. 1.

PS3619.C326T54 2016
813'.6
QBI16-600011

Cover, Map, Lineage Chart, and Interior Formatting by Streetlight Graphics

AUTHOR'S NOTE

The setting of this novel bears some resemblance to the land between Himalaya's kingdom and Ganga's river that some 2500 years ago produced Prince Siddhartha, who became the Buddha. However, this work is a fantasy. The author makes no claim of accuracy, but rather has borrowed freely from the myths, religions, and history of ancient India. Anachronisms, geographical anomalies, and misspellings are intentional. Interpretations of the teachings are those of the writer.

*"… a story is a flame that burns no less brightly
if strangers light their candles from it."*

Wendy Doniger
The Hindus: An Alternative History

PRINCIPAL CHARACTERS*

THE VILLAGE OF GAURI

Mala, an outcaste girl
Talu, her father, an outcaste and a tanner of hides
Sujata, her mother, a village beauty disowned by her family

Shakuni, a Kshatriya or man of the warrior caste

Prakash, the village headman, servant to the wealthy village landlord
Valmiki, the village landlord, a Brahmin or man of the priestly caste

THE CREMATION GROUNDS

Angirasa, the chandala or keeper of the cremation grounds
Kirsa, daughter of Mala and Angirasa
Harischandra, a king without a kingdom, a wandering seeker of truth

VARANASI, THE CITY SACRED TO THE GREAT
GOD SHIVA, THE LORD OF YOGA

Ram, the king of Varanasi's beggars
Addhakashi, the most famous courtesan in the Sixteen Kingdoms
Lakshmi, her servant
Ratna and **Simca**, her young apprentices

* For a more complete glossary of characters, places, and terminology in the **Sadhana Trilogy,** please visit *http://shelleyschanfield.com/glossary/*

Amrapali, a courtesan in Addhakashi's household, lover of Bimbisara
Bimbisara, king of the Maghadan clan
Chandaka, their son

Prasenajit, king of the Kosala clan

KAPILAVASTU, CAPITAL OF THE SAKYAN KINGDOM

Siddhartha, prince of the Sakya clan
Suddhodana, his father, the Sakyan king
Prajapati, Suddhodana's chief queen, Siddhartha's aunt
Maya Devi, Siddhartha's mother, who died soon after his birth

THE HERMITAGE

Asita, an old yogi
Nalaka, his student

THE BANDIT CAMP

Rohit, leader of a small gang of petty bandits

Rohit's gang:
Anu
Ketu
Lanka

THE OUTLAW ARMY

Angulimala, Queen of the Outlaws, worshipped as the black goddess Kali

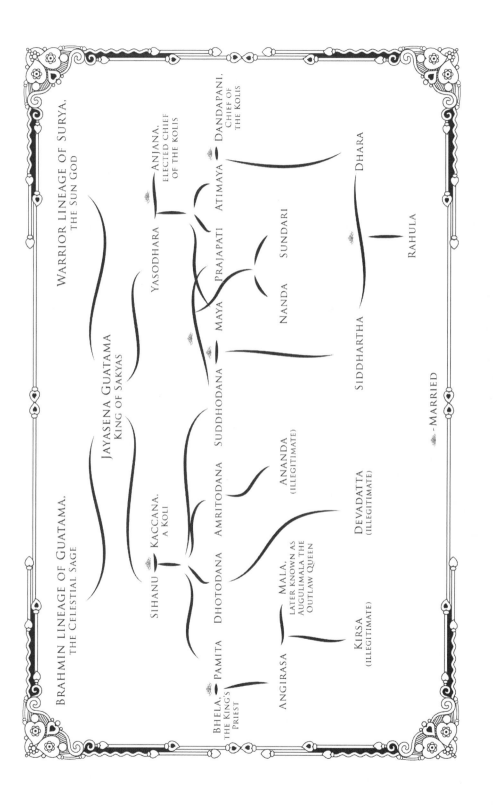

KAMBOJA

GANDHARA

TAXILA

DHAVALAGIRI

KOLI

SAKYA

KAPILAV

KURU-PANCALA

ROHINI

GANG

KOSALA

SURASENA

AYODHYA

Y A M U N A

AVANTI

KAUSAM

VATSA

CHEDI

HIM

INDIA

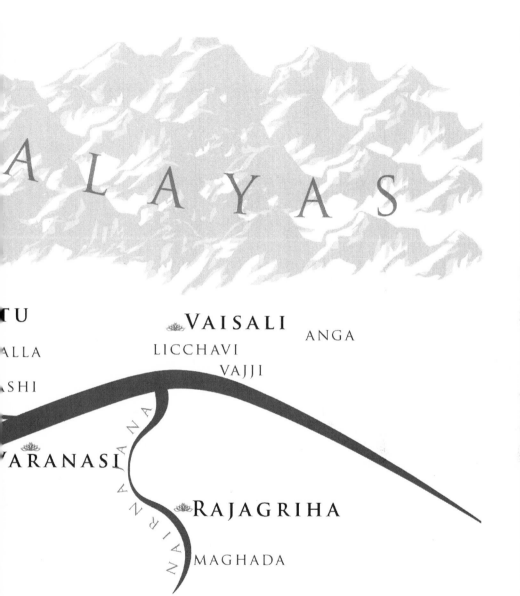

A L A Y A S

TU

ALLA

ASHI

VAISALI

ANGA

LICCHAVI

VAJJI

VARANASI

RAJAGRIHA

MAGHADA

DHAVALAGIRI- TOWN/CITY
KOLI- CLAN
ROHINI- RIVER

PART I

THE TIGRESS AND THE YOGI

THE TIGRESS

A PEACOCK SCREAMED, STARTLING MALA AS she strode along the path from the river. Above, half hidden in the dense leaves, the huge bird flapped to another limb, its iridescent blue tail dragging. It clutched at the branch, nearly toppling, and screamed again, as if to urge her homeward.

Mala had dawdled on Ganga's banks. The monsoon would come soon to the lands of the Sixteen Clans, and the soothing and solitary baths in the goddess's sacred river would stop when the waters ran full and swift. Now dusk was falling fast. Animals rustled in the shadowy underbrush that surrounded the path through the tall sal trees. She hurried to return to her father's hut with the firewood she had collected. Not that he would punish her for staying to bathe. Talu never punished her for anything, but showered her with praise and affection. "One would have to search every kingdom between here and the god Himalaya's peaks to find a girl more clever and hardworking," he liked to say.

Cleverness would not get Mala a husband. She did not take after her round, graceful mother, Sujata. Her father said Sujata was nothing less than the most beautiful earthly avatar of the Devi, the Great Goddess from whom all other goddesses sprang. When her mother smiled, red lips parted to show white teeth. Long, soft waves of hair framed delicate features. Her gold earrings were thin and misshapen, but they glowed against creamy brown skin that smelled like warm earth. Mala had thick lips and a large nose pierced by a small, tarnished silver hoop, and hair like muddy straw. She was only twelve, but already taller than her mother, lanky and ungainly.

No one would ever lie with her like Bapu lay with Ma, murmuring breathless endearments in Sujata's ears when they thought Mala slept.

The trees thinned. Mala quickened her pace. Boys from the nearby village, Gauri, sometimes hid in the tall grasses that grew where the path widened, waiting to jeer and throw clods of dirt. She cringed and clutched the wood to her chest. Lately she had become very aware of how after her baths her damp antariya hugged her body, and how the boys leered, smacking their lips and looking her up and down. She hated them. Thank the Devi that none of them would ever want to marry her.

Even had Mala been beautiful like her mother, she was an outcaste's daughter, an untouchable. Her father was the best tanner along Ganga's river, known even outside their own Kashi clan, but the village shunned her small family. His trade was only a step above the chandala who kept Varanasi's cremation grounds not far downriver. Unlike her father, though, the chandala lived and died in that Shining City that was sacred to the Great God Shiva. To die in Shiva's city meant liberation from the endless wheel of existence, even for an untouchable—or so Mala's father said.

The grasses rustled behind her. Mala clutched the wood tighter. It was heavy, but collecting fuel to help her father was better than stirring hides with him at the curing vats. She hated the stink. Those pits in the earth filled with a reeking stew of human and animal waste, cedar bark, and refuse from the slaughtered beasts' carcasses. It clung to her so that even Ganga's purifying waters could not wash it away. Yet she wanted to help Talu. Not all Gauri's fathers were so gentle and kind. Once, from a distance, she had seen a farmer beat his own child when the boy fell asleep while watching the cows. Kindness, it seemed, was not a matter of caste.

A twig snapped. Mala froze. It must be the boys. She knew she should run, but her legs would not obey her. The forest held its breath. Grasses nearby rustled again, then sharp little teeth and claws sank into her ankle. She dropped the kindling.

"Goddess, protect me!" She twisted around and looked down. A white tiger cub with dark blue eyes was staring up at her.

The cub, hardly more than a ball of white fluff with dark stripes, had left thin scratches on her ankle that were already welling red.

Mala started to smile at the creature, despite the stinging scratches.

14

Then the hair on her neck prickled, and her throat went dry. The mother could not be far.

The cub rose up on its hind legs and pawed at Mala's knee, drawing more blood.

"Ay!" At Mala's cry, it tumbled backward with a little growl that ended up a purr, and it rolled around on the ground, batting at its own tail.

A low, throaty rumble from somewhere in the trees stopped it in mid roll. The cub bounded away toward the sound. Mala couldn't control her shaking, didn't dare look or breathe, certain she would soon feel the mother's fangs at her neck, the animal's long claws ripping her open.

Stillness. Not a sound. Not a movement anywhere. Mala gulped and against every instinct turned toward the forest.

Not more than ten paces away, a huge orange tigress with black stripes emerged onto the path, holding the cub in its mouth. Against Mala's will, she met the great cat's emerald green eyes.

Do not fear me.

Had the tigress spoken? It couldn't be.

I will not hurt you.

It did speak, yet Mala hadn't heard a sound. Shimmering light danced at the edges of her vision. Sparks coursed along every nerve in her body. She had never before felt anything like the energy surging through her at that moment.

The tigress began to walk toward her. The white cub that hung by its scruff from its mother's jaws batted the air helplessly and mewled.

Mala jumped to the path's side. Her knees buckled when the mother stopped next to her, fixing her with that fierce green gaze. The tigress gave another rumbling growl from deep in her chest, then she and her cub disappeared into the forest.

The blood rushed in Mala's ears. Her heart pounded as if it would burst. She had met a tigress! It had spoken to her! Without stopping to pick up the wood she'd dropped, she began to race homeward. Her long legs loved to run, but excitement and fear blinded her. She didn't see the man until too late. They collided and fell to the ground.

Mala instinctively shrank. "Forgive me." When the stranger realized he was in a tangled heap with an untouchable, he would be angry.

A skinny old man with a long beard and matted grey hair streaked with black was sprawled next to her. A dhoti such as homeless holy ones would wear wrapped his loins, but his was smudged and dirty, not the clean white Mala had always imagined a wandering sage would wear. Mala bit her lip. He might be a holy man, but he was filthy.

"What's your hurry?" he asked. The man's eyes, blue as the tiger cub's, were startling in contrast to his sun-darkened face.

Mala put her palms together, touched them to her heart, and bowed. "Forgive me, Holy One," she began, "but I saw a tigress, and I ran—"

"Why bother to rush?"

"Well, I... what?"

The man made a peculiar barking sound. "If the beast wanted to eat you, you'd be a fly-covered carcass right now, dragged deep into the forest so the tigress and her cub could eat in peace. You aren't dead and dismembered, so why should you be afraid?" He gave another bark, almost like a laugh.

"I wasn't afraid!" Mala flushed. "Well, a little. A lot."

He grinned at her. She smiled back.

"It's just as you said, though," she said. "The tigress told me not to be."

"So tigers speak to you?"

She went hot with confusion. Animals spoke to kings and holy men in the stories her father told, but he'd never said they spoke to outcastes. Then she squared her shoulders. "Yes!" It had spoken. She swallowed, a little afraid of her own daring. "That is, I think it did."

"Did it or did it not? If it did, you should heed it. The Devi herself rides the tiger, trusting in its strength and wisdom."

"The Devi rides a tiger?"

"Yes, when she goes into battle as the warrior goddess Durga," the yogi said. Mala had not heard of this Durga. Her mother had never told her the Devi was a warrior, only that the Devi was the Great Goddess and the Great Mother to the whole world, and the Protectress of Children who listened to all prayers, no matter who spoke them. "Have you got any food?"

"No, Holy One, forgive me." She had never had a chance to perform the dharma of offering food to a holy wanderer. No rishi or rishiki had ever come to her family's door. She had always supposed that like everyone else, they avoided outcastes, though if they were all as dirty and strange-looking as this one, it was hard to say why. Her family at least tried to stay clean. "My parents will feed you, though, if you come to our hut," she began, hoping he didn't have magic power to read her thoughts. "That is, if you don't mind…"

"If I don't mind what?" He fixed her with his intense blue eyes.

She did want him to come with her. She had to bow her head to hide a sudden, involuntary smile. He really was filthy.

She looked up to find him grinning and scratching at his matted hair with long, dirty fingernails. "Ah, I see! Who is more unclean, you or me, eh? Bah! That's just Brahmin nonsense about purity and pollution." Mala looked at him with wide eyes, astonished that he dared speak of the gods-on-earth with such disrespect. "They don't want everyone to know that it's purity in your heart that's true dharma," the man continued. "Where food's concerned, I don't care if I'm eating from a Brahmin's skull, like Lord Shiva himself! Take me to your parents' hut—what did you say your name was?"

Still amazed at how he spoke of the Brahmins—what had he said? Purity in the heart was true dharma? Could it be?—she was speechless for a moment. "Mala, Holy One." She bowed again. "Namaste."

"You know the dharma better than many highborn ones, I can tell you," he said with a cackle. He helped himself up with his long wooden staff. "Namaste, Mala." He studied her, but his look was curious, not like the boys' leers. "Garland, your name means in the sacred tongue." She nodded. Though the holy words were forbidden to outcastes, her mother had said Mala's name was an offering to the Devi, and therefore stayed pure. "I'm Asita. Now, which way to something to eat?"

Flushed with excitement and pride, Mala pointed down the path. He strode off. He might look old, but it was all she could do to keep up.

When they arrived at the round hut where Mala's family lived, the cook fire was cold and her mother was nowhere to be seen.

"Please, wait here, Asita-ji," Mala said. "Sit in the shade by our home." She wanted to see if Talu was at the vats, just behind the hut, but she didn't want the sage to see how he made his living. "I will find my parents. They may have gone to gather herbs in the forest. Oh, no." She put a hand over her mouth, remembering the tigress.

"Don't worry. They are safe," Asita said, as if reading her mind. He gazed around. "A good spot, if a bit isolated. That's good thatching." He nodded up at the roof. "Is it your work?"

17

"My father taught me." She couldn't help grinning with pride. "He's very patient. The best teacher! I helped him."

"You honor him." He smiled at Mala. "But there are no other huts," he said. "Where is all your family?"

"There is only Bapu, Ma, and me," Mala said, shifting on her feet. She hoped he wouldn't ask more.

"Surely you have uncles and aunts and cousins," Asita said.

"My father was born into a forest tribe," Mala said with some reluctance. It was not a happy story. "He wandered away from his mother when he was young and couldn't find his way back to his home." Her throat tightened. Talu rarely talked about his childhood to Mala, but her mother had told her some things. It made her heart ache to think of it. The frightened, lost little boy had wandered from village to village, but no one wanted to take him in. His black skin marked him as one of those mysterious folk who had lived there long before the conquering Arya clans came to rule these lands. The hidden ones were savages who offered human sacrifices to the Great Mother, and even the lowest among the conquerors shunned them. Finally a tanner from a squalid outcaste settlement somewhere upriver took him in. He became a slave to a slave, learning his trade from the tanner until he knew enough to escape and live on his own. "So he settled here," she finished, sad and angry. Her father was a better man than those villagers who spat at Talu and his daughter whenever they saw them. She had nothing to be ashamed of, and yet she was.

"Ah. I see." Asita's kindly eyes rested on hers, and she felt as if he did see, he did know how hard it was for Talu as a child and how lonely for the three of them now, being isolated even from other outcastes. "I suspect your parents will be back soon. Let's wait here for them. Fetch me some water, eh, Mala? I have a thirst."

"Oh, oh, I'm sorry," Mala said, all of a sudden remembering more of her father's instructions on offering hospitality to wandering sages. She hoped Asita wasn't angry. He was the first sage she'd met, after all. "I must get kusha grass and make a seat for you, Asita-ji!"

He laughed. "A well-brought-up child." Mala flushed with pleasure. "A drink first, then the grass."

So Mala brought him a water jug and a wooden cup. After she gathered the tall grasses to make his seat, she watched with astonishment as he settled with ease, crossing his legs in one fluid motion so that his right foot rested high on his left thigh, and his left foot on his right thigh.

He finished drinking and wiped his mouth with his forearm, grinning at her. "This," he said, looking down at his legs, "is called the lotus pose."

"What?"

"The lotus has its roots in the dark mud and opens its pure flower to the infinite sky, the way we all have darkness within and struggle to reach the light."

Little needles seemed to prick Mala's skin. He had put into words something she had sensed for a long time, when she awakened in the night, and even sometimes in bright sunlight, when her ears would roar and a red light pulsed around her vision. Although she had always wondered if her parents ever saw this red light, something had held her back from asking them. Maybe she could tell Asita about it. He might know what it meant.

The sage was staring at her. She hesitated to ask about the aura. "May I try the lotus sit?" she said instead. She always crossed her legs at the ankles, but how much harder could it be to rest feet on thighs like that?

"Lotus pose. Or padmasana, if you prefer. Go ahead! No need to ask!" Asita had slipped into it without effort, but Mala had to work at it, pulling one leg over the other. "There. It comes naturally to you," he said. "Well, almost naturally." They both laughed. "It gives a firm base to sit when you want to watch your breath."

Mala was just about to ask what he meant by padmasana and why she would want to watch her breath when he added, "Look at this." He uncrossed his legs and reached for a tiny pebble with his foot. He picked it up between his first and second toes as easily as if he'd used his fingers.

"Oh," Mala said, "I could do that."

"Try it." Asita put the pebble down near Mala's foot.

She stretched out a leg and wiggled her toes, but try as she might she couldn't make them work together to pick it up. "If it was bigger, I could," she said, crushed.

"If it was bigger, anybody could. That's not the point," he said with a fierce frown that frightened her. Suddenly, she wanted very much to impress him.

"The point is to know your body's every muscle and nerve, from your skin to the atoms at the very core of your being."

"A person can do such a thing?" Mala said, and immediately closed her eyes as if to turn their gaze inward at these atoms, whatever they were. Asita laughed, and she opened them again.

"Yes, truly, one can," the sage said. "Within each of us is understanding of the whole universe. You had the right idea—close your eyes to see better! Look within to attain this understanding, and there will no longer be any barrier between you and creation. You become free from all sorrow and unite with Atman."

"Atman?" Mala wrinkled her forehead.

"The Supreme Self."

Then it came to her. Atman was the source of everything, where the Great Goddess and the Great God Shiva came from. It was where people went when they were liberated from the wheel of existence. Of course, she would not go there for many lifetimes. As an outcaste, she couldn't ask a Brahmin to offer sacrifices at the eagle altar so as to gain the gods' favor. She had trouble thinking kind thoughts about all the people who despised her little family, as Talu said she should do, so as to keep her karma stainless. He had also said that to die in Varanasi guaranteed liberation. That wasn't much use to Mala. Though it was not more than a day to the Shining City on the nearby great trade road, for a poor tanner's daughter it might as well have been under the sea or up in the heavens.

Talu had always said they must live humbly and show kindness to everyone. That was the way to better rebirths. "Offer flowers to the Devi with no thought of reward, as your mother does at the family altar, Mala. Sing the Great Goddess's praises in simple prayers, and She may grant you her favor and guide your soul to a better rebirth." Mala loved to gather flowers, but she had little patience for chanting endlessly while the little ball of camphor on the stone altar burned to nothing.

Now here was Asita saying that within each person was understanding of all of creation, and gaining this understanding was the way to unite with this godhead. Did she dare ask if even outcastes could do this?

She must know. "Asita-ji," she began.

Just then, Sujata appeared at the forest's edge. She stopped and put her hand up to shield her eyes. "Mala!" Sujata called out as Talu appeared behind her. "Who is that with you?"

THE YOGI

THE SUN HAD SET AND insects sang as shadows swallowed the
nearby forest. Above the wide clearing where the round hut stood,
the stars began to appear. Mala and her parents knelt side by side
in respectful silence by the cook fire that glowed orange against the growing
darkness. Next to Talu, Asita sat cross-legged on the kusha grass Mala had
placed on the hard-packed earth.

Most days Sujata cooked rice to eat for breakfast and they saved some
to eat cold for lunch. Sometimes if Talu had collected some money for
his hides, they had enough for lentils, too, and Sujata would make dal.
They almost never ate anything in the evening. To honor the hermit, Sujata
fried a few vegetables from their garden with the last precious ghee and a
chopped-up onion and boiled most of their rice. After the day's excitement,
Mala was starving. Her mouth watered, but Sujata offered food only to
Asita, who ate with a good appetite. Mala found it impossible not to look
hungry or worried that they were offering the hermit so much when they
had so little. The old man seemed not to notice and ate it all, shoveling the
food into his mouth with dirty fingers.

When he was done, Asita wiped his mouth with the back of his hand.
"A generous and good meal," he said to Sujata. "What a lucky man you
are, Talu, to have a beautiful wife who's a good cook." He looked Sujata up
and down appreciatively. "Now, will you follow the dharma and give a holy
seeker anything he asks? Let me show your wife the pleasures a yogi knows
how to give a woman."

"A yogi? What is a yogi?" Mala sent a questioning look at her father, but Talu was staring at the sage. His jaw worked and his brow wrinkled. Sujata bowed her head, cast a sidelong glance at Asita, and quickly looked down again.

The realization dawned. "But Bapu! He wants Ma?" Mala gasped. This was too much. Her parents were wide-eyed with dismay, Sujata nearly in tears while Talu kept his lips pressed shut. "But it's—it's wrong! Is that what a yogi does?"

"Ha!" Asita let out his strange barking laugh. Her parents jumped. "You mean what does he do to please a woman?"

"No!" Mala flushed with shock and humiliation. "I mean, forgive me, Asita-ji! It's just—ah, what *is* a yogi?" She was completely discomfited, but she could not change the subject.

Asita grinned. "Ah, yes. What is a yogi? He practices the Great God Shiva's disciplines. The Great Ascetic, he is called, the Lord of Yoga."

"Lord of Yoga...?" Mala asked.

Asita cleared his throat. "Remember what I said about looking within. Yoga is a way to do this. It unites all the powers of mind, body, and soul. One who masters its practices yokes his inner self to Atman, which is beyond the sufferings of ordinary life," he intoned, raising his eyes to the heavens.

The prayers Sujata taught her said nothing about being free from suffering, only how to endure it. Mala looked up, following Asita's glance. Her whole being wanted to leap to the stars. Then her spirits collapsed with such suddenness she let out a little cry. To even think such things was forbidden. "But we can't, can we, Bapu?"

Talu cleared his throat. "It is enough for us to say our prayers to the Devi, to treat all others with kindness, and to hope for a better rebirth..." His voice shook a little. Her whole life, Mala had heard this and tried to believe it, but there was a spark in her that fought against her father's gentle, patient ways.

"Atman illuminates the whole universe!" Asita shouted and they all jumped. "It falls on everyone, not just the highborn, Mala! Let your soul soar to the stars." She looked at him, startled. He wagged a finger at her. "Listen, my girl, a tiger spoke to you! You have no need for the rituals the Brahmins perform! That's not how to attain enlightenment! Anyone can become one with this light by following the Great Ascetic's teachings. Even untouchables."

"Bapu, can this be?" Mala pulled away from her mother. The spark in her burst into flame. She wanted to know more about these teachings that her kind could follow, these teachings that required no priests and sacrifices at the eagle altar. What did he mean by disciplines? And to yoke oneself to the Supreme Self? His words dazzled her.

Talu was watching Asita anxiously and didn't reply.

The yogi smiled. "Don't worry, my friend," he said, chuckling. "Yes, it's dharma to share everything—including a wife—with a holy guest, but I was just teasing about yours, though she's very tempting." Sujata glanced at Asita and lowered her eyes modestly, relieved, but also, it seemed, a little pleased as well. "Lord Shiva can spread his seed wherever he wishes, as long as his pretty blue-skinned goddess doesn't know, but I'm not a god, and I have to save my semen to feed my inner fire. A mortal man can't waste the heat of his tapas with women!"

Talu grasped Sujata's hand in relief and she smiled. Mala looked away, cringing for her father. Would he really have allowed Asita to… she couldn't think about it, and bit her lip so hard she tasted blood.

"Love. Not every man and wife are so lucky." Asita grinned wickedly. "Now, Mala, tell your parents about seeing the tigress and her cub."

"A tiger?" Talu and Sujata said in unison.

Mala put away her thoughts about what her parents did at night and Shiva's seed and stuttered out her story. When she finished, Sujata murmured a prayer over her joined palms.

"*Om,*" her mother whispered. "I bow to the Glorious Mother, Devi Ma, Protectress of Children. She who does not fear, I honor You. *Om.*"

The sacred syllable reverberated in Mala's heart. Though it was the most holy word in all the forbidden tongue, Sujata had told Mala that the sacred *om* was so pure that anyone could say it without polluting its sanctity, and that it was right to begin their simple prayers to the Devi with it. Nonetheless, Mala would sometimes look around after she whispered it, fearful someone had heard. If what Asita said was true, she need not be afraid.

"What do you think it means, Holy One?" Sujata put her arm around Mala's shoulders.

Asita shook his head. "A white cub. Very unusual. Tigers serve the warrior goddess Durga—"

"Tell me about Durga," Mala said.

"Mala!" Sujata admonished. "Let Asita-ji finish."

Asita laughed. "Well, my girl, the Devi has many forms—Sarasvati, the goddess of wisdom; the goddess of wealth, Lakshmi; beautiful Parvati, who tamed Shiva with his own yoga; Durga, the warrior goddess; and dark Kali, who wears a necklace of skulls and dances on Shiva's corpse, to name only a few." He paused and looked into the distance.

The hairs on Mala's neck prickled. A goddess who danced on a corpse. What had Asita called her? Kali? "Please go on, Asita-ji."

"Where was I? Ah, yes. The white cub. Though tigers serve the Devi, they honor the Lord Shiva for his terrible aspect and destructive powers. Now and then they will offer a cub to serve the Lord of Destruction, and they cover it with white ashes and stripes of soot from the cremation ground to mark it as the god's."

"Holy one," Talu said, "do you think the Devi meant to give our Mala a sign?"

"Of course it was a sign." Asita frowned. "As for what it means, who knows? The Great Goddess is as old as Time and as mysterious as Death. She is formless but can take on any form she chooses: warrior, princess, musician, bringer of wealth. Even the avatar of a demoness. A dangerous one, the Devi is."

There was no sound but the fire crackling. Mala sat back on her heels, thinking. Her father taught her that the Devi was also the Great Mother the forest tribes worshipped. "She was here long before the Sixteen Clans came with their sky gods, and the Aryas tried to tame her by giving her their name." So the Devi was not only the gentle guardian of children, but a fierce warrior and a dark, wild deity that danced on Shiva's corpse.

Asita winked at her. "The goddesses can't resist Shiva, you know. He seduced beautiful Ganga. She would have washed the world away with her tumbling waters, but he knelt before her. And what he did then," Asita said with another wink, "well, let's just say he convinced her to let her river run over his head so his strong shoulders would break their fall."

He paused. Mala realized she was holding her breath and gulped some air. She wanted more stories. The few Talu knew he'd told her a hundred times. She never dared get close on the rare occasions when the village's landlord, Valmiki, a powerful priest among the Kashi clan that ruled these parts, came from the city to lead a sacrifice. He would have said she polluted the gods' names just by listening and would have punished her parents and her.

"But what do Shiva and Ganga have to do with Durga?" Mala couldn't contain herself.

"Daughter!" Talu glanced toward Asita. "You will offend our guest."

"No, not at all! She's got a curious mind. Asking questions is the best way to show respect," the yogi said. "It's a sign of intelligence, my girl." Mala's head whirled. She wouldn't have dared look at Valmiki or even let her shadow touch his, much less ask the Brahmin a question. "But I can't tell you everything all at once." He laughed. "So pick one of the Devi's forms and I'll give you her story."

Kali. The dark goddess. Something about her attracted Mala. But no, she sounded too frightening with her skull necklace. "Tell me about Durga." Mala could picture the tigress she had seen bounding through the forest with a shining goddess on her back wielding weapons of fire.

"Ah, well, in an earlier age, there was a terrible bull demon, Mahisa, who tricked the Creator into granting him invincibility as a boon. Not even Indra, the celestial warrior and king of the gods, could defeat him in battle. But the young goddess Durga said if the gods would give her their weapons, she would vanquish him…"

Mala listened, openmouthed, as Asita told how the gods gave their divine weapons to the valiant and beautiful goddess, who carried Shiva's trident, Indra's thunderbolts, and six other weapons in her eight arms, and how Mahisa was so overwhelmed with Durga's beauty that he could not raise his own weapons against her, so she beheaded him and routed his demon army. When Asita finished, she begged for another tale and another, until he kept them awake most of the night with stories of the divine warrior Indra, who offered one hundred horse sacrifices to become king of the gods; of a mighty hero who lost his whole kingdom and nearly made his wife and four brothers slaves in a game of dice with a cheating nobleman; of the mountain god Himalaya's blue-skinned daughter, Parvati, who mastered Shiva's ascetic disciplines and made the Lord of Yoga fall in love with her; and more, until Mala's eyelids drooped.

She jerked awake when Asita's beguiling voice came to an abrupt stop. "And that is enough."

"No!" Mala didn't want to leave the worlds Asita created. "Please, go on."

Talu sighed. "She's tired, Holy One. Forgive her."

"I'm sorry, Asita-ji," she murmured, bereft that he had stopped just when there was so much else to know. Gods and heroes could do anything, couldn't they? Then how could it be that a mighty king wouldn't know he was being cheated? Why couldn't any other celestials but Durga stop the bull demon with their weapons? What were these powers of yoga that Parvati had mastered? Questions bubbled in her mind.

"Ha! Look at that eager face," Asita said, smiling at Mala. "You want more, eh? Well, maybe one day I'll tell you some more. But in the morning I must head to Varanasi."

"Varanasi!" Mala had a horrible thought. He looked so old. That was where one went so that they could be released from the wheel of birth, death, and rebirth and join with Atman. She was devastated. She didn't want him to go. She wanted to listen to his stories forever. "Are—are you going to Varanasi to die?"

Asita laughed. "I'm going to the holy city, but not to die. Not yet, at least. My sins are many. I've the urge to bathe again where Ganga caresses Shiva's Shining City, to plunge into the river in the cool morning and lift my arms to the sky as Surya's chariot rises in the east. When Ganga's washed my karma clean yet once more, who knows where I'll go?"

Suddenly he looked much younger. Mala's crushed spirits rose a bit. "Please, Holy One, come back here to see me."

Asita smiled. "Perhaps one day I will."

THE MURDERERS

F ROM BEHIND A CURTAIN OF purple and white flowers, Mala peered
out across a field of low grasses at her mother, who stood at the door
of their small round hut with its high-peaked roof. Mala smiled.
When they thatched it the previous spring, she had picked just the right
grasses and tied them as well as Talu. "This was the heaviest monsoon in
years," he'd said when the rains were over, "but nothing leaked through
your thatching, daughter."

"Mala!" her mother called.

It was time for the midday meal, but Mala didn't want to go in yet.
She was enjoying being invisible, a dark shadow in the cool shade. Ever
since she was a child, this spot had been her favorite hiding place, and ever
since the yogi Asita's visit, it had become even more important to her. All
through the monsoon season, she sat in the hut in the way he had shown
her, cross-legged with a foot on each thigh. By the time the rains stopped,
she could sit for quite a long time, and she came often to the thicket to
think about what had happened during the day or about the dreams and
visions of the Devi that sometimes visited her at night. In those visions, the
warrior goddess Durga sometimes appeared riding a white tiger, and Mala
woke in the morning feeling she could ride to battle herself.

Sometimes after one of those dreams, she would meet the great cat
with the red-gold coat. Sometimes the white cub, which was growing fast,
was with her. Alone or with her cub, the magnificent black-striped creature
would pause only a moment to look at an awe-filled Mala with those green
eyes lit with yellow flames, then pad away on enormous silent paws.

Her mother called a little louder. "Mala!" There would be no dal to eat today because the warrior Shakuni hadn't paid her father for the hides he had ordered. Talu had gone to the warrior's quarters in Varanasi to ask for his due, but Shakuni refused to see him. Her father came back empty-handed.

So it was that there was only plain rice for breakfast, and not very much at that, but she saved a bit to put on her private shrine to the Great Goddess. The Devi liked simple gifts, her mother had always said, so in the year since the tigress spoke to her, Mala offered many little things here, setting them on the flat stone that served as an altar. Whenever she prayed, she imagined the Devi looked like her own beautiful mother, only in a bright red antariya shot with gold thread, not Sujata's plain, faded red one.

"Ma-al-aa!" Sujata shielded her eyes from the high sun and scanned the forest's edge.

Mala lingered, in no rush to go back. Besides, her hideaway smelled sweet after the stinking pits where she'd stood earlier that morning stirring the curing hides with her father. Though it was obvious he needed her, she had skipped away as soon as he told her she could go. If she stayed long enough, the Devi might whisper in her ear again. The disembodied voice might summon her to the river to bathe, or warn her that the jeering boys were near, or just whisper that all was well. It frightened and thrilled her. It never came during morning prayers with Ma and Bapu at their family altar, and she said nothing of it to them. They seemed to have forgotten Asita's visit altogether.

But the voice made her feel very different from the girl everyone scorned. Whenever the Devi spoke, that energy Mala had felt when she saw the tiger, that Presence, as she thought of it, infused her whole body. The villagers needed the Brahmin Valmiki to intercede with the sky gods like the divine king Indra. It was the Brahmin who said the prayers and offered the chickens or goats to them in rituals Mala was forbidden to attend by her low birth. But did Indra speak to them as the Devi spoke to Mala?

Once, long ago, she had asked her mother if the Devi protected even ugly children like her. "All children are beautiful," Ma had said, and patted her cheek. The passing years and the cruel village boys had not convinced Mala that was true. Still, a real yogi had sat at their fire and told her that a tiger wouldn't speak to an ordinary child, and ever since, her ugliness seemed less important.

Mala's stomach growled. Maybe a bowl of rice would be good right now, but as she rose to go a faint breeze touched her shoulder.

Stay a moment.

"Devi!" Eager to welcome the Presence, Mala sat down, took a deep breath, and closed her eyes, inhaling the flowers' lemony scent and feeling the earth's coolness, still moist though the monsoon rains were long over.

Just as she was about to sink into peaceful stillness, hoofbeats trampled the quiet. Mala's eyes flew open. A man with a long black braid that hung down over the brilliant scarlet silk of Kashi's warriors was cantering down the rutted track that led from Gauri. The earth shook under the hooves of his huge grey horse and a thick cloud of dust followed it. By the hut's door, Sujata pulled the end of her faded red antariya over her head and covered her mouth against the dust.

The rider slowed and trotted toward her mother, stopping a careful distance away so as not to touch her shadow. He said something in a harsh voice and raised a hand that held a rolled-up whip. It was Shakuni, the warrior who had cheated her father. His words were muffled but his tone scared Mala.

Her mother pointed toward the vats and Shakuni disappeared behind the hut.

"Talu! Talu!" Sujata called, but she seemed frozen on the spot.

Once again, Mala started to rise.

Stay!

There was a shout, a cry. A whip cracked and an agonized scream followed.

"Talu!" Sujata cried.

The warrior emerged alone from behind the hut. Sujata stepped toward him but Shakuni raised his whip and gestured angrily. "That will teach him to cheat me!" he shouted. "Let him stew in his own vats." He mounted and jerked his horse around and it took off, hooves drumming on the dusty path.

Sujata bolted around the hut and Mala heard her shriek. "O Devi! He's drowning!"

Mala's heart stopped. Her mind reeled in horror. Those pits were almost as deep as she was tall, filled with a stinking stew that made tough hides as soft as her mother's cheek. What it would do to Bapu...

She rose to a crouch, ready to leave her hiding place, but just then three men emerged from the spot where the track disappeared into the trees. She froze and peered through the vines.

One of the men was Prakash, the village's headman. Just two days ago, Talu and Prakash had fought while Sujata clung to Mala. Mala had shouted at them, "Why are you fighting?" She had ached to do something, anything to come to her father's aid, but her mother clapped a hand over her mouth and wouldn't let go. The memory of that fight held her back.

"*Om,* Devi..." she tried to pray, but her mouth went dry. Prakash and his two companions, strangers unknown to her, jumped aside to let the horsemen pass and proceeded to the hut.

Then Sujata came running from around the back. "Talu! Aieee! Shakuni has thrown Talu in the vats! Help!"

The men did not shout a greeting or say a word as they charged toward her. Mala's stomach dropped. They meant to harm her mother. Faint red light pulsed all around. "*Om,* Devi, *om,* Durga, give me courage," she whispered and went into a crouch.

An invisible hand grasped her shoulder.

No. The Devi's voice.

Mala sucked in a breath.

Prakash, his gold armband gleaming against his bronzed skin, reached Sujata first. Mala's heart thudded against her ribs.

"Help him," Sujata cried.

"Come on!" Prakash seized Sujata's arm. He dragged her behind the hut, the two others following. Then she heard her mother's voice calling, "No, no! You must help him!"

A short scream was followed by Sujata's agonized cries then deep, excited, male voices and raucous laughter. Mala couldn't breathe. Every muscle tensed as her desire to help fought with her fear. The red aura pulsed more strongly.

No, Mala.

The horrible screams went on forever. Just as Mala couldn't bear it any longer and started to rise, they ceased. Prakash and his two companions sauntered into view again and the headman looked around, his gaze falling on the vine-clad trees at the forest's edge.

Do not move.

Mala wanted to scream but managed to remain still and quiet. She shrank into herself, praying her cloak of flowers would keep her invisible.

You are safe with me, the Devi whispered. *Keep still.*

Prakash glanced around once. Then he and his companions walked away, talking in low tones. Even when they disappeared down the track to the village, Mala didn't dare move but stayed there through the long afternoon, listening for Sujata to call. Heat rose in shimmering waves over the field, but Mala was cold, so cold. She shuddered violently. When she tried to rise, her limbs would not obey. She had never felt so alone and helpless. She curled into a ball and buried her head in her arms, and wept off and on.

She wished someone would come then feared someone would. All she knew was that she didn't dare leave her hiding place. In a delirium, she whispered the simple mantra her mother had taught her over and over again. "*Om,* I bow to the Glorious Goddess, Devi Ma who protects all children, She who does not fear, I honor You. *Om.*"

Ma would be all right. Any moment she would appear and call for Mala.

But Sujata didn't appear.

The sun god's chariot had disappeared in the west. A nightjar gave an occasional chirrup and an owl hooted. Dusk came alive with frogs and crickets. She'd never stayed in the forest this late, and she strained with wide eyes to see into the dark. At least the aura was gone.

Nearby, the underbrush rustled. Mala sat up and stared. From a short distance, a pair of green eyes lit with yellow flames stared back through the leaves. A low rumble came from the tigress's throat.

The Devi had sent the great cat to protect Mala.

Another rustle, and a flash of white in the bushes. The cub.

Not fear, but fragile comfort filled Mala. Exhaustion overtook her as she said a final prayer, closed her eyes, and slept.

A shout woke her. Mala sat up, woozy and disoriented. She rubbed her eyes. There was her little shrine to the goddess. Why had she slept here? She looked through the vines. Bright sun poured down over a dozen or so villagers milling by her family's hut. Why had they come?

Then she knew.

"No," she said aloud, and staggered to her feet. "No!" She stumbled from her hiding place.

"There she is!" Someone pointed at her. "There's the tanner's daughter."

"Tell her to keep her distance," another villager said.

"Have some pity!" It was Lal the potter. "Aieee, poor thing." Mala began to walk toward him and he waved his hands as if to push her back into the forest. "You shouldn't see, you shouldn't see." Mala started to run but he stood in her path.

"Ah, poor girl. There's nothing you can do."

She walked around him, her feet like lead.

The villagers stepped away as they turned their horrified faces to her. "Poor girl." "Keep her away from the vats." "What does it matter? She's just an animal, like her father." "Even if she's unclean, she's a child, and she shouldn't have to see them dead..."

"Don't touch her," Lal's wife, Jyoti, said. The potter had reached out as if to grasp Mala's arm, but his wife pulled him away.

They watched in silence as she walked past, step by step. The morning sun was already hot and beat down on her. She was covered with sweat but inside she was cold, cold.

Around the back, not far from the vats, her mother's body was sprawled. Sujata's beautiful face was purple and bloody, her lip split. The sight hit Mala like a blow. "Ma!" she choked, and knelt beside the half-naked corpse, which was already swelling in the heat. "Ma." She would never again rest her head on her mother's breast, feel Sujata's hand stroke her hair.

She looked toward the vats. A body lay face down in the stinking mass of hides and offal. The flesh had already been eaten away to expose the white bones of her father's ribs.

"Bapu," she whispered.

A shadow fell over the sun. Her head throbbed. Red washed over her then receded.

"Mala. Mala. Mala!" Lal poked her with a stick. "Are you all right? Aiee, poor girl. Come along. Your mother's body... the village men will take Sujata to the river. Mother Ganga's waters will carry her away."

A farmer who had sometimes come in the evenings to share a smoke of bhang with Talu came up beside her. "Come. We will lay her on Ganga's breast," he said in a rough voice, not meeting her eyes.

A woman wrapped Sujata in a ragged blanket someone had grabbed from the hut, and the farmer and his son picked up the body and headed to the river, Mala following. When they reached the water, the men let the corpse slide into the water. It floated for a moment, and then drifted away. Mala drifted with it on a river of grief.

She lost all sense of time after that. Somehow they were walking to the village. Mala put one foot in front of another. It was as if her body wasn't hers. She stared down at her bare feet that were not her feet. The very air seemed to resist their steps.

Snatches of conversation came to her. "A good thing his lordship is in the village collecting rents today." "Valmiki'll get to the bottom of this, our wise Brahmin." "Wise Valmiki? Ha, he's nothing but a crafty priest." "Hush, you shouldn't say that about a twice-born one." "He's crafty, all right—he's the royal Brahmin!" "If he can't find the murderers, no one can."

When they reached Gauri, the villagers dispersed. Mala went to the shade of an old pipal tree that spread its branches and aerial roots just beyond the clustered huts. Valmiki would sometimes sit in its shade to tell stories of the gods to the villagers. She shouldn't sit where the Brahmin sat, but she was too tired to care. She leaned against the trunk and fell asleep.

It was late afternoon when she woke. Someone had put a water jug next to her and a few chapattis wrapped in a large leaf. She sat up and gulped down the water, then brushed the ants off the bread and tried to eat it, but it stuck in her throat.

Not long after, Lal fetched her. "Come. His lordship Valmiki wants to judge the matter."

THE BRAHMIN

THE SUN BEAT DOWN ON the well and altar at the center of Gauri's haphazard round huts. Near the altar, a low brick structure laid with geometric precision in the shape of an eagle, a white awning had been set up. The Brahmin Valmiki sat under it on a low dais piled with cushions.

Mala stood before him. The eyes of fifty people bore into her back. She no longer felt disembodied or underwater, but her throat was tight, her heart swollen and painful. Sweat and tears ran down her face as she swayed under the sweltering sun, head bowed. Ma. Bapu. Gone. She didn't want to believe it.

She took a breath and raised her eyes slightly to glance at Valmiki. Never had she been so close to one of the gods-on-earth. He would pass judgment. She must tell him what had happened; tell him who the murderers were. They would pay!

The red aura danced around her. It signaled the Devi's protection, she was almost sure, though it frightened her. But why did the goddess protect her and not her parents? Why did she deserve to be saved? The aura subsided. She lowered her eyes and let her tears flow.

Valmiki cleared his throat and spoke in a loud, clear voice. "From what the villagers say, there is no question but that Shakuni was within his rights. The tanner sold him goods of poor quality." Mala raised her head in astonishment. He was the finest tanner around, she wanted to say, but the words stuck in her throat.

Murmurs rose from the villagers. "That's right." "It's true." "A cheater, that's what he was."

"No, he was an honest man," someone said.

Yes. Bapu was honest. No matter the consequences, she would speak. She straightened and sought Valmiki's eyes, but under his haughty stare her words withered.

Even in this heat, his brow, which was shaved back to the topknot of long hair, was smooth and dry. The sacred thread that signified that he had been born twice, first from his mother's womb and again when he entered into study of the sacred Vedas, and that he would free himself from the endless cycle of birth and death in this lifetime, was pure white next to his skin.

If she was very good and fulfilled her dharma, she might return as one privileged to wear the thread, a merchant's son, perhaps, or even a brave and noble Kshatriya. It was too much to dream of being a holy Brahmin. "To serve others and offer them kindness no matter how they treat you," Bapu always said, "that is our dharma." Since childhood, this had filled her with resentment. The other children were cruel to her. It went against something inside her to be kind in return, but her father had believed this was her duty, and she tried to do as he asked. But Talu was dead. He could not guide her; his kindness would no longer be her beacon, and her mother's love would no longer ease her hurt. A bitter taste filled her mouth.

"It is unfortunate Talu stumbled into the pit of hides while Shakuni beat him," Valmiki continued. "A gruesome death, to be sure, but nothing the warrior can be held accountable for."

Mala's heart thudded in her chest like the hooves of Shakuni's horse. Though it was only yesterday, it seemed like a lifetime ago they had drummed on the dusty path. If she could have been brave and strong, she could have prevented her parents' deaths. But the Devi had held her back—or had Mala only imagined that? Perhaps she was simply weak and cowardly. And now, before the tall, white-clad Valmiki she once again shrank—guilty, impure, just like the village children always said. An outcaste whose words counted for nothing against a Kshatriya's.

If only she had the weapons the gods gave Durga.

Valmiki cleared his throat. "Now, they say Talu's woman was raped and murdered," he said. "As far as we know, she committed no crime, and so this is against dharma. You must identify your mother's attackers, or I cannot mete out the proper punishment."

Heavy silence prevailed over those gathered near Gauri's well. Mala's blood thundered in her ears, and her breath was ragged. The Brahmin glanced at the attendant next to him, who immediately offered him water in a silver cup.

Valmiki reached for the cup and took a sip. Mala suddenly realized she was thirsty. She had a powerful urge to dash up to him, smack his face, and seize that cup and drain it. The red throbbed. Her pulse raced, her senses became very acute. She heard every whisper in the crowd and their slightest moves. Her arms and legs tingled.

"Or perhaps your mother had a lover," the Brahmin continued. "Your father became jealous and murdered her."

Anger and shame choked her, but she managed to cry "No!"

"No, you say?" Valmiki said. "Then once again I ask. Among these good people, do you recognize your mother's attacker?"

Mala straightened and turned, looking for the headman, but at that very moment someone bellowed.

"Valmiki!" Everyone jumped. All heads turned. No one saw or heard Mala. She dropped her arm in dismay.

A tall yogi, his hair and beard matted and tangled and streaked with grey, naked except for a dirty white dhoti, stepped forward and planted a walking stick in the dust.

Mala's dismay changed to wonder. It was Asita, ragged and filthy as when she met him.

"You pious hypocrite," Asita said. "What are you up to?"

Valmiki jerked as if struck. The villagers took a collective breath. He was talking to the golden-skinned priest the way everyone talked to her.

"Scared you, did I, O great billy goat of a Brahmin?" Asita laughed. He looked around.

A nervous titter rose from the watchers but died instantly as Valmiki, struggling to regain his haughty composure, glared at them. For a few moments the only sound was the birds chattering.

"Namaste," Valmiki said at last. He put his palms together and lowered his head over them. "Forgive me, I don't recall your name."

"Of course you do. You haven't forgotten our debate at the courtesan

Addhakashi's banquet," Asita said with a grin. The Brahmin's lips pressed into a thin line. "You'd like to forget I won that debate."

His rudeness to the Brahmin took Mala's breath away. She stared at him, hoping to make him look back at her, but he didn't see.

Sweat beaded on the silent Valmiki's face. "Ah, yes," he said. "I do recall now. You were once a Brahmin, were you not? But you rejected your true dharma. You favor allowing everyone to hear divine words, but everyone knows for even a single syllable of our sacred Vedas to fall on an outcaste's ears pollutes them." Valmiki crossed his arms across his chest and raised his chin.

"But who needs the Vedas?" Asita's blue eyes glinted in his dark face. Gasps from the villagers, then murmurs. "We solitary seekers know that the Forest Teachings, the distilled knowledge of hermits and yogis, words of the highest wisdom, may fall on all ears like the songs of birds. Like sunlight, they confer shining blessings equally, no matter one's caste."

Two red splotches flamed on Valmiki's cheeks. "The goddess of speech herself gave us the Vedas. They tell us how to be holy and pure."

Asita turned. His gaze rested briefly on Mala. Her heart leaped. If only Asita would say something to her, it would break the spell the headman had cast.

But he looked away with no sign of recognition. "You don't need him to pray to the gods for you, or to tell you what's holy and pure. You don't have to listen to me, either, just listen to your own hearts. Look inside your own minds."

Valmiki regained some self-control. "Do not scorn the dharma, Asita-ji." His lips curved into a stiff smile as he signaled his attendant, who filled a cup with water and handed it to Asita with a bow. "And where have you been all these years?"

"On a pilgrimage in Himalaya's kingdom, to a cave on the sacred mountain Dhavalagiri. It is an ancient place, where many sages have practiced the Great Ascetic's yoga, seeking freedom from the endless round of birth and death."

"And you have returned to us to share your wisdom?" The Brahmin crossed his arms.

"To share the wisdom of the ancients. The great sage Kapila spoke to me across the generations," Asita said.

"Pray, what did that voice from the distant past tell you?" Valmiki said, amused.

"He said the Brahmins' time is coming to an end. The old gods are dying, Valmiki, and soon no one will need you to lead the sacrifice." The Brahmin paled. Everyone stood breathless, in utter stillness.

Asita belched. Everyone laughed except Mala and Valmiki, whose mouth turned down in disgust. "How about some food?" he said, patting his stomach. "Send someone to get me something tasty, and while they do, tell me what's going on here. Can't be any ordinary village matter, eh? It takes more than a squabble over stolen eggs to get you away from your mansion in Varanasi. Cattle theft, perhaps? Ah, no. More likely it's time for your tenants to pay their rents."

Valmiki whispered to his attendant, who went scurrying off with a village woman to get provisions for the yogi.

Then attention returned to Mala. The Brahmin explained the situation. Asita watched her, a strange light in his eyes. He did know her. He must tell them.

"So as you can see, this girl has suffered a wrong," Valmiki finished. "And we are civilized, here in Gauri. Even for a crime against an outcaste, we seek to know the truth. How fortunate we are that such a wise sage has appeared to help us judge this matter."

Asita's stern gaze swept the crowd. "Yes, I'll help you judge. You won't find the truth about this crime in your sacrifices. Who knows what happened? Step forward and speak." His words hung in the air, and the villagers all looked everywhere but at the yogi. Asita's eyes came to rest on Mala. His face softened.

Hope stirred. He remembered her. He would help her find justice. But he said nothing, only watched her.

Mala licked her lips.

"Speak up, girl," someone said. "Tell us what happened."

Then someone else whispered, "Prakash always wanted the tanner's fair-hipped wife, didn't he?" "They were even betrothed, but she didn't want to marry him."

More whispers. Mala stiffened and strained to hear. Never had she heard a hint of this from her parents. It struck her that the fight between Bapu and the headman had everything to do with it.

"Hush," another said softly, "Prakash has the Brahmin's favor…"

"She was a good woman. She knew what Prakash was like," the farmer who had taken Sujata's body to the river muttered. "But when she refused him, he, well, I heard…"

The farmer muttered something under his breath. Whispers flitted around Mala's ears like little gnats, and she tried to brush them away.

"Sujata was a slut," a voice called.

"Sujata?" Valmiki was clearly startled. "Sujata you say?" The Brahmin took out a white linen cloth, wiped his forehead.

"She was kind and virtuous," the farmer said. "And beautiful. My lords," he addressed Valmiki and Asita, but before he could say more, a woman in the crowd called out.

"She dishonored her family." Mala turned to the speaker. An old woman stared back with deep, dark eyes that seemed so like Sujata's, except that Ma's eyes were filled with love and this woman's were filled with hate. Mala could not look away from them.

"Priya-ji," the farmer said to the woman. "How can you?"

Priya set her mouth in a grim line and looked away.

"Speak, Mala," Asita said.

Mala turned to him. She desperately wanted to speak. Where was the courage she found in her dreams of Durga?

"The girl will not speak for herself, and no one speaks for her. My hands are tied," Valmiki said, mopping his brow again. "Perhaps… perhaps it is her karma. She did something in a previous life that bears this evil fruit."

Mala despaired. Whatever she had done in a past life, she had no idea what it was or how to atone for it.

"Who can say?" Asita countered.

"The gods can say!" Valmiki said. "They know our deeds in past lives determine our karma. From evil actions, a highborn sinner in one life may be a blind worm wriggling in the muck in the next. All know this. Each must follow the dharma of his birth: a Brahmin invokes the gods; the Kshatriya rules men; Vaishyas are traders and guildsman; and Shudras serve. Outcastes are born such because the sins of past lives follow them. They can only hope for a better life in their next rebirth."

"Mark this, Valmiki. Across the generations the sage Kapila told me this:

A son of the Sakya clan will come and turn the wheel of a new dharma," Asita began. "There'll be no more castes and talk of purity—"

Valmiki interrupted him with an incredulous laugh. "The Sakyas? Those upstarts? Absurd." But then he frowned. "Child," the Brahmin said without meeting her eyes. "Rest assured the murderer will suffer the consequence of his actions, whether it be in this life or the next. Such wickedness violates the dharma, the divine justice that rules even the gods." He glanced at Asita. "Is it not so?"

Asita grunted. "If the law is divine, we humans should keep out of it. Stick to compassion and mercy, forget punishment and revenge."

Hot tears sprang to Mala's eyes. Talu. Sujata. *Gone.* No one else here cared about her. Not even Asita. Valmiki must be right. Mala had sinned in a previous life, so she could not help the two people she loved most in this one. For her cowardice, she would surely be born that blind worm in the next.

"When the one who attacked the girl's mother is caught, the criminal will be punished according to our sacred laws. Now return to your duties, good people."

The villagers remained where they were, hoping for more amazing conversation between the sage and the Brahmin, but it was Lal the potter that spoke.

"Your Honor. O wisest of the twice-born!" The Brahmin stared down his nose. The potter knelt. "O most excellent lord Valmiki, who'll take care of the girl?"

Mala's heart lurched.

The potter scooted forward on his knees, placed his palms together in front of his face, and bowed until his forehead touched Valmiki's feet. "The poor girl. Someone has to care for her, Your Honor." Lal sat back on his heels, glancing up at the Brahmin. "My wife works too hard." Laughter rippled through the crowd. Lal looked confused. "This girl's strong. She can carry clay from the river and water from the well. My wife will be pleased to have the extra hands. I'll take the poor thing in, Your Honor."

"Well, Asita?" Valmiki stared at the sage. "What do you say to that?"

For a moment, her heart soared. Asita would take her with him, back to this sacred peak Dhavalagiri. It came to her that yoga must be what gave him such power over ones like Valmiki. She didn't care if she had to live in a cave. It didn't matter, just so she could get away from Lal, from the village, from this horrible nightmare, and learn yoga's secrets.

"Please… take me with you," she said.

Asita looked into her eyes. The village fell away. She was on a high peak covered in snow, the sun dazzling in a cold blue sky. Wind howled. No, it was a demoness, a being, a woman wearing a necklace of skulls, whirling in a wild dance. Suddenly, the being stopped, and Mala saw burning eyes and a long, red tongue. She cried out in fear.

The mountain disappeared. Mala staggered. She was standing under a hazy, hot sun in Gauri. She blinked and looked around, not sure what had just happened.

Asita looked at her sadly and sighed.

"He must treat her kindly, without thought of reward." He gave Lal a baleful look. "Or I will curse him."

"Oh, yes, I'll be good to her, honored among the wise," Lal said, looking down and twisting his hands.

"Then it's settled. She is yours, potter." Valmiki stood and headed to his curtained litter.

"Thank you, Your Honor!" Lal cried. "I'll take good care of her!"

"The gods rejoice at your compassion," Valmiki said over his shoulder. "Well, wise Asita." He turned to where the yogi had been standing and fell silent. Mala raised her head. Asita was nowhere to be seen.

"He's gone!" a villager cried.

"He used one of the yogi's eight powers and disappeared in a flash of light," another said.

"I saw it!" "So did I!" Everyone began to talk at once. The voices came from very far away and the ground under Mala seemed to give as if she were falling down a deep hole.

"Couldn't have been any ordinary yogi, but Lord Shiva himself."

"Shiva the Auspicious One? Come to Gauri?"

Someone laughed. "You're all seeing things. The gods don't even know this miserable village exists."

"Hush! Don't say such things. His lordship Valmiki will hear."

If Valmiki heard, he gave no sign. His four bearers carried his litter away as the people dispersed. Only the headman remained, along with his two companions, holding Mala in his mad gaze.

41

"Follow me," Lal said. She dragged her feet after the potter while he chattered excitedly. "Your poor mother, aieee, such a terrible thing. You'll be a help to my wife. I liked Talu. He was a good man." Lal shook his head. "Or so I thought. Who would've guessed he sold bad hides? Now, remember, be careful what you touch around the family. There's a lean-to by the side of our hut. You can sleep there. My son is eight, my daughter five. Of course you're too old to have played with them, but you'll get along."

No village child had ever played with Mala. Ever. She only half listened as she followed in a daze, her throat constricted with tears she didn't dare cry. She felt the Devi had tested her courage and she had failed. "But I'm just a child," she whispered. "O Devi who protects all children, forgive me…"

Lal turned around. "Eh, Mala? Did you say something?"

"No, nothing." She didn't know how to fight for herself or anyone else.
You must learn.

The Devi was answering. Mala stopped, waiting for more. Perhaps she was hearing things.

"Show respect," the potter said, clearing his throat. "I'm your master now."

How could she learn? She was a slave. "Yes, Master Lal."

"That's better."

Mala's heart sank like a stone thrown into Ganga's holy waters, and it was as if those waters closed over her head, muting everything.

THE DEVI

Lal's wife, Jyoti, was furious that he'd brought Mala home.

"She can clean up the animal droppings in the yard and take away the night soil," the potter said. "She can dig clay from the riverbanks and bring it back here."

"But she can't sleep in the hut! She's an untouchable!"

"She can sleep there, where the chickens go in the rain." He pointed at a lopsided frame attached to the side of the potter's hut, a flimsy lean-to that had no walls and was covered by rotting thatch. A few clucking hens pecked at the earth nearby. The thought of her own snug home made Mala want to weep.

"Well, I suppose, but she looks lazy."

"She doesn't. She looks strong as a young buffalo."

Jyoti's eyes flicked over Mala and narrowed. Then she looked at her husband with danger in her eyes. "I know what you're thinking."

Mala blinked back tears. Jyoti's tone made her wary.

Lal looked shocked. "What can you mean? She's hardly more than a child."

"She'll grow."

"Jyoti," the potter said, and shook his head.

Shoulders tensed, Mala glanced sidelong at Jyoti. She had wispy dark hair streaked here and there with grey and a thin face with a nose like a mynah's beak. In one bony arm she clutched a bowl of rice, in her other hand a long wooden spoon. She appeared to be a bit older than Lal, who was more pleasant looking, with his plump face and round little belly hanging over his dhoti.

After a whispered, vehement discussion between husband and wife, Jyoti fixed her with a baleful stare.

"Hmmph," she muttered after a moment. "All right. But I think she'll eat too much," she said, shaking the spoon, "and work too little."

Mala's shoulders eased a little.

They put her to work immediately with sweeping away chicken droppings, turning jumbled firewood into a neat stack, and weeding a raggedy little vegetable patch. The tasks occupied her, at least. The horrors of the day before seemed a dream, though her aching heart told her it was not.

Jyoti watched Mala, then took the potter aside. "She is a better worker than I thought," she said to Lal, loud enough for Mala to hear. "But it's just her first day. Time will tell if she's lazy and doesn't earn her food."

By midafternoon Mala had finished with everything the potter's wife asked, and she asked to go to the river for the tall grasses that grew along its banks. Jyoti gave a reluctant and suspicious yes.

Mala took a path that went the long way round the village and into the forest, a path that didn't pass her parents' isolated hut. She began to think about what it would have taken for her to truly name the headman as the murderer.

She didn't know, but she must learn. How to learn? The only way seemed to do it. She would have to face the headman again. She didn't have the strength. But would she get it? Would she ever have the strength to avenge them?

Her feet turned to lead as she approached the river. She envisioned her mother's corpse still floating on the water, her eyes beseeching Mala to help. It took all her courage to proceed. But once she reached the goddess's smooth, deep waters, peace floated into her heart on the current's whisper and the cool breeze that rustled the grasses, and its touch released the sobs she'd held back while she faced Valmiki.

She dried her tears. "Thank you, Ganga." The goddess's waters accepted everyone, no matter their caste. She had carried Sujata away to the Lord of the Dead's realm. Mala did not know any prayers for the dead, but Ganga knew how kind and loving Mala's mother had always been. She would tell Lord Yama. He would send Sujata to a better life on the next turn of the wheel. And no matter what the Brahmin or anyone said, Yama would judge Talu kindly, too. Her father had been a better man than anyone in the village.

Mala plucked a large armful of thick fronds and hurried back. When she returned, the potter and his wife watched her as she tied grasses into the lean-to's thatch. The rest she wove into a mat for sleeping. No sooner had she finished tying the mat's edges when her master sent her back to the river for more grasses. When she returned, they leaned a rickety ladder against their hut and instructed her to climb onto the thatched roof.

"It leaks, and the monsoon is coming," Lal said.

She worked there until time for the evening meal, when Jyoti put a meager plate of food on the ground next to the lean-to.

"Well," Jyoti said. "That's a fair enough job, girl. You can come down now." With hands on hips, the potter's wife watched, ignoring the chickens that approached the plate of food. Carefully, Mala moved to the roof's edge, which was not too far from the ground. She should be able to jump down, but in the growing dark it was hard to see where to grab hold or put her feet for support. Finally she rolled onto her stomach, intending to squirm her way to the edge and lower herself, but she lost her grip and slid down the thatching. She tried to stop herself with her feet, but her toes couldn't gain a hold. She landed atop the food dish. For a moment, she lay stunned, looking at the rice scattered in the dirt.

"Clumsy girl!" shrieked Jyoti. "That's all the food you get! Do you think we have enough to waste like that?"

Jyoti grabbed the twig broom leaning at the hut's door and brought it down over and over again on Mala's head and shoulders. Each stroke made Mala feel more worthless, that indeed she was clumsy and wasteful.

Lal came out and made a feeble attempt to calm his wife, then shrugged and returned to the hut. Jyoti found the most sensitive places to land the blows. Her fat little son and skinny daughter stood watching from the doorway, fingers in their mouths. She struck until her anger seemed spent, then without a backward glance, whirled and strode into the hut, followed a few moments later by the children, who had not said a word.

Lal came out later with a folded leaf that held some rice. "She loses her temper sometimes, but she doesn't mean harm."

Whatever Lal said, there was no doubt Jyoti meant those bruises. Mala hated her. "I'm sorry, Bapu," she whispered aloud. She hated working for the dreadful woman, but she had no choice.

Later, as she nibbled at the rice, Mala remembered what Talu had said. That she was the cleverest and hardest working girl in the Sixteen Clans.

She would not work for that woman. No, she would dedicate her efforts to someone who was worthy. "Bapu," Mala whispered and closed her eyes. "I will work hard to make you proud."

Mala adjusted to life with Lal and Jyoti and their two children, who were so silent she sometimes forgot they were there. Jyoti never called them affectionate names or hugged them impulsively as Sujata had hugged Mala. It struck her that if Talu could see them, he might feel sorry for the way they waited listless and bored for any attention from their mother. He might cluck his tongue, saying something about how their mother was so cold and unloving, compared to warm, laughing Sujata.

Pity did not make Mala care about these dull children, who showed no concern for her. It only made her ache for her own parents. She missed Sujata's simple daily puja at her altar in the hut, the only worship Mala knew, to offer flowers or a handful of berries to the Devi. Though she was not allowed in Lal's home, Mala had glimpsed inside it. It was bigger than her family's hut, but dark and shabby compared to the spare but cozy household Sujata kept. There was an icon in a corner, but she had never heard Jyoti give more than a cursory prayer to the warrior god Indra to throw his thunderbolt and bring rain or to the goddess of wealth Lakshmi to send buyers for Lal's pots and plates.

Mala did everything she was asked, dedicating her work to her father's spirit. That did not always deter Jyoti's beatings, which covered Mala's dark skin with red welts oozing blood. Sometimes Lal tried to help after these outbursts. It did no good. She considered running away. She might find the outcaste village upriver where her father had learned his trade, but Talu had almost never spoken about the place, and never with any fondness. What had Sujata told her? He was a slave to other slaves. No, best to stay with what she knew. Jyoti was cruel, but Lal was not unkind. Like most of the villagers, he was poor, yet he did not starve her. She was more willing to work for him, to be sent to the river for clay, where she could hide herself amid the tall grasses near Ganga's banks and bathe.

The villagers wanted as little to do with her as she with them. They had only one thing in common: fear of her mother's murderer, Prakash, who had a reputation for violence not just in Gauri but in Varanasi, she heard. Her cowardice before Valmiki ate at her, but no one else had the courage to stand up to him either. At least he rarely came to the village. When he did come, she hid from him.

There were small joys. Her favorite task was to gather wood. She took the roundabout path through the forest to Ganga's river to avoid passing her family's hut, now deserted and in her mind haunted. In search of clay, she found a large, flat, dark stone which she put at the bottom of the basket. It was heavy carrying that and the clay home, but worth the effort.

In a secluded little spot just beyond the potter's kiln, Mala made a new shrine with the stone. No one would recognize it as such. The other women in the village worshipped the Devi in the form of a demigoddess that lived in a tree near the well, tying colorful strips of cloth around the trunk to ask for the nymph's blessings. When Mala had once tried to join them, they shunned her.

No matter. She preferred her secret shrine. Though she was given little food, every day she would offer some rice to the Devi and say a prayer that she would learn to be brave. The Great Goddess would know that she was always hungry and understand how hard it was to make such an offering. Yet she rarely heard the goddess's voice. Maybe what the Devi wanted was a different kind of offering, but Mala had nothing else to give.

Then she remembered what her bapu had once said. "Do not perform an action for the reward it may bring. Perform it because it is right; it is dharma." She should make her offerings without thinking of what the goddess would give her, but how she could serve the goddess. Easier said than done, but it felt right to try.

One day, a year or so after she came to live with Lal, she set out in the late morning to bring back firewood. She did not head toward the river but was drawn into the forest, as if it willed her to enter its green depths. As she got further from the village, she found it harder to continue through the thick undergrowth, but still something drew her.

Even though by now the sun was directly overhead, it was very dark.

She heard strange calls that did not sound like animals, and the hairs on her neck prickled. Tree nymphs or worse could be watching from the shadowy undergrowth. Stinging midges hovered in clouds about her head and the huge forest leeches, sensing her body heat, slithered fast as snakes over rotting vegetation. When she hurried to avoid them they sped up.

She scrambled along on an overgrown path, crashing through dry, thorny bushes. At last, covered with scratches, she broke out into open space, lost her balance, and sprawled on soft, cool dirt. She rested her cheek on the earth and inhaled a moist freshness, the scent of her mother's vegetable garden after a rain.

At the thought of Sujata, Mala gave herself to tears. When she had cried herself out, it was strangely silent. No birds sang or insects buzzed. She pushed herself off the soft ground onto her knees and brushed away dirt and twigs.

Fragrant trees shaded the grove, though open patches among the leaves admitted some dappled sunlight. After the thick, dense forest, this place was like a spacious and cool green temple. There was a tall, slender stone pillar set in a circle of stones in the very center. The snake-loving Nagas, the most fearsome of the hidden forest tribes, must have sacrificed here once, though the vines covering the linga indicated it had been some time ago. Nagas had not been seen near the village in years, but everyone still feared them. Sometimes when a village man disappeared, people whispered that the dark ones had offered him to their Great Mother, She who was ancient as the earth and had been here before the Aryas brought their sky gods.

Mala shrugged off a whisper of unease. It was so peaceful and beautiful, there could be no danger. She crawled to a tree trunk and curled up against it to rest awhile. The birds and insects remained silent. Her own breathing was loud in her ears. It felt good just to rest her hand on her belly as it rose and fell. Soon she was aware of nothing else.

Her back against the tree and her head nodding, she slipped into a strange new place of lights and sounds, somewhere between waking and sleeping. At first she was afraid, but the tree's roots cradled her and the earth's coolness was like a soothing caress. Light fell from the leaves above like drops of water. A little squirrel with black stripes came near and opened its mouth and spoke, but she could not understand the words. It gave a little squeak and ran away, and as Mala sat up to call after it, a vision snatched her breath.

On a tigress's back, a many-armed, beautiful goddess sat in radiant splendor. All her waving hands carried weapons, save two. One she held before her breasts in a strange gesture, thumb and forefinger touching. The other she held out toward Mala, and from its upward-facing palm shot a beam of light. Mala spread her body full length before the vision and placed her forehead on the ground.

"*Om,* Great Goddess," Mala said. "*Om!*"

There was no answer. Mala opened her eyes and raised her head. The bejeweled goddess dismounted from the tigress and with her two free hands lifted her ruby and diamond garland from around her neck, smiling as she did so.

I am Durga, Mala. Durga held out the garland. *One day this will be yours.* Durga smiled, but as Mala reached for the sparkling necklace, the red jewels began to drip blood. Mala cried out and woke with a start.

The vision flitted in the shadows of her waking mind like a wild animal hiding in the forest's shadows. Dusk was approaching. In the distance, there was something or someone: a horse whinnied, human voices called and laughed. Or did she imagine it? Was Durga only a dream?

No. Durga was real. The Devi had shown herself in her avatar as the warrior goddess. Warriors had strength and courage. The Devi meant for Mala to be strong and courageous, too. But what did the jewels dripping blood mean? When a warrior fights for justice, blood is shed. That must be it.

Mala wanted to think more about what the blood meant, but there it was again; a horse, voices. Her curiosity about what lay beyond the trees grew very strong.

Then her belly rumbled. She was hungry, but she was no many-armed huntress or warrior, and she was afraid. What lay beyond might be dangerous. She was not yet brave and strong as a goddess. The question was which direction to take, for an anxious look around didn't reveal where she had entered the grove.

Then the squirrel with the little black stripe on its back scampered past her to a break in the shrubbery, showing her the path. In some places it was clearly marked and in others more difficult to follow, but it was headed in the right direction, back to Gauri. Mala did not hurry.

THE WANDERER

S HE HAD LIVED ALMOST A year serving Lal and his family. The moon waxed and waned; the monsoon came and went. Now came the season Mala liked best, the cool season after the rains.

She lay under the river of stars watching the Seven Celestial Sages sparkling as they wheeled across the inky sky, their wives gathered in a winking cluster behind them. She had learned a little more of the gods from Lal's children since she came to live in the village. They laughed at her ignorance but at least would tell her the stories they knew. They said the millions of stars were Indra's many eyes. He must see every living thing, she mused, even her. Not that he would care about a poor outcaste. He was too far away, up there in his heavenly city.

Not like the goddess. She was right here on earth. Mala had seen the Devi's avatar Durga with her own eyes. She remembered the tales Asita told—it seemed so long ago, though it was hardly two years—about how Durga fought the buffalo demon; how Parvati won Lord Shiva's heart; and Kali—what was it Kali did?—she danced on Shiva's corpse.

Yes, that's what Kali did. She danced. Suddenly Mala remembered the moment she asked Asita to take her with him. That instant when the village had fallen away and she was on a mountain, where the wild woman with the skull necklace whirled in the cold air. It had frightened her so; she hadn't understood it, had pushed the memory away, told herself it hadn't happened.

But it had. The wild woman was the goddess Kali. She had seen Kali dancing.

A burst of energy coursed through her so strongly it seemed her skin would give off sparks. It danced from her toes to the top of her head. The trees around her were filled with it, too, gave off the same sparks up and down their trunks and limbs and illuminating their leaves. She was lifted out of herself, borne upward toward the millions of stars and the Seven Sages. She was free.

Then far away, a tiger roared, and the moment passed.

Once more Mala was earthbound. She stared into the starry sky, subdued, even a little bereft, and yet with a strange sense of peace.

One day, she would know how to be brave. She hadn't saved Ma and Bapu, but one day, she might save someone who needed help. One day, life would be sweet again.

The next morning, it was the birds' singing that made her eyes open. She sat straight up and broke into a sweat. She should have arisen long ago to stoke the kiln so Lal could fire the pitchers and bowls he had painted with the glaze that would become glistening black in the fire. Mala liked to watch his skilled hands shape the vessels, imagining one day that she could do it, even that she might leave Gauri and find a place where she could make and fire her own pots. She struggled with the urge to ask him to teach her. She would tell him how much she helped Talu at his work.

She sighed and cursed herself for a fool. Helping tan hides was suitable work for an outcaste. Making pots was not.

The thought roused her. She would not be observing his skill at the wheel today. Her sense of the Devi's power and nearness, so vivid last night, was replaced by fear. It was long past the time she should have risen. It was strange that Jyoti had not come out already with her broom.

As she rolled onto her side to get up, Jyoti's voice interrupted the birds. "They're too fine for the girl, Priya-ji."

Mala peered out of her shelter. Outside the potter's hut, Jyoti stood talking to the old woman who had said Sujata was no good, that day Mala stood before Valmiki. She always dressed in a fine white robe, her silver hair bound tight at her nape. Mala had never seen her at Jyoti and Lal's hut.

Mala's movement caught the two women's attention. Priya gave her a hard, quick glance, and then turned and walked away, leaving Jyoti with a length of cloth folded over her arm.

"Here, girl," Jyoti said.

Mala scrambled up and went to Jyoti with her eyes lowered. She steeled herself for a blow. When none came, she glanced at the potter's wife, who was looking at her with an unreadable expression.

"The old woman wants you to have this," she said. Mala was too surprised to make a move. "Well, here, take it!" Jyoti threw down the cloth. Mala bent down cautiously to retrieve the thick, soft fabric, expecting to feel the broom at any moment. The cotton was not dyed or decorated, but it was sturdy and tightly woven. She clutched it to her chest, then looked down the dusty street toward Priya. The old woman waited, silent.

"Well, what are you waiting for?" Jyoti said. "Go put it on. Those rags you're wearing don't cover you, shameless girl."

Ever since she had come to the potter's Mala had been wearing the same things, which were now falling apart and always grey with dirt, no matter how she tried to clean them at the river. She hurried to her lean-to and crouched inside, unwinding the ragged old clothes and wrapping herself in the clean cloth. It lay soft against her skin like her mother's gentle touch.

She carefully folded the old rags to use as a pillow and ran from her shelter right into Jyoti. The potter's wife looked her up and down and glowered. Mala raised her chin and straightened her shoulders. Her new garment was nicer than what Jyoti wore. Her mistress's eyes widened, then she turned and walked into the house. Old Priya watched from a distance. There was no beating that day. Afterwards, Jyoti did not leave so many welts when she took her broom to Mala.

Later, puzzled by Priya's generosity, Mala asked Lal's children about the old woman.

"Don't you know her?" Mala shook her head. "Priya-ji is the last of her family," the daughter said, giving Mala a strange look. "Her husband was headman before Prakash. Didn't you know that?" Mala shook her head. She had never known or cared much about anyone who lived in the village. "She has an arm's length of gold bangles, so people are nice to her even though she outlived her husband, a sure sign of bad karma. But you should know. Her daughter was your moth—"

"Hush!" Jyoti emerged from the hut. She hurried to the girl and gave her a slap. "Mala, get busy with the night soil."

Mala stood thunderstruck.

Priya's daughter was Sujata. Priya was Mala's own grandmother. All through the day, Mala did her chores consumed with this thought. Maybe Priya would see what a hard worker Mala was, how much she could help the old woman, and would use a gold bangle to free her from the potter's service.

Time went on, though, and Priya never spoke to Mala. She did continue to bring gifts for her: another length of good cloth; a new wooden bowl to replace the cracked one Jyoti had given her; even a pair of sandals, though Mala preferred to go barefoot; and once, a thin golden hoop for her nose. Always the old woman handed the gift to Jyoti and then waited until she had seen the potter's wife give it to Mala. Then she would turn away.

It was plain that her grandmother would do nothing more than provide these few gifts for her outcaste granddaughter. Hope faded. Still, the gifts were welcome.

ॐ

The monsoon came and went. In her fifteenth year, Mala awoke one morning to find blood between her legs. Trembling, she went to the potter's wife, who gave her some rags and told her how to stuff them with the wool from the pods of shaalmali trees and staunch the flow.

"And stay away from the boys now. You don't want to end up like your mother, that slut."

"My mother was a virtuous woman," Mala shot back. Her daring intoxicated her.

Then the potter's wife began to shake with fury. "You dare sass your mistress, outcaste?" She fell into one of her rages, which had grown fewer since Priya began bringing gifts. Jyoti beat Mala as she had not beaten her for months. Mala gritted her teeth. Red rage danced at her vision's edge, but she vowed she would not show fear or anger or cry out in pain.

At that moment, Lal hurried up, and for once, he defended Mala. "Stop it! Don't you think she suffers enough?" The potter's unexpected defiance stunned his wife into silence. "Leave her alone, woman," he finished. He blinked, as if surprised at his own outburst.

Mala raised her head. His action gave her strength. She caught Jyoti's eye and held it, putting all her anger and hate into it. For an instant, she was ablaze with fury.

Jyoti paled. She turned on her heel and hurried into the hut.

53

Mala slumped, terrified by her own fury.

Lal was staring. "Mala?"

"Leave me alone," she said in a shaking voice, and he scurried away, glancing over his shoulder.

By evening, Jyoti was shouting at her the way she usually did. But after that day, the potter's wife was careful not to raise too many welts.

Under a punishing sun, Mala sweated and strained with a basket of heavy, wet clay. No breeze rustled the tall, dry grasses lining the path from the goddess Ganga's river to the village that day. The hot, still air almost suffocated her. Not far ahead, the dense forest was relatively cool, but heat and exhaustion made her stop and the baked earth burned her bare feet where she stood. She shifted from one foot to the other and hoisted the basket high on her back, drawing a ragged breath and letting it out with a groan.

Master Lal needed the clay to make his jars and pots. If only someone would help. But they wouldn't. The villagers shunned her like a mangy dog.

She was filthy, though she'd bathed before she left the riverbank with her heavy basket. She stank from sweating under the cloudless sky, pale with heat. She wanted to go bathe again and rise from Ganga's waters purified and cool, but if she didn't get back soon she would face Jyoti's broom.

"*Om*, Indra," Mala muttered, "god of thunder, they say you bring rain. Send the monsoon right now and wash me clean!"

She shivered at her own boldness and looked at the sky. No lightning bolt struck her. Well, she hadn't offered the prayer with much respect, and certainly it flew against Talu's teaching that one must perform one's duty without expecting a reward. She grunted, adjusting the basket's straps and settling the load. She plodded toward the trees. Then she halted. Something was crashing through the brush at the forest's shadowy edge, and the shade no longer seemed so inviting.

"Who's there?" The words came out as a croak from her dry throat.

More cracking and rustling. Her heart pounded, half with fear, half with hope. Perhaps it was a tiger. Perhaps the Devi was sending a sign that it was time to leave Gauri, to escape this misery.

Then a dark shape staggered onto the path.

It was a small boar, perhaps wounded, and thus dangerous, ready to attack. Impossible to run; she was near fainting. The beast would be upon her in no time, disembowel her with its long tusks.

It didn't move. She peered into the shadows. No, no tusks. It was too small for a boar. It was a dog, a black dog, skinny and unsteady on its feet, with flies buzzing around it and pinkish grey flesh spotting its mangy coat.

Mala stepped back, losing her balance. She dropped the basket and picked up a stone. It was wild, perhaps part of a pack; there would be others. She waited, tense, but heard nothing more. Her tension eased. Plain to see the dog was too weak to hurt her. She didn't want it coming close, though. The smell of its rotting flesh repelled her.

The dog looked up at her and whined. As Mala gripped her stone and began to circle around him, he whimpered and stepped toward her. Wiggling maggots covered his sores. "Ah!" Mala reeled in revulsion. She bolted, dropping the basket of clay.

She raced along the wooded path, past the last line of trees and a few dilapidated huts where women crouched over their cook fires, their children playing in the dirt beside them. She didn't stop when they jeered at her, but kept going until she reached the well where a few boys were chasing each other. Jyoti stood filling her jug at the brick altar. Mala drew up short at the moment Jyoti picked up the jug and raised her head.

The woman screeched. "You! Where have you been so long?"

Now it was too late to run. Mala could already feel the blows.

Then a strange thing happened. The potter's wife looked past Mala. Her arms dropped and the jug slipped from her hands with a thud. Its contents spilled as it rolled at her feet, darkening the earth. She screamed. "Unclean!"

Mala swiveled around. The black dog had followed her.

It stumbled forward. Jyoti's scream drew people from the nearby huts. Mothers called to their children from the doors and beckoned them in, crying "Hurry!" and "Keep away from the evil thing!" The basket maker emerged from under the neem tree where he usually sat weaving and gossiping. He backed away from the dog, who tottered forward a few more steps then dropped and lay as if dead.

The first to throw a pebble at the dog was the basket maker's son. A second boy emerged and hurled another. Another pebble landed on the dark fur, eliciting a yelp, and another and another. The poor dog could not move, but its paws twitched. Each whine made Mala wince. She should do something, but she didn't know what.

"Stop!"

The boys stopped throwing stones at once. Everyone snapped around, compelled by the unfamiliar voice.

A stranger stood at the other end of the path. He was clad in a simple dhoti and carried only a wandering sage's begging bowl. Mala's heart leaped, thinking it was Asita, but then she looked closer. His dark beard was streaked here and there with grey, not like the old yogi's nearly white mane. And he had well-muscled and broad shoulders, in contrast with lean and sinewy Asita or the emaciated sages who sometimes sought alms in the village. He looked strong enough to be a warrior.

"Good people," the stranger said, "whether the dog is alive or dead, each stone you throw marks your karma."

Was he a sage or a soldier? Mala couldn't be sure. She stared in wonder at the golden aura that danced around him. Did anyone else see it?

Perhaps they did. The villagers appeared spellbound as the stranger walked over to the animal, knelt next to it and touched its head. The dog lifted its tail once, twice, and whimpered.

"There, poor thing." He examined the dog without fear or the revulsion Mala had shown. She was ashamed. She'd treated the dog the way most people treated her.

"Namaste," the stranger said to a young mother standing in her doorway with her children huddled behind her. "If you would be so kind as to give me some water…"

He bowed and held out his bowl. The young mother drew back. Mala went hot with shame for the woman, and for herself. She wanted to go snatch his bowl and fetch a drink for him, but she was forbidden to draw water at the well.

Jyoti suddenly picked up her jug and began to refill it. She approached the spot where the dog was lying, took the man's bowl and filled it. Her hands were shaking as she handed it back.

The stranger bowed. "Thank you, thank you." Jyoti shook her head and shrugged as if to say it was nothing, though to Mala it seemed extraordinary that her mistress should perform a kindness for anyone or, even more surprisingly, for a useless, sick dog. Then the potter's wife stood, hoisted the jug onto her shoulder, and scurried away, calling for Lal.

The stranger removed the white cloth that protected his head from the sun, dipped it into the water, and with great gentleness began to wash the dog's wound. The animal gave a short, agonized howl. The stranger sat back on his heels.

The villagers had gathered around him. They gaped as the wanderer bowed his head over his joined palms for a moment, then leaned over the dog and began to remove the maggots from one of the wounds with his tongue. Gasps rose from the onlookers. Some covered their mouths with disgust, but no one looked away. A sweet pain filled Mala. If only things were different, she could be as kind and compassionate as the stranger.

You can be.

It wasn't the Devi's voice. It came from Mala's own heart. Suddenly she felt as clean as if a cool rain had just washed over her. She looked up in wonder, but no cloud had appeared.

When Mala looked toward the dog again, the crowd had gathered in, blocking her view. She stood on tiptoe and peered over their heads.

After he had tended to several sores in this extraordinary manner, the stranger looked up.

"It's the only way to clean these wounds," he said, smiling at everyone. "I learned this from an old holy woman I met in the forest. She was so wise! She had lived for five hundred years. She cured a tiger this way."

The villagers smiled at each other, and at Mala, too, who was too dumbfounded to smile back.

The stranger began again to minister to the dog's wounds. When not a maggot remained, he asked if someone could bring healing ointment or powdered turmeric and neem leaves to make poultices. Shy hands provided what he asked.

"I need a length of cloth, any old cloth. I'll make a sling so I can carry him more easily," he said.

Someone stepped forward with a freshly washed linen, which the sage laid flat on the ground. With great care he lifted the scruffy black dog onto it, tied the ends, and looped the sling over his shoulder like a mother carries a baby.

"Ho, poor thing," the stranger murmured as he walked away, as if talking to a child. "Come along. I'm going to the Great God Shiva's Shining City to wash away my sins, and you'll be a good companion…"

A shower of golden light blinded Mala for a moment. The still, hot air dissipated as a sweet, cool breeze eddied around the villagers, who exhaled as one, smiling with pleasure. "Ahhh…"

When the light faded the stranger was disappearing into the forest with his burden, but it was not the dog he carried. It was a radiant childlike being, its head surrounded by beams of light.

The sight stunned Mala. The light hurt her eyes. She blinked hard, looked away from the brilliance.

When she looked again, the two had vanished into the trees.

For several days, the whole village smiled at each other, even at Mala. The villagers could not agree whether it was Jyoti who brought the cloth or the headman's miserly wife, Priya. Each woman denied the simple act and said it was the other woman who deserved the merit for it. The boys stopped throwing rocks at each other. Jyoti gave Mala more rice and even sometimes a little chicken. Even in the heat of the day, Lal helped her carry clay from the river and stoke the kiln. Their children, who had always looked at her with distaste, greeted her with a pleasant "Namaste, Mala." It all made her uncertain and shy.

Not a month later, Jyoti spilled a pitcher of fresh milk and lost her temper. Down came the broom on Mala's back. Normal scuffles resumed among the village boys, with the usual split lips and black eyes. Two men came to blows when one man's cow trampled another's vegetable garden. Accusations of cheating and other familiar quarrels began again among the people.

Everything went back to what it had once been. Everyone seemed more comfortable that way. Even Mala. She had never been able to shake the sense that all the kindness would turn to blows, and to be right about that was somehow reassuring.

Yet when she next trudged back from the river with a backbreaking load, the memory of the stranger's compassion for the dog and the villagers' kindness to her, however brief, remained. Things could be different. She had seen it. Somewhere there was a place where people were always loving and kind to each other.

One day, she would find that place. Until then, she must be satisfied with the memory.

PART II

THE DARK GODDESS

FLIGHT

ANOTHER ROUND OF SEASONS PASSED. Mala worked hard without expectation of reward, but dedicating whatever merit her actions might have to a better rebirth for Talu. She grew tall and strong. At sixteen, she was lean, slim-hipped, and muscular from carrying bundles of wood and heavy loads of river clay. Since she began her monthly bleeding, the village boys followed her more often as she went to the river, though she was no beauty. Her face was not a delicate oval like Sujata's, but broad, with high, angular cheekbones and full lips. Then she realized it didn't matter what she looked like to them. They didn't really see *her;* they saw prey, an animal to torment.

Well, hunters do not always catch their prey. She had ways to defend herself. She always returned from the river with stones that her strong right arm hurled with deadly aim, and they kept their distance. They never followed her far into the forest, fearing the young white tigress that had been seen near a neighboring village. Last year it killed two cows and the young son of the sole farmer who had showed any kindness to Mala. Parents cautioned their children against straying too far, and the children obeyed.

Mala, though, sought the white cat, sure it was the cub she met the day she met Asita. Each time she went into the forest to collect good wood for Lal's kiln, she explored the hidden path the squirrel had shown her until she made her way to the grove of fragrant trees. Whenever hope and strength faded, she went there. There was a faint Presence, not strong, but more a sense that the Devi was watching. She always left with her courage renewed.

Mala sought the white tigress without success. The months passed, and it was time for the annual soma festival: the sacrifice celebrating the rescue of divine King Soma from the demons and the return of the nectar of immortality to the gods. Jyoti was preparing her finest curries and even stewing a chicken for the celebration. The smell of onions frying in ghee was wonderful, but Mala wouldn't get any.

Her mother, who had been born into the Vaishya caste, had seen the sacrifice as a girl. She told Mala it was best to keep away during the festival's wild nights. Before the ritual, the priests gathered the soma, a plant that only they could find in the forest, and pressed its life-giving juice to make the holy nectar that brought divine visions, and that only they could drink. The Brahmin Valmiki almost never came to the village to perform the rite but stayed in Varanasi to celebrate it with the king. This year he had come to collect rents and had decided to stay and lead the ritual. In all likelihood, his presence would not stop the people from getting drunk on barley beer and rutting with each other's wives. After all, the gods themselves celebrated with drunken carousing when the celestial soma once again filled the full moon.

Mala was glad to stay away from such festivities. Still, she wanted to feel clean for the day of sacrifice. Jyoti was distracted with cooking, so she decided to steal away to Ganga's waters to bathe.

To avoid troublemakers, she skirted the midden heap, taking a meandering path that was rarely used by other villagers. As she made her solitary way, she recollected the days when her parents were alive. Talu would send her to the river after a long morning's work at the vats, and her mother would look up from the cook fire to wave as Mala headed into the forest. Lost in this bittersweet reverie, she emerged from the forest near the riverbank, and Dilip, the trader's son, and his two friends, Anil and Ragosh, leaped at her.

She had no chance to struggle as Anil grabbed her arms from behind. Dilip pulled at her antariya. She always wound it tightly around her legs, and he fumbled with it as the other two jeered.

"Hey, boys," he said, grinning at her. "She's not half bad-looking. Your mother was a whore for a filthy tanner. Are you going to follow in her footsteps? Or would you like to try something better, like me? Want to taste my love?" He leaned close and pressed his hips against her.

Bile rose in Mala's throat. Clammy sweat covered her skin.

"Eh, boys, look at her pretty clothes," Anil said.

Ragosh gave a low whistle. "Maybe she's a queen in disguise."

"And has to be chaste for the soma sacrifice." Dilip slipped his hand under her clothes, feeling between her legs. His touch set off a wave of furious disgust that mobilized her frozen muscles. She struggled to twist from him. Anil tightened his grip. They all laughed.

Dilip leaned closer, as if he would kiss her. If only she could spit at him, but her mouth had gone dry. "You don't want me," Mala managed to croak, her whole being shrinking from his touch. Red lights began to dance.

"My lord Valmiki wouldn't approve, but Ganga's waters will wash away our sins," her tormentor continued, stepping back and looking her up and down.

Everything was suddenly sharp and clear and still.

Mala took a breath and thrust her knee into his groin.

"Oof!" Dilip crumpled to the ground, moaning and clutching at himself.

The others whooped and howled. Anil was laughing hardest of all and couldn't hold onto her. This was her chance. As if lightning had struck her, she bolted.

"Wait, you little bitch!" Anil shouted behind her, but her feet flew. Not until she arrived at the hut, panting, did she looked behind her. No one had followed.

ॐ

That night, she lay in her lean-to by Lal's hut listening to the revelry. It kept her awake, but was reassuring, in a way. The boys would be in the middle of the drunken orgy and not thinking of her.

At some point she must have fallen asleep, because a roar awakened her. For a moment, she thought she had dreamt it. The festivities were over and the night was quiet. Instinct made her remain still. There was a drunken laugh, then jocular catcalls.

"Dilip... she's over there..."

They were out there in the dark, not too far away. A twig snapped and the leaves of a nearby bush rustled.

"Mala... oh, beeeauuu-ti-fool Mala..."

The low call raised the hairs on Mala's neck. Another roar. It was no dream. The tigress. She was sure.

65

"What was that?" one of the boys said in a low, urgent tone.

"Aw, 's nothing…" There was a loud hiccup and another rustle.

The tigress let out a third roar. It echoed in the night, then all became silent again.

"No, there's something out there." It sounded like Anil. "Let's get back to the fire, tell the hunter."

"You afraid of tigers?" A giggle. "Or Mala? Mala, Mala," he sang out drunkenly, "do… d'you want my loving…?"

Come away into the forest, Mala.

The Devi. Every nerve seemed to come alive. She held her breath. Nothing moved.

"I'm hard as a rock for you, Mala… C'mon… I know you wan' me…"

I will protect you.

Mala did not hesitate. She sat up, trying not to make a sound, but she couldn't suppress a groan at the pain from a muscle she had sprained when she fled from the boys. She crouched under the lean-to's thatching, preparing to run.

Thunder rumbled. Clouds covered the moon, and whoever was out there could see no better than she. She knew the path into the forest so well that her feet would go where they had to. She must get to the trees faster than her tormentors. She waited, tense and afraid. The snap of a branch nearby spurred her to leap and flee.

Behind her, a single hoarse shout rang out. "There she goes!"

The white tigress leaped from nowhere and sailed past her with a snarl. There was an agonized shriek. "No—"

Mala didn't look back. She ran faster, no longer aware of the pain of her bruises, crashing through the brush at the forest's edge. Deeper and deeper into the tangled trees and shrubs she raced, heedless of the thorns and branches that scratched her, until her lungs burned. She burst through the undergrowth and stumbled into the grove just as she felt she could not take another step. At last. Her refuge. No villager knew of this place.

She stopped to lean against a tree. Her pounding heart slowed and the roar of blood in her ears lessened. Nothing moved. Not a tiger, night bird, or cricket. Every nerve was taut. Something was wrong. Utter silence bore down on her.

The heavy stillness seemed about to crush her when everything began to shake. The earth heaved and buckled, knocking her off her feet. It tossed her up and then caught her with a painful jolt. Up and down she went in this way, helpless. Solid tree trunks waved like kusha grass in the wind. Leaves and twigs rained down.

"Devi!" she managed to cry. The ground rippled again and again.

Then as suddenly as the quaking started, it stopped. Nothing stirred. Mala was motionless, too, trying to grasp what had happened.

A breeze rustled through the leaves. Thunder rumbled in the distance. A nightjar gave its familiar croak. These ordinary sounds calmed her a little. She patted the ground, half expecting it to give way under her hand. Was it real? She'd been tossed like a boat on the current of Ganga's waters in flood. The trees had waved back and forth in ways thick wood couldn't, shouldn't move. Maybe she didn't know what wood was at all. She patted the tall sal tree's trunk nearest her. Solid.

At last, she reined in her racing heart and thoughts. Her aching body crumpled to the ground in exhaustion.

There was a low growl. The white tigress padded into the grove and walked up to Mala. She held her breath. The huge cat chuffed in her ear.

You are safe now. We are far from the village.

"You... the cub." Mala's voice failed her.

Yes. I am grown now. I am called Rani.

"Rani...?"

A queen of the tiger race. I will watch.

The tigress's eyes caught the starlight and glittered blue-white in the dark. They drew Mala in, and for a time it seemed that the tiger's senses were hers. Every leaf and twig was illuminated with greyish light though it was moonless, a myriad of sounds sorted and separated into the faint thud of a faraway deer's hooves and a birdcall that was no birdcall but a Naga hunter signaling a fellow tribesman that he had found game. She tasted salty blood in her mouth—Rani's mouth—and through Rani's senses knew it was human. Perhaps the tigress had killed one of her tormentors. Good. She wished they all were dead.

Talu would disapprove. So be it. Revenge felt sweet. For an eternal moment she stared into the tigress's glowing orbs. With a trembling hand, she reached out and stroked Rani's silky yet rough fur. The white cat was a wonder.

Mala's lids drooped. She lay down and rolled over onto her back. Above the leafy branches, bright stars glinted between thunderheads. She slept.

THE BANDIT

"**H**O! YOU THERE! OUT OF the way!"
Shouts startled Mala from exhausted sleep. She looked around in a panic. No one was there. The tigress was gone. The taste of blood came back to her, and she wiped her mouth with the back of her hand. It was a dream, she told herself, knowing it was not.

"Move along!" "That's right, get going."

Voices came from beyond the tangled shrubs that hid her. Mala rolled over and got on her knees, wincing from the cuts and scratches acquired on her headlong flight. As she crouched and moved forward through the concealing thicket, creaking wheels and shouts muffled the twigs that snapped underfoot. She stayed well hidden as horses, men, and oxen moved past.

A road. The secret grove was almost right next to the Uttarapatha, the legendary, magical great trade road. If she had only known! She might have escaped Gauri, taken it east to the mist-covered lands east of the mighty Brahmaputra River or west across the forests and plains at Himalaya's feet to Taxila, a city that was the gateway to wondrous Parsee and the West. Her father had spoken of golden-haired people who dwelt in lands rich with silver and precious gems, beyond the Gandharan desert. They built fantastic stone temples on mountains that rose from a calm blue sea, in which they worshipped their gods as supreme above all others.

Out of a memory, Talu spoke. "But their mountains are mounds of dirt next to King Himalaya's peaks, Mala. And their gods bow to Brahma the Creator, and nothing there is as fair as these lands that lie between the mountain god's palaces and Ganga's waters."

Mala moved forward to see better, but remained hidden. Three men on horseback had halted in front of a line of oxcarts laden to the brim and covered with oiled leather tarps such as her father used to make. In contrast to the white dhotis of the ox drovers, the riders wore emerald green antariyas and brilliant rose-pink sashes. They had long Kshatriya braids hanging down their backs and short swords in jeweled scabbards hanging at their sides.

"Move out of the way, I say!" a warrior shouted. "Lady Addhakashi must pass." Wheels creaked and groaned under their loads as their drovers urged the ox teams to the side of the road.

A strange vehicle followed. It was a long platform resting on six wheels, drawn by heavy horses with thick legs. It groaned and cracked at each rut. The platform had a low railing around the edge and was strewn with shiny fat pink, orange, and red pillows of various sizes.

Over it all extended a yellow canopy, and under the canopy sat two women: a plump one with grey-streaked dark hair, dressed in bright, rich blue; the other so radiant she must be a goddess. The plump woman was tending the hair of this goddess draped in vibrant rose-pink cloth shot through with gold. She wore a diamond and ruby necklace, like the garland the Devi herself had worn that day in the grove. Mala couldn't tear her eyes away. Then the vehicle jounced over a rut and came to a halt.

"Ah! Ouch!" the goddess said in a very human voice. "The great serpent Shesha makes the earth tremble today as he did last night."

A sweaty, half-naked slave scurried back to look at the wheels and was joined by the drovers of the other carts. They all began pointing and talking at once.

"No, Addha, my dear," said the grey-haired woman in blue, pulling roughly with an ivory comb. "These oafs don't know how to drive the wagon, that's all. Ah, this is impossible!"

"You're hurting me, Lakshmi," the woman called Addha said.

"How will I untangle this mess while we're knocked about like this?" Lakshmi replied.

"We're stuck, my lady Addhakashi." The bearer came up to the wagon's side, wiped his forehead with a dirty rag, and scratched his head. "Now what'll we do?"

"Ask the captain," Addha replied. "Captain Shakuni! Do something."

Shakuni.

Mala's every nerve thrummed. Talu's agonized scream rang in her head. Shakuni, the warrior who knocked her father into the vats with his whip and killed him.

Her chest contracted as if an invisible hand were twisting her heart inside her body.

"O Devi," she prayed under her breath, "I need you now…" She wished Rani would appear, but with so many people about, even the queen of the tigers might stay away.

Mala was on her own. In fear, loathing and rage, she watched from her hiding place as guards and bearers milled around. The warriors gave conflicting orders, gesticulating at the servants who looked at each other, nodded their heads and shrugged.

Lakshmi took a little bottle and poured oil in her hands, and then resumed dressing her mistress's hair. "A fine mess this is. We should have left for Varanasi earlier."

Lady Addhakashi tossed her head and smiled, disturbing Lakshmi's attempts to dress her unruly hair. "But how could I leave?" She held up her left hand and wiggled a ringed finger.

The gem caught the sun, dazzling Mala for a moment. Her eyes regained their focus.

Lakshmi cocked an eyebrow. "Just because he gave you Sarasvati's sapphire, it's no reason to think King Prasenajit is your friend. What will our former king think when he sees his favorite wearing a gift from his enemy?"

"Poor King Brahmadatta. He didn't have a chance against Prasenajit."

"Because he spent half the kingdom's revenues on you, my dear."

Addhakashi smiled. "Brahmadatta will think that I was very clever to extract such a price from that miser Prasenajit."

"Or he'll think the Kosalan has bought you," Lakshmi said.

"That was the whole point. I negotiated a very nice arrangement for our former king precisely because our new king thinks he bought me."

"I never understood the game of politics," Lakshmi said.

"It was you who taught me that it's the most important skill for a courtesan to learn."

"Perhaps it's better to say that I never played the game particularly well. Not like you, my dear."

"Oh, Lakshmi. I could never have come so far if it weren't for your instruction—"

"My lady," Shakuni interrupted.

"What is it, Captain?"

"There's a village not too far away. I'll send a couple men to find help. I'll stay with you to make sure these worthless fellows don't run off." He sneered at the drovers and bearers.

Mala tensed as two guards galloped off and disappeared around a bend. Gauri was not on the trade road, but the path to it was well marked.

"Get busy," Captain Shakuni said, and the men resumed their efforts to free the vehicle.

Lakshmi put down her brush and stared into the forest. "Look, Captain. Do you see someone in there?"

Mala ducked behind the bushes. Shakuni gave a quick glance in her direction, squinting into the shadows. She held her breath.

"You're imagining things." He went back to ordering the men about.

Mala was shaking. He was so close, but how to take revenge?

"Put your shoulder to it," the captain called. They gave the vehicle a feeble push.

"Perhaps we should get out," Addha said.

"No," Shakuni said. "You two stay where you are. The road is too dusty for your pretty feet, Lady Addhakashi. These fellows are just lazy." He resumed shouting out ineffective orders.

"Captain Shakuni," Lakshmi said, interrupting him. "There are gangs of bandits on these roads. I think you should have kept another guard here."

Addhakashi shrank against Lakshmi. "You promised to keep us safe, Shakuni." She slipped off her sapphire ring and put it under a cushion. Then she put a hand on her necklace.

"Are you the warrior?" he snarled at Lakshmi. "I told you, it's all rumor and nonsense. Nothing but cowardly robbers on this road, my lady. I could take on a half dozen with one arm behind my back. You shouldn't upset your mistress, old woman. There's not a thing to worry about with me here."

He shouted for the drovers to get busy, but the skinny bearers shifted from one foot to the other and shook their heads, no closer to freeing the wheel.

"'There's not a thing to worry about,'" Lakshmi mimicked. She tugged at her mistress's hair with the comb. "Take on a half a dozen, indeed. I don't care what he says. With all the fighting between the clans, the wicked prosper. Deserters make the roads worse and worse; that's what everyone says. We should have brought more guards."

"But he will keep us safe," Addhakashi said uncertainly, fingering her necklace.

A drover spoke up. "The cart is too heavy, my lord. If my lady would step down..."

"Nonsense," the captain snapped. He dismounted, muttering. "Weaklings. By the gods, I could do it myself, and not wait for any help. Here, I'll show you where to push." He put a muscled shoulder to the wheel.

At that moment, a shout rang out and a short man with a pockmarked face and bulbous nose jumped from behind the trees on the road's other side, waving a short sword. Addhakashi shrieked. The drovers and bearers disappeared as if by magic. Mala would have cried out, but someone grabbed her from behind and clapped a hand over her mouth. Panic paralyzed her.

"Shhhh!" her captor whispered. His breath was hot in her ear. "I won't hurt you."

His accent was strange. She twisted to face a dark-haired stranger with a mustache. He grinned down at her. Her knees buckled, but he held her tight.

"Shhh," he whispered again. He put a finger to his lips and asked with his warm, dark eyes if she would remain quiet. Mesmerized, she nodded.

He released her. Strangely, she didn't want him to let go. Her skin burned everywhere he had touched her. The handsome, mustached stranger crept past and, still hiding in the shadows, pulled out his sword.

On the road, Shakuni's weapon flashed from its scabbard as he faced the pockmarked bandit.

"I'll slice through that pathetic blade like it's a twig," the captain said. The pockmarked man hesitated with his dull sword half raised. "Then I'll slice through you the same w—"

At that moment, Mala's captor leaped onto the road behind the warrior, but not fast enough. As if he had eyes on the back of his head, Shakuni whipped around and met the bandit's blade, nearly knocking it from his hand. The pockmarked man attacked, and now the captain fought both bandits, stepping lightly as a cat and parrying the robbers' awkward strokes with ease. The one with the mustache was more of a challenge than the other bandit, but still not up to the captain's skills.

"Where did you learn to fight, you useless curs?" Shakuni danced around, lunging and feinting as he mocked.

Be careful, Mala almost shouted, as the one who had held her stepped to the side to avoid a lunge from Shakuni and in the next second was sprawling face down on the road, tripped by the leg of a cowering bearer hiding under Lady Addhakashi's vehicle. His weapon flew from his hand.

"Hnnh," he grunted, the air knocked out of him by the fall.

The captain brought his sword down on the pockmarked man's blade, knocking it from his hand. He jumped back, and Shakuni prepared to finish off the mustached bandit. Mala was terrified. She didn't dare fight Shakuni. The warrior would kill her, too.

He was her father's murderer. She wanted revenge.

"Rohit! Watch out!" the pockmarked one shouted.

The mustached man turned toward his companion for a second, then rolled face up and reached for his weapon. That glance cost him. The captain stepped on the blade.

A rock. She needed a rock. Mala stooped and found an oval stone that filled her palm. She hefted it. It felt warm in her hand.

The captain paused to smile his triumph at the women in the wagon. "You see, ladies, these cowardly thugs don't know how to fight—"

Mala stepped from her hiding place. "Shakuni!" she cried. Her boldness astonished her. The familiar energy shot through her, and as it did, the red began to pulse. Its power intoxicated her.

Shakuni gaped. Rage flooded Mala. It guided her hand as she hurled the stone, scoring a direct hit on the bridge of his nose.

"That was for my father," she said, breathless and shaking with fierce joy as he fell backward against the wagon and landed with a heavy thud.

For one horrible moment she waited, sure Shakuni would get up and come after her. Thick, dark blood trickled from one nostril. The captain lay slack-jawed and still. She had killed him. She had killed her father's murderer. She felt faint.

The pockmarked man approached slowly. "By Indra's balls, that was a good shot," he said. He turned to Mala. "Who are you?"

Rohit got to his knees gulping for air. "Many thanks!" he said when he could stand. "May the gods bless your strong arm!" He saluted her. White teeth flashed under his mustache.

Overcome at what she had just done, Mala couldn't move or respond.

Rohit turned away and took the reins of Shakuni's horse. "Get the jewels, Anu. This warrior won't be needing this fine beast anymore." He grasped a handful of the animal's mane and gave a little jump across the horse's back, but not far enough to mount. The horse tossed its head and stepped away and Rohit nearly slid off, barely managing to hold on to the mane.

Meanwhile, pockmarked Anu leaped up onto the wagon. "Get on with it! Your rings, your bracelets, everything. And that necklace, my lady." Lakshmi and Addhakashi took off their rings and Anu stuffed them in a white sash that was wrapped tightly over his protruding stomach.

"You can have everything—here, here, take this chest, it's full of jewels," Addhakashi said in a trembling voice. She pulled a gold cuff off her upper arm. "But don't take the necklace. It was my sister's... it's all I have left of her..."

"Give it here," Anu said.

"If you take the necklace from my lady, I'll hunt you down, you ugly sow," Lakshmi said, shaking a fist, "and roast you over a slow fire!"

Anu scowled at her but hesitated. Rohit finally succeeded in getting a leg across the horse's back and sat up like a warrior. "Just take it, you fool!" he said.

At the sound of hoofbeats, Mala regained the power to move. "Wait," she said, but Anu and Rohit paid no heed and looked at each other.

"Forget it," Rohit said. "Take the chest, and let's go."

But as he pulled the horse alongside the wagon, Anu grabbed the necklace and gave a yank. It broke, sending diamonds and rubies flying like drops of water and blood onto the road. Addhakashi's hand flew to her neck. She let out a sharp cry that pierced Mala's heart.

Anu cursed. He fumbled with what remained of the necklace, trying without success to stuff it in his sash. He flung it away and grabbed the chest. He tucked it under one arm and half fell onto the horse's back behind Rohit.

"Unh," he grunted. Rohit tapped his heels against the horse's flanks and the animal broke into a trot. The bandits bounced up and down on its back. The horse began to gallop. Anu looked about to fall off. In short order, the jewel chest dropped from Anu's arm. As it landed, multicolored jewels spilled over the road. They dazzled Mala as they scattered, flashing in the sun. The thieves, their curses wafting in the air, disappeared just as the returning guards came round the bend from the other direction.

Pandemonium broke out as the servants scrambled to pick up jewels. Mala leaped back into the dark woods and crouched. No one seemed to notice. She peered through the shrubs.

The guards brought several men from her village. She huddled deeper into the brush, afraid they would see her. The rage that gave her courage to throw the stone evaporated. Her heart was pounding so loud they must hear it; her breath was hoarse and ragged in her throat. She pressed her lips together, trying to be quiet. They would seize her and take her back to Gauri.

But no one was giving her a thought. Lakshmi scrambled off the wagon and waddled to the chest and its scattered contents. "Give me those!" she ordered a bearer who was holding a bangle, gazing with wonder at the treasure in his hand. "All of you, make way. And give me what you've picked up, or I'll have you whipped." To a man they dropped whatever they held, and Lakshmi pawed through the dust and gathered them up.

"Captain Shakuni! By the gods, is he dead?" a guard asked. "Who did this?"

"Bandits attacked us," Addhakashi said in a quivering voice.

"How many? Where have they gone?" The two warriors looked around uneasily.

Lakshmi grunted in disgust. "Two inept robbers were too much for that incompetent fool Shakuni."

"It's bad, Vijay." A guard had dismounted and gone to the captain's side. "He's bleeding from his nose. At least he's breathing."

"Just two bandits overcame the famous Shakuni?" Vijay stared at the still form. Mala stared, too, wondering if she really had killed him.

"There was a rakshasa, too, sir!" cried a bearer, emerging from his hiding place under a wagon. "I saw her! She flew out of the woods!"

Mala bit her lip. They took her for a demoness. It was a heady thought.

"Did anyone else see her?" Vijay said.

The other bearers and drovers looked around and shrugged, then glanced nervously into the woods.

"I see," he said sarcastically. "She flew back into the woods." He shook his head. "We should move out. More could be on the way."

"A demoness?" someone said.

If only she were a rakshasa. Mala felt a tingle of power.

"No, you fool," a warrior said, a little too loudly. "More bandits. Now, Mistress Lakshmi, you'd best get back in her ladyship's wagon."

A few bearers glanced into the woods with worried looks. Mala shrank.

"But where's the necklace? It was Moti's—" Lakshmi said.

"We need to get away," Vijay said with a stern look.

"But my lady's necklace!" Lakshmi exploded.

"Get in the wagon!" Vijay ordered. "Come on, you." He swept his arm around, indicating that all the men should get to work.

Lakshmi clambered in. Now all the bearers came out of hiding and began to push on the stuck wheel, helped by village men.

There was a creak and a lurch, and the wheel climbed out of the rut onto the road, heading east. Everyone shouted and cheered.

"You! Over there." Vijay pointed to two men. "Load the boxes from that cart onto my lady's wagon. Put Captain Shakuni's body on the cart." As they lifted him, Shakuni groaned. Mala gritted her teeth. He was alive. "Careful with him now."

Mala backed farther into the forest and huddled near the ground, thinking they would come after her. But the one who would have been most interested in finding her was unconscious, and the others perhaps feared what they thought was a rakshasa. Addhakashi's bearers and the villagers rushed about until the unconscious captain was settled. The little caravan began to move.

As soon as the courtesan's party had disappeared from sight and earshot, the drovers of the other carts that had pulled aside to let her wagon pass began to prod and whip their oxen.

"Hurry, hurry," said one. "The demoness will get us."

"There was no demoness," another laughed. "Though she was a great strapping girl. Had good legs, even if her breasts were small."

"She could be a tree nymph who will turn us into monkeys..."

"I'll bet your lovely nymph is still close by, there, in the woods, waiting for a man like you."

"Not me." The man stared wide-eyed into the forest.

Mala pressed behind a tree.

"Let's get on." Slowly they began to move westward. The wheels cracked and creaked.

"Ever been so close to Kashi's finest whore?" a drover said.

"She's no whore," someone called out. "Addhakashi's the best courtesan in all Kashi—no, in all the Sixteen Clans!"

"So you'll make a bid for her favors?" another asked.

"I'll get a big fee when I deliver this fine Kashi muslin to those Kosalan oafs in Sravasti."

"Won't be enough! Only the king can afford her price. You'll get a street girl—"

"Go off and find that demoness. She's still close, I'll wager, and won't cost so dear."

Mala peered out as the carts disappeared around a curve in the road. The voices and laughter faded. When everyone was gone, it seemed that she had dreamed it all: the beautiful woman in the luxurious vehicle, the bandits, Shakuni unconscious in the dirt, everything.

Beyond the forest's shelter, the road shimmered in the heat.

THE CHANDALA

MALA HUDDLED IN THE SHADOWS. Her mind spun until she was exhausted. She feared that the villagers would come back and find her, but she feared stepping onto the road and heading into the unknown. She wished for a sign, to hear the Devi's voice to tell her what to do. Or perhaps now Rani would come. Yes, Rani would come and show her a safe place to go.

But as the afternoon wore on, Rani did not appear. Mala's jumbled thoughts gradually returned to the lady Addhakashi and her servant. An idea formed: Mala could go to Varanasi and seek them out, ask for their help. It was half mad to think they would take her in. Yet she was strong. She didn't fear hard work. She had skills and was quick to learn. To return to the village meant only more of the same; Jyoti's beatings, the drudgery, Dilip's and Anil's leers. Dilip. Anil. Rani had attacked them. Mala had seen it, tasted it, felt it through Rani's senses. The knowledge gave her courage.

She would journey into the unknown. She took a first step onto the road. In the terrible heat, thirst gripped her and her head swam. Her mouth was thick and dry and she swayed a bit where she stood.

The cicadas sang a strange song that rose and fell in the stifling afternoon. She tried to quiet her own breathing to listen to it. Gradually, the insects' song became human. Someone was chanting. Her blood sang in her ears. She should head back to shelter, but something held her.

"Shantih, shantih, shantih."

A dark silhouette appeared. Her pulse raced. *Run,* she said silently, but she was desperate for water. As she stood swaying, the figure became a slender and fine-boned young man, head down, bent double under a heavy load. He wore little more than a ragged dhoti that hung on his hips. He was some years older than she, well-muscled if lean, but he did not look strong enough to carry so much.

Her unease lessened. "I'm thirsty…" Mala stumbled out. He started. He searched Mala's face, as if looking for something. "Moti? Moti! Is it you?" His marvelous golden eyes widened in wonder.

Mala, hypnotized by those eyes, at first couldn't respond. "No… no… I'm not Moti."

"Ah." His joyful expression disappeared.

"Do you have some water?" she said at last. "If you'll give me a drink and some food, I'll help you carry the wood…"

With a sigh, he slung his bundle of sweet-smelling branches off his back and onto the ground. He handed her a gourd. "Drink."

Mala grabbed it and gulped the warm water.

"Not so fast. You'll get sick." The man put one arm around her back to support her, and with the other reached to push the water away from her lips. Too late to tell him she was untouchable. She had already drunk from his gourd. He was ragged and dirty, too, though. Maybe it didn't matter.

He did not remove his supporting arm, but led her to a tree. "Sit." She glanced around. What if someone came from the village? He followed her eyes. "What frightens you?" he asked.

She didn't answer. She was too hungry and tired to do anything but sit down with a thud. No one was coming. She leaned her back against the tree with a sigh.

Some small rocks dug painfully into her thigh, and she resettled herself, feeling under her leg for the stones. She pulled out the broken strand of red and white jewels. It sparkled on her palm. She forgot to breathe.

"What have you got there?" With sudden interest, the man grasped her palm in his and studied the gems. "By the gods…"

"What's wrong?" The look on his face scared her. The gems suddenly burned in her hand.

"But these are like the rubies in the necklace I gave my Moti! Where did you get them?"

Mala shut her eyes a moment. "They belonged to the woman in the cart. Lady Addhakashi, they called her. She was as beautiful as a goddess…"

"Addhakashi?" He wrinkled his forehead. "My Moti was Addhakashi's sister."

Mala didn't care whose sister she was. "Please, do you have food? I'm so hungry…"

"Tell me what happened," he said as he fumbled with the sash tied at his waist and drew out a cloth, which he unwrapped to reveal some crumbling flatbread and a few withered wild plums. He held it out to her with one hand.

"Thieves attacked." The gems glittered so dazzling white and angry red in her hand it seemed they were alive. She thrust them at the man. "Here. They were yours…"

He shook his head. "The gods took my beloved Moti from me, and now they have given the necklace to you."

I gave it to you, Mala. The vision of Durga on the tiger rose in her mind's eye.

"Not the gods," she whispered. "Durga… Durga gave it to me." Her hand shook a little, and light shot from the jewels.

"How so?"

"She… she appeared to me… at a shrine in the forest. It was the same necklace."

"Truly? The Devi appeared to you as Durga?"

Mala could hardly respond. It all suddenly overwhelmed her—her visions of the Devi in her many forms, the escape from the village, the tigress, the bandits—and now this man.

His eyes searched hers.

She nodded. "Yes. Yes, she did."

With his free hand, the man folded her fingers around it. "It is your karma to keep it. You must hide it. And not tell anyone." She fumbled at her antariya and tied it in its folds as he turned his calm golden eyes to her, studying her. She had never wanted so badly to be as beautiful as her mother. He must think her very ugly, dirty and scratched as she was. Then he smiled. The light in his eyes sent sparks down her spine. "Don't be frightened. We are alone. Eat a little."

She could not help shoving the bread into her mouth. It tasted like the food of the gods. She barely chewed before she swallowed, took another bite and another, until the bread and plums were almost gone. "I'm sorry," she said mumbled through a full mouth. "I am greedy." Talu would be embarrassed.

"No, you're hungry. Do you live near here? I can help you find your way home," he said.

She stood up hurriedly. "No!" She swallowed. "No, I have no home."

He shrugged and rose to retrieve the bundled wood.

"I can help you with that," she said, reaching for it. It gave off a scent like her grove back in the forest.

"I can carry it. But if you wish, you can walk with me. I'm going to Varanasi." He was kind. He had asked her to go with him. There was no one to say yes or no but her. It was astonishing, intoxicating that she, Mala, could choose. "Yes! Yes…" Trembling, she helped him hoist the wood onto his back. "It smells good."

"Sandalwood," he said, "for funeral pyres of the rich. There's none near the cremation grounds. I had to walk to find some."

Mala's eyes widened. A chandala. A keeper of the cremation grounds. If she had thought about it at all, she had thought of a chandala as wrinkled and old, not young and so good-looking as this man was.

No village boy could compare with him. He was more like a noble, with his strange amber eyes shot with green and gold that were dark yet shone with light, and his chiseled nose and cheeks and narrow lips. He wore a white cloth wrapped around his head with a flap hanging down to protect his neck from the sun. It contrasted sharply with his golden-brown skin. His dhoti was streaked with dirt. Sweat glistened underneath smears of what looked like ash. He could be the god Shiva that Asita had told her about years ago, who lived at the burning grounds. An urge to touch him swept through her. She blushed.

"What is your name?" he said, not noticing her embarrassment.

"Mala. What is yours?"

"I am known only as the chandala."

Without another word he began to walk. Mala hurried with him, stealing curious glances at her benefactor. He raked the ashes. She tried to imagine it.

"Burning the dead must be even worse than a tanner's life," she said, then instantly regretted it.

"At first, I hated it. But now I think it's the best work."

"Why?" she asked, astonished.

"Because it never allows me to forget that one day I will die."

Mala blinked. One day she would die.

Time stopped in mid stride.

The forest's green was suddenly brighter; the headcloth the chandala wore became brilliantly white. Everything looked sharper: a banyan grove at the side of the road whose myriad trunks disappeared into the forest gloom, each of its thousands of leaves hanging still in the breathless heat; a quail with her chicks scurrying across the dusty road.

Underneath Mala's senses there was a subtle roar, a hum that had always been there, in her hiding place near her parents' hut or in the night's silence as she watched the stars wheeling above. All this time she had hardly dared admit she heard it. Now the urge to understand it seized her. What was it? Would it become louder or disappear when she died? What was beyond the trees, the earth, the heavens' deep blue? For a moment, there was nothing but blackness too deep to look into. In an instant, complete terror gripped her, then just as quickly it was gone. She closed her eyes and took a deep breath.

The chandala had taken a step ahead. She caught up, more curious than ever. Her father had said that everyone stood before Yama Dharmaraja, the Lord of Judgment, when they died. "Does—does a chandala know what it's like, the kingdom of the dead?" she said.

He shrugged. "Not anymore than you do. Hideous for some, paradise for others. Or so it's said. Not much different from this life. But it is also said no one stays there forever. Some say you'll be reborn, again and again until you attain moksha."

"I've always wondered, how do they know?"

"How do they know what?"

"That one is born again and again?" Mala asked. "I can't remember any of my former lives."

"Ah." The chandala looked amused. Mala blushed. "There are learned Brahmins who study the Vedas for years but never dare ask themselves that question. They simply believe what their teachers or their fathers tell them. Never believe someone who says he knows for certain what comes after death. If there are those who truly do know, they stay silent about it."

Mala was about to ask what he believed when he began to sing in a strange language, gazing up at the sky. It made Mala shiver, like when her mother sang the sacred *om*.

"... *so anga veda yadi va na veda...*"

The sacred language. Her ears burned, but no thunder clapped, no celestial being appeared to drag her to Yama's seven hells. And this man, an outcaste just as she was, had learned the words, even spoke them. This gave her courage. "What does it mean?"

"It is the Nasadiya, the Creation Hymn. *Whence this creation has arisen—perhaps it created itself, perhaps it did not—the One who looks down on it, from highest heaven, only the One knows... or perhaps knows it not...*"

"How did you learn the hymn? How did you know what it means?"

They walked in silence a bit. She had offended him, the last thing she wanted. "I've... I've heard the word moksha," she said, giving him a timid glance.

"You have?"

"A long time ago. From a holy seeker." Perhaps someone like Asita had taught the chandala. "He said anyone could attain it."

He nodded. "Indeed anyone can. The wise say if you follow your dharma in each life until your karma is stainless, then you might find a fortunate rebirth where you become a sage or a rishi, one who through supreme knowledge succeeds in uniting the self that lives in his heart to the great Self, Atman, that encompasses all. It is beyond the comprehension of most, but one who attains this union knows he is part of everything and everything is part of him. He becomes the animals, the plants, the wind, the stars. The sages say *Tat tvam asi*." He paused.

Mala had been lost in his voice, barely understanding. "What? Tavamasi?" she blurted, then pursed her lips. There. She'd spoken the sacred tongue. She shrank a little, anticipating celestial wrath.

None came. Her heart lightened.

The chandala spoke. "*You are that.* When you know in your heart's deepest corner that you are connected to everything, that you *are* everything, that's moksha."

This is what Asita knew. She was sure of it. He had said she could let her soul soar. "And a woman could know this—this—*tat tvam asi?*" There, she'd said the words again. It made her dizzy.

He looked thoughtful. "Some say no. But there are many tales of wise rishikis in generations past. And I could never understand why not. After all, when a woman gives birth to a child that has taken all its nourishment from her, lived by her very breath, she can truly say, 'I am that child.' It is the man's seed, true, but it grows in the woman's womb. What man knows another being in such a profound way?"

"But an outcaste?"

"Some say no. Others say only an outcaste knows true freedom."

"Why?"

"An outcaste has no dharma as Brahmins, Kshatriyas, Vaishyas, and Shudras do."

Mala looked at the chandala suspiciously. "My father told me our dharma was to be kind to everyone. And he told me to expect no reward."

He laughed. "Then you were well taught."

Her knees went wobbly with embarrassment and pleasure. Those eyes. She must keep talking so he would keep looking at her with those golden eyes. "What—what happens when you know you are everything, and unite with Atman?"

"When we die, our souls travel up to the moon, which catches them by the karmic imprints—the traces of our actions—that follow them. The silver moon sends them back to earth in the rain. The rain nourishes the earth and all that grows on it until the soul finds the seed of the creature—animal or human—into which it will be reborn. But those souls that are pure pass right through the moon and beyond to the stars, into the timeless eternity. There is nothing to hold them to this existence. Suffering ends."

"Suffering never ends," she said with sudden and intense bitterness, thinking of her life since her parents died. What did this man know about pain? What was she doing following him?

Because chandala or not, he had an aura that reminded her of the mysterious joy that infused her when she made offerings to the Devi. She had felt something similar long ago, when Asita told his tale. Sadness washed over her. That joy never lasted. Asita had left her in the village. Sooner or later this man would leave her on the road.

"Suffering never ends, you think." His voice broke into her thoughts. "Even so, we may always hope to transcend it." The chandala gave her a beautiful smile. Her heart skipped a beat.

"Come with me to Varanasi, Mala."

Her heart bounded. Every syllable he spoke was like sacred music. He wanted her to go with him. It was a miracle.

Without another word, they walked east toward the sacred city, the chandala chanting softly. *"Shantih, shantih, shantih..."*

Mala limped along at his side. Her heart was light. Everything that came before receded in her mind. She took in everything around her with new eyes.

"Shantih, shantih, shantih," the chandala chanted. "Peace, peace, peace."

They arrived at the burning grounds after dark. By starlight the chandala led her along a path through barren ground to a little hill. A small thatched hut stood atop the rise, leaning toward a tall tree next to it. The doorway yawned pitch black, and she hesitated, not knowing what she might find inside.

"I'll sleep out here," he said.

She wanted this mysterious and gentle young man to touch her, caress her, to make her moan with pleasure as her mother had under her father's hands. Did he want her?

Show him you want him, a voice whispered in her ear. *Have no fear.*

She took his hand in her trembling one. With a slight smile he led her inside. He must have guessed right away that it was her first time and was gentle and slow with her. A sweet pain and then the most exquisite pleasure she had ever known. Afterward, they rolled apart. He was quiet for a time, and she was afraid to say anything.

"I... I never dreamed," she breathed at last. "I never knew..."

"Ah." He raised himself on an elbow. His face was shadowed so she couldn't see his eyes. "There is pain for a woman, the first time," he said. "I—"

She put her arms around his neck and pulled him to her. "There is pleasure, too," she said, and kissed him.

Later, when he slept, she stared down at him in the darkness. This was love. And she didn't even know his name.

THE CREMATION GROUNDS

I N THE MORNING, THE CHANDALA helped her wrap the necklace in
a cloth and bury it beneath some bricks, which they built up so that
there was a hollow center where they could build a fire. Atop the bricks,
they placed a dented metal basin that held their food over the cook fire.

"It is well hidden there," he said, looking at her steadily. "But you can
take it any time and go…"

But go where, and alone, without him? He was the first truly good
thing that had happened to her since her parents' deaths. She shook her
head. "I'll stay here."

Thus began her new life. Nights were delight tinged bittersweet. Mala
remembered the sighs and endearments Talu and Sujata had shared. She
had a waking dream sometimes that they were still alive, that she and her
lover would take a little boat—one like those she saw on the river, shaped
like large wooden bowls bobbing up and down on the water. They would
paddle west against the current toward Gauri; it would be a day's journey,
perhaps. When they got to the spot where she used to bathe when she was a
child, they would take the path to the clearing where she had lived with the
full, happy heart that died when they did, and there Bapu and Ma would
be, standing smiling in front of the hut.

As for the days, that happy heart was coming alive again.

Initially, the place shocked her. Remnants of pyres dotted the barren
ground and bone shards lay everywhere. It took some getting used to, the
daily procession of the dead, but she was beginning to understand what the

chandala meant when he said this was the best work. Life was short, and death fell on everyone equally.

They built pyres for rich nobles and for those of the poor who could scrape together enough to buy the wood for a beloved one. When the priest or the eldest son or a brother put fire to the wood underneath the white-wrapped corpse, the world became sharper, clearer; the blue sky, the circling vultures, the flames crackling, the sickly sweet smell of burning flesh, the blackened body.

Over time, the fire seemed to catch in her heart and expand in her chest. She grieved for what she had lost, and in letting the grief out she made room for the happiness she found with this man who looked so noble and yet raked the ashes.

Yes, in its way it was the best work. Certainly there were worse things than raking the ashes of the dead. It was hot and hard, true, but she was used to that, from stirring the vats with her father and firing a potter's kiln. The smell was not pleasant, but it was in no way worse than the tanning pits. The consuming fire left little but ash and some bone, purifying everything.

The first day after they came to the cremation grounds, she had once more asked his name. Once again, he gave no answer, and an odd, cold feeling had settled in her stomach, as if knowing his name would somehow be dangerous. The feeling was so strong that she didn't ask again, telling herself that in this world they were creating at the cremation grounds, there were just the two of them. No need to call him anything other than "love." Mourners who brought their loved ones' corpses never spoke to them. What need had they of names?

Other concerns absorbed her. Food, for one. The earth around the dusty neem tree was hard, dry, burned, like the large expanse where they built the fires. There was no place on the barren ground for a little vegetable garden such as the one that Sujata had carefully tended. Mourners brought rice and flour and sometimes other food as dana to pay them for building and tending the pyre. If these gifts were fresh they were often about to spoil and had to be eaten right away. Some mourners were more generous than others, and would bring a basket of onions or dried fruit tied up in an old cloth. Those gifts lasted longer, and the cloth would be useful when they needed new clothing. There was never plenty, but mostly there was enough.

Now and again they went to sleep hungry, but that was no different from what Mala had always known.

To supplement what they were given, she fished. When she was a child Talu had shown her how to make a little net from hemp, to stand in the shallows and toss it. She had never been as skilled as he, but she was good enough. Early in the morning, she would scramble down the little bluff that overlooked Ganga's waters, which at this time of year were narrowed to a small channel surrounded by sandy riverbed, and catch a fish or two.

When their work was done, Mala and the chandala would gather roots and delightful sweet berries and fruits from the forest across the river. They could walk across the sandbars and swim the narrow stream to the inviting, dense green on the other side, laughing and splashing each other. Anandavana, the chandala called it, the Forest of Bliss, the home Shiva created for his wife Parvati, the mountain god Himalaya's daughter.

"Are there altars to Shiva and Parvati in Anandavana?" Mala said to him one day as the sun was setting and they were making their way home from the forest's cool green shade.

"Yes, though Shiva's true followers know the enlightened person has no need for shrines or priests or rituals. They scorn the grand Vedic sacrifices the Brahmins perform," he said with harsh contempt. "Those dreadful spectacles. In a king's name they offer a buffalo to Indra for victory in battle, or an ox to Kubera for a rich merchant who wants to get richer, or a flock of doves to Kama to help a lover win his love." He plunged into the water that reflected the purple and pink sunset.

Mala, taken aback by the bitterness in his voice, dove after him, but in the murky coolness she couldn't see him and surfaced. He was standing in the shallows, his hands raised to the sky. His eyes were closed and his lips moved in prayer.

"How do you know so many prayers?" Mala asked when he had finished and scooped water over his head three times, shaking his long, tangled hair. Not for the first time, she thought it was impossible that he was an outcaste.

"There are sages who will teach worthy seekers. The man who was chandala here before me taught me much."

Mala cocked her head. "He was a sage who lived among the ashes? How can that be?"

"Lord Shiva lives among the ashes."

"But he is a god."

"True. But he does not differentiate between purity and pollution. So it is with his followers. You might call yogis and holy wanderers casteless. Some were once Brahmins or Kshatriyas or the tradesmen of Vaishya birth who have renounced their dharmas in order to seek wisdom. Even a lowly Shudra can perform asceticisms and become a sage."

"What dharma did the chandala who taught you renounce?"

"I never asked. There was no need to know."

"Now you are the sage who builds the pyres. What dharma did you give up?"

His face twisted into an ugly frown. Mala froze. If she made him angry he would cast her out. She was afraid to be alone. She only wanted to please him so he would let her stay. "I didn't mean—"

He took her face in his hands. "There is no need to know." He searched her eyes. "The only thing you need know is that I never thought I would laugh again. Then our paths crossed."

She swayed toward him, raising her lips. He slid his arms around her. "I am no sage, but a fool who wants to kiss you." He did so, softly. "And what does my past dharma matter? Now our duty is to each other."

Mala's heart soared. She embraced him. They kissed again, then tore themselves apart and raced through the shallows, back to the hut where they fell together onto the hard ground, breathless.

The next day when she returned to the river to fish, she noticed that a little farther down the bank, just beyond some tall reeds, a small shaalmali tree was growing between several large, flat boulders. She was glad to see it. She could make a drink from the lush red flowers that came after the rains. The seedpods that came after the flowering season held the fiberlike silk-cotton that she used to catch the blood during her courses, and that she could also use to stuff pillows for their bed, which was nothing more than mats she'd woven from the tall grasses that grew near the river. The tree was a generous gift from the Devi, and a good place for a private little shrine. At the tree's base she stacked a couple smaller rocks. As the days passed, she offered food she saved from her meals on the altar. It pleased her that she could give more than she ever had back in Gauri.

One day they found a live chicken in the wooden box at the entrance to the burning grounds where mourners left their payments. Its legs were tied and it fluttered its wings.

Mala picked it up. It was scrawny and half dead. "Poor thing! But we'll feed it and soon we'll have fresh eggs."

"A chicken wouldn't last a night out here," he replied, amused. "Haven't you heard the jackals?"

She had heard yips and calls in the night, but so distant that she hadn't thought anything of them. "But we could keep it in the hut while we sleep."

"They'd just come take it while we work."

"In the daylight? I've never seen a jackal."

"They hide in the scrub, keeping low, watching us to see if we neglect our duties and leave something unburned for them." Mala shuddered a little. "But mostly they stay in the forest. Especially when they accompany a tiger on a hunt."

Of course. She had forgotten that jackals did not fear the great cats. She recalled that her father said the two races had lived in relative harmony since ages past, when all mortals spoke to gods and animals. In that ancient time, a jackal had tricked a hunter into freeing a tiger from one of his traps, and out of gratitude, they were allowed to follow the tigers and feast on leavings of their hunting.

"You could offer it to the Devi," he said.

Mala flushed. He had watched her at her little shrine.

"Cut off its head, catch the blood in a bowl, and pour it over those rocks by the shaalmali."

"But you said what the priests did was a disgusting spectacle."

"There's one thing about offering an ox. The priests divide the food among the worshippers," he said with a strange laugh. "We could eat the chicken."

Mala didn't know what to make of his strange laugh, but in the end, she did as he suggested. She slaughtered the chicken the way she'd seen Jyoti do it and put it on to cook, then took the blood to the river. The chandala did not come along, and she was glad of it. She felt there was something between her and the Devi that he didn't need to observe.

After she had made her offering and said her little prayers, she looked toward the forest. Maybe the tiger those jackals followed was Rani. Rani was queen of her race, she had said. Asita said white tigers were dedicated to Shiva, so perhaps Rani hunted in the god's forest.

"I will watch for you, O Rani," she said softly and headed back to the hut.

From then on, whenever Mala went to the river to bathe or fish or say a prayer at her altar she would squint into Anandavana's shadows, hoping to see a flash of white. She went a few times to the forest to collect wood and searched for a grove like the one she'd found near Gauri or a shrine to Shiva and Parvati, but the chandala had told her that the forest was dangerous. She shouldn't go alone, maybe even not at all. Not only sages at their hermitages but bloodthirsty outlaws lived in its tangled depths. It brought the two bandits who had tried to rob the courtesan to mind. Perhaps Asita had a hermitage there, or those outlaws camped somewhere in its shelter.

Those possibilities didn't engage her for long. A few more times she went to explore Anandavana but felt unfriendly eyes on her. Best to return to her work at the burning grounds and give up her quest for the time being.

The days rolled by until a moon passed. Mala was content and happy, yet occasionally an uneasy restlessness seized her. Her lover never spoke of leaving. She hesitated to ask, fearing it would displease him and he would turn away from her. She couldn't bear that.

One night as they lay on their grass mats, she gathered her courage. "I wondered, love, are you bound here until another comes to take on your task, as you did for the sage who was here before?" He didn't answer, so she rushed on. "Because, you see, I wondered, why not sell the necklace? It would surely fetch a great price. We could start a new life somewhere else."

"This is my place, my penance," he said. His voice had a hard edge to it. She had displeased him, just as she had feared. "I committed a great sin against a powerful Brahmin," he said. "If I am found, I will be punished, and you may be, too, if they find you with me. Now you know. You need not stay, Mala."

"I don't want to go."

"Think carefully. You could take the necklace. You must not try to sell the whole thing, especially here in Kashi or in the Sakyan kingdom. It would bring down their wrath on us." Whose wrath, Mala wondered again, but had no chance to ask. "You might sell a few of the jewels that came loose. Or take it to Maghada, or other places in the east where the necklace would command a good price, or in the far west, the kingdom of the Ghandaras or the Surasenas. I will not stop you," he finished in a rush. "I would not blame you for going." He turned to her, his eyes glistening in the dark.

She melted. "I wouldn't know how to sell it!" She didn't know much at all about the wide world. She wanted to learn how it worked, but if she were on her own she wouldn't know where to start. She could end up a slave again.

After so much loneliness and suffering, she had found some happiness in this most unexpected place. Though he said she risked punishment if she remained with him and these powerful others found him, no matter that she raked the ashes to live, she felt safe at the cremation grounds. If someone from Gauri was even bothering to look for her, well, who would think to look in this place? Aside from her parents, no one had ever treated her so kindly as the chandala did. It was hard not knowing his past, but she loved him here and now.

She didn't know if he loved her. He kept so much hidden, and he never asked about her former life. It hurt, but she didn't tell him her sorrows. There was much she wanted to forget. No doubt it was the same for him.

"I don't want to go," she said again.

What was done was done; they should only look forward. With that thought, the weight in her heart shifted, lightened. This was her karma, to serve this man, serve with him in this place of death.

"If you stay, we will keep the jewels hidden," he said, his arms behind his head. "It is a famous necklace. If you go, remember what I said about the Sakyas and the Kashis; if you tried to sell it, they would recognize it and someone would find you..."

Desire swept through her. She wanted to rock underneath him, to make him want her to stay, need her to stay. "Love," she said.

"Hmm," he replied.

"Love, teach me the things that... that would please you most..."

He turned away and for a long time said nothing.

His long silence made her heart heavy. "I—I'm sorry. I only wanted—"

With startling force, he pulled her to him with one arm and rolled on top of her. His hips ground against hers. She gasped, and he covered her mouth. His eyes glinted in the dark, frightening her, yet somehow she sensed he did not see her. He buried his face in her neck, biting so hard it hurt. She gasped again. Then he thrust his fingers in her mouth, and she began to suck on them as he moved down to kiss her breasts, sucking and nipping at her nipples while he loosened the antariya wrapped around her hips and felt for her sex. He murmured in her ear how to touch him, where to kiss, what he wanted.

What he asked she gave, things she had never dreamed of doing, things that would fill the gods themselves with ecstasy and that filled her with fire. Breathless with desire, she returned his every touch and kiss, and they writhed and rolled on the grass mats. At last he entered her, and she squeezed her legs around his back. She wept with joy.

"Moti," he cried as he finished, then whispered in her ear, "Moti, my dark pearl."

She tensed. Her throat constricted. Moti, his old love. "Oh, love. Why?"

He pushed against her embrace. A little red light flickered around her. No—she didn't want to let go. But she released her legs, almost choking with tears. The red flickering died away.

He rolled off to lie on his side, facing away from her. It was not long before his breath came slow and even, though she was not sure he really slept.

"Love." She leaned over him. Her whisper was hoarse and trembling.

There was no answer. She rolled the other way and stifled her sobs. When she had cried herself out, she lay awake a long time, trying to imagine their future together. But she could not.

The next day, though, they worked companionably together. When the pyres had all extinguished, they sat around the cook fire sharing their observations about the mourners and talking about pleasant nothings. They made love again that night, but from that time on, no matter how passionate their lovemaking became, he never called Moti's name. But neither did he call out "Mala!" at the moment of ecstasy.

Still, as time went on, she sensed he gave her all he was capable of giving. It had to be enough.

THE LORD OF YOGA

T HE MONSOON CAME. MALA'S COURSES stopped. The rainy months passed while life stirred within her and filled her with power. This energy seemed to surge up from the earth itself through her feet and right to her heart. There were no flashing lights, there was no pulsing aura, only the feeling that she wanted to weep and shout with joy at the same time.

She was afraid to tell the chandala, and for a time he seemed not to notice. Then one night as he fondled her breasts, he said, "How is this that they seem to have grown?"

She smiled in the dark. He knew the world better than she, yet he was so naive in some ways. Then her smile faded and apprehension took hold. She didn't know what he would think. "I am pregnant, love."

In the dark, she could not read his face, but his silence said volumes. He was angry; he would say this was no place to bring up a child; he would send her away. At the last thought, her eyes filled with tears, and she took a shaky breath.

He took her in his arms. "What's this? Are you crying?"

"No... yes." She sniffled. "Are you angry?"

"How could I be? New life in the ashes..." He kissed her forehead then went silent again. She wanted him to say something, anything. Nestled in the crook of his arm, she wiped her eyes and looked up. She couldn't see his face. "It is strange," he said, and his voice was full of wonder, "that Shiva has sent a child as a blessing, here amidst all this death. That he's sent a child at all, really."

"What do you mean?"

"Shiva was not much of a father," he said with a laugh.

"Love! The gods hear everything."

"Why should we care? The Great God is terrible, but also merciful. And he loves truth."

He was merciful. Asita had said Shiva broke the flow of Ganga's waters to keep the earth from washing away. She smiled in the dark. She hadn't understood then what Asita meant when he said the god knelt before the goddess, but the chandala had shown her. A great rush of desire made her shudder. "I think he was also the Great Seducer. The yogi who came to my parents' hut long ago said even the Devi couldn't resist him." She traced the chandala's collarbone with her finger.

"In some of her forms. Ganga, for instance, and Parvati. The most chaste of mortal women are helpless before the tapas that emanates from the Lord of Yoga and his followers. For mortal yogis, the challenge is to resist the nymphs who seek them out in the forest."

"But are you one of the Lord of Yoga's followers," she said, "that you must resist?" She let her hand wander down his chest and stomach.

"I live among the ashes seeking the wisdom he can bestow." The chandala turned and grasped Mala around the waist, and with one surprising and fluid motion lifted her so she straddled him. "But I have taken no vow of celibacy," he said as he entered her, "and I don't have to resist my nymph."

Their lovemaking was long and slow, then urgent and hard. Then they lay spent in each other's arms.

"Tell me, why did you say that he was not a good father?" Mala asked.

"He did not want to give his wife, Parvati, a child," the chandala said. "And when she kept begging for one, he tossed her the tiger skin he sometimes sat on during his meditations and told her the skin would beget a son on her while he practiced his yoga."

"That was cruel!" She didn't care if the god heard.

"Well, he should have been more careful what he said. Her husband's thoughtless words made Parvati weep, and when her tears fell on the tiger skin it softened in her hands, and she shaped it into a boy child. She called him Ganesha, the Lord of Hosts, in hopes he would one day be a great ruler. She told him to guard her door and be an obstacle to anyone who would enter without her permission. When Shiva had finished his ascetic practices, he wanted to make love to his wife, but Ganesha wouldn't let him into Parvati's chambers. So Shiva struck off his head."

Mala gasped. "But that's horrible."

"Parvati was grief-stricken and outraged, and told Shiva she would never lie with him again. Now, Shiva took great pleasure in making love to Parvati, who knew how to give divine satisfaction to her lord." Mala nuzzled his neck. "What's this? Haven't you had enough?" He laughed.

"Like Parvati," she said. "I know how to satisfy my lord."

"And he is well satisfied," the chandala said. "And a bit weary."

"All right. Finish the story."

"Shiva is powerful, but he even he cannot undo what is done. So he rushed out and found the head of the first animal he saw, a young elephant, and struck off its head. Then he put it on Ganesha's shoulders, and from then on, the boy had an elephant's head. This was not entirely a bad thing; elephants are very intelligent animals and Ganesha became very wise."

"It turned out all right for Parvati, then, although I'm not sure how I would feel if our child had an elephant's head. But I think Shiva would be a difficult husband. He was mean to Parvati."

"And yet he defended women. Once, he helped the dawn goddess. When four-headed Brahma looked on his beautiful daughter Ushas dressed in dawn's brilliant purple, red, and orange robes, he was filled with lust. In a panic, Ushas ascended heavenward. Brahma grew a fifth head to find her. Seeing this unseemly behavior, Lord Shiva cut off the Creator's fifth head. Now, Brahma was the first Brahmin, and according to the dharma, to kill a Brahmin stains one's karma black. As Shiva's punishment, the other gods decreed the skull of Brahma's fifth head be fixed to the Great Ascetic's hand. He would have to eat and drink from it until he purified his karma. So he came to Ganga's banks to practice austerities in the cremation grounds, and that is how he came to live in the ashes."

Shiva defied the dharma to protect Ushas. Mala's skin prickled. A god who defended helpless women was a god worth praying to. "But he didn't kill Brahma," she said, thinking aloud. "Gods are immortal! He just cut off one of the Creator's heads."

"Gods die, too, though their existence spans thousands of mortal lifetimes. But you're right. Brahma didn't die. Still, my dear, it is no less a crime to cut off a god's head."

"But he had four others."

The chandala shook his head and smiled. "Ah, enough, Mala. You should go to the Maghadan kingdom and study the dharma. I think you might be able to argue the law with the students at Maghada's great ashrams, where they study it in a different way."

"What does it mean, to study the dharma in a different way?"

"In Maghada's ashrams, scholars compare how other peoples make laws, to take what's good from them. The Maghadan king, Bimbisara, wants his kingdom to be the most just among all the Sixteen Clans."

"Don't all kings want to be the most powerful?"

"To rule justly confers greater power than any army could."

"But a woman can't study the law," she said.

"Maghadan law gives equal status to women. And to all castes. They have a saying: A man is noble not by birth, but by deeds."

Mala put a hand on her stomach. A place where her child would grow up equal to a Brahmin. "That yogi who came to our hut said something like that," Mala murmured. "I'd almost forgotten. Something about a prince of some clan would turn the wheel of a new dharma." She yawned and settled into the crook of his arm again. "Who did he say—the Sakyas? Yes, it was the Sakyas. You spoke of them."

The chandala tensed. "Do you want to learn more or not?"

"Yes, yes. Go on about Shiva and his punishment."

"Lord Shiva burned with such great tapas," he began, but his voice was still harsh. He took a breath and relaxed a little. "He burned with such spiritual fire that where he sat became a tirtha between the worlds of gods and men. Sometimes it is possible for mortals to pass through that gate and enter Indra's heavenly city…"

Mala's eyes drooped. The chandala began to breathe soft and even next to her, and she drifted until all of a sudden there was a light, a white, hot light, brighter than day, and she was building a pyre for her chandala, lighting it, letting it purify this dark stain on his karma. But suddenly, a goddess with skin as black as night rose from the flames and began to dance on the corpse. Kali, it was dark Kali. Red flames leaped and roared around her. Mala wanted to drag her lover's corpse from the fire, but the goddess vomited blood—

She jerked awake. What could this terrible vision mean? Was he going to die soon? She laid an arm across him, felt his chest rise and fall and heard his heart beat. No, it couldn't be. Perhaps it meant her karma was to fulfill this duty to him when he died. Yes, that must be it. And Kali, why was Kali there?

Her thoughts wandered and her eyes began to droop again. Sleep took her.

Once again there was brilliant light, brighter than day. Once again her lover's white-wrapped corpse was laid atop a pyre, but a man was holding out the flaming torch to set the wood aflame. She strained to see this man, feeling she recognized him, but she couldn't quite make him out. Somehow, though, it comforted her that he had taken the task to set the fire from her. Released from this duty, she began to dance and dance and dance until the stars began to fall from the sky.

THE DARK GODDESS

A LOOSELY WRAPPED ANTARIYA COVERED MALA from shoulders to knees. With a hand on her growing belly, she watched the chandala, who a short distance away was arranging sandalwood logs in a neat geometric pattern for a wealthy merchant's pyre. He had insisted that she stop helping him with this hard work. Her time was a few months off, but already he was anxious that she not exhaust herself.

She busied herself with practicalities, washing and folding rags, keeping the water jar full, weaving a basket to hold the baby. There was no midwife who would tend to her near the burning grounds, which lay on the sprawling city's western edge. She might find one in the outcaste settlements where tanners like Talu, carriers of night soil, butchers, and other untouchables lived, but those were far downriver, on the eastern side. But she had helped when Gauri's cows calved; she had watched the midwife and taken away the bloody rags when the village women gave birth. She was nervous, yes, and yet she had a deep sense, a different form of sacred energy, that all would be well when her time came.

Today something had drawn her to watch her lover at his work. When the pyre was ready, the mourners lifted the litter that carried the corpse—white-wrapped and strewn with red, yellow, and orange marigolds so it appeared already aflame—atop the stacked logs.

Puffing a little, the chandala walked over to her, wiping the thin film of sweat off his forehead then putting his hands on his hips. A breeze ruffled his hair. The monsoon had ended but the air remained fresh and cool. "This is not good," he said, shaking his head.

"Whatever do you mean? The logs are properly laid." ·

"I heard them talking."

He indicated the merchant's three grown sons, who stood on the other side of the unlit pyre. They were large, fleshy men, wrapped in richly patterned antariyas, rings flashing on thick fingers. They were whispering with their wives, three equally richly attired women with gold bangles from wrist to elbow and necklaces flashing with jewels. The finery did not improve one wife's beaked nose or another's fat chins. Nor did the shining adornments dim the palpable aura of hate those two emanated toward the third wife, a haughty beauty. Mala shaded her eyes with her hand, studying them. They were surrounded by children of varying ages, who stood with their shoulders hunched, a position much like the one she used to take when she expected Jyoti's broom on her back. Sure enough, when one of the younger children asked a question, the fat woman gave him a slap that made her chins quiver and silenced the child.

A few steps away from this group stood a fourth man, who was younger than the other three and did not resemble them physically. Their clean-shaven faces were jowly and bore sour expressions. The fourth man's visage was tanned and lean, and he had a well-trimmed beard. His plain, dark blue antariya was wrapped only around his waist. Over it he wore an odd garment of unbleached linen or cotton. It was made from pieces of cloth so that it fitted over his shoulders and covered his arms. One side folded over the other on his chest, and a dark blue sash, the same color as the antariya, held it closed.

Next to this man an old woman in voluminous white robes, probably the merchant's widow, leaned on a cane. Her unkempt grey hair fell around her shoulders, over her thin arms and almost down to her waist.

"Talking about what?" Mala asked, but before the chandala could answer, the priest, a man as round and short as the Brahmin Valmiki was lean and tall, began the prayers and poured ghee over the corpse and the sandalwood until both were soaked. The sons joined the chanting, then one with grey-streaked hair took a flaming torch and touched the woodpile.

The flames licked around the lowest logs, gradually working their way up the pyre, until with a sharp hiss they exploded around the corpse and up to the sky. They burned with a low thunder that was like the subtle roar that filled Mala's ears at very quiet times. The yawing sensation that sometimes came over her, the sense that she was about to fall into a black chasm, made her sway and reach for the chandala's arm. But at this moment he let out a cry.

"Stop!"

"Stop!" The lean young man echoed his shout, and both rushed toward the white-clad old woman, who was all of a sudden next to the fire with her arms outstretched. She looked heavenward and cried out. She would have stepped into the flames but the young man reached her, seized her arm and pulled her back, but not before her white robes had caught on fire.

Mala's lover and the young man looked at each other. The young man drew up short, shocked recognition in his eyes. The chandala shook his head then he turned and raced toward the hut. He seized the waterskin they kept hanging from a low bough of the neem tree and ran back. The young man was brushing at the flames, trying to put them out. It could not have been a minute before the chandala was back and squirting the water over the woman's flaming robe.

"How dare you, Bhallika," the oldest son shouted from across the pyre. "She is our mother, not yours! Let her have her noble death."

"Noble death?" The young man brushed at the smoldering white garments and then enveloped the old woman in his arms. "For shame, that you should wish your own mother to suffer such an agonizing end! Dhuma does not want to die. She does this because she knows you will cast her out with nothing."

Dhuma struggled to break away from Bhallika. "I do want death, my friend," she said, and started to weep.

"You see," the beauty said, "she knows the dharma. A woman who outlives her husband brings misfortune to the family. Better to die. Is this not true?" She turned to the priest, but he was already hurrying away, his duty to the dead and the mourners finished.

"And what if Deepak should catch a fever, die young, and leave you, Ghita?" Bhallika retorted, his green eyes flashing. The beauty drew herself up and gave him a cold look, but she did not reply.

As the pyre burned hot and steady, Mala stared through the heat waves at the strange tableau the merchant's family made. The sons and their wives looked into the flames with their jaws set. The children, tired from standing for so long, shifted from one foot to another. They rubbed tears and ash from their eyes and for a while sent imploring glances to their grandmother. She did not even look in their direction.

She seemed unaware of anything. Her struggles had subsided, but Bhallika did not let go. The sons gathered their families and walked away while the pyre turned to coals, not waiting for the fire to die as respect for the dead required. Several children looked over their shoulders, their faces wet with tears, only to have one or another mother snatch their hand and pull them along.

"You should bring her to the hut," the chandala said to Mala.

She was shocked at everything that had happened, but this astounded her. "But how can we offer them hospitality—"

"It's all right," Bhallika said. "The chandala and his wife stay to help this woman, while the priest runs. Who is the Brahmin?" He spat. "Not him. He's a worthless cur. Come," he said to Dhuma. "You need water, and we must see if you're burned."

The old woman allowed him to lead her. Mala hurried ahead and brought the mats from inside the hut and set them under the tree. Bhallika helped Dhuma sit down while Mala took a wooden bowl and dipped it in the water jar. She offered it to Dhuma, who didn't look up, so Bhallika took it.

"I have some dry clothes," Mala began.

Dhuma raised her wrinkled face and gazed at Mala with deep-set, dark eyes. "You are kind, but I don't need them. You see, I'm not injured." She lifted her singed, wet robe from her legs to show there were no burns.

"You're sure?" Bhallika asked, sitting back on his heels. "The nights are cool. You could catch a chill."

"And start coughing and die? I wish for it." She sighed and patted his leg. "You care more for me than my sons ever did." He said nothing. "But then, what was our example? We neglected our own parents on the way to acquiring our wealth. And I… I… what dark sacrifices I made…"

"What are you talking about? You and your husband are the epitome of dharma," Bhallika said. "The fire on your family altar never goes out, and it is covered with flowers and fruits always."

"There is much you don't know, my friend," she said, and looked away, toward the river. "But I am grateful to you. You brought my husband such joy on the travels you took together. They were by far more profitable than

102

any caravan he undertook with our worthless sons, who only cared to stay home and spend his money."

At that moment, the chandala returned. The pyre had burned down, the embers scattered. He was carrying a sack that the merchant's family had left as dana. He slung it to the ground and opened it. His eyes lit up. "Rice. Good quality, too."

"Then it cannot be from my sons." She looked at Bhallika, who smiled and shrugged.

"We have spices and oil, and some lentils," Mala said. "I can make a good meal for you. And please, I have a good length of cloth that you could wear while those things dry."

"No. These clothes are all I need," she repeated. "I am exhausted. I would like to rest…"

"I have pillows to make you more comfortable," Mala said.

"I wish I had a daughter-in-law like you, my dear," Dhuma said, smiling.

Mala fetched the pillows and helped the old woman settle down, then busied herself with the fire, all the while glancing sideways at the chandala and Bhallika.

Bhallika's strange green eyes were locked on her lover's amber ones. "Odd to find one such as you here," he said after a time.

"One such as I? What do you mean?" Her lover gave Bhallika a warning look, then glanced in her direction and lowered his eyes.

He murmured, "I mean, one of your lineage…"

"One who rakes the ashes has no lineage," the chandala snapped, glaring at the young man. "But what of yours?"

"As you like," Bhallika said in his soft voice. "As for me, like you, I have no need of a lineage to prove my worth. A merchant determines his own by how rich he makes himself and his investors. Nowadays I serve the Sakyan king."

The chandala stiffened. As Bhallika's voice dropped again, Mala strained to hear.

"…I have learned it was stolen from Addhakashi," Bhallika was saying. Mala's neck prickled. "Some say thieves… but King Suddhodana thinks it's here in Varanasi. He senses it. The Gautamas have a gift for these things… but no one seems to know where the necklace is… no trace on the black market."

The necklace. Mala held her breath and ceased frying the rice. Out of the corner of her eye, she watched the chandala listen in silence, expressionless.

"You must look elsewhere than Varanasi then," he said after a time.

"Indeed," Bhallika said. "But for now, I think I will bathe in Ganga's waters."

Mala felt his glance fall on her, but she poured water into the pot and stirred it as if her life depended on it. The necklace was underneath the cook fire's coals. She could see it so clearly in her mind's eye, she thought the merchant must, too.

ॐ

The old woman slept. The others ate in silence though Mala's head spun with questions. Dark fell, and the chandala stood up. He held out a hand to help Mala rise, nodded in silence at Bhallika. They walked toward the hut.

Mala turned back. "If she wakes, I kept a little rice in the bowl with the wooden cover."

Building the pyre with such heavy wood had exhausted her lover, and he fell asleep at once. Mala couldn't stop thinking. Bhallika had recognized the chandala, that much was clear. She must find out more. She rose in silence.

The night air was a cool caress after the hut's stuffiness. Ganga's river of stars flowed across the black sky. Dhuma sat by the fire, stirring it with a stick so that little flames gave off an inviting yellow glow in the surrounding darkness. Near it, Bhallika had flung himself among the pillows and was snoring softly. Mala's shoulders slumped.

"Looking for him?" Dhuma said.

"Yes," Mala began.

"Your man doesn't satisfy you?"

"No! That is, yes." Mala stepped over to the fire and got down on her knees next to the old woman. "I don't want that from Bhallika. It's that I—I want to know what he knows. About my man." She glanced at the sleeping merchant. "He's taken the place I made for you to rest."

Dhuma smiled. "I don't need it. I told him I would sit by the fire a while." She put a hand on Mala's belly, and the baby kicked. "All will be well."

"Do you think so?" Mala broke into a smile and trembled with relief. "I know it in all my bones, but I don't know how."

"Certain things are plain. You are young and healthy. A bit narrow in the hips, but you are strong enough to push. But also I feel Kali Ma will watch over you."

"Kali." Mala's skin prickled. "I saw her in my dream, wearing a skull necklace."

"I knew it."

"How do you know? She frightens me…"

"Good. You should fear her. If you cross her, she will show no mercy in her anger, but if she bestows her favor on you, she becomes Kali Ma, the Mother whose love is deep and wide as an ocean."

"Why would Kali favor me?"

"Kali is within you." The fire's soft, golden light surrounded Dhuma's wrinkled face. "You can think of it this way. There are goddesses in every woman, forms of the Devi that guide us on our lives' paths if we let them. You could say a courtesan personifies Sarasvati, the goddess of the arts and learning and beauty. Or a woman who follows her husband to a forest hermitage personifies Parvati, who mastered Shiva's yoga and lightens his solitude at his lonely retreats." She paused. "Or in my case, Lakshmi. The goddess of wealth once favored me. Thus my husband's fortunes grew and our household prospered." The old woman stared into the flames. "Now I have nothing…"

Excited by a sudden realization, Mala ignored this remark. "So Kali is the goddess within me?"

Dhuma's forehead wrinkled. "Perhaps. Perhaps it is she who drew you here, for she often appears to mortals at the burning grounds. If she is your goddess, I cannot tell you if you are blessed or cursed."

"How do I know whether she will favor me? What offerings should I make to her?"

"Offer the things you hold dearest," Dhuma said. She fell silent.

Mala thought a while. She had nothing of value. Except the necklace. She pushed the idea away. She did not want to think of offering that. "Does she have temples in the city? Do people worship her there? Are there priests who make offerings?"

"Priests, ha! She has no need of them. Besides, men fear her. The Brahmins fear her most of all. She is too powerful. Even Shiva could not truly tame her. She is no god's consort, as Lakshmi is to Vishnu the

Preserver, Sarasvati to Indra, and Ganga and Parvati to Shiva—but Kali, no god rules her."

The priests feared Kali. No god ruled her. It excited Mala. "My man says Shiva's followers have no need of priests, either. Is it like that?"

"So many questions. I don't know the answers. I only know that to worship Shiva or Kali is very dangerous."

"How so?"

"Those who perform Shiva's highest yoga gain powers of mind that can corrupt as easily as they enlighten. Those who sacrifice to Kali without a pure heart will use the powers she bestows toward perverted ends."

In the fire's red center, a black spot began to spread. Mala couldn't look away. Time stopped. A demon hissed. Red coals became eyes that bored through Mala. She lost all sense of time.

A snap. A crack. Mala blinked. Disoriented, she looked around. Bhallika stirred under the tree, but Dhuma was nowhere to be seen. The sky was silvering.

Bhallika sat up, stretched, and yawned. "Where is Dhuma?"

"I... I don't know," Mala answered. Then in her mind's eye she saw a white-clad figure head down the embankment to Ganga's waters.

"The river," she gasped. "She is going to the river."

Bhallika jumped up and began to run toward Ganga. "It's too late," whispered Mala as she watched him disappear down the bluff.

A red sun was rising in the east when he returned. "She walked into the river," he said, his face grim. "She disappeared before I could reach her."

"A better death than the flames," Mala said. It was true. It was what Dhuma wanted. "Please, sit. I will give you something to break your fast..."

Bhallika stared at her. She met his eyes. There was nothing she could do for the old woman now. She was bursting with questions about the chandala, but the grief on Bhallika's face kept her silent.

He shook his head. "I will go now," he said. "Thank your man for me." He walked away without another word or glance.

THE CHILD

T HE TIME HAD FINALLY COME. Nine moons had passed since her last blood. Her belly was huge. The pains had begun that morning. Mala had never known such agony.

"What can I do? What can I do?" the chandala asked, helpless with concern as she writhed and moaned.

"Boil some water," she gasped. The little task was enough to make him feel useful and for Mala to stop worrying about him and pay attention to the child demanding to be born. In the midst of this agony she struggled to remember what they did in Gauri. She had thought it would all go smoothly, but in the moment, she forgot the charms and incantations the midwife said to coax the infant from the womb.

In the end, the baby came like a miracle. An enormous push, and the child slid out from between her legs in a pool of blood. A girl! The sudden cessation of pain and the sight of her tiny daughter were wondrous beyond words. Everything about the baby was perfect; the tiny hands and feet, the long lashes, and sparse black curls plastered down with the waters of birth.

One more push, and the afterbirth came. With weak and trembling hands, she cut the cord while the chandala watched with his mouth gaping and brow wrinkled, caught between awe and disgust. Men never attended births in the village. That the chandala had asked to help was extraordinary, but it was plainly too much for him.

"Love." Her voice was weak. "Love, help me… clean her."

"Oh… yes… here." He wrung out a large rag, and as he tried to hand it to her he dropped it in the dust, picked it up and wetted it again, then wrung it out. It was grey with dirt, but it was clean enough to swab her baby. The newborn took breath without a midwife's slap and gazed at her parents with strange, knowing eyes.

"You're not disappointed," Mala said, weary but happy.

"No, why?"

"I thought all men wanted sons."

"She's beautiful," he whispered.

"Like my mother, Sujata," she said, in woozy amazement. "Such a perfect little creature came from such an ugly mother." She shook her head.

"But Mala. You are beautiful," the chandala said.

Mala's head spun. He'd never said such a thing. She would never have expected him to. She had looked at her reflection in the river many times and seen the same broad cheeks and thick lips she'd always seen, though her eyes looked back deep and lustrous.

"But she is so skinny. Aren't babies fat?"

She laughed aloud at the wonder in her arms and the wonder that he'd said she was beautiful. "Skinny? Yes, I suppose she is."

"We'll call her Kirsa, the thin one."

"Kirsa, my skinny little one." The baby stretched and yawned.

The chandala touched Kirsa's cheek with his finger. "Shouldn't you feed her?" he asked. His brow was still wrinkled, but now he appeared not so much revolted as frightened. He blinked several times then stared with eyes wide open. "So helpless... the poor creature... is she—will she—will she be all right?"

"Yes, love, yes." Mala soothed him as she put the baby's mouth to her nipple the way she'd seen the midwife help village mothers. She'd watched only from a distance, but it seemed simple enough. Once again wonder filled her, as little Kirsa took it right away and sucked contentedly. It was so simple, so right. So beautiful. That's what the chandala had meant.

Kirsa's mouth worked for a few moments, then fell away from Mala's breast. A drop of milk remained on her pink lip. She fell asleep almost at once. What did the midwife say? Something about how it was auspicious for the baby if the mother's milk came in right away.

"A good omen," she whispered.

That night the dark goddess Kali came, dressed in rags and around her neck a garland of white skulls that dripped blood, vivid against black skin. She had four arms that held a discus, a mace, a trident, and a silver cord. Around her waist was a belt from which severed arms hung. A red aura blazed around the goddess.

Mala shook so hard she could not speak. As if to hide Kirsa from Kali's presence, she pressed her baby closer. What had Dhuma said? When the goddess bestowed her favor, her love was a boundless ocean. "O Kali Ma…"

You are a fool, Mala.

The voice rang in her head. "O Kali, why…?"

Kali opened her mouth wide, revealing sharp teeth, and let out a shriek of laughter. Mala winced and glanced down at the baby, who impossibly remained asleep. "Protect my child, O Dark One, and I will give you everything I have…"

Kali shrieked again. White teeth flashed in the dark face. Her tongue was the color of bright red blood. *I am Kali, the Power-of-Time. There is nothing you have that is not already mine.*

Mala was stricken. "Don't take my child!" she cried.

She sat bolt upright. There was no dark goddess with a blazing red aura, only Kirsa sleeping peacefully at her side. Where was the chandala? Frantic, she looked around, then saw the fire flickering outside. It would soon be dawn; he must be cooking their breakfast rice.

Mala settled down on her side, close to Kirsa. She shivered a little, once again, remembering the skull necklace dripping blood. She was not certain she wanted to ask the chandala what the dream meant. She was afraid of what he would tell her.

Kirsa yawned in her sleep. She looked so innocent and peaceful.

Mala's uneasiness passed. She studied the baby beside her, a pure new being with her golden skin in folds at the wrists and the perfect little fingers, the tiny mouth with its red lips, the dark, curly tendrils on Kirsa's head, soft as silk.

"How funny, my skinny little one," Mala whispered. "Such a huge head, like a melon, and such a tiny body." Gauri's midwife always bemoaned a newborn's ugliness in a loud voice, in case any demons or jealous nymphs were nearby, ready to steal a healthy son or do other mischief. To Mala, Kirsa was beautiful, though she wondered at the gods' craftsman, Tvastr.

He made a tiger cub that could jump and play almost as soon as it was born. Yet when he made a human baby, so oddly shaped and helpless, it seemed like he had not finished his work.

Then her heart constricted. Kirsa's helplessness appalled her. No one could protect her from all life's dangers.

She pulled the little bundle into the crook of her arm. "O Kali, you spoke the truth," Mala whispered. "I have nothing that is not yours. I can only offer you my love for my child." Tears spilled down her cheeks. Frightening as it was, the vision brought wisdom. "Only you can keep her safe from harm. Be kind to her, I beg you."

Outside the door, she could see dawn's silver light. She should get up now and help the chandala, but her lids were too heavy, and she slipped into dreamless sleep.

Eerie chanting awakened Mala.

"Om, bhur bhuvah svaha
Tat savitur varenyam
Bhargo devasya dhimani
Dhiyo yonah prachodayat."

Disoriented, she raised her head. The sleeping baby was still nestled in the curve of her arm. The chandala was not by her side. Then she remembered; he had been making breakfast rice.

"Om!" The chanting started again, sometimes full and then hesitant, cracking unsteadily.

The baby mewled. Mala held her precious newborn closer and yet with even more tender care, and eased toward the door. A low fire danced near the little clay stove and made shadows in the neem tree's leaves. The sky was just beginning to silver.

Her lover knelt before the fire. *"Om, bhur, bhuvah, svaha!"* He began again, dipping a ladle into a blackened wooden bowl. The *om* reverberated in Mala's heart as it had when her mother sang it. Then a beautiful hymn poured from his lips as if he'd spoken them all his life.

He held the ladle aloft, then poured liquid into the flames as he chanted. Golden ghee, a special treat carefully saved to cook their rice when the baby

110

came, sizzled on the charred wood. He dipped and poured again. The ghee hissed and smoked as it hit the fire.

"Love?"

He made no sign of hearing. *"…Tat savitur varenyam…"*

She went to his side. "Love, what are you doing?" Though she was right next to him, he gazed into the fire with eyes that seemed to see nothing, but reflected the light of the flames.

"Bhargo devasya dhimani… dhiyo yonah prachodayat…"

His voice rose, despairing and full of awe. In Mala's arms, Kirsa cried out, as if to echo her father. The sound made him gasp and frown. He looked at Mala and Kirsa. "Who are you?"

Mala went cold. She touched his arm. "Love?"

He brushed her hand from him. She drew back and held Kirsa tighter. He shook his head and looked into the flames again, blinking in confusion. "I… where am I?"

"My love, what's wrong?" she whispered.

"Moti!" he cried. Then his eyes focused on Mala and Kirsa. He burst into tears and covered his face with his hands. "Oh, Mala! Forgive me."

Kirsa started to cry again. A chill shook Mala, and she turned back to the hut. Seating herself near the door, she put Kirsa to her breast. Nursing calmed them both.

The chandala cried for a long time. Mala was too angry and hurt to comfort him. At last he lay down next to the dying fire as streaks of pink across the east announced the dawn goddess. The baby slept, too. Only Mala stayed awake as the sky went from grey to blue. She rose and made a sling of a long strip of clean cloth and tied Kirsa to her. Though she was sore and weak, she began to cook the breakfast rice, pouring the last few drops of ghee into the bubbling pot.

When it was almost ready, the chandala stirred. She avoided his eyes and knelt, picking up the wooden ladle and spooning some rice into a bowl. Head lowered, she held it out to him. He touched her shoulder, but she shook off his hand. Her throat was full of tears. It chilled her, the way he had looked right through her and their child.

"I should serve you. I am not worthy of what you've given me."

"What are you saying?" Mala stifled a sob. She put the bowl down.

"What can possibly be wrong? We brought a beautiful daughter into the world."

His face was twisted and tears coursed down his cheeks. "The gods forgive me... I should never have brought you here, never have conceived a child on you." He looked at Kirsa with sorrowful tenderness. "Who am I to deserve a father's happiness?"

"You're a good man," Mala began.

"A good man." His lips curved in a bitter half smile. "You fool. What kind of a woman would bear my child and not ask my name?" he said in a harsh voice.

It was as if he had struck her with these words, this man who had never raised a hand to her. "You said... I didn't want to... we didn't need to know each other's past," she whispered, struggling not to burst into tears. "You didn't want to tell me..." She hadn't wanted to hear, but since she had seen the recognition in Bhallika's face she felt it wouldn't be long before he could no longer run from his past.

He hid his face in his hands for a moment. "Forgive me." He touched her again, but Mala leaned away. He sighed. "I was grateful that you didn't ask. But I think the time has come. I was not born an outcaste."

"I've known that from the beginning. You're not like any village boy, or anyone I've ever met." She sniffed and wiped one hand across her eyes. "Eat. Soon someone will bring their dead, and we'll need to work."

"Oh, no. I would not have it, after all you did to bring our daughter forth." He reached a tentative finger to touch the top of Kirsa's head where it emerged from the sling. "No one's come. Our services aren't needed as yet. Come, sit. I will fetch water from the river."

He took the pail and hurried away on the path to Ganga's waters. When he disappeared into the tall grasses, Mala had a terrible foreboding. Dhuma had gone to the river to drown, never to return. Perhaps he wouldn't return either. She sat in a stupor of anxiety. What would she do then? She couldn't think.

Then he returned, sweaty and panting, with water sloshing from the jug on his shoulder and sluicing over his thin chest.

When he had set the jug at the entrance to the hut, he sat next to her. Neither spoke for some time. Finally, Mala gathered her courage. "The words you chanted, what do they mean?"

"It is the mantra a Brahmin says every morning and every evening, the Gayatri, the most sacred meter of any chant. *Om, the earth, the sky, the heavens. Let us meditate on the divine light of the sun. May it illuminate our minds...*"

"You are a Brahmin." She had always known. "One of the gods-on-earth."

"I committed one of the worst crimes a Brahmin can." He covered his face. "I slept with my guru's wife."

ANGIRASA'S TALE

I F SHE HAD NOT BEEN so stunned, Mala might have laughed. "Crime? In our village, men slept with other men's wives all the time. No one cared."

He dropped his hands and settled himself cross-legged, facing her. "Not a guru's wife and his pupil. It's a great sin."

"Was it Moti?" Mala asked quietly. He looked away. "You called me Moti. When we first met, on the road," she continued, "you thought I was someone called Moti. When I told you the courtesan Addhakashi was wearing the necklace, you said Moti was her sister."

He rested one palm atop the other in his lap. "If I'd told you, you could have taken the necklace and left."

"I wanted to stay. Remember? It was my choice." A choice made out of fear and love at the same time.

He exhaled. "My name is Angirasa. I am a Sakyan nobleman."

"A Sakyan?"

"I'm a kinsman to King Suddhodana of the Sakyas on my mother's side. On my father's side, I am descended from celestial sage Angirasa himself."

She recalled the feeling she'd had not so long ago, that to live here with the chandala, do their duty to the dead, and, when the time came, to light his pyre was enough. This changed everything. He was royalty. Descended from immortal beings. She looked down at sleeping Kirsa. That meant a great deal for their child.

"My father Bhela is King Suddhodana's royal priest, and my mother is the king's sister. They sent me to Varanasi to study under my father's famous kinsman." Angirasa took a deep breath. "I was his best student. Valmiki singled me out for praise—"

"Valmiki!" Mala jerked. The baby mewled. "Hush, hush, little one," she said. With shaking hands, she offered Kirsa a breast. Thankfully, the baby quieted at once.

"You know him?" Angirasa asked.

"He was the landlord of my village," she said. "When a warrior murdered my father, he said it was my father's fault. That was a lie!" A wave of pain and shame washed over her. She'd failed the test of courage then. Valmiki had made her feel worthless, guilty before his gods.

"Murdered... how terrible." His face was full of compassion. "When was this?"

"Years ago. I was only twelve."

"You kept secrets, too."

"You never asked!" Her lips trembled. "And I told myself it was better... it was clear you had suffered, and so had I. You don't know what it's like to be untouchable, a slave. You begin to believe what everyone says, that you pollute everything you touch, that you deserve the beatings... If it hadn't been for the Devi's voice, I would have been crushed to nothingness."

The fire snapped. Mala's skin tingled. A faint bluish aura danced around Angirasa. The dark came alive with the Presence, and she realized what the Devi was trying to show her through her visions of Durga, of Kali. It was like Dhuma said. The goddess was within her.

"I wish I had known," the chandala said.

"Angirasa," she said his name for the first time. It was sweet on her lips. "Angirasa, no matter my caste, you could take our child to your family." They both looked down at sleeping Kirsa. Mala's thoughts began to race. "You could say that her mother had died." She swallowed. "I would pretend to be your servant, to be near her, so through you she would have riches—"

"I could never deny her a mother's love, or you a daughter's." His voice was firm.

Mala was near tears. To live such a lie would be horrible. And yet. "Do you really think this is better?" The cremation grounds were bleak and grey in the morning light.

He looked down at his hands. "I can't go back. And so neither can my child."

"You shouldn't be punished when you only slept with Valmiki's wife—"

"That isn't all." He cut her off again. "Listen, and you will see why I can't go back."

Mala would listen. If she knew the whole story, she might be able to change his mind. They should return to his kingdom. They could give their daughter a better life.

"The Brahmin Valmiki is famous for his knowledge of the Vedas," he said. "No one could sing the hymns so beautifully. He is a passionate scholar, too. He wrote beautiful verses about the prince Rama of Kosala, the incarnation of the god Vishnu, and his princess, Sita. When I was six years old, my father sent me to Valmiki to begin my studies as a brahmacharin."

Mala held Kirsa tighter. "Six! How could your mother ever say goodbye to you at six?"

"Such is the way among nobles. Of course I was lonely for my family, yet even young as I was I went gladly. Valmiki seemed the wisest and most wonderful guru a boy could have. For many years I was happy living at his ashram in the Shining City, learning the sacred hymns from his lips. As I said, I was his best student, and the other boys didn't always like me, but Valmiki was like a father to me. He had a weakness, though, one that I didn't understand until I'd been with him for ten years."

"Such a long time!"

"Not long enough. A noble youth spends twelve years at an ashram, learning from a guru the sacred science of the Vedas," he said, musing. "If I had followed my caste's dharma, I would have completed my studies six years ago. Then I would have returned to my clan, taken a wife. By now I might have had sons." He reached out and stroked Kirsa's cheek with one finger. "But I'm happy to have this daughter." He raised his hand to Mala's cheek. "If every man could see what I saw when you gave birth to our child… to bring forth life, a woman risks death. You match a warrior's bravery…"

If only she were brave. But perhaps she was. She had born a child almost alone. She had only thought of getting through it, but now she felt very brave indeed.

"The way of it is that some years on, I would send those sons to study, then to marry and become householders themselves. Then I would have retreated to the forest and lived a simple life in my old age, meditating on union with the great soul, Atman." His mouth pressed into a bitter line. "The rare man will become very holy at this time. I dreamed I would be such a one, that I would become a sannyasin, one who renounces all material possessions. I would take to the road with only a begging bowl and a staff, not caring where I ate or slept but waiting only for death and moksha. It requires only that one give up everything."

Mala shook her head. "The rich want to have nothing and think then they will become holy. But those of us born with nothing, we're considered the very opposite of holy, impure, paying the price for sins in another life, people to be shunned."

"Very clever," he said with a half smile. "Poverty doesn't necessarily bestow wisdom and virtue. But perhaps, in a way, it would be easier for the poor than the rich to become holy, if the poor could hear the teachings of wise sages…"

"The yogi Asita said something like that. The teachings fall on everyone equally, like sunlight."

Angirasa looked surprised. "You knew Asita?"

"I met him in the forest near my village when I was just a girl of twelve. I brought him to my parents' hut, and he told us stories. Like yours. I could have listened to him forever. He was the one who first told me about moksha."

"I heard Asita debate Valmiki once. Valmiki was not easy to fluster, but that old yogi did it." Angirasa stared into the east, where the sun was already coloring the clouds of Ushas' garments pink and violet. Mala looked down the path to the entrance to the burning grounds, but so far there was still no one with a fresh-wrapped corpse and no need to build a pyre.

"That doesn't surprise me," Mala said, turning back to Angirasa. "In front of the whole village, Asita talked to Valmiki as if he were an outcaste." Suddenly she laughed.

"What is it?"

"It's just that, he treated my parents and me—that day he came to our hut—he treated us like his equals, like—like people! But he treated Valmiki as if he were the outcaste."

Angirasa nodded. "He liked to shock people, to make them think. I was sixteen when I heard their debate, eight years ago. It planted the first doubts about what Valmiki taught. It took place at Addhakashi's mansion."

"Addhakashi. The woman I saw on the road to Varanasi," Mala said. Angirasa nodded. "At first, I thought she was a goddess. Go on."

"Some men worship her like one. In those days, the young Addhakashi was Varanasi's pride; its greatest, most educated and refined courtesan, not yet even in the prime of her beauty."

"I have heard Varanasi is very proud of its courtesans, but it seems they are just… just prostitutes."

Angirasa looked thoughtful. "Strict moralists say that a courtesan is nothing more than an expensive prostitute. And it's true she places a price on her body, but no one would confuse a woman like Addhakashi with the woman on the street who must sell herself to live."

"Tell me more."

"To practice the courtesan's trade, a woman must be very intelligent. In Varanasi, the apprenticeship is very arduous. She is trained in the Sixty-Four Arts of Love and in the profane sciences. Men pay for her companionship and to share her bed, and—"

"Intelligent? But surely she must be very beautiful, too."

Angirasa laughed. "Not if she's clever enough. The greatest courtesans understand many things besides love: politics; military sciences; medicine. Even, I've heard, the engineering of roads and palaces. Brahmadatta, who was king of Kashi until Prasenajit's treachery, paid more attention to Addhakashi's advice than his own councilors. For such companionship, the king pays dearly."

"I see." Mala thought for a moment. "She must be of a noble caste, to sleep with a king."

"A high-caste woman who has no family or dowry, perhaps, might follow the profession. Usually a courtesan's lineage is a mystery. That way, a man like Valmiki can pretend he's not marrying someone who in fact defiles him."

"So—so she might be an outcaste?" This astounded Mala. "And yet, because she is trained in all these things men pay a high price to sleep with her?"

"The most powerful nobles in the land vie for her favors."

An incredible notion flashed through her mind. "And the money? It's hers to keep? She doesn't have to give it to a father or brother or someone like that?"

"It is hers." Angirasa looked amused. "Some squander it on trifles, but the wise ones invest it with merchants or buy land, so when their beauty is gone they remain independent."

"I've never heard of such things," Mala said slowly. "It almost seems like a good life for a woman… except… if she doesn't want to sleep with a man who comes with lots of money."

"It's the price the courtesan pays until she has enough wealth to choose her lovers. Addhakashi has reached that stage. She is considered one of the greatest of her kind. The only one better, perhaps, was her older sister, Moti." Mala closed her eyes. The pieces of the puzzle were coming together. "The Black Pearl, they called her. Dark-skinned, enormous dark eyes and black hair that fell like a waterfall to her waist. She never wore it bound or braided, even after she married Valmiki. He defied his powerful family to take her to wife."

She flushed and trembled. Angirasa had loved this beautiful woman. No wonder he spoke Moti's name in his sleep and thought of this black pearl when he caressed Mala. Heavy sadness enveloped her. "He defied his family, you say, marrying outside his caste?" she said, turning away.

"The Vedas do not forbid it. In some places, like in Maghada's kingdom, it is common. It's not unheard of among us Sakyans, but here in Varanasi, no. Valmiki's proud family was as shocked as you."

Kirsa roused a bit. Mala kissed the baby's forehead. In the Sakyan kingdom, she could be a princess. "You were telling me about the debate between Valmiki and Asita."

"Several kings, including my uncle King Suddhodana, were present at this banquet as were Varanasi's greatest scholars, and many nobles," Angirasa said. "Even at the rich Sakyan court, I had never seen anything like this gathering dressed in brilliant clothing and loaded down with jewels. Addhakashi was resplendent. At her right side, in the place of honor, sat the dark, matted-hair Asita, dressed only in a ragged dhoti. He was quite a sight in that grand crowd."

Mala smiled at the thought. "I can imagine."

"Valmiki and Asita debated the merit gained by sacrifice versus the tapas one generates in ascetic practices," he continued, "and argued over which was more holy, the hymns of the Vedas or the Upanishads, the Forest Teachings of sages who reject ritual and tradition. At first, I listened enthralled." His face took on a look that was at the same time rapturous and pained.

"But then my attention was distracted. A boy's life at an ashram is a sheltered one. Only a few girls embark on the study of the sacred sciences of the Vedas, and there were none at Valmiki's ashram. Nor did his wife, Moti, serve, as the wives of some gurus do, as a surrogate mother to the students. Indeed, we rarely saw her, though one glimpse was enough to remember her forever.

"When Moti made her entrance at the debate, she was dressed much more seductively than a Brahmin's modest wife should. You might think Valmiki would be angry when she swept in late and interrupted the proceedings, but he liked it. Everyone had to look. Such a woman would arouse any man's lust and envy, even Addhakashi's patron, King Brahmadatta. She glanced my way, and Kama's arrow pierced my heart.

"I was so young, and everything I felt in that instant, Moti saw on my face. It amused her for a moment, then she forgot me, an insignificant student in the glittering crowd. But after that night, her beauty possessed me. I couldn't eat, study, or sleep. Valmiki had no idea of the source of my unhappiness, but out of concern sent me to visit my parents in Kapilavastu—"

"Asita spoke of Kapilavastu."

"A city of wonders," Angirasa mused. "I should have liked for you and Kirsa to see it. What would my mother have thought of this little one?" His smile faded. "But she will never know you, Kirsa."

Mala's thoughts churned. Her daughter, a princess, and she, Mala, could she pretend to be a servant? Watch someone else mother Kirsa?

Angirasa went back to his story. "I had become so thin my mother thought I would die. I knew only one thing: I had to have Valmiki's wife. That was when I conceived the idea of stealing the necklace."

Mala pressed her lips together. They rarely spoke of the necklace, but it was always there, in the back of her mind.

"It was a beautiful thing, a priceless jewel that had belonged to the Gautamas for generations. I stole it from my uncle Suddhodana." He grimaced in shame. "It was said to have belonged to a divine nymph and to bestow special power on its owner."

"Couldn't we take it back to your clan?" Mala said. "Surely if you brought it back, they would welcome you." Even as she spoke these words, she was troubled. She did not want to give up the garland of gems.

"The time to return it is long past. And the theft was not the worst of my crimes."

"So you fell in love with your guru's wife. You did not steal her from him," Mala began.

"But I did." Angirasa took a deep breath. "I took the garland of rubies and diamonds back to Varanasi. I planned to search out Moti in Anandavana, where she often went to picnic with her poets and musicians. It's said that Parvati entertained the courtesans of Varanasi in Anandavana and told them the secrets with which she won Shiva's heart. That is why the city's courtesans are the best in the Sixteen Kingdoms." He closed his eyes again. "As I well know."

So that is where you learned, Mala said to herself. How could she ever have imagined he would love her? Mala could never compare in beauty and skill with this woman.

"On the day I knew she had planned an outing in the forest, I asked permission to visit a wise old Brahmin whose hermitage was there. But instead of going to his hermitage, I followed Moti's party. I waited while they ate and drank and then took their rest. When all were sleeping, I woke her. I offered her the necklace, and her eyes lit up with greed. She accepted my gift, and my attentions. At first, she toyed with me. But then, she became obsessed, too. We were fools in love; we risked all and lost. I was found in her bed. Valmiki threw us out. Moti asked her sister to take us in, but Addhakashi was too afraid of Valmiki's wrath. We lived in a forest hermitage for a brief time. One day I went out to seek alms and food. I returned and found—" He stopped abruptly and turned his face away. A vein in his neck throbbed.

"Love?" Mala said after a long silence. She reached out and touched his arm.

He turned back. His eyes were full of tears. "I found her dead." His voice was low and shaky. "She had been stabbed many times, and was covered in blood."

"Oh, Angirasa, my love." Mala wanted to touch his cheek, yet feared somehow her touch would hurt him. "But who would do such a thing?"

He straightened. "Earlier, I had seen a man hurrying down the path. By his gold armband, I recognized him as the village headman where Valmiki owned property who sometimes delivered messages at the ashram. Prakash, he was called."

A great shudder shook Mala. Angirasa stroked her arm. "What's wrong?"

"Prakash murdered my mother."

"I'm sorry." Angirasa looked down at his hands that rested in his lap.

"The workings of karma are strange." Strange, indeed.

"I hardly remember what happened after that." He looked into the dying fire. "Somehow I got her body to the cremation grounds. The chandala was an old man. I told him I would become his servant if he would cremate her. It was my penance. In time he died. I cremated his body and became the chandala in his place. That was four years ago. Whether Valmiki knows his servant is his wife's murderer I cannot say, but I believe if he knew what became of me, he would come for revenge—"

"Hush!" The sleeping Kirsa rustled and took a deep breath. "Look," Mala said. "Someone comes."

"Rest here with the baby."

Angirasa walked off to build the pyre, leaving Mala with her heart torn in two.

INTERLUDE

DHAVALAGIRI

One.
Atman, the Absolute, the Universal Self.
Blinding light. Bliss. Peace.
Eternity.
Then... One becomes Two-in-One.
Divine Consciousness and Divine Energy. The primordial
ground and the forms that arise from it.
Two-in-One divides, Two come into being.
The Person within and Nature without.
The Great God, the power of destruction, and the
Goddess Mother, the power of creation.
The linga and the yoni.
Shiva, pure knowledge, and Shakti, the maelstrom
through which knowledge becomes the world.
Male and female.
Pain.
A splinter, a shard of Mind breaks away.

THE SPLINTER TUMBLED THROUGH THE howling maelstrom, out of Atman, into...

... where? There... red... pulsing... the heart, where jivatman, the separate, small self, dwells. Warmth. Consciousness grew into...

... who?

A gale. Buffeting. Something cold: stinging, pelting... what?

A body. Whose? His.

"Om... om..."

The wind snatched the sacred syllable from his breath before he could speak it. Something creaked. Tree boughs swaying in the gusts.

Ice, little needles on his skin. The hard ground frozen beneath him.

Asita shuddered; lost concentration. The snow quenched his burning tapas, his spiritual heat. Smothered the hard-earned fruit of his meditation. Every vein and nerve went frigid. He gasped. Opened his eyes. A blizzard whirled around him. He couldn't see the cave. He shivered so that he could barely uncross his legs. When he did, he struggled to stand.

The wind abated slightly, and he got his bearings. Something glowed through the blinding snow. A fire? In the cave?

He tottered where he stood. He had stoked no fire there before he left to make his seat on the flat rock, his favorite spot for yoga. It had been a warm spring day. There had been no blizzard, not a cloud in the sky, only the magnificent view over the ridge that filled his eyes before he closed them and began his plunge into deepest samadhi. Who had built it?

He staggered toward the light in confusion, then stopped. A form appeared at the cave entrance. Was some creature from one of hell's fiery realms awaiting him there?

"Better get in here, you old dog-eater," a familiar voice shouted. Only one person had the strange, bandy-legged gait of the man running to him. Anjana, the chief of the Koli clan. Asita nearly collapsed with relief.

"Begone, hideous demon!" Asita managed a laugh as his old friend put an arm around his waist. Then struggling against the wind and whirling snow, Anjana half-carried, half-dragged Asita to the cave, and deposited him, wet and cold to the marrow, in front of the cozy fire.

Snow blew in and hissed on the flames as the chief tended to the patchwork of hides stitched together for a door, tying the leather strips attached to it to the twisted roots that grew out of the living rock. He threw a blanket over Asita's shoulders, one his daughter Atimaya had given to Asita the previous fall on one of the yogi's visits to the Koli village before the snows set in. It had served him well these many winter months. Atimaya was a skilled weaver, and the multicolored blanket was warm and soft though Atimaya was a sharp, cold young woman. Perhaps the child she was expecting would change that.

"Nnnnnn..."As his limbs thawed, Asita could only groan. His fingers and toes, thick and swollen and white, tingled as if stuck with thousands of needles. He rocked back and forth as the firelight illuminated the crude figures of yogic poses drawn on the cave walls. A gust of wind forced smoke down the long fissure in the cave's roof that served as a chimney, making their eyes water. Then another gust sucked the smoke back up and out with a sharp whistle.

Asita pulled the blanket closer as Anjana stirred the clay pot that hung over the fire. "Smells good," he said to the chief.

His friend's almond-shaped eyes crinkled as a smile spread over his smooth, broad face, which was bronzed a permanent copper color by years of hunting and patrolling under the brilliant mountain sun. "You old fool," Anjana said. "Sitting on a rock in a blizzard. The goddess laughs at you." The chief picked up a wooden bowl and filled it, then handed it to Asita, who cupped his trembling hands around the steaming vessel, grateful for the warmth.

"Call me a fool? Who scoffed at Dhavalagiri and climbed her breasts in this tempest?" He swallowed and glanced up at the chief.

Anjana met his eyes only briefly. There was concern in them. "I felt this one last storm brewing, and my old bones told me it was going to be a bad one, even though it's late for such fury. I had a sense I should come to make sure you were all right."

There was more to it, Asita was certain, but he held his tongue.

"By the time I got here," Anjana continued, "the snow was falling so heavily I almost couldn't find the cave. And then you weren't in it. Couldn't believe you'd be sitting out there in the midst of it."

"I would have been all right," Asita began. And he would have, normally. The wind could have beaten around his naked torso for days. Well, maybe not days. He was getting older. But he would have been able to come out of his trance smoothly. "You distracted me," he said. "I didn't have time to emerge properly."

Anjana busied himself with the barley. "Are you angry?" His voice was tense. The Kolis understood the dharma of giving food and shelter to wandering sages and yogis seeking supreme wisdom. They also understood that to disturb holy seekers during their ascetic practices was to risk rousing their anger and to invite their dreadful curses that pursued a man the rest of his days.

"Probably a good thing someone came, even if it was a drunken lout like you," Asita said with a mock growl.

"That's the thanks I get? I should have stayed in my warm hall in the village and let the vultures have your frozen corpse."

"Hmmph."

"Anyway, Yasodhara was worried, too."

"Ah. I see. Your wife kicked you out. She needs a good beating. Show her who's chief."

Anjana grinned. "Beat her? Not even that evil brother of hers"—he paused and spat— "may he dwell in the hell realms until Shiva dances the end of the universe—not even he dared lay a hand on her."

Asita grinned back and shook his head. "But you tamed her."

Anjana snorted with amusement. "I wouldn't say that!" He filled his own bowl and began to eat.

Asita shook his head, smiling. No one would have predicted that the rough, sly chief of the Kolis and the imperious Sakyan princess would have been happy with each other. Certainly not Yasodhara's scheming brother, who made the match to get her out of his kingdom. No one would have predicted, either, that a princess of the royal Gautama family, raised with every luxury in the wealthy Sakyan court, would have taken to the harsh, simple Koli life. "She could have ruled her clan better than her wicked brother," Asita mused aloud.

"He was mad."

Asita frowned. "Madness preys on that lineage." The firelight darkened for a moment.

"In the men of the line. I'm glad I didn't have sons."

It was Asita's turn to laugh. "Not another man in the Sixteen Kingdoms would say that. If any Arya warrior's wife couldn't give him sons, he'd take another until he had progeny to light the pyre and say the prayers for him."

"Imagine Yasodhara if I took another wife. And I don't care much for prayers. You know that."

They laughed together. Asita felt warm from the inside out now, and they ate in companionable silence. In all his wanderings through all the Sixteen Clans, he had met many people, become fond of a great number of them, but called only one a true friend.

Their friendship had grown over the many years Asita had returned to

Dhavalagiri, the mountain goddess, as the peak was known. Of all the solitary hermitages he had made in the forests of the lowlands, none compared to this one. He loved to practice yoga on these magnificent heights.

Anjana finished his barley gruel and set the bowl down. "Asita." He hesitated. "Yasodhara... she doesn't have the madness. But she does have some of the gifts of her lineage." His smooth brow wrinkled. "She can see into the future sometimes... and she has foreseen that one of our daughters may... will... is in danger, when it comes time for her confinement."

Asita was well aware of Yasodhara's abilities. He took them seriously. Atimaya was not the only one who was pregnant. Her sister Maya's child was due near the same time. He opened his mouth to ask more, but just then the wind beat at the patchwork of skins, and one of the leather thongs that tied it shut snapped. A frigid gust brought in a swirling mass of snowflakes.

After securing the cave opening, the chief sat down at the fire. "It looks like this storm will last a while, my friend," he said. "Sleep now. I'll tend the fire. We'll have plenty of time for talk after you've had some rest."

Despite what Anjana had said about the storm the night before, as quickly as it rose it abated. The next morning, the sky was lapis blue and the blinding white snow was already melting under a blazing sun. Anjana and Asita shoved off the piled drifts and sat on the boulders flanking the cave entrance, enjoying the returning spring warmth. Anjana had loosened the long scarf wrapped around his neck, and Asita let his blanket slip off his shoulders. Though a ridge hid the village, they could see smoke rising from the cooking fires. Two eagles, the yogi's companions over the winter months, circled nearby, watching for unwary hares.

Anjana cleared his throat. "Yasodhara sees difficult births for both, and death for one." He paused. One of the eagles dove then rose carrying an indistinct bundle of fur in its talons. "She cannot see the children," the chief said. "What do you know?" There was palpable pain underneath his calm, flat tones.

Asita sighed. He didn't want to look into the future. He didn't want to think about the past. He had come to spend the winter months at his practices, sitting in utter stillness, progressing step by tortuous step along the path to mastering each sense until he had stripped away all layers of consciousness. Then only the present would exist, and he could lose himself in its limitless bliss.

Difficult enough under any circumstances. Even more difficult because the conflicts between the lowland kingdoms vying for power had come as far as Koli territory. Other clans saw the forests that covered these lands and the game that lived in them as tantalizing riches, though somewhat hard to seize from Anjana's wily warriors, and skirmishes resulted from their encroachments. One skirmish had taken place very close by. A small patrol of Anjana's skilled archers made swift work of them. A surviving enemy warrior said they had come for the god Himalaya's treasure that everyone knew was hidden in fat wooden chests in Dhavalagiri's famous sacred cave. Anjana's men had laughed at this, for if there were jewels so easily to be had, the Kolis would be much richer than they were.

But what made it most difficult to focus on his yoga was that Asita knew this much: the karma of the boy growing in Maya's womb and the girl in Atimaya's were entangled with each other and with the struggle between old and new; between the powerful Kosala clan and its rivals, the rising Maghadas and Sakyas; between the Brahmins and their rigid rituals and those like himself who sought spiritual freedom. Asita wanted to know how they fit together, but he could not quite see. All he knew were possibilities.

A brisk breeze tugged at the blanket, and Asita drew it closer.

"Well?" Anjana said. The breeze caught several strands of hair that had escaped his braid. He and Asita gazed at each other.

Asita closed his eyes. He had studied yoga for years, beginning at the feet of several gurus. They taught him how to meditate, turn his consciousness to the study of his own mind. They taught him that his true nature was one with everything that humanity called reality, the world and everything in it, and that reality was only a dream. They taught him that his true self was one with the Universal Self. *"Tat tvam asi,"* they said. "You are that."

Tat tvam asi. When he understood what it meant, his last teacher kicked him out of the hermitage, saying: "You don't need me. Go, find a tree deep in the forest or a cave high on a mountain, and perform asceticisms. From now on, your practice is your guru. Sit until your senses still. Focus on your breath until you can control it. Let your heart slow unto stopping." He had heard of Dhavalagiri and its cave. Drawn to it, he'd gone there more than twenty years ago for the first time, and it was there he mastered many of the

THE TIGRESS AND THE YOGI

yogi's powers of mind. He understood the speech of the animals. He could be in two places at once.

He could see into past, present, and future, though imperfectly. He didn't want to look and see which of Anjana's beloved daughters the chief would lose. And the children. Would they both survive? He found the threads of their lives on the loom of time. They were strung close to each other because of their common lineage that went all the way back to the sun god Surya and the celestial sage Gautama. His mind the shuttle, he wove back and forth along their threads.

Each child might have extraordinary abilities. Each might rule the world or become a buddha, an awakened one. Or each might fail, and there would be chaos and suffering.

Then suddenly there was a third thread. A girl. Who was she? Her thread lay close to the other two, her karma intertwined with theirs. What bound her to them? The lineage? Was she a Gautama? There... the mother... he could see something... he knew the mother...

"Old friend," Anjana said, breaking Asita's concentration.

"Twice in two days." Asita opened his eyes and fixed a glare on Anjana.

Anjana's gaze didn't flicker. "Well, then. I'm ready for your worst curse. But what did you see?"

Asita laughed, once again grateful for the friend who didn't fear him. "This is what I saw. You'll have two fine grandchildren come spring. Atimaya will have a girl. You should name her Yasodhara."

"That will please the old woman," the chief said.

"Maya's son will be known as Siddhartha. 'He who achieves his goal,' in the sacred tongue."

"Hmmph. Doesn't sound like a name Maya would choose." Anjana brushed a strand of hair from his cheek. Or was it a tear?

Asita glanced away. The Sakyan king would pick the name. That much he knew. He hadn't seen what would happen to Maya. Not for certain. "Would Atimaya choose to name her child Yasodhara?" he said lightly.

Anjana gave a half smile. "It's a mouthful. We'll shorten it to Dhara. I wonder if it will be Atimaya's karma to have as much trouble with her own daughter as my wife had with her." He smiled. "And what fond little name will the Sakyans give Siddhartha?"

Asita trembled. He didn't dare say what he hoped: the Buddha, the Awakened One.

So he said what he knew would be true. "Prince Siddhartha."

Several days later while he sat meditating in the warm afternoon sun, Asita remembered the third child. The mother's face rose before him.

"The little outcaste from Gauri?" He was so surprised that he blinked and spoke aloud, startling the eagle perched on a branch of a nearby dead tree.

The eagle turned a disapproving yellow eye on him. *What little outcaste from Gauri?*

"Mala!" Asita said, still speaking aloud, though the eagle could have understood his silent thoughts perfectly well. "Why, how time passes. She must be sixteen now, at least, and a baby on the way. But how is her child linked to Siddhartha and Dhara?"

Perhaps you should go find out. The eagle turned its head and raised its beak. *Haven't you been sitting up here long enough?*

PART III

THE HORSE SACRIFICE

THE MAIDEN DEATH

"*OM, ASATO MAA SADGAMAYA.*" A short distance away, a priest lit the fire and began the chant for the dead in a ringing, melodious voice. Mala stiffened and glanced at Angirasa, who was raking through the smoking ashes of an earlier cremation.

As she feared, Angirasa started to murmur the prayer soft and low. They were not out of earshot. For the time, though, the crackling flames and hiss of burning fat hid the sound.

"Louder, Bapu," Kirsa lisped.

"Kirsa!" Mala put a finger to her lips. The child loved her father's singing, but if he was heard, all was lost. "Hush, Angirasa."

He ignored her. Lately he had begun to chant louder as he worked, as if he wanted someone to recognize his beautiful voice.

Mala moved her rake back and forth in silence, glancing at the mourners, a noble family. Yama Dharmaraja had snared their daughter—a child of seven, only a year older than Kirsa—with his silver noose. Did the Lord of the Dead regret taking the young and innocent? The mother's grief would break even a god's heart.

Kirsa stayed near her father, poking at smoldering embers of an earlier fire, breaking them apart and scattering them, humming along with him, very low. In the six years since her birth, she had lived with the burning grounds' harsh sights and breathed its malodorous air as if they were unremarkable.

What was remarkable was her beauty. She had silken waves of hair like her grandmother Sujata's, and her father's strange amber eyes flecked with green and gold, and his high cheekbones and perfect, straight, narrow nose.

Such beauty was wasted here.

Their little family was isolated by their work and where they lived, there on the city's western side. They had no friends among Varanasi's outcastes, who lived outside the city's eastern gates. And how could they marry Kirsa to one of them? In comparison to their desperate poverty and the awful work the untouchables performed, her life among the ashes was sweet.

The need to maintain Angirasa's anonymity deepened their isolation. They had no friends at all, save the fisherman Matsya and his wife, Matsyani, a childless older couple who plied the river, free as the birds that lived on Ganga's reedy banks. Now and then they came by in the evening to listen to Angirasa's tales of gods and goddesses. They cared nothing about caste, and would bring a fish for dinner. They doted on Kirsa.

"Tamaso maa jyotir gamaya!"

The Brahmin's voice rose to a crescendo. To Mala's relief, Angirasa's low chant trailed off. He wrinkled his brow. Gradually his raking ceased. He stared past Mala and Kirsa at the flames of the child's pyre. Mala recognized the signs and put a hand on his arm. Over the years she had become used to that empty stare, told herself there was nothing she could do, though it pained her to watch him sinking into a dark world only he could enter. Lately, his empty eyes and weary demeanor took over more often more often. Sometimes not even his beloved Kirsa could bring him back, and he would perform his duties like a sleepwalker for days.

So many times she told herself to flee. If Angirasa wouldn't come, she would dig up the necklace, take Kirsa.

She never did. Fear of the unknown stopped her. And she could not bear to break the bond between Kirsa and her father. He adored the girl, who was the sun and moon and stars to both her parents.

"Mryityo maa amritam gamaya!" The Brahmin finished the prayer. The chandala came out of his trance.

"Om, asato maa sadgamaya."

"Om, lead us from the unreal to the real…" The Brahmin's singsong voice started the mantra once more. The mourners wept. He raised his hands and voice to the heavens.

Before Mala could stop him, Angirasa let his voice rise with the priest's.

"From the darkness to light, from ignorance to knowledge... From death to immortality!"

"Angirasa," Mala hissed.

The mourners, lost in their grief, seemed not to have noticed. All except one, a man standing a little aside from the family. There was something odd about him. He didn't look like the other richly dressed family members. He wore a plain antariya around his hips and had wrapped some striped cloth around shoulders like an old woman's shawl, covering his head. It cast a shadow on his face. He looked in their direction through the waves rising from the fire's heat. Mala wished he would look away.

The fire crackled. Orange flames consumed the tiny white-wrapped corpse. The sickly sweet smell of burning flesh filled the air. She took Kirsa's hand and led her away to the hut, and sent a fervent request to Shiva to make the pyre burn fast, for the mourners to leave, and for her little family to be alone with the spirits of the dead.

In the evenings, after their day's work, Angirasa would tell the tales that had so enraptured Mala in their early time together and that mesmerized Kirsa now. Sometimes he spun grand visions of the soul's journey through many lifetimes, facing Yama Dharmaraja on his throne at each death. Mala wondered if there really was a kingdom of the dead, where beyond the cremation fire Yama sat in judgment. She could not picture it. Even if there were, just as Yama's kingdom was beyond this world, there must be something beyond the land of the dead, beyond the bliss of Atman. Every time she followed this thought, she arrived at the edge of a chasm so dark it made her reel and sent her back to the practical prayers her mother had always spoken to protect their little family. She made offerings to Kali at the shrine by the shaalmali tree, but rarely felt the Presence.

When the flames of the little girl's pyre began to subside, Mala and Kirsa joined Angirasa a short distance from the pyre. It was said the child was around Kirsa's age. The goddess Sitala had sent a deadly fever and the girl succumbed, in spite of the prayers and rituals and many offerings. No matter what form the Devi took, it was hard to know how to please her, Mala thought with a shiver.

The wings of circling vultures cast a shadow over the mourners and passed over the chandala's head. The dead girl's mother looked up. She stared at Kirsa, who hid herself behind a fold of Mala's faded antariya. The priest poured more ghee on the fire. Flames leaped and the wood crackled. Soon, the girl's family would leave and take their bitterness with them.

"*Om, shantih shantih shantih…*" Kirsa whispered.

"Hush!" Mala said, feeling the eyes of the man who stood apart watching her and Kirsa.

"*Om,* may you have peace." This time Kirsa spoke too low for the mourners to hear as she peered at the grieving woman from the shelter of Mala's body.

ॐ

"Bapu, why is there death?" Kirsa asked that night, as the three of them lay awake under the night sky. It was breathless hot, too hot to sleep in the hut; too hot to sleep at all, so they brought their mats out and lay watching the stars, Kirsa in the middle, Angirasa and Mala on either side. A short distance away in the darkness, sweetish smoke hung over the cremation grounds, no breeze to blow it away. At least no breeze meant no ash and grit to sting their eyes and fill their nostrils.

"Why aren't you sleeping?" Angirasa said.

"Because I'm sad."

"Sad?"

"For the little girl's mother," Kirsa said. "Her eyes were so sad! She will never hold her little girl again. If there was no death, they would never be separated. They could hold each other forever."

A little tremor shook Mala. The things that sometimes came out of her child's mouth.

"Well," Angirasa said. Change the subject, Mala thought, tell a tale to disperse the lingering image of the little white corpse they'd burned earlier. But he was always so patient with her questions. "What do you think it would be like, if there were no death?"

"No one would cry when somebody they loved died, because nobody would die."

"But think, what if no one died?"

Oh, Angirasa, Mala thought. Why can't you give her a tale of the love god Kama's mischief? "Love—" she began.

But Kirsa interrupted. "There wouldn't be keepers of the burning grounds. We wouldn't have to rake ashes."

"What would we do then?"

"Um… we could fish on the river, like Matsya and Matsyani," Kirsa said. Mala sometimes imagined that the old couple would take Kirsa, give her a new and better life among the fisher folk. If she could not convince Angirasa to return to the Sakyan kingdom, it offered a way out for Kirsa. Perhaps Mala could fish, too. The thought was pleasant, but then she wondered who would care for Angirasa.

"That sounds pleasant," Angirasa said. "But perhaps not. What would happen here on earth if no one ever died?"

"There would be a lot more people." Kirsa paused. "Everyone would just keep getting older and older, wouldn't they?"

"Exactly…"

"Oh!" Kirsa sat up. "But what if people still got sick, and didn't die? Would they all get better, Bapu? Or would they be sick and in pain forever?"

Kirsa's questions always pleased her father, and as much as they sometimes irritated Mala, she was amazed and proud of how much the child seemed to understand of his answers. "She has an old soul," Angirasa liked to say. The child loved the sound of his musical voice as much as the meaning of his words. If only he wasn't telling a tale of Death. It made her uneasy. Mala rolled to her side, moving closer to her lover and child in spite of the heat.

"An interesting question," Angirasa said. "One that troubled the Creator himself…"

The girl snuggled against her bapu. A bittersweet ache filled Mala's heart. She loved these two more than anything in this life.

"You see, daughter, in the very beginning of the universe, before there was death in the world, the Creator Brahma became aware of the suffering of his creatures. He began to meditate on this, and he generated such fiery hot tapas that intense, black smoke poured from his nostrils. This smoke coalesced into a dark being, the maiden Death.

"Brahma was mesmerized by her exquisite beauty. *O my daughter,* he said to her, *my creatures are suffering. You must grant them release.*

"*O Father,* Death replied, *I dare not. To take life would blacken my karma forever.*

"*Nevertheless, you will do as I command,* Brahma said sternly.

"But the maiden refused to obey the Creator—"

"She disobeyed the Creator." Kirsa's eyes were round. "She was very brave."

Mala gazed over at Kirsa. Yes, little one, she was very brave. Very brave indeed. The maiden had stood before the god Brahma and defied him. Mala's throat constricted as she thought of the day she stood before Valmiki. She had not dared to speak, to name Sujata's murderer, to fight for Talu's good name. If Kirsa knew how her mother had quailed, would she be ashamed?

"The gods themselves wondered at her courage," Angirasa said, and Mala turned her attention to the tale with an almost childlike hope that somewhere in it, there would be a key to how to find that sort of courage. "While Brahma fumed, Death pondered his request to bring release to earth's creatures. She climbed Mount Kailash to seek the Lord of Yoga, Shiva, who had mastered the highest knowledge. When she appeared before him, Shiva emerged from his deep meditation. Death's beauty nearly overwhelmed him, he who the other gods called Destroyer, whose final dance would end this universe.

"*Teach me your disciplines,* she said to Shiva. And from the Great Yogi she learned to practice austerities with such complete concentration that even he could not have done better. First, she stood utterly still on one foot for fifteen million years. The gods watched in wonder as the tapas she generated became hotter and hotter, enough to purify the sins of thousands of lifetimes."

Of course. The maiden had embarked on a quest, a spiritual quest. She had mastered her fears with yoga. Asita's long-ago words sprang to Mala's mind: *One who masters yoga's practices yokes his inner self to Atman, the Supreme Self, which is beyond the sufferings of ordinary life.*

Mala was rapt. Her nerves tingled.

Angirasa continued. "Her father once again commanded her to do as he decreed. Brahma said, 'My daughter, mortals need you! Listen to them cry out, trapped in their misery. Their suffering never ends, for they cannot die. Let them know the ecstasy of release in your arms.'

"But lovely Death, with her fathomless black eyes and red lips, refused him again. Her obstinacy threatened the universe with chaos. 'Even we gods may not live forever,' Brahma said in anger and despair. 'You must teach us all how to die.'"

140

"The gods die, too?" Kirsa interrupted.

"They, too," Angirasa replied.

"The stars will disappear one day, too, won't they, Bapu?"

"So say the wise," he said patiently.

At these words, the old black chasm opened up before Mala, but the tingling remained. Asita had said it was not forbidden to let her soul soar to the stars. She knew with utter certainty that this was so, that anyone, even she, could study yoga as the maiden did.

"Well, if everything dies, what then?" Kirsa said, matter-of-fact.

Mala's heart twisted. Wandering the roads or making a hermitage, a life like Asita's was a solitary one. It took courage. A child would hinder someone who wanted to take that path. No mother could leave her child for it. And yet...

Mala shrank from her own thought in horror.

Angirasa, who had been silent, thinking about Kirsa's question, suddenly spoke. "Not everything dies. The essential word endures always, the syllable *om*." His voice began to rise. "When its sound emerges from nothingness, a million suns explode out of swirling darkness. Though each age of creation may endure for eons beyond counting, all one day will collapse into darkness again, into the irreducible vibrating particle. So it goes on forever!"

His words rang out over the ashes. Then quiet reigned, except for the blood roaring in Mala's ears. What would it be like to experience that infinite forever?

"Go on, Bapu." Kirsa's calm little voice brought Mala up short. She stepped back from the abyss. Love was another path to courage. It arose from the chamber in her heart where the little self dwelt.

She would do anything for Kirsa. She rolled to her side again, propping her head with her hand and gazing at her daughter.

"The gods waited as Death posed on the other leg for many ages. Tens of millions of years, she drank and ate nothing but air, but she would not obey Brahma the Creator's command to bring death to man."

"Bapu, how long has the earth existed?"

"So long that only those who understand sacred geometry can calculate the years."

"How many years?" she insisted.

141

"So many questions, daughter," Angirasa said. He turned his head slightly, glanced at Mala with an amused smile. She was happy to see the stars' sparkle reflected in his eyes. "Four billion years the ages of this universe have lasted, and some say it will not be long until it ends."

"Not long?" Kirsa said, a little anxious. "How long?"

Angirasa laughed. "Not until all the stars are extinguished, and you can see how many still blaze brightly, daughter. Now, may I continue my story?"

"Yes, please." Kirsa stared up at the night sky.

"Death continually asked herself: 'How can I put an end to so many lives, how could such acts not blacken my karma forever?'

"For twenty thousand more years, beautiful Death dwelt in water, which boiled and steamed from her tapas. The creatures of the three worlds multiplied until there were three hundred and thirty million gods in the heavens and three hundred thirty million mortals on earth, and all the creatures in the waters and the forests and the skies between.

"'The tapas you have generated will burn all your sins for ages without number,' Brahma said in desperation. 'You will be free of any evil karma.'

"Still she refused. At last Brahma said, 'My daughter, to help you in this terrible duty, I will make man desire release from the suffering of this life more than anything.'"

The chandala's voice quieted to a whisper.

"'But he will be ignorant of his own true desire, of his own thirst for you. He will seek women, or power, or riches, thinking that the obtaining of these will quench his yearning for you, for Death. But women and power and riches are only passing pleasures, mere distractions. Not understanding this, he will bring about his own destruction. Rape and adultery, war and betrayal, insatiable greed! All in pursuit of that elusive thing called pleasure.'

"Hearing this, the compassionate maiden Death wept and her tears became the diseases that afflict we who dwell on earth. 'I will do as you ask, O Brahma,' she said..."

Angirasa fell silent. The sparkle had gone out of his eyes. Mala tried to read his face in the dark. All of a sudden she was angry. What could he be thinking to tell such a story to Kirsa? The child couldn't possibly understand it.

"Oh, Bapu, I hope Lord Shiva dances and it all ends soon." Kirsa sighed.

"Kirsa! Why, little one?" Mala reached out to stroke her cheek, to soothe her.

"Then no one will be sad, Ma. Even Death," she said.

Angirasa and Kirsa fell asleep very soon after. Mala dozed. When she woke, she was surrounded by a red mist. Terrified, she sat up and tried to brush it away. Then suddenly it was gone.

She closed her eyes and fell into fitful visions of a beautiful dark maiden, before whom even dark Kali bowed, until the goddess Ushas colored the dawn sky pink.

VALMIKI'S ASHRAM

"NALAKA! IF YOU'RE DONE EATING, clean this," the cook said, holding out a crusted kettle with rice burned to the bottom, "or get the broom and sweep the corridor to Valmiki-ji's chamber."

Nalaka preferred to sweep. Though he was too old for such a childish game, he still liked to pretend the broom was a magical weapon. He was a young god, flexing his muscles. With his first wide stroke, he scattered the dried leaves that flew off the stone floor, imagining they were the guru Valmiki's other students, his merciless tormentors, whirling into infinite space.

Very soon he felt a fool. He was a man, not a god. Past twenty-one. He should have left the ashram three years ago, at eighteen. Valmiki said that if he would only attend to his studies, he would have already mastered the Vedas, which was to be like a god. But he had come to the ashram so late. He was fifteen when he arrived; the other boys had been reciting the hymns and ritual rules since they were six years old.

Nalaka had never caught up. At first he tried, but it was boring and hard and embarrassing that he never seemed to get them right. So here he was, still trying to master what boys half his age knew. Nalaka hated it. But he stayed, not knowing where to go and not wanting to give students like arrogant Kapur, three years his junior but vastly more learned, the satisfaction of seeing him give up.

Swish. He swung the broom back and forth. Swish. Though dharma required every student in the ashram to do their share of everyday chores, the rich boys never did anything.

He paused, took an end of his worn white antariya, and wiped it across his sweaty forehead. Ever since he had arrived at Valmiki's ashram, he'd been treated like a servant. No matter that he was a Brahmin's son, born into the highest caste just like the others. No matter that his mother was the famous guru's distant relative.

He flushed. He remembered as if it were yesterday the humiliation when Valmiki failed to recognize Nalaka's mother's name. Nalaka had to stand and recite his lineage while the brahmacharins, noble sons of the Kashi clan's most ancient and powerful Brahmin families, tittered behind their hands. He hated the other boys from that instant, especially Kapur, who even back then was able to assist in the rites. He had led the others in tormenting Nalaka, trying to goad him into fights.

Valmiki forbade fighting between the brahmacharins. From Nalaka's point of view, that was a pity. The other students were pale, flabby creatures who might know the sacred Vedas by heart but didn't know how to throw a punch. This skill Nalaka learned from the boys he grew up with, the Koli clan's rough-and-tumble warrior youths. After every scuffle, Valmiki would reprimand him and assign long, seated meditations in the courtyard's hot sun, or three-day fasts where Nalaka was allowed only a few cups of water, or other strict austerities. It was worth it.

At first, Nalaka survived these penances by convincing himself that to master austerities was vastly superior to memorizing hymns. Gradually, he did master them, finding the physical discipline rewarding in itself. One day he would live simply, like a true sage, a hermit pursuing solitary meditations at a rustic retreat deep in the forest, not at a great white mansion on the highest bluff overlooking Ganga's river.

On the other hand, the white mansion had its pleasures, like its sweet-scented courtyard garden and fountain and the delicacies the cook prepared. Whenever Nalaka thought of leaving, he knew he could never go back to his clan as a failure, and he lacked the courage to leave the ashram to find a forest sage and ask for teachings. Besides, Valmiki was famously wise and learned. What guru could compare with him? So he stayed. Every now and then, he would answer one of Kapur's insults with a punch, which would lead Valmiki to assign him fasts and threaten to one day expel him. Thus six years passed.

Swish. Nalaka resumed his rhythmic strokes. *Sweep away these troubling thoughts.* He knew how. Focus on the golden light filtering through the curtained doorways of the rooms that lined the corridor. These rooms had a pleasing view of the river. Breezes that wafted through latticed windows brought the scent of the flowering jasmine vines that twined over the mansion's outer walls, while his own room near the hot kitchen smelled of curry and rancid cooking oil.

Let them have their river view. It was nothing compared to the magnificent Himalayan peaks and the vast green forests of his home on the slopes of Dhavalagiri, the mountain goddess. Not that he had really missed the impoverished Koli clan's little village, a collection of huts the villagers shared with their animals. He had never missed the smell of the goat that shared his parents' house, or his strict Brahmin father and clinging mother, but he did miss mountain air.

The grass broom sent dust motes swirling in the shafts of light. Nalaka had never minded the work as such. Life in the mountains was hard and everyone worked. It was the way the ashram's other students looked down on it that bothered him. He hated himself for a coward who kept sweeping and sweeping and taking their abuse when he should have left years ago.

A voice broke into his thoughts.

"Fifteen days until the final rites. At last, my dear Valmiki, the year of the Ashvamedha is near finished."

Nalaka moved quietly to the curtained doorway and cocked his ear. Someone was in there with the guru.

"Yes, Your Worship." Valmiki's response sounded tight and high-pitched. "Everything has been done to perfection."

Your Worship. Must be the Brahmin Yajna, the new king's closest advisor, who knew the Black Veda's incantations and spells better than the holy hymns.

"I marvel at how well you've performed all year. Every prayer of the Horse Sacrifice perfect, every ritual flawless."

Nalaka's skin prickled. Yajna could turn a man into a monkey with a glance.

"Your detractors say you've got it all written down, but I've never believed it."

Nalaka nearly dropped the broom in surprise. His heart began to race, but he couldn't help edging closer to hear better. Several months ago, Valmiki had ordered him to carry a number of wooden boxes to his chambers, saying, "You're the oldest and strongest and can handle these heavy things. You must be very careful with them. The contents are fragile. And private. Do not under any circumstances look inside them."

It took several trips and he strained under the weight. When he finished, Nalaka couldn't resist. He opened a box. It was filled with stiff, oiled palm leaves on which the hymns and rituals of the Vedas were written. He opened another. The same.

He had been stunned. Such a thing was virtually forbidden. Though his own father had defied tradition and taught him the secret of lettering, many Brahmins considered it against dharma to commit the sacred Vedas to writing. Yajna, like all the Kosalan priests that King Prasenajit had brought with him to Varanasi, was violently opposed to the practice.

Nalaka never told anyone he knew his letters. Nor did he tell anyone about the boxes' contents. In truth, it increased his wavering faith in Valmiki to know about the guru's secret rebellion. Yet now, resentment over all the wrongs he'd suffered gave rise to a vengeful thought. Yajna might be interested to know what those wooden boxes stacked neatly in Valmiki's chambers contained. Could this finally, after all these years, be a way out of the ashram?

Then Nalaka flushed. What had he become, that he would think of betraying his guru?

"You could not possibly favor copying down the verses," Yajna continued. "I told the king that you know the holy language must not be read but heard in all its glorious beauty. You know that the Vedas have been passed from mouth to ear since the goddess of speech Vac revealed them to the Seven Sages."

Valmiki must be in a cold sweat. Nalaka's resentment was replaced by fear for his teacher, who after all had tried very hard to teach him.

"To use the same tainted scratchings the merchants use to track goods and money for the divine words is heresy, wouldn't you say, my dear Valmiki?"

"Of course, Your Worship," Valmiki said in that same tight voice. "The guru must chant them to the student and keep the transmission pure and unbroken forever."

"Oh, these degenerate times." Yajna let out a huge sigh. "This dark Kali Yuga, the Age of the Black Goddess. One day we will wake up to find Kali dancing on Shiva's corpse and the universe will end. Until then, we must cling to what purity we can. What, my dear Valmiki, will happen to memory, that most important instrument of mind, when your students no longer need to remember everything but can read the hymns like a merchant reading his accounts?"

Valmiki cleared his throat. "What indeed?"

"Fifteen days to the ultimate sacrifice," Yajna said, "and Indra himself will bless King Prasenajit's rule."

Nalaka's stomach was churning, his mouth dry. It had been a great honor for Valmiki to be chosen to lead this grandest and most ancient ritual, the very one that the celestial warrior Indra had offered to secure his rule of heaven. Only the gods and a few of their mortal sons ever dared perform it. Not in living memory had anyone seen it. Until now.

Everyone in Varanasi followed the ritual's progress avidly. For a year, the consecrated stallion had been roaming through the Arya clans. During this time, hundreds of priests had sacrificed animals by the thousands, and under the great Valmiki's guidance not a single syllable or step in the rites was forgotten or performed wrongly.

If anything went wrong with the final rites, all would have been for nothing.

"The sacrificial horse has roamed through every land," Yajna said, "and all kings have chosen not to fight its passage."

Nalaka suppressed a snort. Of course no one had chosen to fight. The Kshatriya "honor guard" prescribed by the ritual was a whole army of the best Kosalan warriors.

"Under divine law," the priest continued, "they have bowed to the stallion and thus shown their submission to King Prasenajit."

"Not the Sakyas and Maghadas," Valmiki blurted in surprise. "They fought the Kosalan army and won. They did not bow to the stallion."

Neither had Nalaka's Koli clan. But then, the horse hadn't wandered into Koli territory. Perhaps it was the mountain goddess's protective grace, but more likely it was not deemed worth it to fight the tough Kolis, who had no vast treasuries filled with gold and jewels to plunder.

There was an ominous silence.

"They will submit." Yajna's voice was low and hoarse. "They will! Continued perfection is essential. Then Indra himself will force them to touch their foreheads to Prasenajit's feet!"

There was another pause. Nalaka licked his dry lips. He didn't much care who ruled. The Kolis despised all the lowland clans, especially the Sakyas, their close neighbors and cousins. But Valmiki would surely suffer if the Ashvamedha failed to bring Indra's blessing. In spite of everything, Nalaka loved his guru. He didn't want to think of how the Kosalan king and his sorcerer would punish Valmiki for such a thing.

"As he looks down from his heavenly city, Indra marvels at what we have achieved thus far," Valmiki said quietly.

"The final rite is key. No one must doubt that Indra blesses his majesty Prasenajit's rule."

"Of course, Your Worship."

The Kosalan pulled the curtain aside. Nalaka ducked behind a column. His heart pounded. Had the sorcerer seen him?

"Until the final ceremony, then," Yajna said. "I will show myself out."

The curtain dropped. It was silent in Valmiki's chamber. Yajna's footsteps faded. Nalaka waited until his heart slowed, then crept away, broom in hand.

KALI'S WARNING

MALA SPENT THE WHOLE NEXT day obsessed with the idea of leaving the burning grounds. The little girl's funeral was a warning from Kali. The fading feeling of safety she'd once had here disappeared overnight. Though she felt ill-suited to devise their escape, she knew she must try.

That night after Kirsa went to sleep in the hut, Mala and Angirasa sat under the stars. "We must leave here," she blurted.

Angirasa stopped poking the fire's embers. "What?"

"If you keep chanting, you'll be recognized."

He frowned. "I have a duty here. I must do it until karma sends someone to take my place, as I took my predecessor's."

Mala took a deep breath. She had expected this. "Not long ago, Matsya told me that there is a man in the outcaste settlements who got drunk and set his own hut on fire. His wife and children burned to death. He told Matsya that he wanted to do a penance."

"Well… he may be worthy… but I would need to stay for a while, to teach him what to do, as the chandala before me passed along his knowledge. But even if this outcaste wishes to take on this dharma, where would we go?"

"Anandavana. For a time, anyway."

"The Forest of Bliss? But there are outlaws—"

"What do we have that they'd want to steal?"

"The necklace," Angirasa said. A little flame sprang up, and she caught his eyes in the brief light, then looked away, flushing.

"There are a thousand hollow trees in the forest. We will find one, hide it there, under an owl's nest, the way we have it hidden under the cook fire's bricks," she said in a rush. Since the day she arrived at Angirasa's hut and they buried the necklace, they had never taken it out. Yet the flashing diamonds and rubies were more vivid in Mala's mind in that moment than the first time she held them in her hand. Lately, she had been thinking about the necklace more and more often. In waking visions she saw Kirsa dressed in gold and blue silks, the jewels around her slender neck. Or she saw herself attired like Durga, seated atop the white tiger and carrying the goddess's divine weapons, the gems sparkling between her breasts. Or she was powerful, black-skinned Kali, filled with mother love.

Angirasa gave her a strange look and his ensuing silence made her squirm. At last he spoke. "We would be found as easily in Anandavana as here."

"Bandits hide in the forest because the king of Kashi's soldiers can't find them in its depths. The soldiers won't find us, either."

"I couldn't possibly go now. The final rites of the Ashvamedha will take place soon..."

Mala froze. Angirasa had spoken of this grand sacrifice that the Kosalan was offering, which had not taken place in living memory. She had a horrible feeling he wanted to go and chant along with the priests. "You're not planning on going..."

"No... no, of course not..."

His answer didn't allay her fears. "Listen, my love," she said, "you've talked about how hermits live there, too. I've been thinking—I don't know, of course, but I have this—this feeling—one of those hermits might be Asita!"

"Ah, Asita," he said. "Possibly."

"Yes, it is possible! We could try to find the old yogi! We could live with him, care for him, as if we were his students... even Kirsa could learn from him..."

"We don't know where his hermitage is, if he even has one. While we wander we could be attacked by a boar, or a tiger, or some other wild animal. Or demons..." He drifted into silence and looked out over the distance.

"I don't think there's a danger of that. Listen, Angirasa, do you remember when I told you how I met Asita all those years ago, that I saw a tigress and her cub? I saw that cub again, when she'd grown up and become the queen of the tigers. Rani, she is called." Mala paused. Perhaps she should tell him everything about her visions. She hardly knew where to start.

But he seemed distracted. "What? You know a tigress? Come now, Mala…"

"I do! Truly. I—I don't know, but I think Rani might live in Anandavana. She would protect us…"

"You're imagining things. Even if Asita has a hermitage in Anandavana, would he disrupt his ascetic practices to give us shelter? And outlaws, they can sense when someone has a treasure. They'll be drawn to the necklace no matter where we hide it. And even if this Rani happens to live in the forest," he paused and gave her an indulgent smile, "why would she protect us from beasts or demons? Or men, for that matter?"

Mala wished she'd told him more about Rani earlier. "She will, I know it," she said, but to her own ears she sounded uncertain.

He paused. "You say we won't be found, but someone found Moti and me…"

She had no response to this. They sat in silence until he stood up and held out a hand. "Come," he said softly.

His sweet voice sent a shiver of desire through her, but their lovemaking didn't satisfy her. He took his pleasure and fell asleep after, but Mala was wide awake. He was right. She didn't know that Asita lived in Anandavana. She didn't know that Rani would protect them or was even anywhere near. She only felt it was so. Even more strongly, she felt they must leave here. They must.

ॐ

But the next day, Angirasa acted as if they hadn't talked.

Frustrated, Mala sat with Kirsa, who was absorbed in stringing dried seeds on thin hemp twine to make necklaces. The sun was still high in the west. The last fire had gone out, the mourners had gathered the ashes.

"Look what I have," Angirasa called out. Mala looked up and shaded her eyes with her hand. He was walking slowly across the burning fields to the hut, carrying something. "A mourner left them as dana," he said when he reached them. He knelt on the hard dirt and held out two folded lengths of faded but good quality Varanasi cotton.

Kirsa stared with her eyes wide, speechless for a moment. "So pretty," she said at last.

Mala nodded. No one had ever left such a gift. Flowers and vines covered the cloth in pale yellow, reddish pink, and light blue like wild flax blossoms. Once the flowers must have bloomed bold and brilliant on deep green vines. Now the fabric was faded, but the design was beautiful still, and the cloth only gently used.

"But... it's too nice to wear, isn't it?" Kirsa looked anxiously at Mala.

"Of course you can wear it. But let's go to the river and bathe first," she replied.

"Ah!" Kirsa smiled wide. "I can offer my old one to the Devi. We could tear it in strips and tie them around the shaalmali tree."

"A good offering, darling," Mala said.

"Let's all go," Angirasa said. Kirsa ran into the hut and got the jar that held the soapberry and herb extract they used to wash. They set off, Kirsa skipping ahead, until they descended the low bluff to the sandy stretch to the river, which had shrunk to a narrow channel in the summer heat.

They placed the new cloth by the silk-cotton tree, which had already given its fruit and now stood bare, only a few brown leaves clinging to the branches. Kirsa and Angirasa ran ahead. Mala took a deep breath and paused under the sparse shade, watching them until they reached the water. She needed a few moments alone to think.

She would not try to convince Angirasa to leave. She would just go. She would wrap up the necklace, tie it in a corner of her antariya and tuck it at her waist, and take Kirsa's hand. If he would not come with them, they would leave him. They would find somewhere to stay. Perhaps if she found the courage to take this step, the Devi's voice would whisper encouragement in her ear, or Rani would appear to protect and guide them. Then still holding Kirsa's hand, Mala would arrive in a clearing where stood a hut that needed thatching, and there would sit Asita. Or some other hermit. Or even a gang of thieves. Mala would offer to thatch the hut, to find food and cook, and they could stay...

She sighed. What would thieves do with a woman alone and her pretty child? Not all answers to that question were pleasant. Nor was it pleasant to imagine a boar charging, or a green-skinned demon with white fangs leaping from the shadows, or encountering a troop of Kashi warriors searching for renegades.

A shriek made her heart stop.

Then came laughter. Angirasa had wound Kirsa's soapy hair atop her head. "Now duck!" he cried, and Kirsa held her nose to plunge under the surface. He pulled her up out of the water and swung her around, and she shrieked again when he tossed her back in the river. A splash, and up she came, laughing. Mala's heart twisted. Even if she could overcome her own doubts to leave, she could not bear to part those two.

OUT OF THE DARK

NIGHT FELL OVER THE BURNING grounds. Angirasa sat with legs crossed, poking at the cook fire's dying coals with a thick stick.

Kirsa had been fidgeting, trying to be patient, but she couldn't contain herself any longer. She wanted her story and it was getting late. "Bapu?"

Angirasa prodded a coal and roused a few small flames. "Hmmm?" he murmured.

"Are you going to tell a story?"

"Ah. Well, I suppose I could, if you really want me to."

"Bapu!" Kirsa frowned at him.

Mala was edgy. *Tell the story. At least take us away from here with your tales,* she wanted to say.

"Oh, all right. Let's see. What kind of story shall we tell tonight?"

"The one about the poor girl that the king fell in love with," Kirsa said, smoothing her new antariya over her knees. Her eyes shone with anticipation.

"Hmm." Angirasa poked until the remnants of a small log split with a hiss and sent sparks up to the stars. "Which poor girl and which king? There are so many…"

"You know! The king gave her his ring and said he would be back, but a wicked demoness cast a spell on him so he forgot, and when the poor girl came to his kingdom with her baby he didn't know her, and so she threw herself in the river and the ring fell off her finger and a fish ate it and then a bird ate the fish and found the ring and took it to the king and he remembered everything and ran to catch her and he thought she was drowned but she wasn't and they all went back to the palace and ruled according to the dharma forever and ever."

"Ah." Angirasa set his stick down. "That story." He brushed off his hands. "As you know it perfectly, my dear, I won't bore you by telling it again."

Kirsa pursed her lips. "Then the one about the nymph who fell in love with the sage and asked Indra to make her mortal so she could die with her beloved and be united with him forever and ever in Atman."

"But they both die in the end. Isn't it too sad, little one?"

"Not so sad. They are together in Atman, aren't they?" Kirsa thought again. "Then how about one about Prince Rama? How he married the beautiful Sita and the demon Ravana kidnapped her so he had to rescue her."

Two embers flared then subsided. They were like demon's eyes. Mala sat up straight. Had she heard a noise in the darkness? She glanced over her shoulder.

"Too long," Angirasa said, to Mala's relief. "It will be time for you to go to sleep before we even have Sita married to her beloved Rama."

Or kidnapped by the demon Ravana. No, not that tale. Not tonight. There it was again. A jackal? So close? Mala craned her neck. A charred piece of wood fell to pieces with a faint hiss and crack. Just the fire. Still wary, she resettled herself.

"Oh, all right." Kirsa looked down at her hands. Angirasa had something more instructive in mind than her favored tales of princesses and their lovers, and the child could tell. "What story do you want?"

"Well, I was thinking about a tale of the noble warrior Karna, who wanted to learn secret martial arts that only a certain Brahmin knew—"

"But Brahmins don't know the warrior's arts," Kirsa interrupted. "It's a Kshatriya's dharma to kill in battle and a Brahmin's to say the prayers that remove the stains that shedding blood leaves on the warrior's karma."

"So the ancients said," Angirasa said. "Think of Lord Krishna's words to the hero Arjuna, the night before the great battle of Kurukshetra: better to do your own dharma badly than to do another's, no matter how well. But may I continue?" Kirsa nodded. "You see, long ago a band of warriors had cut off the head of a Brahmin who was a humble and well-loved sage, in order to steal the sage's magic cow. His son wanted to take revenge. So though he was a Brahmin, he set himself to learn powerful charms and

156

weapons to make himself invincible, and he became a notorious killer of Kshatriyas. The warrior Karna knew this, so he concealed his own lineage so he could study at the feet of this powerful Brahmin, who taught him a magic mantra that would make him invincible. But when he discovered Karna was a Kshatriya, the Brahmin cursed him. 'You will forget the mantra just when you need it,' he said, and—"

"Better you should listen to my tale." Out of the darkness came a harsh voice. "A tale about the Brahmin who stole his guru's wife."

ॐ

Mala leaped up. A man emerged from the shadows. On his arm, a gold band glowed in the firelight. It was Prakash. Her mother's murderer.

Everything slowed. Step by step he approached the circle of firelight. Rooted to the spot, Mala could only stare at him.

Angirasa stepped in front of Kirsa. "Stay away from my child," he said in a shaking voice.

Prakash smiled and tapped his large club against his open palm. "The Brahmin who hides his lineage," he said, tapping slowly, "so that he may escape justice."

Angirasa eyed it and stepped back, reaching behind to move Kirsa back as well. "How did you know I was here?"

"Your chanting. People are talking."

"Did Valmiki send you?"

Prakash laughed. "No. His lordship doesn't know that I found you. He's too holy a man to do it himself, so I'm taking vengeance for him."

Find a rock, instinct told Mala. *Knock him out.* She could do it. Her aim was good as ever. But it was as if time had thickened. She could not move fast enough. She was seized from behind before her body could begin to obey her will. There was no chance to resist.

"Ma!" Kirsa cried. Angirasa turned to look at his daughter.

The headman laughed. "Now take your punishment, chandala." He swung his heavy club. It cracked against Angirasa's skull so loudly that Mala screamed.

Angirasa hadn't even seen the blow coming. He fell to the ground and lay still. Prakash rolled him face down and secured his hands behind his back. As he finished tying the hemp rope, Angirasa let out a groan. She

157

despaired. There must be something in her karma that brought trouble to those she loved.

"We meet again, eh, Mala?"

Mala glanced over her shoulder. Dilip, her tormentor from the village, pinned her arms behind her and pressed against her back. He bore scars on his face and body. Mala remembered the great cat's roar and the screams the night she ran from Gauri. Rani! If only she knew how to summon the tigress, how to summon the Presence—but she did not.

Prakash stoked the fire, his gold armband glowing in the flames that licked the bottom of the blackened little kettle. He took a gourd from his sash and poured a thick liquid into it. As he stirred the pot he smiled, now and then glancing at Angirasa, who struggled weakly against his bonds. Prakash grasped an arm and wrenched him up. "Sit there," he said. Angirasa collapsed and the headman pulled him up again, half dragging him to the woodpile. Angirasa managed to sit atop the low stack of logs, head lolling, blood pouring out of his nose, wrists bound behind him.

"Don't... don't hurt... my child..."

Kirsa clutched Mala's leg. "Ma..."

Prakash, who was stirring the bubbling contents of the pot, looked up with cold eyes.

The hairs on Mala's neck rose. "Shhh, shhh."

"Who would have guessed you ended up here, Mala," he said. "They have missed you in the village. Thought that wicked white tiger got you."

Dilip shuddered. "Is it hot enough?" he asked. "Let's just get it over with and go."

Prakash stuck his finger in the pot and pulled it out with a yelp, then shook his hand and blew on it. Dilip snorted with nervous laughter. The headman filled a ladle with the bubbling oil, stepped in front of Angirasa, seized his lolling head by the hair and yanked it to one side.

"Kirsa, don't look!" Mala cried. Kirsa pressed her face against her mother's leg. With a steady hand Prakash lifted the ladle and poured a stream of scalding liquid into Angirasa's ear.

Angirasa's face twisted into a hideous grimace. He opened his mouth wide but could only mewl like an injured kitten. Little rivulets of fat and tears ran down his cheek and neck.

"He's never hurt you." Mala was shaking with rage and fear. "He's never

158

hurt anyone!" The flames seemed to leap and tinge everything red. Then it covered her, and her strength surged. She writhed, trying to free herself from Dilip.

"Don't you know?" Dilip said into her ear. "He killed his woman, Moti. Maybe we're saving you, Mala. How long before he might kill you?"

"He's not the murderer! It's Prakash."

"What?" Dilip breathed in her ear. His grip loosened.

Prakash raised his hand as if to strike her. Mala mustered all her courage and met his cold stare. He revolted and terrified her, but she held his gaze.

"I'll deal with you later," he muttered and bent to pick up a rope. He bound Angirasa's ankles and with muscles bulging yanked his limp prisoner off the stump and dragged him through the dirt to the neem tree, where he threw the rope's other end over a branch. As the headman hoisted his victim up, Angirasa made no sound, and his silence seemed to lessen Prakash's satisfaction. He secured the rope around the tree trunk and stood back, watching his victim sway upside down at its end like a slaughtered animal.

"Ma!" Kirsa wailed.

"Quiet," Prakash said, and grabbed the child, tearing her away from Mala's leg and throwing her to the ground. Kirsa shrieked and curled up in a ball.

"No! Kirsa!" Mala struggled, but Dilip's grip only tightened.

"Aren't we going to kill him?" Dilip asked.

"Can't kill a Brahmin. My lord Valmiki wouldn't want that, especially during the Ashvamedha," Prakash said. "Let the vultures finish him. They'll tear his guts out before long."

"Then let's take care of this one," Dilip said. He released Mala, spun her around, and punched her, sending her sprawling.

"Ma!" Kirsa rushed to her mother. Mala tried to get to her knees and Dilip kicked her in the stomach, knocking the wind from her. She tumbled back down. Lights flashed before her and her head swam. Kirsa shrank away.

Dilip straddled Mala and struck her across the mouth. As he raised his hand to strike again, a new voice called out of the darkness.

"O honored headman!"

Prakash whirled around. Kirsa scrambled to throw her arms around Mala's neck, weeping. Mala fought a wave of nausea and sat up to put one arm around Kirsa and put the other hand to her swelling eye. She squinted to see who was coming.

A short man, round as a melon, entered the firelight's circle.

"Ho, your honor. I crave a word."

Prakash watched him. "Who are you, fat man?"

"Namaste, O most wise and just headman," the man said, with an exaggerated bow over joined palms. "I am here on behalf of someone…"

"Who?" Prakash said.

"Someone who has an interest in a certain jewel."

"What jewel?"

"You know perfectly well. The necklace."

Prakash stared. "Necklace…?"

"Yes, the Sakyan necklace. That a youth called Angirasa gave to the courtesan Moti. It has magical properties that would be useful to any rival to the Sakyan clan."

Angirasa had said it was a powerful gem, even in pieces. Mala glanced at the spot under the cook fire, half expecting to see a ruby glow. She looked away at once.

Prakash looked the round man up and down. "Bandits stole it years ago. They would have sold it. It's long gone."

"So some say," the round man said. "But if anyone would know that a thief was trying to sell it, it would be me. And in all these years, I've heard nothing concerning its whereabouts."

"Even if bandits hadn't sold it, why would it be here?"

"A magical thing like that has its own will. Perhaps it found its way back to its owner." He nodded toward the swaying figure. "The necklace may be here."

Mala did not know if the necklace's magic was intact. She only knew she could not let these evil men possess it.

"What makes you think this ash-covered outcaste is its owner?" Prakash jerked his head toward Angirasa and snickered uneasily.

"Well," the man said, rubbing his hands, "like you, I'd heard about the chanting chandala." He chuckled. "And so, apparently, had King Prasenajit's priest, Yajna."

Prakash waved his hand. "Would Angirasa have stayed here, lived like this, if he had such a jewel? No. The bandits got it. Probably sold it in

Taxila years ago, and it's hanging around some Parsee lady's neck. Who are you, anyway?"

"Permit me to present myself. I'm King Ram, the Lord of the Beggars."

Mala shook her head to clear it, swallowed bile. The Beggar King, the man who ruled Varanasi's underworld. Even the real king was said to pay him tribute.

Prakash gave him a shaky smile. "I swear, I don't know anything about that necklace. You can go now, and leave us to finish our job."

King Ram narrowed his eyes and studied Prakash, who straightened his shoulders and lifted his chin. "I can see you know nothing about it. I'll come back later with Yajna himself, perhaps, and we'll find it."

Mala's eye throbbed, but she tried to think through the haze of pain. Could King Ram help her child? She could make a deal, offer him the necklace. As if he heard her thought, he turned to Kirsa.

"But I've come all the way out here, and I don't like to leave empty-handed. The child, there." King Ram gestured at Kirsa. "She's a pretty thing. I'll take her." He turned to Mala. There was no trace of kindness in his eyes.

"The child and the woman are mine," Prakash growled.

"Surely we can agree to share these spoils. You take the woman, I'll take the child. She's worth a piece of silver," he said, reaching into the broad sash that circled his enormous belly and bringing out a small sack. "If you'd like to reconsider about the woman, I could afford an extra coin or two. She's not all that bad-looking under those ashes. Of course, you could satisfy yourselves first, my good sirs, at no charge, just to seal a transaction among friends."

"Hah." Dilip let out an amused grunt. Prakash said nothing.

Ram shrugged. Silver coins glinted in the firelight as he paid the headman. Prakash weighed them in his hand. Satisfied, he jerked his head at Kirsa. "She's yours."

Mala tightened her arm around her daughter, but Dilip seized Mala's hair and yanked. With a cry, she let go. Dilip yanked again and sent her sprawling. Ram picked the girl up.

"Ma!" she cried. "Ma!"

"I—I know wh..." I know where the necklace is, Mala was going to say.

161

But even as Ram's cold eyes stabbed her, some inexplicable force kept her silent. A faint tingle, the merest wisp of power ran along her nerves.

Om, Kali, Mala prayed, *you who protect all children, who does not fear, I honor You. Om, Kali, help my child, help my child, help my child, help me...* Maybe somehow this man was sent by the dark goddess to help them.

"I'll take good care of her," Ram said with a gentle smile. He pulled a sugarcane from his sash and offered it to Kirsa. "Have a sweet, little thing." She didn't take it, but she stopped crying. "What's your name?"

Kirsa looked up at Mala. Mala begged him with her eyes: *Save the child.*

"Tell her it's all right," he said, still smiling.

Perhaps there was kindness there; perhaps he would help. Yes, if he took Kirsa now, Mala could go get her later, get the necklace, take it to him, get Kirsa back. But no, how would she get away from Prakash? She groaned. There seemed no way out. "It's... it's all right, Kirsa," she choked out.

"An odd little name. Skinny one. There, Kirsa, see? Your mother says it's all right."

Kirsa took the sweet cane with one hand. The round man carried her over to the tree stump where Angirasa had sat earlier. Angirasa. The branch on which he hung creaked. Was he alive or dead?

"A knife? Will someone be so good as to lend me a knife?" Ram said.

What did he need a knife for?

Prakash proffered a knife. "Ah, thank you, Your Honor." Kirsa sucked on the sugar cane and let the Beggar King hold her other wrist to the stump, watching wide-eyed as he raised the blade high.

Suddenly Mala saw what Ram would do.

With a sure stroke, he brought the knife down, swift and sudden. There was a dull thud.

Kirsa's shriek split the air. Blood spurted. The beggar had severed two fingers of her left hand. A flicker passed over Angirasa's face.

Blood spattered Kirsa's new antariya.

Mala would kill this man with that knife. She forced herself up, took a swaying step.

Dilip seized her arm and whirled her around, then struck her on the face with the flat of his hand. She fell to the ground, struggled to rise but couldn't. Everything was going dark.

"Don't worry," the Beggar King said from a growing distance.

A numb little piece of Mala watched everything from a long way away as Kirsa's wails stabbed at her heart.

"Just two fingers gone," Ram said to Mala from a great distance. He was taking her child away. She couldn't bear it. "Enough to get a little extra sympathy... She's a lovely child... She'll be a good little beggar..."

That was the last thing she heard before everything went black.

It could have been a minute or an hour before she came to. She tried to roll over but pain stabbed at her ribs. Her head ached. One eye was swollen almost shut, but through the other she could see Prakash and Dilip talking in low voices.

"Ram said this necklace was a powerful jewel," Prakash said.

"Not much chance it's here," Dilip said.

"Ram said something like that priest Yajna knew it was. He's a sorcerer. He knows things like that."

Dilip looked nervous. "I don't like sorcerers."

Then a high, keening sound filled the night.

"Did you hear something?" Dilip said.

The keening sounded again.

"What *was* that?"

"Shhh," the headman said, peering into the darkness. "Who goes there?"

A short silence. A blood-curdling whoop, and an enormous demon leaped out of the dark and knocked Prakash to the ground. Dilip bolted, shrieking, his cries fading into the night.

The demon faced Prakash, who was frozen with terror. The thing's head was covered in snakes and its face was hideously misshapen and green, with three white stripes across his forehead, the mark of one who serves Shiva.

Mala suppressed a groan.

All of a sudden, it laughed. "Rohit, look what I've got!" it said in a very human voice.

Rohit. That name. She raised herself on her elbow. Another man approached from the shadows.

The creature kicked Prakash. "M-mercy," Prakash said, scrabbling across the ground.

"What have you got there, Lanka?" the other man said. His mustached face was familiar.

"That snake Prakash."

Mala almost cried out when the demon started to pull off its green face. It was only a mask. Underneath was an ordinary human, broad-nosed and clean-shaven.

"Have mercy, Lanka," Prakash said.

"Get up, headman." The mustached man weighed a knife in one hand. A jolt ran up Mala's spine. Rohit. The bandit with the mustache who fought Shakuni that day long ago.

"Rohit, I beg you. Protect me from Lanka. Let me go in peace. I won't tell anyone I saw bandits here, I swear by Indra."

Rohit hesitated. Prakash got slowly to his feet. Rohit spat. "Go." He jerked his head, and the headman ran into the night.

"Why did you do that?" Lanka said.

Rohit shrugged. "This woman is hurt."

"Look!" Lanka rushed to Angirasa. "I think he's dead," he called.

Rohit knelt beside her. "Check that hut. See if the jewels Anu talked about are in there."

"Help us," Mala whispered, looking toward Angirasa. "My daughter..." She rolled to her side and gasped as pain shot through her chest.

"Shhh," Rohit said. He shook his head. "Don't move. Let me look. They beat you very badly." He touched her side and she winced. "Maybe broke some ribs."

An owl hooted.

Lanka looked into the darkness. "I don't like being here at night."

"Oh, Lanka, you're such a fool. Go. See if you can find the necklace."

Lanka disappeared into the hut.

"Please," Mala whispered. "Help me... my child..."

"A child? Is she hiding somewhere?" Rohit half rose to look around, then halted, studying Mala from head to toe. "I know you." He knelt again. "I know you... by the gods." He let out a low whistle. "You're the girl who threw the rock. What happened here?"

Before Mala could gather the strength to answer, Lanka came out of the hut, shaking his head. "Nothing."

Rohit grunted. "Anu and his stupid visions."

"Whatever made him think there were jewels here?" Lanka said.

"A couple nights ago he had one of his dreams. Something about the ruby and diamond necklace that he tried to steal from Addhakashi. The day this woman helped us." He nodded at Mala. "You was hardly more than a girl," he said, "but long-limbed as a colt."

Lanka came over and looked down. His broad face was kind and open, but he looked over his shoulder and it was clear he was afraid. "This is the one? Who threw the rock that knocked out that bastard Shakuni?"

"Saved Anu's life and mine." They both looked at her. "Strange that I should find her here now."

"The fire…" She would tell them the necklace was buried under the fire. She would tell them and they would help her…

An eerie hoot came out of the dark. The owl flew out of the tree, a flash of white wings at the edge of the fire's low light and disappeared in the darkness.

"Maybe Anu's vision did mean we'd find a jewel here," Rohit said. "Put her on a mat, Lanka." He pointed to a grass mat Lanka had tossed out of the hut while looking for the necklace. "We're taking her with us."

THE KING OF THE BEGGARS

WHEN KIRSA AWOKE, THE SUN was beating down from a pale blue sky. She was lying in the dirt. Her hand throbbed. She lifted her arm. A bloody bandage covered the stumps of her missing fingers. There were strange voices, nearby shouts and screams of laughter, like nothing she'd ever heard at the burning grounds. Where was she?

"Is she awake?" a man said. The pain in her hand was so intense she almost groaned, but instead she shrank into herself, stifled the moan, and shut her eyes. He was dangerous. She didn't want to let him know she'd heard. Where was Ma? She must find Ma. But how? *Om, Devi, Great Mother, help me...*

"Yes, King Ram, she is."

Kirsa could not help squinting at the speaker, a skinny little boy with a patch on one eye.

"So she is. Namaste, pretty thing."

King Ram. The one who had taken her from Ma, the one who cut off her fingers. Why had he done that? Why had Ma given her to this man? She put her good hand over her eyes, but then she saw Bapu swaying from that branch, so still, so silent. Her eyes flew open.

Why had those men attacked Ma and Bapu? Maybe Ma was tied up like Bapu had been. That's why she hadn't come.

"Time to get up," Ram said. "The sun is high overhead."

"Maybe she's hungry," the boy with the patch said. The thought of food made Kirsa want to vomit. She gagged, and a little bile came out of the corner of her mouth.

"Help her sit, Rebha."

She sensed the boy kneeling next to her. He touched her uninjured hand. She opened her eyes.

"Come on," he said. She struggled to rise. Rebha blinked at her with his one good eye. How had he lost the other one? Kirsa suddenly knew the answer and tried to push it away. "That's better, isn't it?"

King Ram held out a bowl of rice and lentils. "Here. A special treat. Your first day. Eat it, and then time to get to work. You'll go out with Mitra." Still laughing, he bowed and handed her the rice. She shrank. He might hand her food, but he was not a good man. Maybe she had done something wrong so that those men attacked her family.

But what could Ma have done? One of the men had hit her and kicked her. Kirsa should have helped, but she was too small.

"Don't be shy." King Ram thrust the bowl at her. "Eat, or I'll give it to Rebha."

Reluctantly, Kirsa reached out and took the bowl, placing it in her lap. Rebha's shoulders slumped a bit. He turned and walked away. She took a few grains of rice in her fingers and put them in her mouth but couldn't swallow.

"Mitra!" King Ram called. A boy much bigger than one-eyed Rebha broke away from a group of children standing a short distance away. They looked at her then glanced at each other. Her stomach fluttered. "He's the best of the beggars!" Ram said, patting Mitra on the back. "He knows all the tricks."

Kirsa shrank and glanced sideways up at Mitra. At least he didn't look mean. The other children's stares scared her.

"He's more grown up than you, and stronger, so no one will steal my pretty Kirsa away."

"Off with you now, pretty one," the Beggar King said, and left her with Mitra.

"You going to eat that?" Mitra said. He was slender and taller than she, and wore a white cloth wrapped around his head and an dirty antariya wrapped around his hips. It might have once been orange. He studied her with heavy-lidded brown eyes. She shook her head. He sat down next to her and with three scoops emptied the contents of the bowl into his mouth. He tossed it at another child then stood and put his hands under her arms. She stood up, swaying. He looked at the bloody bandages. "Oh, they'll be sorry for you, poor little thing," he said. "Can you walk?"

Kirsa nodded. Her head spun a little at first. She swayed, but somehow standing made her feel a little better. The pain in her hand receded a bit as she followed him through the beggars' camp. They passed other children, who quieted and stared. Mitra called out now and then, and one would respond with a wave or a shout.

Away from the camp, they threaded their way through crowded streets. Mitra might not look mean, but he wasn't gentle. When she stumbled he grabbed her good hand and jerked her up. It was hard to protect her injured hand from the people who jostled her. She tired quickly and began to feel queasy again. The sun's white glare hurt her eyes so she looked down. The crowds swimming at the edge of her vision terrified her.

For her whole life, Kirsa had admired Varanasi glittering high on its distant bluff. When the rising sun struck the white walls of its houses it was like Indra's heavenly city. It looked so pure and beautiful, but here inside the Shining City it was no paradise. She'd never dreamed there were so many people in the world. And it smelled dreadful—the burning dead didn't give off such a foul miasma of waste and dirty bodies and terrible filth.

Mitra came to a busy square. "There's a shrine to Indra over there." He nodded toward a tall wooden structure. Two priests robed in white stood in front, accepting gifts of flowers and food from a gaggle of worshippers. "People like to look generous to their gods. I make good money there," he said. One of the priests narrowed his eyes and watched as they approached.

Rebha was leaning against a wall nearby. Mitra gave him a shove. "Find another corner." The boy's one visible eye, huge and tear-filled, looked at Kirsa with a mute plea. Kirsa could do nothing for him. If only her ma was here, maybe she could help him. Ma was strong and beautiful... but those men had hit her, and then she had given Kirsa to King Ram. But surely Ma was going to come back and get her. There was a reason for all this, even if Kirsa didn't know what it was. But she wished she did. She wanted to cry.

"You see the way he cries?" Mitra said. "They give you more money when you do."

Kirsa had tears in her eyes. With a tentative look at Mitra, Kirsa held out her throbbing, bandaged hand.

"You're good!" he said. "People feel extra sorry for a sweet little girl that's hurt." He took the injured hand and gave it a quick squeeze.

She bit her lip to hold back a cry. The tears in her eyes spilled down her cheeks.

"You catch on quick," he snickered.

Just then, a plump woman in blue stopped. "Wait," she said to a servant following her, who had a basket of ripe fruit hanging on his arm. The smell nauseated Kirsa.

Mitra held out an open palm. "O beautiful, good Lakshmi," he began.

The woman shook a finger at him. "Not for you, Mitra, you rascal. You're strong enough for real work. But who is this poor little one? Here, child." She dropped a handful of coins in Kirsa's lap.

The angry look Mitra gave her as the woman in blue walked away turned Kirsa cold. The whole day, as she gave him all her coins, she tried to smile. At first he just glared, but as time passed he softened. "They like you. You're such a pretty little girl." He stroked her hair. She didn't dare pull away.

That night when Mitra showed him the coins King Ram laughed and smiled, but his eyes were cold. She got extra rice. That was good. Though she hadn't really stopped feeling sick all day, she was starving. Still, she took little mouthfuls. *Eat slowly,* Bapu always said, *and thank the gods and the rain and the sun for the food with each bite.* At the thought of her father hanging from the tree limb, she squeezed her eyes shut. The rice turned to sand in her mouth.

"Not hungry, eh?"

She opened her eyes. It was Mitra. He snatched her bowl, chucked her under the chin, then walked away. She scrambled to her feet. Little pinpricks of light danced in front of her, and she nearly fell. Mitra had disappeared around the corner of a ramshackle hut. Despite her pain and hunger and dizziness, Kirsa noticed that the hut's roof badly needed thatching. She looked at the bloody bandage. How would she ever help Ma and Bapu thatch their hut once she was home again?

Home. That was it. She had to go home.

She steadied herself. She must escape. Her stomach rumbled. First, though, she must eat. She took a breath and wiped her sweaty forehead. She would find Mitra, get her rice back.

In the beggars' camp, children were eating or playing at dice. No one paid attention to her as she slipped past two girls who seemed about her age. One had oozing sores all over her face. The boys and older girls threw garbage at this girl. She looked at Kirsa once with dead eyes, then looked at the ground without a word. The other girl had legs no thicker than the sticks her father used for kindling. A boy was pulling Skinny Legs around on a sledge as she shouted and laughed with everyone, even the older boys, who terrified Kirsa.

They were bigger than Mitra and sauntered about, naked to the waist. Thick, bulgy muscles covered their arms. Some had scars on their faces or crisscrossed on their backs. She stole glances at them. Skinny Legs was very brave to talk with them.

Kirsa wandered in a daze. Where had Mitra gone? Dark was falling; everyone was settling for sleep. She had never felt this way before, so alone, with no one to help her, no idea where to go. She found her way back to the ramshackle hut, fighting tears. Not far away there was a sort of lean-to, long and low, where some of the prettier older girls were sitting on pallets. They had lined their eyes with black and painted their lips red.

Maybe one of those girls would hold her the way Ma did when she was sick, let Kirsa share her pallet. Maybe she could offer to thatch the lean-to in return.

She swallowed hard. That would never happen. In this dreadful place, there were no grasses. Just mud, all the way down to the riverbank. "Oh, Ma, where are you?" she said softly.

Ma was tied up with Bapu and couldn't come to Kirsa. Kirsa must go rescue her. If she could get to the river, she could go find Matsya the fisherman and his wife, Matsyani. They would do anything they could for her and Ma and Bapu. But two men stood between the edge of the camp and the water.

King Ram appeared by the lean-to where the girls with painted lips sat. Kirsa crouched low. Men and boys walked up to him, pointed at a girl and handed him coins, just the way Ram had handed that bad man coins and taken Kirsa. She stared in horrified fascination. The man who had given coins would lie down on a girl he'd chosen and bounce up and down. Bapu lay like that on Ma when they thought she was asleep, but when they did it, Ma's eyes were closed, and she smiled and crooned.

Some painted girls lay there silent, their faces fixed. Some giggled while the men bounced, others groaned or cried out. Kirsa turned away, dread filling her aching and chilled body.

A few children lay down not far from her. She wanted to talk to them, but they whispered behind their hands, their eyes in shadow. She'd never been around anyone her age. She had imagined other children, played with them in her mind, but she was afraid of these real ones. She leaned against the hut and curled into the tiniest ball she could so as not to bother anybody. She was shivering and hot all at once. She closed her eyes against the pain and the sights and sounds of the camp.

ॐ

The next day, Kirsa's hand felt worse. Mitra came and led her away to a different temple. All day she went hot and cold and shook, like the time the fever goddess Sitala cast a spell and made her sick. Ma had never left Kirsa's side until Sitala's spell was broken.

She couldn't stop the tears rolling down her cheeks. Lots of people gave her coins. Mitra was very pleased, but it didn't lessen her lonely misery. By the day's end she felt very weak and he had to drag her up and half carry her the rest of the way to camp, muttering all the time.

That night Mitra came to where she lay shivering with pain and fever.

"Shhh!" he said, putting a finger to his lips. "Hush, pretty thing." He took her good hand and pulled her up and led her, tripping and nearly crying, toward the river. Was he going to help her? She trembled. He put his finger to his lips again as they approached a well-made hut with a piece of cloth hanging across the entrance. Kirsa's heart pounded as she followed Mitra, step by careful step.

Just as they reached the entrance, King Ram jumped out from behind the cloth. Kirsa shrieked. "Where do you think you're going?" He seized Mitra's arm.

"I—I—"

Before Mitra could say anything, Ram smacked him on both cheeks.

"Off with you." They glared at each other. Without a word, Ram took Kirsa into his hut. There was a low, narrow pallet. He lay down. "You can sleep with me." No, no, she couldn't ever sleep next to this monster. "Come on, now," he said with that evil smile, and beckoned. She didn't dare refuse. She curled up with her back to him, not quite touching. "It's all right." She started to cry, and he stroked her hair. Could it be that he would be kind? No. She hated his touch, but in her exhaustion she couldn't keep from closing her eyes.

She woke from a troubled dream to find King Ram was holding her tight to him and rubbing and pushing his fat body against her. He panted in her ear. She cried out.

"Quiet!" he said in a hoarse whisper, clapping a hand over her mouth.

For an instant, she froze.

Bite him!

She bit hard.

"Ouch! Brat!" Ram said, releasing her and shaking his hand.

Kirsa gathered her strength, clenched her teeth against the pain, and clambered to her feet, stumbling out of the hut. The sky had turned silver. The calls of the fishermen floated over the nearby river as they launched their boats. She staggered toward Mother Ganga.

"Ho! Come back here!" King Ram's voice called from behind her.

"Ah!" she gasped. There were the guards. They would catch her, but no, their heads drooped on their chests. They were sleeping. She could slip by, get to the water.

"Ho!" Ram called again. Against her will, she glanced back. He was waddling after her, clothes asunder, stumbling and tripping. A sleepy child raised his head, then one of the guards looked like he was rousing. "Catch her!"

"Wha...?" The guard shook himself. Her legs buckled, but then something or someone, or she didn't know what, buoyed her up as if she was floating on a breeze.

Run!

Her wobbly legs obeyed. Rocks pierced the soles of her feet but didn't stop her. Her wounded hand felt huge. She was almost at the river. Oh, just a few more steps. Icy water numbed her feet. There was a boat moving from the shore. Could it be Matsya's? The old fisherman and his wife would take Kirsa back to Ma and Bapu. If she could only get back to them everything would be all right. The bad men who came to their hut would be gone, and everything would be the same as it always had been and always would be.

"Catch that little brat!" Ram's voice came from very far away.

"Matsya!" she gasped, splashing forward. The river swept the boat away too fast.

Men and women stood in the water near the riverbank. The sun's rays were just breaking over the horizon, and the people plunged under Ganga's waters and emerged with arms outstretched as Surya's fiery chariot blazed on the horizon. It was beautiful.

"Get her!"

Kirsa glanced back. Ram's guard was stepping into the water behind her. At that moment a man emerged from the river, hiding her from the guard. Water ran in silver rivulets down his beard and off his matted locks over his skinny chest. He seemed unaware of her but burst into a chant like one her father liked to sing.

Then someone else took up the chant—*Bapu!—could it be?*—that way, toward those steps.

Bapu, I'm coming! Kirsa lost herself among the worshippers ducking and rising. She fell. The cold, shallow water shocked her but didn't stop the fiery pain as she caught herself with her wounded hand. She tried to get up, struggling against the soaking wet folds of her antariya. If she could only reach those steps, the ghats where Bapu had said wise rishis who knew the answers to every question sat. Maybe he was there. Or maybe the rishis would know where she could find Matsya and Matsyani. So many bathers stood between her and the steps. It was so hard to move. She would never reach the fishing boats. Her wet clothes were heavy against her shivering limbs.

Then all of a sudden there was the woman in blue—what had Mitra called her? *Lakshmi*. The one who dropped coins into her lap. Lakshmi was ducking her head in the water. She stayed under a long time, then emerged to raise her hands to the morning sky. A surge of hope sent Kirsa farther into the river. The kind woman in blue would help, if only she could reach her.

Beware the current!

Now the river itself was pushing her farther and farther from shore, but she had almost reached Lakshmi. There was the antariya floating on the surface—so close—as the plump woman submerged again. Just a little farther—her fingertips nearly touched it, but her clothes were dragging at her. The water was so cold. She reached once more. Lakshmi rose with her hands extended, pulling the cloth away from Kirsa.

Her feet lost the bottom and she sank into Mother Ganga's arms.

THE FOREST OF BLISS

"MALA. MALA."

Someone or something grasped her shoulder. Mala tried to break free so she could keep up with Kirsa. They were running away from King Ram, running toward Ganga's banks. Kirsa stumbled.

"Mala—"

Whatever it was shook her. "Leave me alone!" She pulled Kirsa up with one hand and lashed out with her other arm. Her fist struck flesh.

"Ouf." The grip on her shoulder slipped. "The hell! You wake her up, Rohit."

Wake up? Was this a dream? No. She must help Kirsa escape that loathsome Beggar King. They were almost safe. At the river, many people plunged below Ganga's surface and emerged to salute the sun. Kirsa raced ahead into the water. *Beware the current,* Mala cried, but Kirsa didn't hear. The current was too strong—

"Mala!" She opened her eyes and looked into Rohit's compassionate ones. "Let me help you," he said, and slid an arm behind her back to lift her to a sitting position.

"Ah!" Pain stabbed her chest.

"You're hurting her!" The man who had worn the demon mask—Lanka, that was his name—was looking over Rohit's shoulder.

"She hit me." It was pockmarked Anu standing next to Lanka, rubbing his jaw.

"It's all right," Rohit said. "You were having a nightmare."

"I wasn't!" It was so real. "I was saving Kirsa, then Mother Ganga took her." Kirsa might be drowning. Mala looked around, frantic. "Where am I?" Daylight showed through the ramshackle wooden walls and filtered through holes in the disintegrating thatch roof. Rohit, Anu, and Lanka surrounded her.

"You're in Anandavana," Rohit said. "The Forest of Bliss. This is our camp."

"It's an old temple, see, that some say is haunted," Anu said. "By demons." He smirked at Lanka, who frowned.

Mala struggled to get up. "I must find my daughter. She was drowning!" She broke into sobs.

"Easy." Rohit pushed her back gently. "You haven't been able to open your eyes for two days. You're hardly ready to get up, let alone look for your child."

"Two days..." She was very weak. She began to wipe her eyes and winced. The left one was swollen from Dilip's blow. Her jaw hurt, too.

Rohit took her chin and studied her bruised eye. "Hmm. I have an idea of something we can do for it. I learned about healing herbs from a yogi who sometimes takes a retreat nearby."

"I don't need herbs..." She needed her daughter, but when she tried to push herself up, pain shot through her whole body.

"I need help, too," Anu said in a sarcastic tone. He scowled at her over Rohit's shoulder. "She almost gave me a black eye."

"I found her." Mala choked back tears. "I was helping her escape... it was so real."

"Shhh," Rohit said. "It was nothing but a dream."

"Dreams can be real," Anu said. "Like I dreamed the chandala had that necklace."

Rohit tossed him a disgusted look. "And look how that turned out."

Mala pursed her lips. Anu's dream had been true. She shuddered. No. Ganga had not taken Kirsa. It couldn't be. She must at least try to get up so she could find her daughter. "Help me."

Rohit took her arm. She managed to stand, and he supported her as they left the ramshackle structure. Tangled undergrowth under tall trees surrounded a clearing of hard-packed dirt. At its center a fire crackled. A

176

slender young man with kohl-lined eyes sat on a flat rock, holding a stick on which a hare's carcass was impaled over the fire. It smelled delicious.

"I'm glad you're awake," he said. "My name is Ketu."

She needed some food if she was going to get away from there. She eased herself down on the ground next to him. Ketu passed the stick to Rohit and picked up a wooden bowl, filled it with some dirty-looking rice from a thoroughly black dented pot, and handed her the bowl.

Rohit examined the hare. "Looks done." He put it on a rock and cut it in five pieces. Anu grabbed a haunch and started eating where he stood; Rohit handed the front leg and part of the breast to Mala and a similar piece to Ketu, then took the back for himself. Lanka took the other haunch.

"Thank you." Mala took hesitant bites at first then tore at the hare while the others ate in a silence broken only by monkey chatter and birdcalls that floated down from the trees.

"Three nights ago we went to the burning grounds and found you," Rohit said when he'd finished. He avoided saying anything about what they were doing there. "You were kind of woozy when we carried you away. We brought you here. We're in dense forest, but not far from the river. Just across Ganga are the cremation grounds. It's safe enough here. No one comes to this temple—it's been deserted for a generation. For the last two days and nights you've been unconscious or delirious and babbling about getting your daughter from the Beggar King."

"It's plain that devil Prakash attacked you, but why?"

There was no reason to hide Angirasa's identity anymore. She told them who he was and what he had done, and said Prakash was taking vengeance for Valmiki. Her memory of the attack was disjointed, but the horror that Angirasa and Kirsa suffered was vivid and difficult to tell.

"The poor little thing!" Ketu exclaimed when she choked out the way Ram had cut off Kirsa's fingers.

"It's not just the Beggar King that maims little ones," Anu said. "Some parents do it, too. But that is probably all Ram'll do."

Mala burst into tears.

"Very comforting," Rohit said, giving Anu a glare.

Anu shrugged. "Just tellin' the truth. You was going on and on about finding your little Kirsa but if you do, Ram will want payment for her."

"It's true," Rohit said. "He'll want a lot, assuming he's willing to give her up. She could make money for him for the rest of her life—"

"Could be a very short life. I've heard some of them die from the maiming," Anu said.

Mala looked at him in shock while the other three glowered.

"Could we steal her back?" Mala whispered. Thieves could surely think of a way.

"Ram has eyes everywhere," Lanka said. "The city is huge. It's hard to find your way around, much less look for one little beggar. Even if we found her on a street corner and took her, whoever was with her would run to the Beggar King right away. We'd never make it out of the city." He went back to chewing a bone.

Rohit nodded. "There are so many alleys and slums. Down each one of them is at least one of Ram's people. Even if you find her, his people would tell the Beggar King. He wouldn't let her go. Your only hope would be to buy her, and that will cost."

The necklace would buy Kirsa's freedom. "I know where the necklace is."

"What?" Lanka was astonished.

"You see, I was right!" Anu's eyes lit up.

"Take me back to the burning grounds and I'll show you where we hid it." She paused. "But we must build a pyre for Angirasa…"

"Let's go get it now. The body hanging there would've kept anyone except vultures away," Anu said. "Must be just bones left now. No time to waste before someone else goes looking." He half rose.

Rohit scratched his clean-shaven chin. "The city guards have probably found it already."

"It was well hidden," Mala said, desperate to enlist their help.

"I suppose we could go at night," Rohit said. "Even if someone has taken the chandala's place, we could wait till whoever it was slept. But we have to consider that King Ram may have come back for it. Ram's people may be guarding the place. Even worse, Kosalan soldiers, if this priest Yajna is involved. We can't just rush in. We need to scout it out."

"We should go now," Anu said, and the men all began arguing with each other over the fisherman's trustworthiness.

Mala watched their bickering in despair. They were no use. Exhausted as she was, maybe she should go to the burning grounds alone. Angirasa's cruel fate tormented her as much as Kirsa's uncertain one.

At last Rohit said, "We should make sure it's safe to go look for it. We need to know what's happening there. Maybe tomorrow Lanka and I will get as close as we can. Then we'll see."

"What will we do in the meantime?" Ketu asked.

"I say we go to that shrine today," Anu said. "You know, the one where all them rich pilgrims go. It's where the priests open the gate to the gods' world. Rich folk want to catch a glimpse of Indra's heavenly city."

The bandits stood to gather weapons and prepare to go. Mala watched them in silence. As soon as they were gone, she would leave, too. Ganga was close. She could swim it when the waters were slow and shallow, as they were now. Somehow she would get to the hut, dig up the necklace. She would figure it out when she got there. Then she would take the necklace to Varanasi and find the Beggar King and Kirsa.

As if he'd heard her thought, Rohit turned to Mala. "Have you ever been to Varanasi?"

She shook her head. From the distance, it looked immense. She didn't know the first thing about finding her way in such a place. "I've never been to any city."

"Well then, don't think of going to Varanasi alone! It's a maze. You have no idea how easy you'll get lost. It's dangerous, too, even for men like us who have weapons. For a woman alone..." He gave her a warning look. "You're not well, either. For now, you should rest."

It was true. She was exhausted just from eating a meal. Her bruises made it painful to breathe. Her head was aching. Yet she had no intention of following his suggestion.

As soon as the bandits disappeared, Mala tried to stand. Her legs wobbled and she had a splitting headache, but the thought of Kirsa and the food in her stomach gave her strength.

She took off, her excitement carrying her along until she reached the riverbed and there she halted.

Varanasi's white walls gleamed. It was so far, so huge and unknown... she didn't know if she was strong enough to make it. As she stared, the shimmering city seemed to rise on a bank of golden clouds, getting farther and farther away, rising to the heavens. "Kirsa!" She started to run, but her legs gave out. She fell flat on the damp sand. Too weak to get up, she started to crawl, but her head began to spin. Stars whirled in front of her, then nothing.

No, there was something. Someone. A beautiful, pale-skinned woman wrapped in a rich blue antariya floated toward her. A net of diamonds held her long dark hair at her neck. A long rope of pearls fell between her bare, round breasts, and bangles studded with blue and green gems covered her arms from wrist to elbow.

Kirsa is safe.

Mala gaped. "Who are you?" she managed to ask.

Lakshmi.

Mala blinked. Lakshmi?

I am the Goddess of Wealth and consort of Lord Vishnu.

When Mala looked again, a plump woman with greying hair, so familiar somehow, wearing the same rich blue antariya as the goddess, stood in front of her holding Kirsa, whose sleeping head rested on her ample breast.

Mala lost consciousness.

ॐ

When Mala woke, she was still lying on the sand, but her headache was gone. She got up on all fours. Her dizziness abated. She was soon able to stand.

The woman in blue filled her mind. The Devi had appeared to her as Durga riding a tiger, carrying weapons, radiating courage. Kali had shown a face of fearsome love. Now Lakshmi was offering safety and security for her child. Mala's heart wanted to believe that someone rich and generous had rescued Kirsa. It was the plump woman on whose breast Kirsa rested. Maybe Mala should go to the city and seek them out.

Or was it madness to believe this? How among those thousands would she find one little girl and one round woman dressed in a blue antariya?

Though her whole being wanted to go to Kirsa now, she could not go alone to find her. She needed to gain the trust of Rohit and his men and enlist their aid in rescuing her when the Devi gave her a sign the time was right. Slowly, she began walking toward the forest.

When she got back to the clearing, she set to work. She swept out the decrepit old temple to make it more habitable and examined the roof. It would cave in with the first monsoon rain. She would thatch it, make the temple a dry and cozy shelter. When the Devi gave a sign, she would go to the city and find Kirsa, bring her here. In the meantime, Mala would make herself indispensable, and they couldn't fail to help her.

Her stomach growled. She needed food. Dusk was coming. She noticed a large rough-hewn wooden box not far from the fire, its lid weighted down with stones. A sack of rice, another of dal, a small bag with—wonder of wonders—cardamom pods and another star-shaped seed unfamiliar to Mala, but good smelling. And more wonders: a little jar filled with oil. She rinsed the dented kettle with some water from a large half-filled water jug and began to cook. As the oil heated she dropped in the spices, and on the heavenly fragrance that rose she sent a prayer to Lakshmi, who offered abundance and safety to her daughter. "Protect Kirsa," she said, "keep her safe." She stirred in the rice and lentils and added water, and as it boiled and steam rose, she saw Lakshmi's face in it, smiling at her.

Her heart was eased, but her headache, which had subsided for a time, returned with great force. She couldn't ignore the stabbing pains around her ribs or the throbbing around her eye. Rohit had mentioned something about a yogi at a nearby hermitage who knew healing ways.

Asita. It must be. Or perhaps that was too much to hope for. She considered trying to find him but feared getting lost. Rohit and his men would return hungry. It would please them to have a meal ready.

Not long after she started the rice, the men filed into camp in dejected silence. Mala glanced at them as they gathered by the fire. Anu's straggly hair was full of leaves. Ketu had a long scratch on his cheek as if a bramble had caught him. As soon as he sat down he began to dab at it with a square of clean cotton. Lanka was disheveled and subdued, and Rohit's face was sullen.

Anu pulled a piece of cloth out of his sash and let it flutter to the ground. "Fine treasure." He glowered at Rohit.

"It's not Rohit's fault," Ketu said. "Who knew there'd be so many guards?"

Lanka flung himself down in front of the fire and sighed. "Remember the coins and bangles and rings we used to get..."

Anu spat. "Been a while since I tied coins in *my* sash."

Mala pressed her lips together. She would ask the yogi's name and the way to his hermitage later. "The food is ready," she said. Ketu smiled at her and picked up a wooden bowl. Lanka did the same, but Anu and Rohit made no effort to eat. They ate in silence as the sky darkened.

Lanka put down his bowl. "These days," he said with a full mouth, "it's warriors everywhere. Anyone who doesn't have a guard has nothing worth stealing."

"It's because of deserters," Anu said. "They're vicious! Ruined things for honest thieves like us. That's what I say."

Mala would need to know how to avoid these soldiers when she and Kirsa left for… for where? She would think about that later. "Where do these deserters come from?" She filled a bowl and handed it to Anu. He took it without a word.

"From Prasenajit's armies," Lanka said, swallowing and wiping his mouth with the back of his arm. "Like the Surasenas. They don't like fighting for their Kosalan master." His face glowed with sweat from the fire's heat and the warm night air.

She filled another bowl and crouched, leaning toward Rohit. He had stretched out on his back at the edge of the firelight, his arms crossed behind his head, and stared up at the stars. "The Kosalan king seems to have conquered everyone," she said. "Why would soldiers desert a winning army?"

Rohit raised himself on his elbow. "It's true that he's defeated most of the western clans. And some southern ones, too, except the Maghadas." Rohit reached out and accepted the bowl from her. "Thank you," he said in a soft voice.

In spite of her pounding head, a little flush of pleasure rose to her cheeks. She wanted him to talk more.

"These Maghadas," she said, hesitating. "My Angirasa told me they lived by different laws. More just, he said. You say their kingdom is south…?"

"Some say that the king's own bodyguard is made up of women," Ketu said.

"Huh. I'll have to see it to believe it," Anu responded.

"What do you think, Rohit?" Mala asked, hoping he would verify what Angirasa had told her. She had already thought of going there with Kirsa.

"One thing is certain," he replied. "Prasenajit didn't dare attack them, and King Bimbisara helped the eastern clans turn away the sacrificial stallion." Rohit licked his fingers.

182

Anu, who had gobbled his food, held out his bowl. "I'm glad old Prasenajit is doing that sacrifice. Plenty of rich pilgrims and powerful barons coming to pay their respects at the final ceremony. It'll be good hunting for us."

The city would fill with pilgrims. In a crowd, Mala and Kirsa could blend in, make their escape. She had to find Kirsa first. For that she needed help. She studied the men.

"During the year of the Ashvamedha," Lanka chimed in, "the king is supposed to sleep between his chief wife's legs without rutting. That's what the Vedas say." He looked around with a proud smile.

No, not him. Lanka was like a bullock with a good disposition, lots of strength, willing to work, but not clever. She needed someone clever.

"Since when are you readin' the Vedas?" Anu sneered.

No, not Anu. She needed someone who could weigh risks, think before he acted. Besides, she didn't trust him.

"Not too difficult for Prasenajit," Ketu said with a wink. "His chief queen looks like the horse." Laughter rose with the smoke into the surrounding trees. An owl hooted nearby. Ketu cringed. "Of course, she is a noble lady."

No, not Ketu. Kind, like Lanka, but much too timid.

"But no beauty," Anu said. The men laughed again.

Rohit sat up. "We'll see. Maghada and his losses to the eastern clans aren't Prasenajit's only troubles."

It had to be Rohit. He was the gang's leader.

Mala slumped. Six years ago, when they'd encountered each other and the courtesan Addhakashi on the road, he'd been a rather inept bandit. Not much seemed to have changed. But he was the most intelligent. She would tell him her idea of going during the sacrifice, when pilgrims packed the city, which would make it easier for her and Kirsa to escape. He knew his way around; he would be able to think of an escape route.

But she still had to find Kirsa.

"In the North," Rohit continued as Mala became lost in thought, "the Sakyas get richer and more powerful by the day. King Himalaya protects their backs with his high peaks, and it's hard for Prasenajit to wage an effective campaign against them."

Mala snapped to attention. "The Sakyas?" Angirasa's people. Kirsa's people.

"There's some story about the Sakyan prince. That he'll rule the world." Anu polished off his second bowl and belched. "Maybe he'll bring peace to the Sixteen Clans. Like I said, this fighting's not good for honest thieves."

"The trade road isn't safe anymore," Ketu said, nodding, "what with armies moving east to west and back again, plundering and raping and murdering."

"Hard to tell the difference between a real army and those gangs of deserters," Lanka added. "Some say if the bandits united, they'd be as powerful as the Kosalans."

"An outlaw army," Anu said. "That's a good one."

Firelight swam. The warm night was suddenly too close. Red mist rose around her.

"Mala," Rohit said, reaching out a hand. "You look sick."

"I... I need to rest," she said. Rohit pulled her up. The mist faded.

Ketu grabbed a brand from the fire. When they entered the temple, he held the torch up and looked around. "Good enough for a priest to live in," he said in surprise.

Rohit helped her onto her pallet. "You're a useful woman to have around."

She gave him a wincing smile.

"Come on," Ketu said. "Let her rest."

The temple's stifling air pressed against her swollen eye, but exhaustion soon overcame discomfort. She slept and dreamed she was a many-armed woman riding a tiger, wearing a necklace of bloody rubies, and one of the weapons in her many hands was a rock.

A NEW CHANDALA

NALAKA SWAM UP FROM A stuporous sleep and sat up on his charpoy, covered in sweat. He rubbed his eyes. From the position of the sun's rays on the dirt floor of his stifling little room, it must be midafternoon. He had fallen asleep after eating.

He leaped up. The whole ashram would have gathered in the courtyard by now. This afternoon, everyone was to observe another rehearsal. With only ten days until the priests led the stallion to the eagle altar and commenced the concluding rite, normal lessons had ceased. Valmiki and the Brahmins who would assist at the Ashvamedha practiced endlessly. The students watched, instructed to try to catch errors, but in fact no one knew as much as Valmiki, not even Kapur, so no one ever offered any corrections.

Nalaka rushed down the passage from the kitchen to the courtyard. It was a few days since he'd overheard Yajna and Valmiki talking. In that time, he'd obsessed over what to do with Valmiki's secret. The guru had been particularly dismissive lately, which rekindled Nalaka's resentment and desire to cause trouble. He would send an anonymous message to Yajna about the boxes filled with writing. But then he would think that to remain loyal was the highest good.

When he got to the courtyard, the rehearsal was in progress. The other students sat sweating under the hot afternoon sun while the fountain splashed nearby. They would be feeling occasional cool drops on their hot skin, which worsened the torture. Nalaka didn't want to draw attention, so he stopped in the ashoka tree's shadow and leaned against the wall. He crossed his arms over his chest with studied insolence, enjoying the cool shade as he watched the others swelter.

"Thou, O sacred stallion, companion of the gods," Valmiki chanted. "Thou dost not die through this sacrifice, but thou art made immortal."

The three Brahmins who would assist at the sacrifice gave the response. "Thou dost not die. Thou art made immortal!"

"Let not the fire darken thee, let not the cauldron split while thy limbs cook."

"Let not the fire darken thee!" the priests repeated.

In all his time at the ashram, Nalaka had never seen Valmiki sweat under the hot sun. If he sent that message to Yajna, though, the guru might soon lose his cool composure.

"Let thy soul burn bright as thou goest on the smoke of Agni's fire to the dwelling of the gods." Valmiki raised his hands to the heavens.

Did Nalaka truly want to do something that would harm Valmiki, who still awed him with his learning, his power, his wealth?

"Do not fear the slaughterer's ax; it will do no lasting harm to thy body."

The priests raised their hands, imitating Valmiki. "Do not fear!"

Not everyone could remember and recite everything perfectly. Nalaka was a prime example. How many years had he tried to commit the hymns to memory? It would be good to have it all written to refer when no learned Brahmin was present to ask about this prayer or that.

Why should he threaten Valmiki? Nalaka could help him. He would reveal he knew how to write. He would gain the Brahmin's favor, at long last be the star pupil, make the others burn with jealousy.

"Let not the slaughterer be clumsy as he slices through thy thirty-four ribs, but cut them cleanly—"

"But, Valmiki-ji!"

Someone had dared interrupt. Valmiki gaped, hands still raised to heaven. A stunned silence ensued.

"A horth hath thirty-thix ribs!"

Titters began to rise. Heads turned to little Shukra, the orphaned son of Valmiki's stablehand, even more a misfit at the ashram than Nalaka, but for charity's sake the guru let him stay. Nalaka had a soft spot for the boy and had taught him to wrestle. In return, Shukra worshipped him.

Valmiki lowered his hands. He was shaking. The laughter died. The

Brahmin, his mouth working, glared at the students one at a time until his gaze rested on Shukra. The boy looked miserable. He didn't have a true brahmacharin's shaved head and topknot, and his mop of dark hair was plastered to his head with sweat. Tears filled his eyes.

Everyone watched with bated breath. In many ashrams, Shukra would receive a sound beating. Valmiki preached the philosophy that one shouldn't strike a student, but he had used his cane on Nalaka often enough. Maybe Nalaka deserved a beating now and then, but it seemed unjust to beat poor Shukra, who had not chosen a brahmacharin's life. Besides, anger destroyed tapas. If Valmiki did beat the boy, it would reduce his spiritual heat and affect the upcoming rites.

To Nalaka's relief, Valmiki lowered his hands.

"There will be no evening refreshment for anyone," the guru said hoarsely. "To your quarters, all of you. No one is to come out until tomorrow morning's puja."

ॐ

Night had fallen. The cook had prepared fruit and lime water for Valmiki, but he was afraid to take the tray to the Brahmin's chambers. The guru's anger might still burn strong after the afternoon's disruption. Whoever brought him food risked a curse for disobeying his order not to come out before morning. "You take it." The cook handed Nalaka the tray.

As Nalaka hurried across the courtyard, he thanked the goddess of learning under his breath. "*Om*, thank you, Sarasvati, *om*." She must have sent him this opportunity to tell Valmiki that he knew what was in the boxes, but that the secret was safe. No one would hear it from his lips; indeed, he would confess that it was his secret, too, that he believed in writing the sacred words. They would share this; he would work hard to become Valmiki's best student so they could work together to advance the cause of writing, of learning, of progress.

An oil lamp burned outside Valmiki's chambers at the corridor's end, but shadows hovered near the boys' quarters. Nalaka walked quickly by until he heard tense whispers outside his nemesis Kapur's room. He stopped to listen outside the curtained doorway.

"How many ribs does a horse have?" Kapur hissed.

"Thirty-thix."

187

"Let's beat him." "Bend over." There was a thwack and a cry of pain. "Ow!"

"Shhh!" "What's your name, Shukra? Say your name!" A thwack, another yelp.

Shukra said, "Thukra."

"Thukra, Thukra, can't say his own name Shukra!"

Nalaka's anger rose with the taunts, which though still whispered were getting louder.

"Now, Thooookra, how many?" Snorts and giggles.

"Thirty-thix…" This time, there was just a brief little gasp following the blow, but no cry.

"Thirty-four, not thirty-six," said Kapur with typical arrogance. "The Vedas tell us so."

"Shhh, I tell you! Valmiki will hear." "Hit him again, Kapur."

Another thwack. Nalaka seethed. Kapur would be enjoying this.

"Do you doubt the sacred Vedas, you little dog-eater?"

"Thirty-th—thix!" Shukra cried out. "My father taught me!"

Blows rained down. Nalaka dropped the tray with a clatter and thrust the curtain aside. Kapur looked up in surprise, a cane in his raised hand. Nalaka seized it.

"I'll show you what it feels like," he shouted. Years of enduring Kapur's taunts exploded in full force on the elegant brahmacharin's shoulders. Another older boy grabbed the cane and twisted it from Nalaka's grip, handing it to Kapur.

Kapur faced Nalaka, shaking with fear and anger. Everyone else stood back.

Except Shukra. He seized Kapur's antariya. As Kapur looked down stupidly, Shukra yanked, once, twice, and it fell to the floor. The youth stood naked. Laughter filled the room. Kapur turned bright red.

Nalaka drove his fist into Kapur's handsome face. He fell, screaming in pain.

"Stop!"

Valmiki stood in the doorway. His face was red and sweat stood out on his brow. His hands shook. "Who is responsible?" he said, very slowly.

The whole room turned to Nalaka.

Except Shukra. "I am, Valmiki-ji."

188

Torchlight flickered at the postern. It cast shadows over Valmiki's face.

"You think I am casting you out," he said in a stern voice, "but I am giving you your freedom."

Nalaka hung his head. He gripped the walking staff he'd made from the broom handle. His throat was so tight he couldn't speak.

"You stayed though you never felt you belonged here."

Nalaka nodded.

"That's something to be said for you. You will need endurance to survive in the world. You are a misfit, my boy," Valmiki said, more kindly. "That is your curse and your blessing. You have a hard path to follow before you find a home. But you will find one."

Nalaka raised his eyes. "Valmiki-ji," he began. This was his last chance to say what he knew about the writing. Perhaps then he wouldn't have to leave.

"Yes?"

No. He wouldn't tell him. Valmiki was giving him his freedom. He felt a strange elation along with fear. "About Shukra," Nalaka said in a rush. "He didn't know what he was saying. He believes in the Vedas, I'm sure of it. He's just a boy. He doesn't understand. The others were so cruel to him. I should be punished, but not he."

"You presume to tell me how to deal with my students?"

"No, Valmiki-ji." Nalaka looked away. "But he was very brave! Even if he is wrong, he stood up for what he believes."

"Are you quite finished?"

The sky began to lighten. A nightjar chirruped as it settled in a nearby bush.

"Yes, guru-ji."

Nalaka waited, head lowered, his heart hammering. Then Valmiki put a hand on his shoulder. "I'm glad you defended him. But now you must begin the homeless life. Beg your meal each day. Sleep under the stars at night. Seek an enlightened teacher and follow him."

Nalaka feared he would burst into tears. "But Valmiki-ji." He suddenly saw how he'd resisted Valmiki's best efforts to teach him. Now he all he wanted was to sit at his guru's feet and listen. "You are an enlightened teacher."

Valmiki was silent for so long that Nalaka raised his head. "Once, I could have been." His face was weary. "But worldly things distracted me. Now go." He raised his hand as if to confer a final blessing. "And Nalaka."

"Yes, Valmiki-ji?" Nalaka whispered.

"A horse does have thirty-six ribs." He shut the postern.

Nalaka stood there, astounded. He had so many questions. Why did the Vedas say one thing if the truth was another? Was solving this riddle a part of Valmiki's teaching? What could it possibly mean? His head spun. Was Valmiki telling him the Vedas were not true? It couldn't be. Or could it?

His shoulders slumped. At the very moment his intellect awakened, he had no guru to guide him.

He had no idea where to go.

ॐ

Aimless, Nalaka wandered Varanasi's crowded streets all day. Now that he was no longer Valmiki's student, he suddenly felt that no one else was as learned or wise. He had often gone to listen to the sages who lived in Varanasi's sacred grove, but they were charlatans compared to Valmiki. He would never ask them for teachings.

At last, at the end of the day, not knowing where he would sleep, he went to sit on the ghats along Ganga's river. Once he got to the wooden steps that led to the water, he felt he'd made a mistake. All around were the homeless poor, sometimes whole families, fighting over places to settle for the night. There was nowhere to sit. Whenever he tried, someone would shout or shove him away, staring after him with hostile, hungry eyes. He gripped his walking stick and hugged the tied sack that held his food to his chest. His mouth curved in a bitter smile. The broom handle had truly become a weapon.

He moved away from the ghats' wooden steps, farther along the riverbank to where the fisherfolk pulled their boats in on the sandy bank. They glanced as he passed, then went back to folding their sails and coiling ropes and nets. Beyond this he found a place on a soggy tussock and took out the little meal the cook had prepared for him. "You will have to beg your food from now on," he had said, "but here is something to get you through the first night."

As Nalaka took his first bite, a wiry man in a filthy dhoti splashed through the muddy water. "You there, don't I know you?"

Nalaka looked up. There was something familiar about him, but so many beggars came to the kitchen gate at Valmiki's mansion. He chewed and swallowed. "No, I don't think so."

"How about some food?" The beggar sat down next to him.

Nalaka sighed. It was dharma to share what he had. He held out the leaf-wrapped rice and vegetables.

The beggar ate it all. When he had finished, he wiped his mouth. He studied Nalaka with bright blue eyes. There was something very familiar about him. "This swamp is no place to sleep, my boy. I know somewhere dry."

Nalaka, suddenly wary, stood up and stepped into the shallow water. The man wanted something. Nalaka obviously had no money, so it could mean only one thing.

The beggar let out a laugh that was like a dog's bark. "Foolish boy," he said, as if he'd read Nalaka's mind. He shook his head, chuckling. "That way. The burning grounds." He pointed toward the setting sun.

"The burning grounds?" Nalaka's stomach turned.

"The first stop on your journey. You'll want to get there before sunset."

ॐ

A flock of vultures tore the strips of linen from the white-wrapped corpses left near the entrance to the cremation grounds. Odd that no one had come to take them and burn them. Was there no chandala?

They ceased their feasting, watching as Nalaka passed with an uneasy glance over his shoulder. His senses were painfully heightened. Hideous smells burned his nostrils, grit scratched where clothes met skin, and the setting sun cast a fiery orange glow that brought tears to his eyes. He hurried down the path to a hut on a little rise, next to the only tree in this barren field.

There was an incongruously cheerful fire burning in front of it. There was someone there, too, but dusk obscured him. It must be the chandala, but why was he shirking his duties?

A skinny black dog separated himself from the man by the fire and ran up to Nalaka. He gave a short bark.

"Ho, Kumar," the man said. "Friend or foe?" Kumar sniffed at Nalaka,

191

who drew back in revulsion. The dog let out another bark. "Well, bring him here. We can use some help."

The dog raced back to the hut, zigzagging here and there, chasing clouds of dust and ash. Nalaka followed at a slow pace. He had imagined someone who tended the burning grounds as a small dark creature, hardly a man at all, but resembling a dark Naga tribesman. This fellow was tall and strong, just past his middle years, his black hair and black beard streaked with grey. He had thick muscles, like a trained warrior. If he was some sort of sage, he was well groomed, compared to the usual filthy and skeletal ascetic.

"Who are you?" the man asked as Nalaka walked up to the hut.

"Nalaka." He bowed over joined palms. "Namaste. And you?"

"Namaste." The man paused. "Call me the wanderer. I've come to do penance. When I arrived, I found him." The wanderer indicated a bed of dry grasses where a slender man lay. He stank of urine and feces, and horrible burns covered one cheek.

Nalaka shrank in disgust. "How terrible. What happened?"

"I don't know. I've only just arrived and he's been unconscious. The workings of karma! Lord Shiva told me I was needed at Varanasi's burning ground. *Thou wilt be its chandala,* the Great God said. I'm sure the god means for me to find out what happened here. I need water to clean this poor man. Can you go to the river with this vessel?"

The man on the ground began to moan. "Kirsa... Kirsa..." His eyes opened wide. They were a color Nalaka had never seen before, a glorious golden amber. The wounded man stared at the wanderer with desperate intensity. "Harischandra?" He tried to seize the wanderer's arm. "Harischandra, is that you?" He stared. "It is you... His Majesty Harischandra, of the Surasenas..."

Nalaka looked at the wanderer, astonished. He'd heard of the Surasena clan's former king, who lost his kingdom to King Prasenajit through treachery. Rumor said he was dead.

"By the gods, Kumar," the wanderer or Harischandra or whoever he was said to the black dog, who sat by the fire, his tongue hanging out. "By the gods. It's Angirasa." The dog whined.

"Who?"

"Angirasa the Sakyan."

Nalaka couldn't believe his ears. It had all happened a few years before

THE TIGRESS AND THE YOGI

he arrived in Varanasi, but everyone at Valmiki's ashram knew the story of Angirasa and the guru's wife, Moti, though no one spoke of it except in whispers.

"Take that jar. There, by the cook fire." The wanderer pointed. "That will be a path to the river. Please, take it and fetch water."

"Ah, yes." Nalaka didn't relish walking alone in the gathering darkness. He glanced at Kumar, who seemed perfectly happy to sit by the fire. The dog was grinning at him, tongue lolling.

It was a short, terrifying walk to the river past shadows that held demons or ghosts that would emerge at any moment. Nalaka scrambled down a steep bluff, looking around with wide eyes. He filled the jar but as he climbed back up much of the water sloshed out. Back at the hut, breathless, he handed it to the wanderer, who poured it into a kettle set over the cook fire.

"I'll need more."

Twice Nalaka braved the darkness to fill the kettle. At last, the wanderer finished cleaning Angirasa. He was badly beaten and burned, but his amber eyes were beautiful. No wonder the famous courtesan Moti had preferred him to old Valmiki.

"Harischandra, you must help my daughter. Help her..." he repeated, delirious as the wanderer and Nalaka tried to soothe him. At last he slipped into unconsciousness. The dog lay down with a groan and put his head on his paws. "You will stay the night?" the wanderer said. "I have some food in my sack."

Nalaka nodded. He was exhausted and hungry and had no desire go back into the darkness alone. Besides, an idea had been forming. The wanderer said that the god Shiva had spoken to him. He was compassionate and on his travels he had no doubt gained much wisdom. Perhaps this was an ashram among the ashes. Perhaps this man was meant to be his guru.

"While you went to the river, Angirasa told me his story," the wanderer said. "Much evil has happened here. But first—"

An animal yipped nearby. Kumar raised his head and pricked his ears. The hairs on Nalaka's neck rose. The wanderer looked at the black dog, who let out a huge sigh and resettled his head on his paws.

"Only a jackal," the wanderer said. "Nalaka, what Angirasa said is true.

193

I am Harischandra, king of the Surasena clan. But I beg you to tell no one you saw me here."

"Don't worry," Nalaka replied, settling next to the fire and crossing his legs. He studied his hands. "I have no one to tell." Harischandra looked at him with such kindness that it all came pouring out, everything that had happened in his year at Valmiki's ashram. Tears poured down his cheeks, and when he came to the moment Valmiki sent him away, he found he was angry. "He sent me away, knowing I had nowhere to go."

"But where are you from? Could you go back home?"

"No." He would be too ashamed, but he didn't want to say that. "I can't. You see, Valmiki told me I must find an enlightened teacher. I... I thought it might be you..."

"Ah. Well. I am no sage or yogi. So it cannot be me."

Just then Angirasa roused. "The Beggar King," the wounded man said, "the jewels... buy her from the Beggar King..."

"What jewels?" Nalaka said.

"While you were at the river, he spoke of a necklace," Harischandra said softly. "A famous necklace."

Angirasa raised a weak hand and pointed to the cook fire's stacked bricks. Then his hand fell, and he breathed no more.

ॐ

In the morning, they built stacked wood to burn Angirasa's corpse. At his father's side, Nalaka had seen many pyres lit for dead Kolis, but never one that burned so hot and fast as this one. There was nothing for the vultures.

After they took Angirasa's ashes and threw them on Ganga's breast, they went back to the hut and dug underneath the cook fire, flinging bricks aside until they found an old, dirty cloth. When Harischandra untied it, he held a diamond and ruby necklace of surpassing beauty. Its jewels sparkled in the sun.

Nalaka couldn't take his eyes away. The desire to seize it struck him. He reached but stopped with his hand in midair. "There's something evil about it, isn't there?" he whispered.

"No. But there is magic about it," Harischandra said.

"What will you do with it?"

"Find Angirasa's daughter. Give it to her. I have a good idea where to look." He folded the cloth and tucked it in his sash.

There was nothing to do now but go. Nalaka gathered up his walking staff. Only one day since he'd left Valmiki's ashram, but it was a lifetime. Once again the unknown loomed before him, and he was terrified.

But then he looked out over the barren, dusty cremation grounds. A group of mourners was already approaching the entrance, carrying a white-wrapped corpse. He shivered. This was not his place.

"Go with the gods," Harischandra said. "May you find your teacher."

AN OLD FRIEND

THE NEXT MORNING, MALA WOKE to a touch on her cheek. She opened her eyes. A man with stringy, matted grey hair looked down on her with eyes that burned bright blue in a tanned and wrinkled face. Rohit stood behind him, arms crossed.

"Asita!" she cried.

"You recognize me, eh?" The old yogi smiled. He was sitting on his heels next to her pallet, a wooden bowl in his hands.

"You know each other?" Rohit's eyes were wide.

"It's Mala from Gauri, who ran from a talking tigress. As if that would have saved her if the tigress had wanted to eat her!" He let out that peculiar barking laugh Mala remembered from the night he sat with her parents and her around the fire telling tales. "But she was littler then. Perhaps she's bolder now."

As if she would have forgotten him. "How did you find me?"

"My hermitage is nearby."

She wanted to laugh, to weep, to shake him in anger. He had awakened her heart with his story of Shiva and Parvati and their lovemaking. He had awakened her outcaste's mind to the possibility of liberation. But he had done nothing when she stood before the Brahmin Valmiki hoping to find justice for her murdered parents. Why hadn't he helped her?

A thin beam of daylight poured in through a hole in the roof and pierced her eyes. She squinted and put a hand to her face and groaned. The swelling seemed hotter and more painful than yesterday.

"Don't touch it," he said. He dipped bony fingers in the bowl and scooped out a kind of paste. "This will help."

With great gentleness he dabbed the cool plaster around her eye. It gave her almost instant relief.

"I've something for you to drink," he said, setting the bowl aside and picking up a clay cup. She rolled to her side but as soon as she pushed herself from the ground dizziness struck. "Rohit, help her." Rohit took her shoulders while Asita held the cup to her lips. She sipped at the bitter liquid. "All of it." She drank. "Time to let her rest again." Rohit eased her back down onto her pallet. Asita watched Rohit leave, then sat down and crossed his legs and studied Mala with a steady gaze. "Little Mala. All grown up."

The pounding had already eased. "Why... why didn't you help me? Back then?"

"You were too young. Not ready." Before she could ask what he meant by not ready, he continued, "Besides, if I had taken you with me, you would never have fallen in love with Angirasa or known the joy of having a daughter."

"You know about them?" she asked in stuporous surprise. The drink made her sleepy.

"I know everything," he said. "I know Kirsa is safe."

"So it's true!" Mala reached for his hand. "The goddess Lakshmi told me..."

"Yes. She is well cared for," Asita continued. "She will live like a princess if she stays with the people who saved her."

Well cared for. Mala closed her eyes. *Thank you, O Lakshmi.* But behind her closed lids, it wasn't the goddess of wealth who appeared, but Kali, who fixed a bloodshot gaze on her.

Mala's eyes snapped open. She hadn't been able to care for Kirsa, to protect her. She should have trusted her instincts. If they had fled into the forest, they would have found this place. They would have found Asita. But they hadn't left the cremation grounds, and so Angirasa was dead and Kirsa stolen from her, and her plans to rescue her daughter from this terrible fate were all just wishful thinking. Go find the necklace, go to Varanasi, then run away with Kirsa. Her fantasies evaporated in reality's cold light. "Where is she?" she whispered. "Where is my daughter?"

"You don't know?"

"Lakshmi didn't tell me..." Sleep tugged at her. She floated above her pallet like the dust motes floating in the beam of light that came through the temple roof.

Asita wrinkled his brow. "If the goddess didn't tell you, then I cannot. I propose you leave her there and come with me. You alone. I will show you how to free yourself from suffering."

Mala struggled to stay awake. "Free from suffering..."

Kali's words on the night Kirsa was born came back to her.

A child means nothing but suffering for its parents.

All the love she had given Angirasa and Kirsa had turned to anguish. She couldn't care for her daughter. Maybe it was safer for Kirsa to stay where she was. How could she face Kirsa, having allowed all this to happen? She didn't deserve her... but to follow Asita?

It seemed an eternity had passed. Asita was watching.

She wanted her daughter. She would take her to the Maghadan kingdom, where there was no such thing as an outcaste, or to Angirasa's people, these Sakyans..."I—I want to find her."

Asita stood. "Perhaps that is your karma. No need to decide now. Come see me. We will talk." With that, he was gone.

Perhaps it was her karma to follow him.

Or perhaps not.

Who had spoken? It was a low rumble in her head, like a tiger's growl.

Mala blinked. "Asita?" she whispered. She struggled to sit up. He said he would show her how to be free. How? What did freedom mean?

The yogi couldn't have gone far. "Asita!" she tried to shout, but it came out a croak. She collapsed onto her pallet. There was no calling him back.

Kirsa is safe.

Beautiful Lakshmi shimmered in the beam of light. As she smiled at Mala, the rope of tiny white pearls between her breasts began to change. It became a necklace of skulls, and Lakshmi's serene face was replaced by the dark goddess's fearsome grimace.

Follow me, Kali said, *and Kirsa will be avenged.*

"Kirsa!" Mala called. She walked on a cool stone floor through enormous rooms with high-beamed ceilings. There were people everywhere, all finely

198

dressed, but everyone was shrouded in a haze, their faces turned away. They knew she was an outcaste. She shouldn't try to find Kirsa. They would find out Kirsa was her daughter, and an outcaste, too, and they would banish her from this place.

But then Kirsa and Mala would be together. A man in a blue and gold antariya stood with his broad, muscled back to her. She wanted to run her hands down that back. She touched his shoulders, and he turned around. He was faceless. A ghost. Mala looked around frantically. Everyone in the palace was a faceless ghost.

Mala fled down a long passageway, screaming. "Kirsa! Kirsa!" This place was full of ghosts. She must find Kirsa, take her away. Lakshmi came floating down the passage, smiling, the necklace of pearls falling between her breasts. "*Om*, Lakshmi, bestower of wealth, where is Kirsa?" Mala cried. Lakshmi smiled, and her pearls became diamonds and rubies, and she became Durga with her many arms, and then the flashing red and white jewels became skulls dripping with blood, and Durga faded into black-skinned Kali. Kali laughed, her tongue lolling, her bloodshot eyes flashing with love and fury. In one powerful arm the dark goddess held a sword, and she raised it, poised to strike off Mala's head.

"Stop!" A little boy stepped between Kali and Mala. He was dressed in blue and gold, and he had a face. He was not a ghost. He had a sweet, kind face with amber eyes just like Kirsa's.

"There are many paths to truth and peace, Mala," he said.

Mala sat up with a gasp. She had not awakened once in the night. Asita's potion had let her rest. But it gave her that dream.

Her bruises ached less, but her mind was churning. She felt she must go right away to see the yogi.

When she walked to the cook fire, the men all looked at her in astonishment.

"You slept well?"

"Where is Asita?" she said, not bothering to answer.

"That way." Rohit raised his arm and she was off, feeling their curious eyes on her as she hurried away. She stumbled a little as she hurried down the narrow path Rohit had pointed to; she was better, but she was not healed.

When she arrived in the clearing, Asita was seated on a platform built into a huge banyan's aerial roots, trunks, and thick foliage. He beckoned her closer.

"You like my hermitage? Rohit and his men built this for me." He knocked on the roomy platform with his fist. It gave off a solid sound. He clambered down.

They sat on the dry ground next to a circle of stones where a little fire burned. Some tubers were baking on a flat rock next to the embers. Asita's tangled hair fell around his shoulders, and he had drawn three horizontal stripes of grey ash across his forehead, signifying the third eye and Lord Shiva's trident.

"I had a dream," Mala said, her voice shaking. When she had told him everything, he wrinkled his forehead. She waited, holding her breath, for him to speak, to illuminate the dream's message.

"What do you think it means?" he said.

"What do I think it means? But how can I know?"

Asita laughed. "I cannot tell you! It's between you and the Devi."

Mala's jaw worked. The yogi was infuriating. How was she to know? She needed someone to guide her, to help her.

"You think you need guidance. I can guide you on yoga's path but as for the Devi, well, do you remember what I told you that first night?"

"Yes. Yes. You said, 'The Great Goddess is as old as Time, and as mysterious as Death. She is formless but can take on any form she chooses: warrior, princess, musician, bringer of wealth. Even the avatar of a demoness.' Those were your exact words," she said, surprised that they came back to her after all these years.

"The Devi has given you many signs, Mala, but if you are going to follow her, you must choose the form and the direction. There are those who could help you on that path. I am not one of them."

"But where am I to find that person?" She thought of Dhuma's words, that those who sacrifice to Kali without a pure heart are in danger of doing evil. She wished Dhuma had not walked into the river. The river. Ganga. Maybe Ganga would guide her.

"Go to the river," Asita said. It was unnerving how he knew what she was thinking. "Sit. Think of the forms in which the goddess has appeared to you. Think of what she is asking you to do. Then come back, and I will tell you my way."

Mala wandered back to camp in a daze. Lanka was sleeping under a tree and Ketu was starting the midday meal. She was about to ask where Rohit was when he came walking up the path from the river with Anu. When they saw her, they exchanged a look.

"Mala," Rohit said. "I want to talk to you. Anu and I went last night to the cremation grounds."

"Without me?"

"You could hardly have come! See, we wanted to know if we could somehow get the necklace."

The three of them sat on the worn wooden steps of the temple.

"And?"

"It won't be easy," Rohit said. He was absorbed in cleaning his fingernails with the tip of his knife. "There's someone there now, tending the fires."

"Someone new?" Mala wondered if the new chandala was that outcaste who got drunk and burned his family, and if he had cremated Angirasa's body and said any prayers.

"Big, strong looking fellow," Anu said, scratching his belly. "No half-starved outcaste, if you ask me."

Rohit nodded. "I'd guess he was once a warrior. No doubt there's a tale behind why he's ended up at Varanasi's burning grounds."

"Probably doing some kind of penance," Anu agreed. "But whatever the story is, I wouldn't want to fight him for your necklace." He spat.

"Ah." Mala was almost relieved. Whoever this man was, he might serve as a deterrent to Prakash and the Beggar King. The necklace would be safe, at least. And she didn't need it. "It doesn't matter."

"What?" the men said at the same time.

"How are you going to buy Kirsa from the Beggar King?" Rohit asked.

"Kirsa is safe. The goddess Lakshmi gave me the sign. She's with good people. Asita saw it too, with his third eye. She's not with that evil Beggar King. So we don't need the necklace for a ransom."

"Where is she, then?" Rohit said. "Did Asita tell you?"

"No." She frowned. "He said if the goddess didn't tell me, he couldn't."

"Maybe that's for the best."

"She's my daughter! I want to find her." Mala suddenly wanted to get to the river, to sit and let the Presence come. She felt certain she would learn where Kirsa was. "How can it be for the best if I don't know where she is?"

Rohit studied her face. "Mala. When I was a child, my parents were cast from their home, and I was torn from them. The tale is too long to tell. All that matters is that strangers found me and cared for me. I learned later that my father is likely dead, and I know nothing of my mother. But I survived."

"What strangers? Bandits? Is that how you learned your trade?"

He shrugged. "There are worse lives. As I said, they were kind. If Asita says your daughter is safe and with good people, well, maybe that's the best thing you can hear. Maybe it's her karma to be with those people."

"Didn't your mother look for you?" Stupid question, she thought as soon as she spoke it. Cruel, too.

Again, he shrugged. "How would I know? In a way, I hope she didn't, or at least not for long. I think the search would have caused her much suffering. If she lives, I hope she found a way to be happy in the world." He looked at her with compassion and deep sadness. "You're much luckier than she was. You know your daughter is safe."

Tears sprang to Mala's eyes. She would like to know his story one day, but not now. "I know that if your mother possibly could have, she would have tried to find you. And I must try. Will you help me?"

"Varanasi is enormous. You are going to knock on every door?"

"No, of course not. I think the goddess Lakshmi was trying to tell me who rescued Kirsa. Lakshmi turned from a beautiful goddess into a plump woman with grey-streaked hair who was dressed in blue. I think she must be someone wealthy. We can knock on the doors in the nobles' quarter, try to find a woman in blue called Lakshmi..."

"Oh, Mala." Rohit shook his head. "You look like a beggar. The guards will never let you wander in the wealthy quarters."

"Hey," Anu said. "She can't help she's in rags. You might offer yourself to a soldier, though, and see if he'll help you."

"Shut up, Anu." Rohit jumped up and raised his hand.

Anu shrank back, grinning. "Well, she's a good-looking woman. I seen you looking at her."

Rohit flushed and turned on his heel. Mala went hot, too. She stood up, looked after Rohit, then turned in the other direction, toward the path to the river, and hurried away.

She found a spot to sit under the trees atop a little bluff overlooking the river. Ganga had begun to deepen and swell with the rains that were already falling in the mountains and would soon reach Varanasi.

She crossed her legs, right foot on her left thigh and left foot on the right one, and closed her eyes to pray, wishing she had Asita's ability to see the past and the future. Angirasa had tried to teach her how to see with her third eye, but she had never had the confidence that she could master the technique. Dreams and visions came to her, but she couldn't will them.

Then suddenly her heart pulsed in the cavity of her chest, bloody red. She was tumbling toward it—how could she fall into her own heart?—and a yawing sensation overwhelmed her. She rushed toward the sacred chamber where the little self dwelt, yearning for Atman. At the moment she would crash into it she spun away, and there was the open wound that was her love and fear for Kirsa. Her inner eye turned from it as if seared with a flame. It came to rest on a cool, blue vein that calmed her. She breathed, and prana coursed along her nerves. It carried her to a purple bruise that contained everything she felt for Angirasa. Just as the prana touched that bruise, there was a flash of light, and when the light faded, there was a twisted pink scar over it.

With a gasp, Mala opened her eyes. Had it been real? She hardly dared to believe she had seen own heart. She staggered across the sand to the river and plunged into a forest of underwater grasses, tendrils of Ganga's hair, the dark green water of the goddess's garments. Mala swam through them like a fish to shallower water then broke the surface, stood, and stretched her arms toward the sky.

"*Om!*" she cried. "Give me courage, Devi, you who are Kali, Lakshmi, Durga, Ganga, Parvati, you who are mother, wife, and daughter of all the gods and of the universe. Grant me courage to find my daughter. *Om.*"

THE CHOICE

FOR THE NEXT FEW DAYS, Mala didn't even bother to look for the fisherman Matsya, but instead headed to Asita's hermitage, where he had begun to teach her about yoga.

If she decided to follow him, they would live at the hermitage; they would spend mornings on meditation techniques and yogic exercises. Asita might go to the city to seek alms, but Mala would stay in the forest, gathering food and tending their shelter.

"Let's begin with some simple lessons."

At the start, she tired easily, and even sitting and meditating according to his instructions was difficult. At first she thought it was her injuries that made it hard to concentrate, but as the days passed and she improved physically, she only found herself more bored and restless. His instructions confused and frustrated her. First he would say that she should focus her attention on all her senses, then he would say that the goal of yoga was to withdraw from all sensation. He would ask her questions about what he had just told her, but her attention was always wandering to Kirsa. When she couldn't answer, he lost his temper.

The main hindrance was that she couldn't stop thinking about Kirsa. She ached for her child in a way she didn't think the yogi could ever understand. The urge to find her was too strong to dismiss.

Then Kali appeared in a dream.

Follow me, and avenge the wrongs done to you, the dark goddess said, just as she had before.

Mala woke with a start, feeling she must decide, once and for all, what she would do.

"I want to know more."

"Good. You will be learning yoga for a lifetime."

"No. I want to know more about Kirsa." She ignored Asita's frown and settled on the ground before him, crossing her legs. "These people love her, yes?" she said after a long silence. "This woman in blue, she's rich."

"Oh, Mala." Asita leaned against the banyan's trunk and rubbed a hand over his eyes. "As you wish. I will tell you what I have seen. I hope it will help you decide what to do." He sighed. "The wanderer who now tends the burning grounds found the necklace. He took it to the courtesan Addhakashi. Her servant Lakshmi is the woman in blue you see in your visions. She rescued Kirsa."

"You said if the goddess didn't tell me, you couldn't! Why are you telling me now?"

He shrugged. "That was then. Now I see you can't choose if you don't really have a choice. The Sakyan king is due to meet Kirsa at the courtesan's house within days. Angirasa gave Kirsa her amber eyes. Only Gautamas have them. And only if the father is a Gautama. So King Suddhodana will recognize her."

"Suddhodana. The Sakyan king," Mala murmured. "He will take her to his kingdom. What a life she will lead." Her eyes filled with tears. "I have nothing to give but my love."

"To you, love is nothing?" His face was a mask.

Self-pity welled up. "A life with me would be filled with uncertainty. Her future would be assured there. How could I take her from that?"

"The rains will be here soon," Asita said as cloud passed over the sun.

"What has that got to do with it?"

"The thatching needs repair, or we'll be meditating soaking wet."

"We? You and I?"

"You were wondering how you could deny Kirsa a royal life," Asita replied. "I thought you were deciding to stay."

"I don't know," Mala said, rubbing her temples. She wanted to weep. "Oh, please tell me what to do."

"I can't," he said.

He was right. It made her angry. "You old fool. You wander the roads or sit here in your retreat, taking offerings the rich and poor bring you just for a few crumbs of your so-called wisdom." Mala could hardly believe these words were coming out of her mouth. Beyond the respect he and every sage was due, he had told her the Devi had given her a sign all those years ago. She owed him something for that.

Then she thought of how he had left her in the village after her parents died, and her anger increased. She owed him nothing. "You give nothing to those who really need help. You're—you're a selfish old lecher."

Asita raised an eyebrow. "Selfish? My wives said so when I left our fine mansion. But lecher? Where did you get that idea?"

"I remember the way you looked at my mother."

Asita chuckled. "The thought is far different from the deed. Consider this: I slept between my two, plump young wives and never touched either one."

Her anger drained away for a moment as she considered the emaciated old man between two voluptuous maidens.

"No, no," Asita said, reading her mind. "I was young and handsome in those days. The heir of a great fortune, a brilliant future as a high Brahmin ahead of me, but it was no good. None of it made me happy."

Mala blushed then scowled, the anger back stronger than ever. "You don't know what happiness is. You don't know what love is." A flicker in his eye told her she'd struck a nerve, and an evil joy filled her. "There's something wrong with you, isn't there? Couldn't make love to your wives, isn't that it?"

Asita sat silent and still. Only his eyes moved, or maybe it was just a trick of the light, glinting off their blue depths.

"That's why you left your family. You haven't known anything like what Angirasa and I had."

"What *you* had, maybe," he said softly, "but whose name did Angirasa call in the moment of passion?"

The morning light dimmed. Red pulsed around Mala. She stepped toward him and raised her hand, but Asita sprang up before she could strike. She wouldn't have dreamed he could move so fast, but he seized her arm. He twisted it and somehow her whole body twisted, and she was flying head over heels. A glimpse of blue sky through the banyan leaves, and she landed on her back on the hard-packed dirt with a heavy thud, the wind knocked out of her. She gasped for air. It was a moment before she could take a breath.

"You're right." Asita offered her a hand and helped her up. "I don't know what you and Angirasa had. I didn't make love to my wives. But that's not why I suffered. I loved another man."

This revelation took her breath away just as if he'd thrown her once more. "You loved a man? But that—it's wrong—the gods forbid it... don't they?" She paused, uncertain. She'd never heard Angirasa speak of such things.

"In some places, like among the Maghadas, it is tolerated. Among other clans, it is reviled. My people forbade it. But what mortal has the right to say where love should fall?" He shook his head. "It would dishonor my family if anyone ever knew, and truthfully, I never knew if he loved me, too. What could I do? When I thought it through, I saw I couldn't help but hurt all the people I cared about, no matter what I did. I had to find a way to hurt them as little as possible. There was one choice. My dharma, the right thing, the thing I must do."

"I think I understand." Mala's rose on unsteady legs and brushed herself off. "The only thing to do was to leave." She had trouble meeting his eyes. "I'm sorry."

Asita shrugged. "Soon you will know what you must do."

She waited for him to say more, but he remained silent, so she bowed over her hands and walked back to the outlaws' camp.

THE COURTESAN'S MANSION

B Y NOON THE SUN WOULD make the rooftop too hot for sitting, but it was early in the day. A few branches of the neem tree hung over the roof, and underneath them it was shady and cool enough. Kirsa liked it there. It was a quiet, private place. From this spot, she could see over the houses of the courtesans' quarter to the river.

"I had a place like this at Addha's old mansion," Ratna had told her. "When I began my apprenticeship, I used to look out over the river to the Forest of Bliss, where I grew up. My father was a holy hermit there. He had just died, and it soothed me to be alone." Kirsa liked Addha's beautiful, kind apprentice instantly, and to know that they both had lost a father made her feel closer to her. Right away Ratna took to calling her "little sister," which increased her adoration for the lovely young woman.

Ratna said she didn't often come up there nowadays because of her duties serving the house's patrons, but the very first day when the last guest left she had fetched Kirsa and brought her up to sleep under the fading stars. Ratna said she would leave the ladder propped in the corridor so that Kirsa and Chandaka could easily climb through the opening to the top.

Chandaka was eight, almost two years older than Kirsa. He was the slender, quick, and cheerful son of Addha's senior courtesan, Amrapali. On the first day, when Kirsa thought she would die of her fever and her grief, he had sat next to her pallet and told her stories to distract her. She couldn't help but smile when he made funny faces. He was full of mischief.

The Brahmin cook didn't approve of them climbing up to the roof. It didn't take more than a day for Kirsa to see that the cook didn't approve of anything Chandaka did. He complained to Lakshmi that the boy was leading Kirsa astray, but Chandaka smiled at Lakshmi, and she gave them a halfhearted scolding and told them to be off and behave themselves.

It seemed ages since Lakshmi had pulled her out of Ganga's waters—though it had only been nine days; Kirsa had counted them. She remembered running from the Beggar King's camp into the river. Some presence helped her. Then she had seen Lakshmi bathing and saying her prayers, but the presence was gone, and Kirsa was sinking into Ganga's watery breast. She would have sunk forever if the plump woman hadn't seen her struggling to stay afloat and hauled her dripping and gasping to the riverbank. Kirsa had shivered with cold and exhaustion while her rescuer cooed over her hurt hand. "You'll come home with me," Lakshmi had said. "Let King Ram just try to get you back!"

As Kirsa sat in the pleasant shade, she thought about the burning grounds. A whole different life, as if she'd died and been reborn. The luxuries showered on her almost seemed commonplace now, but despite them and the all the attention from the household, she ached for Ma and Bapu.

She tried not to think about Bapu, about that terrible night, about Bapu screaming silently. When she did, sobs would shake her. If Ratna was nearby, she would come and cuddle and caress Kirsa. Or Lakshmi would envelop her in a hug, crooning mantras to the Devi, and the terror would diminish. They asked her what was wrong, but she wouldn't speak of what had happened.

Kirsa scanned the distant water for the fishing boats that went out at dawn and were just now returning. She searched for Matsya's vessel, but its triangular sail looked like all the other boats. It was impossible to know which was his.

To her great joy, on the first day she arrived at Addha's mansion, Matsya came to the kitchen gate selling his fish. Thereafter she waited for him, certain that this would be the day he would bring her mother. They would hug each other and never let go. Lakshmi would insist that Ma live with Kirsa in the courtesan's house. They would sleep under the neem tree in the kitchen courtyard, or on the roof during the hottest weather. During the day, her mother could sweep and gather wood, the way she had at the burning grounds. Kirsa would wash and fold Ratna and Simca's fine silks,

209

take towels and perfumed oils to them in their bath, and help Lakshmi prepare the garden for the evening's guests and entertainments.

Matsya had been appalled when he learned of what happened. He promised to go to the burning grounds and find Ma. But the next day he had come looking very troubled and saying that he had not seen any sign of Ma or Bapu there. Someone new tended the fires now, a big, strong man who had a black dog, and who was too busy tending fires to talk to him. Matsya promised he would go back, but so far he hadn't had a chance.

A loud knocking on the back gate roused Kirsa from a daydream that was so real she could almost feel Ma enfolding her in her arms. Her heart began to pound. Could it be?

"Coming," Lakshmi called from the kitchen garden as the knocking was repeated, louder this time. In the distance, the boats were still coming ashore. Surely there had not been time for Matsya to come from the river with his fish to sell. Kirsa rushed to the ladder and scrambled down, nearly falling off in her excitement. She slipped through the kitchen and past the cook as he ground the spices together in the fragrant masala for which he was famous. Or so he liked to think, Ratna had told her with a wink.

In the herb garden, Kirsa came to an abrupt halt. The high gate had been rolled aside, opening the little courtyard to the back alley. Lakshmi stood with one hand covering her mouth, staring at a broad-shouldered man with thick dark hair streaked here and there with grey. Kirsa ducked behind the trunk of the neem tree.

The man was covered in dust and ashes like Bapu used to be after raking the fires. Kirsa's heart almost leapt from her chest. Although in stature the stranger was nothing like her gentle, slight father, for an instant she saw Angirasa, transformed by his ordeal to this commanding presence. He had come for her; she should run to him, but she couldn't let go of the tree trunk.

"Is that any kind of greeting for an old friend, Lakshmi?" The man's eyes sparkled.

"Oh, my lord," Lakshmi said at last, putting her hand to her heart. "We feared you dead! How many years has it been? Ratna! Come quickly!" She recovered enough to bow over her joined palms. "But what has happened to you!" She tsked-tsked and shook her head. "Covered with dust and ash. You look like one of Shiva's followers, not the King of the Surasenas!"

Kirsa's hopes plunged. Lakshmi knew him already. Besides, he was really nothing like her father. Still, she couldn't look away. She had overheard her parents talking one night, something about the palace where Bapu was raised, a king who was his uncle. But Lakshmi called this man king of the Sursas or Sursnas, not the Sakya clan that Ma and Bapu had talked about.

"But you'll explain later," Lakshmi continued. "Now you're hungry and thirsty. Ratna! Simca! Where are you?"

"I'm here." Ratna's dusky face appeared in the kitchen doorway. It looked as if she had just come from her bath. Wet hair was flowing over her brown shoulders and the yellow silk band wound round her breasts. Her wavy locks were so long the ends brushed the matching antariya wrapped low around her hips. To Kirsa, she looked like a divine nymph. Ratna bowed to the dust-covered stranger, giving Lakshmi a sideways glance. He examined her with appreciative eyes, which made Kirsa somehow proud to be Ratna's "little sister."

"Namaste, my lord..." Ratna said, pressing her palms together.

Lakshmi waved an impatient hand. "Not now. Prepare the bath for our guest. Oh, but first fetch Addha. Tell her King Harischandra is here."

"Shhh." The man put a finger to his lips. "You shouldn't speak my name so loudly, especially here in Varanasi. Prasenajit thinks I'm dead, which is for the best." He glanced over his shoulder. "In fact, I think I've been followed."

Kirsa pressed her body against the tree and craned her neck around it, trying to be invisible yet wanting to be seen.

Just then a dog barked and Chandaka came scurrying in. His straight black hair was plastered to his sweaty forehead, and his creamy white antariya was smeared with something that looked red and sticky. "There's a wicked-looking dog out there!"

"Chandaka, where have you been?" Lakshmi said, seeming to forget everything else. "Your mother was looking all over for you! It's hard enough to get the tabla master to come, and she couldn't find you anywhere. King Bimbisara will be here tomorrow for the Ashvamedha, and what will he think of your playing! You'll shame your mother." She put her hands on her hips and narrowed her eyes. "You went to the market, didn't you? And where did you get the money for those sweets that are smeared all over your good clothes!"

Chandaka ignored her and put his shoulder to the gate and pushed, but it refused to budge. "Help me, Lakshmi! The dog will come in."

With a low growl, a black dog stepped into the courtyard. "Chandaka," Kirsa cried, "watch out!"

"Ho, Kumar. Sit." As soon as the man spoke, the dog sat on his haunches. Harischandra put one hand on the gate and slid it shut while Chandaka gaped up at him. The hair on Kirsa's neck stood up as the dog caught sight of her and pricked up its ears. Matsya said a man with a black dog tended the ashes at the burning grounds. She stumbled backward and fell hard on her bottom, letting out a yelp of surprise.

"Kirsa! Are you hurt?" Chandaka rushed to her side. He stood between her and the dog, trying to toss his sweaty hair out of his eyes. He trembled but glared at the animal.

"Ah." The stranger looked at her. "Kirsa."

Everyone turned and stared at Harischandra.

"My lord! You know the child?" Lakshmi said.

"Your dog is scaring her," Chandaka said in a shaky voice.

"Don't be afraid," he said. "Come. This is Kumar. He's been my best friend for, well, how long has it been, Kumar? Seven years since we met at that village? Gauri it was called, I think."

Kirsa brushed herself off and stood. Chandaka took her hand. She raised her eyes to Harischandra's, which glistened with tears. Her vision blurred. Everything and everyone but the stranger dropped away. In her mind's eye she saw this good man in front of her family's hut, kneeling near the cook fire where her father lay on the ground on a bed of soft kusha grass. He bathed Bapu's face with oh, such tender, tender care. Then he sat back on his heels and the dog began to howl, and the scene faded.

Every fiber of her being said this vision was true. Kirsa's heart knotted in her chest.

"What is it, Kirsa?" Chandaka held her hand to his slender chest and looked from her to Harischandra. "Why are you looking at her like that? You're making her cry! I don't like you."

"It's all right, Chandaka." Kirsa brushed her free hand across her eyes as Harischandra knelt before her. He put his hands on her shoulders.

"I... I saw something," she said. "I don't know how... but... he is dead. Bapu is dead."

Harischandra's brows rose. "You saw rightly. Your lineage has a gift for such things." He sighed. "I gave him the rites."

"Thank you." Kirsa gave him a solemn nod. Later she would ask what he meant by her lineage's gift. She kissed his cheek. She had spared him the pain of saying that Bapu was dead. Knowing that undid the knot in her heart, and it swelled with sweet pain until her arms opened and she flung them around Harischandra's neck and wept while he held her tight.

"Well." Lakshmi sniffed and touched at her eye with a corner of her antariya. "What can possibly happen next?"

What happened next was that Harischandra bathed. Lakshmi recovered her composure and called Simca to fetch his dirty clothes. Simca thought herself the favorite of Addha's two apprentices but was not at all as gracious and lovely as Ratna. Furthermore, she treated Kirsa like a servant. She came dragging her feet. Kirsa would rather die than let that lazy, spoiled creature have anything to do with the man who had cared for Bapu. She took Harischandra's dust-covered dhoti and washed it with great care, her eyes blinded by tears. When she returned to the bathing court, he was seated on a cushion in the shade of an arch covered with jasmine vines, dressed in a borrowed antariya of plain but very fine Varanasi linen.

Kirsa wanted to know everything that had happened at the burning grounds and what he meant by her gift, but she was all of a sudden too shy to ask.

"Ah, little Kirsa." Harischandra smiled. "And where is my dhoti? These clothes are too fine for me."

"But you're a king!"

He wagged his finger at her. "Remember. No one must know."

"Besides, the dhoti is still all wet, and I'm to take you to Addha's garden now."

He frowned. "I mustn't be seen."

"No patrons will come this evening. Addha says two kings are coming tomorrow, and we must prepare for them."

"Ah. I will be gone first thing in the morning. There will be dead waiting for their pyres."

Kirsa nodded solemnly. She knew this well. "It will be a nice little feast tonight," she said. "We'll eat by the lotus pool." She couldn't hide her excitement at eating by the fountain. "Sudhir is preparing the dishes you like best, he says."

"Wonderful." Harischandra smiled. Kirsa took his hand to lead him to the heart of the house, an elegant courtyard with a magical fountain that Kirsa never tired of watching. Harischandra swiveled his head as they walked. "I'm not the only one somewhat fallen in the world," he said as if to himself. "A long way from the grandest palace in the courtesans' quarter."

Kirsa couldn't imagine what kind of a palace Addha had lived in before. This place was grand enough to be in Indra's heavenly city.

"But this house has its charms." Addha's musical voice came from behind them. Harischandra jumped and turned. She bowed as if he were her most honored guest.

"As long as you are in it," he said. "Namaste, my dear Addhakashi. Forgive my rudeness." The bow he returned to her was kingly.

The courtesan parted her reddened lips in a smile, revealing small white teeth. "You speak the truth. I always liked that in you."

He looked her up and down. She had dressed herself in her elegant green and pink silks, and her dark hair was loosely bound at the nape of her neck with a matching strip of cloth. She wore simple emerald earrings and a single white pearl at her nostril that caught the whites of her dark, dark eyes, enhancing the contrast. "You wear the years well."

"You're too kind, my lord. So much has happened since we last met, I feel bent like an old crone with age and grief." Addha cast her eyes down.

"Nothing of the kind. You are ever fresh as a girl. It must be witchcraft."

Addha's lips curved in a little smile. "Asita taught me some of yoga's tricks to keep the years at bay. But come. My garden waits, and you will tell me honestly if it compares favorably with the place you now dwell."

"And I will tell you what I know of this child," he said, and stroked Kirsa's head.

Then Harischandra told a tale Kirsa only half understood, about a Sakyan king who was Bapu's uncle, about an evil man named Prakash who worked for a Brahmin called Valmiki, and much more, long into the evening while Kirsa's eyes got heavier and heavier. She put her head on his lap and dozed while he talked, until she couldn't tell what was Harischandra's story and what was a dream.

But she did not dream the necklace. She awoke when he shifted and said, "But I think you will recognize this, Addha."

She sat up, yawning, as he took a dirty cloth from his sash. He unfolded it, and there, in the palm of his hand, were sparkling red and white stones, such as she had never seen before.

THE SAKYAN KING

"SIMCA! RATNA!" LAKSHMI BREEZED PAST Kirsa, who had just arrived outside Ratna's room, hoping to help the young courtesan finish dressing. "Stop dawdling. Their majesties will be here at sunset!"

"I'm here," Ratna replied, pulling aside the thick cloth at her door and stepping into the cool passageway. She smiled down at Kirsa, revealing just a glint of her white teeth. Her hair was tied back with a ribbon of pink and green, the house's colors, bright against the dark waves. She wore a green antariya wrapped low at her hips and a band of matching silk wrapped around her breasts, simple gold hoops at her ears and nostril, and one gold armband around her dusky arm. Even this simply attired, she looked like a goddess.

"I'm sorry I was late!" Kirsa exclaimed, crushed to have missed her part in creating this vision. "You're so beautiful."

"I think I look as dull as a pea hen." Ratna smiled. "Green doesn't suit me at all."

Lakshmi cocked her head to the side. "No. Just right. Lovely, but you won't outshine Addha."

"Now we must dress Kirsa," Ratna began. The apprentice knelt and gave her a squeeze. "Are you excited to meet your great uncle, little sister?"

Kirsa tensed. She was to meet this Sakyan king, this great uncle tonight. She had overheard Ma and Bapu whispering about him before. She didn't know why they had kept it secret from her. Maybe because they were afraid the king wouldn't like her.

Chandaka had tried to learn exactly what the mystery was all about. Though he was very clever, he hadn't been able to uncover much. He told her she shouldn't worry about meeting any kings; his mother's patron, King Bimbisara, was kind and jolly. But Kirsa feared the Sakyan king would be stern and cruel and wouldn't like her at all, and she was terrified to meet him.

Lakshmi brushed the suggestion aside. "We'll not dress her yet. Chandaka will have her climbing on the roof and getting her finery dirty. Now, remember, Ratna, you and Simca must be like shadows and not catch my lord Suddhodana's eye while Addha entertains him."

Kirsa wanted to be a shadow, too. Lakshmi said the Sakyan's lineage went all the way back to the sun god Surya, who had endowed the line with martial prowess, and the celestial sage Gautama, who bestowed his name on it and whose great wisdom infused its sons and daughters. It was rumored some of those sons and daughters were mad and prone to demonic possession. Between the divine heritage, the sage Gautama's wisdom, and the madness, Kirsa imagined the Sakyan as a godlike being with many arms carrying terrifying divine weapons and shooting fire from a fierce red eye in the middle of his forehead like the god Shiva. Chandaka scoffed at her fears. "If he's anything like my mother's patron, King Bimbisara, he'll be round and smiling and bring you sweets," he had said. Nevertheless, she imagined King Suddhodana had sharp teeth and could gobble her up if he wanted.

Ratna gave a low, lilting laugh. "We have no choice but to be shadows. Who could compare with the great Lady Addhakashi?"

Lakshmi arched an eyebrow. "One day you will, my girl, one day. That is, if we survive life under the Kosalan clan's king." She heaved a sigh. "Things are not like they were under our good King Brahmadatta. Only a true man of the Kashi clan should rule in Varanasi. How he showered Addha with jewels."

"No, they're not like they were under Brahmadatta," Ratna said. "The Shining City is dying. It's the Maghadas or the Sakyas who will rule next, no matter how many Horse Sacrifices His Majesty Prasenajit offers."

"You are safe in these walls," Lakshmi said, then pressed her lips in a thin line. "Nonetheless, my girl, I thought I'd taught you better than to say such things in front of certain folk." She looked from Ratna to Kirsa and back again. Kirsa felt she had somehow failed Ratna and her cheeks flushed.

"Then let's leave Varanasi." Ratna tossed her beautiful head. "Addha will seduce the Sakyan and convince him that he should be her royal patron and bring her to his capital. They say it's beautiful."

Kirsa's throat constricted, the way it did every time someone mentioned this.

"From what I've heard, King Suddhodana's not the sort to be seduced. More likely he's the seducer."

"Let him brag that the greatest courtesan of the age is his swooning slave," Ratna said. "Addha will work it to her advantage. She's more intelligent than any man, even this upstart Suddhodana Gautama with his supposed divine attributes. She'll make sure he thinks it's his idea to help us. And wouldn't he be inclined to do so anyway, given how we have helped our little Kirsa?"

The look Ratna and Lakshmi gave Kirsa made all her fears rush back. No, she did not want to meet King Suddhodana.

Ratna stood and smoothed her antariya. "Varanasi used to be the center of learning. My father always said that no true sage considered his life complete without coming here to give teachings on Ganga's banks, but now the Kosalan Brahmins won't let anyone who displeases them speak."

"The Maghadan kingdom would suit me." Lakshmi tapped her chin. "Or any of the clans allied with them. But I don't know about these Sakyas and all their talk about the prophecy that the kingdom's precious little Prince Siddhartha Gautama will conquer the world."

Ratna laughed and shook her head. "Armies conquer the world, not prophecies, but no doubt that's why the Sakyan was invited to the Horse Sacrifice. Prasenajit wants everyone in the Sixteen Clans to know that he will be a world emperor." She curled her lip. "As if offering a stallion on the fire altar will make him so."

"Didn't I just tell you to be careful what you say? Prasenajit's Brahmins will not tolerate any talk against the Ashvamedha."

"Then let's be off to the Maghadan kingdom or the Sakyan capital, where we can say what we please about the gods without fear."

Kirsa's lower lip began to quiver. She didn't know how Ma would find her if they left.

"Enough." Lakshmi straightened her shoulders. "We won't be going unless Addha completely enchants His Majesty Suddhodana. Everything must be perfection. Simca! Where is that girl? Kirsa, run off and find her."

Kirsa didn't want to show she was upset, so she hurried away without a word. Addha's apprentice wasn't in her room, nor was she in the little courtyard with a small bathing tank where she liked to laze away her afternoons in the cool green water. Where could she be?

No matter where Kirsa went or whom she asked, no one had seen Simca. Not in the storeroom stealing some of Lakshmi's precious scents, or in the garden by the fountain telling the other servants how they should set up the low couches and the oil lamps. Kirsa circled back around to Simca's room, mystified. She had noticed before that the door to a tiny neglected garden was slid half open on its tracks, but Simca never went out there. If it were Ratna's room, the little garden would have a little shrine to Parvati and Shiva surrounded by flowers, but Simca was too lazy to take the time for such things. It was unlikely that she would be there, but there was nowhere else to look. Kirsa slipped through the opening.

Under a scraggly tree, Simca was on her knees, her back to Kirsa. In front of her was that horrible warrior Shakuni, Simca's lover, leaning against the tree trunk with his face contorted and eyes closed, moaning.

Kirsa gasped. Whatever they were doing was not right, not right. Simca jerked and tried to draw away from Shakuni, but he pressed her to his groin and cried out.

Kirsa wanted to run. Shakuni slowly opened his eyes and fixed her with his crazy stare as he adjusted his clothing. She couldn't move. He was a violent man, prone to murderous outbursts; the effect, Lakshmi had told her, of being struck in the head by a rock many years ago while defending Addha from robbers. Addha had to banish him from the house because of his temper, but he wouldn't stay away from Simca. Not a week ago, Lakshmi had to chase him away with a broom, and here he was again.

Simca turned around, wiping her mouth with the back of her hand. "You little fool!" She glared at Kirsa. "If you tell Lakshmi or Addha, you'll be sorry."

Kirsa turned and ran, her mind reeling.

"But where is this child, this daughter of Angirasa you speak of?" King Suddhodana's deep, warm voice filled the darkening garden. It demanded obedience, but despite the care Lakshmi and Ratna had taken dressing her, Kirsa was sure he would only see her injured hand and be disgusted by her. She shrank into the shadows behind a tall clay urn and pressed her hot cheek against its cool surface.

"She will be here any moment, my lord."

Kirsa couldn't see from her hiding place near the passageway from the kitchen, but could imagine the torches glowing in the sconces and the lily pads with their tiny oil lamps floating in the pool, their reflections broken by the ripples the fountain made. Addha would be in her green and pink silks, her dark hair braided and bound with ribbon and pearls, looking up through her eyelashes at the Sakyan.

"Please, have some more of this Parsee wine," the courtesan said in a wheedling tone.

"You promised me a little kinswoman, my lady Addhakashi."

Other men stammered in Addha's presence, awkward and eager for her approval, but the Sakyan king sounded cross and impatient.

"Perhaps Chandaka has distracted her." The other monarch, Bimbisara, the patron of Chandaka's mother, was speaking. "The lad's irresistible. Mark my words, my dear Amrapali, women will fall at his feet in a few years."

Amrapali plucked a single, pure note from the instrument. "Even Lakshmi can't say no to my son."

Kirsa's stomach twisted into knots. Now she had gotten Chandaka into trouble, too. Things were not going at all perfectly on this evening that was so important to everyone of Addha's household. It had begun with seeing horrible Shakuni with Simca, then Simca's threat. It all made her want to cry.

Then everyone was in such a rush, she couldn't even tell Ratna what had happened. She had wanted her "big sister" to dress her in green and pink so they would look alike, but Lakshmi and Addha had shooed the apprentice off to do other things. Addha insisted on this creamy silk antariya. "It would be too much to dress the child all in Sakyan blue and gold," Addha had said, "but this hints at her heritage. It's just the right touch." Lakshmi had nodded in agreement and hurriedly dressed her, then bustled off, leaving Kirsa feeling uncomfortable and awkward.

"Are these children always so disobedient?" Suddhodana didn't bother to mask his displeasure. "My son would never dream of such behavior."

Though she hadn't seen any of the guests yet, she already disliked this Prince Siddhartha, whose unexpected visit was throwing the house into a tizzy. She disliked him even more for making her and Chandaka look bad.

"Ah, well, my lord," Addha began, but Bimbisara interrupted.

"Come now, my royal brother," the Maghadan king said, "You were a child once. This little girl is not accustomed to meeting kings."

Now Addha and the kings all talked at once, their voices jumbling together with the fountain's splashes so Kirsa couldn't understand what they were saying. With damp, trembling hands she smoothed the folds of her elegant outfit, then looked in dismay to see if she had spotted or wrinkled the soft silk, which was embroidered with flowers in yellow and blue. They bloomed off green vines woven in a subtle pattern of swastikas, the symbol of the Sakyan king's divine ancestor. In the dark she couldn't really see, and could only hope she'd left no mark on it.

The slap of Lakshmi's footsteps and the lighter pat of Chandaka's sounded in the nearby passage that led to the kitchen.

"Foolish boy!" Lakshmi was saying with hushed urgency. "You knew you were wanted in the garden! And Kirsa, too. Where is she?"

"Ow! I don't know. I had to find my tabla..." He held up the little drum in one hand.

"That's what you get for leaving your things about. King Bimbisara is going to be very angry that Amrapali's son was not there to accompany her when it was time for her to sing!"

"But... I didn't mean..." His voice cracked. If Chandaka was afraid, things were very bad indeed. Kirsa felt awful. Everything was her fault. She must somehow make it better. She stepped from behind the urn.

"There she is!" Chandaka's cry echoed against the garden walls. All talk ceased. Kirsa could feel everyone look toward the passageway.

"Child, where have you been?" Lakshmi hissed like an angry snake and glared, which tied the knots in Kirsa's stomach even tighter. The plump woman eyed her, pulled at the antariya and smoothed Kirsa's hair, then yanked at Chandaka. She attempted to straighten the white headdress Chandaka wore that couldn't completely cover the shock of unruly hair that always fell over his eye. "Now, the two of you, don't disgrace us."

Chandaka took her hand, and they entered the garden, sweaty palms clutched together. Her eyes were drawn first to the faint radiance that surrounded a tall, handsome man. Though the radiance awed her a bit and his face wore a frown, he was not the many-limbed demon with a fierce third eye she had imagined. In fact, he possessed only two strong arms and two long legs, like any ordinary man.

"Here," Chandaka squeaked. "Here we are, my—my lady Addhakashi."

King Suddhodana's eyes fell on Kirsa. She leaned against Chandaka, who trembled a little.

"Ah. You see, my lord, they are here." Addha gave them a sweet smile, but there was an edge to her tone.

The king's frown disappeared. He stared at Kirsa. His eyes were amber like her father's and her own that she had seen in Ratna's polished tin mirror. Around his neck was a dark gold necklace inset with deep blue lapis and on his upper arm a matching wide cuff. He wore a circlet of brilliant yellow gold around a high brow which was also much like her father's, from which long, dark hair flowed over his bare, muscled shoulders and chest. His silken antariya was blue and worked with gold thread at its edge with the sun god Surya's swastika.

His lips parted in surprise, but before he could speak, Chandaka let go her hand and bowed deeply over joined palms. "Namaste, King Bimbisara. Namaste, King Suddhodana."

"Well, there's my little musician. I hope you've been practicing, Chandaka," said a round man with short, rather unkempt hair who was dressed in a simple antariya the color of fresh saffron with one end draped over his shoulder. He looked very unlike a king; more like one of the sages who stopped at Addha's kitchen gate for alms, except that he wore a great silver ring set with an enormous green stone on the forefinger of his right hand. It flashed in the torchlight. Chandaka had always said that Uncle Bimbisara wasn't only his mother's patron, but loved Amrapali and him. To judge by the fondness in his smile, Chandaka was right. Bimbisara turned to Kirsa. "Ah, child." He studied her a moment. "She is so like her father," he said, turning to King Suddhodana, who cleared his throat and opened his mouth as if to speak, but remained silent.

A memory popped into her mind out of nowhere of her father and her sitting around their dying cook fire one night after her mother had gone to sleep. "Remember, Kirsa," Angirasa had said, "you are of the sun god's lineage."

Kirsa squared her shoulders, took a step into the garden, and prepared to bow. Then she saw a boy, about her age and size, dressed in the same gold and blue as the king. He had the king's high brow and cheekbones, and dark, curly hair framed his face under a smaller gold circlet. He was all golden: the skin of his slender chest and arms, the aura that surrounded him, the eyes that swept over her and sent a little shock through her when they met hers. Any thought of disliking him vanished.

Chandaka moved ahead, but when she didn't follow, he turned around. "Don't be afraid," he said, taking her hand again and giving a gentle tug. "It's all right now…" He followed her gaze to the boy and wrinkled his forehead.

"Look at her, Father," the boy said, breaking into a smile. "She is ours!"

The king cleared his throat again. "She is so like my nephew," he said in a voice tight with emotion. "My sister will be overwhelmed…"

Kirsa stepped away from Chandaka and walked up to the king. "Namaste, my lord Suddhodana," she said, loud and clear and unafraid. She put the palms of her good hand and her bandaged one together and bowed. "Namaste, Prince Siddhartha," she said, turning to the boy. Her smile felt as wide as his, and his face seemed as familiar to her as her own, and her heart, though it ached for Bapu and Ma, knew it had found a home.

"But her hand," King Suddhodana said, all tenderness gone. "What is wrong with her hand?" He reached for Siddhartha's shoulder to pull him back.

The prince shook it off and in one motion moved next to Kirsa and touched the bandage. "Someone has hurt her, Father." He looked at her with a serious expression. "We will find him and punish him."

THE SAKYAN KING'S SON

ROUND THE GARDEN, THE TORCHES sputtered and smoked.

"Tell me what happened when you escaped the Beggar King," Siddhartha said. He shifted on his cushion and recrossed his legs, settling again, and took her maimed hand in his. Kirsa, who had been sitting on her heels next to him, looked at their joined hands. She didn't like anyone looking at her wound or touching it, not even the healer Lakshmi had sent for. But when he held it, somehow it ached less.

"There's not much left to tell." Kirsa leaned forward and traced the fingers of her good hand over the water. The few little lamps that still burned on the floating lily pads bobbed on the ripples. She had already told the prince more than she had ever told anyone at Addha's about the attack on her family and her brief captivity at the Beggar King's camp. "Lakshmi rescued me," she said. "Just yesterday a man came and said my father was dead." Her throat tightened.

"What man?" the prince had begun, when there was a shout.

Kirsa bit her lip. Harischandra had said they should keep his name secret.

"Hey!" It was Chandaka. He stood at the entrance to the passage that led to the courtesans' chambers, his headdress askew and a frown on his face. "Are you two still talking?"

"Oh!" Kirsa had only been vaguely aware that the music had stopped and that Addha, Amrapali, and the two kings had left. Half-empty dishes littered the table. "Where... where have you been?"

"With the guards. Gambling." He puffed out his chest. "You didn't even notice I was gone." He stuck out his lower lip.

"My father forgot about me!" Siddhartha said in astonishment, swiveling his head.

"You weren't paying attention. They were talking about things," Chandaka pulled off the white headdress and tossed it on the ground.

"What things?" Kirsa asked.

He sauntered over to where she and the prince sat and stared down at them with a superior air.

"What things?" Kirsa repeated, mystified by Chandaka's sullen expression.

"Come on. I'll tell you." He extended his arm to help her up and nodded toward the low table. "There's a whole plate of honey cakes left. Let's take them up to the roof."

She grasped his hand and stood up, brushing off her fine antariya. "Lakshmi will be angry. And what about Siddhartha?"

Chandaka curled his lip at the prince, then gave Kirsa a mischievous grin. "Everyone is in bed."

She flushed. "Chandaka!" She didn't like it when he gave her that grin. While she was sitting with Siddhartha and talking, she'd been able to ignore the excited male laughter that wafted through the mansion. It was the way feasts ended. The courtesans and their guests retired, and soon the laughter would end in cries and moans that frightened her.

The night she arrived at Addha's house, there was a feast, and when it was over she heard Amrapali shrieking and shouting "Oh, stop, my lord," as if she were being beaten. It sent Kirsa into a terror, but she gathered her courage to run for help and came across Chandaka splashing in the lily pool, a forbidden activity. "Robbers are attacking your mother!" she had said, breathless. Chandaka let out a short laugh. "Don't be stupid."

He had apologized right away. Kirsa hadn't asked what was going on or why his voice sounded so bitter, but all of a sudden tonight she thought of what Simca had been doing earlier today with Shakuni. She didn't want to understand.

Siddhartha interrupted her thoughts. "But where are all the servants? Where is my guard?" He seemed alarmed.

"We get by without them." Chandaka glared at the prince, daring him to criticize. "Before, we lived in a huge mansion, as big as your palace, I'll wager, with a hundred servants." He raised his chin. Ratna had told Kirsa that the old mansion was beautiful and there were eight gardeners and five kitchen maids and not just Lakshmi and the cook and one old porter; and a dozen guards, not just two. She blushed for Chandaka's lie. "Your guards are gambling with King Bimbisara's men in the kitchen garden. I was with them." He crossed his arms over his thin chest and looked down his nose at the prince. "You're not afraid, are you?"

"I always have a guard at my father's palace." Siddhartha looked up at Chandaka with wide amber eyes. "And a servant to carry my white parasol," he added.

Chandaka snickered. Kirsa wrinkled her forehead in confusion and looked at him. "Only kings and queens and princes and princesses can have a white parasol," he said to her. "Isn't that right, Your Majesty."

Siddhartha's golden skin turned dark with embarrassment. "I'm not a majesty, I'm a highness." Chandaka rolled his eyes. "I mean, I hate things like that! But at my father's court... we—the royal family—oh, it's stupid... my attendant follows me with one. Even at night." He paused, as if surprised at his own words. They all looked at each other.

"A parasol at night?" Chandaka began to titter, then exploded, laughing harder and harder. The look of consternation on Siddhartha's face changed to puzzlement, then he began to laugh, too. Chandaka threw himself on the ground and clutched his stomach while the prince howled with delight, mouth wide open. Kirsa was reduced to helpless hiccups. At last they quieted.

"I've never laughed so hard." Siddhartha wiped tears from his eyes.

"Really?"

"Really."

"Hmmm. I laugh all the time."

Siddhartha glanced at Kirsa. She nodded. "He made me laugh the first day, when I was so sad."

"Come on," Chandaka said, a pleased grin on his face. "Let's get the honey cakes and go look at the stars." They jumped up and grabbed handfuls of sweets from the platters and wrapped them in a cloth, then raced down the passage to the ladder, giggling and whispering. At the top they dropped their stolen treats on a low, weathered table and sat on faded cushions, stuffing their mouths. Without thinking, Kirsa wiped her sticky fingers on her flowered antariya. Her heart fell when she saw the dark smear. Addha and Lakshmi would be furious.

"I want to look at the city," Siddhartha said, not noticing that Kirsa had gone very quiet.

They walked to the parapet on the roof's edge. Chandaka stood on Siddhartha's left, Kirsa on his right, and they looked over the few winking lights.

"Varanasi is very dark," Siddhartha said. "They say night never falls in Kapilavastu, there are so many lights. People feast and drink until the third watch ends."

"Varanasi used to be like that. That was under the old king. This new one doesn't approve of courtesans and drinking houses," Chandaka said.

"But Varanasi is still famous for its sages," Siddhartha said, his eyes shining. "One of my teachers says that Shiva himself taught on Ganga's banks, and it's still where the wisest gurus go to teach. I want to go see them."

"What? Listen to a dried-up old yogi? The marketplace is much more fun." Chandaka grabbed Siddhartha's arm. "It's hours till dawn! We could sneak out and go see."

"Oh, no!" Siddhartha looked horrified.

"Are you scared?"

"My father would be so angry."

"Who cares? I'm not afraid of him." Chandaka gave an exaggerated shrug. Siddhartha gave him a dubious look. "But if you never go out, how do you know what Kapilavastu looks like at night?"

"My guards sometimes take me to the gates and let me climb to the top of the palace walls. They pretend to disobey Father, but I'm sure he knows about it, or they wouldn't dare. I've never been so far from home, ever! I hardly even leave the palace, except for sacrifices. I hate them, unless we just offer fruits and flowers, and not an animal."

"My father said that killing an animal was as wicked as killing a man," Kirsa said.

Siddhartha studied her with wide eyes. "You know, it's your grandfather who is my father's priest," Siddhartha said, looking at Kirsa, "and who leads the sacrifice."

Addha and Lakshmi had told her this. She didn't understand how it could be, but now Siddhartha said it, too, so it must be true. She imagined a very tall man all in white, with his head shaved except for the topknot a Brahmin had on the crown of his head, who would look at her with disapproval.

Chandaka changed the subject. "But it's stupid. You can't be king if you don't lead your army in battle and go out in your city to give alms and travel to visit other kings."

"My father and the queen say it's dangerous." Siddhartha's amber eyes turned wistful.

"During the feast your father said something about your mother being powerful."

"My mother?" Siddhartha looked confused.

"You and Kirsa were talking, so you didn't hear. He said the queen is powerful, but he thought Addha could stand up to her. She sounds scary."

The prince's face became grave. "The queen is not my mother, but my aunt. My mother is dead. Aunt Prajapati can be kind, but she scares everyone, from generals to kitchen maids."

"Scares generals!" Chandaka burst into delighted laughter. Kirsa gave him a furious look. Couldn't he see the prince was upset? He clamped his mouth shut. "Um, sorry."

"It's all right. You didn't know." He paused a moment, then words came rushing out. "My mother was my father's favorite wife. She was from the Koli clan. They live in the Himalayas. When it was her time, she went back to her home. I was born in her clan's sacred grove."

"So she died there?" Chandaka said. Kirsa gave him another furious look, but she was curious, too.

"You don't have to tell us," she said, touching Siddhartha's arm.

Siddhartha's eyes filled. "The tale they tell in the palace is that I came out of my mother's side—not like babies are usually born." Before Kirsa could wonder how babies were born, the prince rushed on. "An ashoka tree burst into bloom, even though it wasn't the season, and bowed in front of her so she could hold on to a branch. Flowers fell from the sky. Or so they say. The gods did magic for her."

"The gods did magic? I don't believe that." Chandaka began to scoff, but seeing Siddhartha's face, he stopped.

"I don't think I do, either. If the gods favored her, why didn't they save her? She died seven days after I was born." He sighed. Kirsa thought of the prayers Bapu had chanted and the flowers and fruit she and Ma had offered at the shaalmali tree, and she, too, wondered why no god or goddess had helped them.

"This is wonderful," Siddhartha said, and Kirsa looked up, startled. "I have a half brother, and a baby sister, and lots of cousins and playmates, but I don't have any friends. No one really *talks* to me. Like you just did, Chandaka. I feel like I could tell you anything." The sorrow lifted from his face. He gave a shy smile. "And you, too, Kirsa."

"Hunh." Chandaka wrinkled his forehead. "You don't have any friends?"

"There's a—a prophecy. It makes people act different around me. Only my nurse told me the truth about when I was born," he continued. "And only after I asked and asked, and then she made me promise I wouldn't tell anyone what she told me."

The two boys fell silent. Despite Siddhartha's sad story and the way it made her think about Ma and Bapu, Kirsa was strangely happy. She suddenly felt she would be content anyplace, as long as she was with these two: Chandaka with his mischievous grin and Siddhartha with his golden eyes and golden aura.

"Ah, look!" Chandaka pointed. "Look at those little lights floating along. What is it?"

"It's just lamps on Ganga," Kirsa said, peering into the dark. "No... wait... it's on the streets." They all strained their eyes in the dark. More and more lights gathered on Varanasi's streets and headed toward the great park on the river where the priests made sacrifices.

"They're going to the Ashvamedha," Siddhartha said. "It's the final day today. When they kill the horse." He swallowed. "And lots of other animals. Father says I have to go, but I don't want to."

"We're all going," Chandaka said. "That's what Addha and your father said, Prince."

"All of us?" Kirsa was perplexed.

"King Suddhodana says you're a royal Gautama," Chandaka said, with peculiar emphasis on "royal Gautama." Kirsa looked at him but his face was a mask. "And you must go, too, Kirsa. I think it will be fine! All the warriors and pretty women and all the animals that will be sacrificed. I heard there would be a lion from somewhere far away in the west."

"The animals suffer!" Siddhartha shuddered. He and Chandaka exchanged a glance. "But let's not talk about it." He looked down for a moment, then brightened. "I want to hear about the places you go in Varanasi, Chandaka."

After that, there was no end to the talking, at least for the boys. Addha had warned Kirsa not to say anything about Bapu working in the cremation grounds. The king would think she was impure and not take her to his kingdom. Before she met Siddhartha, that hurt her, and she hadn't wanted to go to Kapilavastu. Now, even though it pained her to think of leaving Varanasi without finding Ma, she wanted to go with Siddhartha to his palace. So she kept quiet.

Chandaka boasted about his pranks in Varanasi's market. A recent foray swiping fruit from half-blind farmers' wives became stealing sacks of gold from thieves, and the time the other day that he hit Shakuni with a stick for shouting at Kirsa became a grand sword battle.

Then Siddhartha described his father's palace: the many-storied wall encompassing the palace and grounds the size of the whole of Varanasi, the multitude of peacocks wandering the gardens, the vast fountains and lily pools with swans floating on them, cool stone bathing tanks deep as lakes, and a sacred grove filled with the wisest sages in the world. There had even been a white tiger sighted in the wild park that stretched into the Himalayan foothills.

"I don't believe you!" Chandaka snorted, but Kirsa felt in her heart that Siddhartha could never lie.

"Then you'll have to come and see for yourself," the prince replied. "After the Horse Sacrifice, I'll convince Father to bring you to Kapilavastu with me."

"You don't have to convince him," Chandaka said.

"What do you mean?"

"It's another thing Addha and your father talked about. We're going with you to your kingdom," Chandaka said. "All of Addha's household. He said he would give her a grand mansion to live in."

Kirsa's heart beat fast. She must somehow send word to the fisherman and his wife, tell them to hurry and find Ma, then they would all move to—to—her mind reeled, trying to imagine this mansion. "All of us?"

"Not my mother," Chandaka said, his eyes cast down and his mouth in a sullen pout. "She's to go to the country of the Licchavis..." His lip trembled.

"Amrapali won't come?" Kirsa was stunned. "But why?"

"I can't tell you." Chandaka frowned and looked away.

"But we're all friends," Siddhartha said. "You could tell us."

Chandaka looked near tears. "I can't. Let's not talk about it anymore."

Kirsa had never seen him cry. It was unthinkable, going away without Amrapali. She couldn't imagine why.

"We'll all be motherless," Siddhartha said. "But we'll have each other."

They fell silent. The sky brightened with the dawn goddess's approach, and the clouds that robed her turned purple and pink and orange. Below, merging from every street, pilgrims massed in a slow-moving river, flowing toward the eagle altar to witness the Ashvamedha.

ASHVAMEDHA

"Ketu," Mala called, her heart beating hard against her ribs. How could he disappear so fast? "Ketu, where are you?"

Wherever Mala turned, whichever way she tried to go, the throngs that filled Varanasi moved the other way. Like a great river taking her in its current, they forced her to follow them. Ecstatic faces surrounded her, pilgrims murmuring prayers, some weeping, others swaying and stumbling as if drunk, their staring eyes fixed on Indra's heavenly city, or perhaps the hell realms of Yama, Lord of the Dead. She had never been among so many people before. All she wanted was to escape the heat and closeness of the bodies. Under the already scorching sun, the air was suffocating from all the human smells of the teeming city: sweat and perfumes, feces and food.

When Rohit and his men had decided to try their luck in the city, he warned her not to come. They would be making the most of the unguarded shrines and houses emptied of their occupants as the whole city made its way to the eagle altar.

Mala ignored his advice. She knew this was her chance to find Kirsa.

"What are you going to do?" Rohit had said. "Go to the city and start asking anyone if they know where a woman in blue named Lakshmi can be found? Unless you know more than that, the crowds will work against you. But don't listen to me."

He was right. Mala had felt strongly that the goddess Lakshmi would appear and guide her as soon as she entered the city. Instead, Ketu disappeared almost the instant they passed the gates. One moment he was there, the next she was squeezed among these strangers babbling amongst themselves or chanting hymns to the gods. Her eyes filled with tears. She couldn't fight the crowd. The goddess had betrayed her. She would never find Kirsa.

"*Om!*" A well-fed man in the Kosalan colors with a red antariya and a black sash wrapped around his waist shouted in her ear. He stared ahead of him in a sightless trance, his eyes wide and bloodshot. "*Om!* Let the stallion bring us strong cattle and strong sons!"

A chorus of voices answered him. "*Om! Om!* Let the stallion bring power to our king and wealth to our clan!" "Jai! Victory! Victory to the Kosalas!"

"Kosalan bastards," someone on Mala's other side said. A sweaty, smelly man in a stained dhoti jostled against her, muttering to himself. He was lean, almost skinny, with stringy muscles running up bony arms. Greasy matted hair framed his narrow face. He could have been a sage, but he gave off the stink of dead fish. "Blasphemers," he muttered a little louder. His eyes darted this way and that, and he blinked rapidly. Mala was about to ask if he knew Matsya the fisherman when he raised his fists over his head. "Only the heroes of old could perform the Ashvamedha!" he shouted. "The gods will punish King Prasenajit."

At this, the man in red and black blinked and started. "You dare call our king a blasphemer?" The stew of humanity stilled like a bubbling pot taken off the fire. Everyone stared at the man in the stained dhoti.

A soldier shouldered his way through. "What's this? Did you call our king a blasphemer? Everyone knows he is descended from Prince Rama himself." He grasped the smelly man's arm.

"Kashi scum!" someone said. Many murmured assent.

"Come along, come along," the soldier said, dragging his captive behind him as he pushed through the crush.

"The Kashi clan will rise and throw off the Kosalans!" The shout came from somewhere nearby. Everyone turned and looked to see who said it, but it was impossible to tell. Then more people began to exchange shouts.

"You Kashis don't deserve to rule." "Your king ran from the city like a cowardly jackal."

"He was betrayed." "Prasenajit's a usurper!" People shoved this way and that. The pot was bubbling again, and the hostility was palpable. Mala couldn't breathe.

233

"Indra himself will bless King Prasenajit's sacrifice. The Kosalan king will be a world emperor!"

"Yes! Chakravartin Prasenajit!" "Hear, hear!" "Svaha!" "That's right."

She must get away, she must. Kashis and Kosalas looked eager for a fight. Several guards wearing Kosalan black and red began to work their way in from the edge of the crowd.

"Move along. Move along, I say!" one of them said.

Mala couldn't bear another minute. She gritted her teeth and pushed toward a dark alley off to the side of the broad, crowded street.

A peddler selling betel nuts accosted her as she broke from the crowd, but he turned away when she asked, "Do you know a little girl named Kirsa?" Then someone tugged at her arm.

A spindly, filthy fellow held her with one hand and stretched out the other one for alms. Pus was dripping from one of his eyes.

Mala swallowed. Maybe he knew the Beggar King or had seen her daughter. "Do you know a little girl named Kirsa? With two fingers missing?"

The beggar opened his mouth. There was something wrong with it. Mala staggered back.

Someone caught her. "He can't speak," the man who held her said. "Missing his tongue. What did you say, you're looking for a little girl? Come with me, maybe I know where she is."

Mala was certain the man did not. She tried to wrench free, but he dragged her into an alley where a still figure lay under a white cloth. He fumbled at her antariya. "And I'll have you."

He pushed her against the wall, but that morning she had wound her antariya tight around her legs, and he yanked and tugged without loosening it, cursing her all the while. Sudden strength surged through her. She tried to twist free, but he smacked the side of her head and pressed harder against her, immobilizing her with the weight of his body. The blow made her dizzy. A wave of revulsion washed over her.

Just then there was a low rumble, like a growl coming from a deep well.

The man stepped back. Then he gasped and released her.

There was nothing under the dirty white cloth, and over it stood a white tigress, its blue eyes fixed on Mala's attacker.

It was Rani.

Leave or be eaten.

"You—you spoke! The gods preserve me from demons!" The man staggered backward down the alley a few steps before his legs crumpled under him. His jaw worked and his eyes bulged out. "I... stay away..." Another low rumble came from deep within the tigress's throat. The man crawled away as fast as he could without a backward glance. When he reached the end of the alley, he managed to scramble up and was swept away by the surging crowd.

Follow me. The tigress padded away down the twisting alley. Its white-striped tail disappeared behind a ramshackle hut.

"Wait!" Mala ran after, and as she turned the corner around the hut, a whirlwind took her. There was a howling like demons and a feeling of being squeezed so tight her bones would shatter.

When the whirlwind stopped, she was astride Rani, who was padding along a sort of dark tunnel. She seized the fur on the great cat's neck to keep from falling.

Hold on with your legs.

In stunned silence, Mala obeyed.

That's right, like you were riding a horse.

No sooner did the thought occur to Mala that she had never ridden a horse than the tigress said, *You will. One day. You will.*

Who... how... Mala couldn't even articulate her questions. This strange tunnel wasn't real. This was all a dream. It must be. She would wake to find that she had been raped and was lying on the filthy ground of a Varanasi alley. "Where have you been?" Mala was almost weeping.

Do not try to understand. It is enough for you to watch. Watch and learn.

Mala pressed her legs around the tigress's warm fur as they continued past the rippling walls of this tunnel or whatever it was. The darkness began to lift and the walls shimmered with light, and through them all of a sudden shapes appeared. As they became clearer, Mala realized they were pilgrims. She and the tigress were quite literally walking *through* the crowd, which seemed oblivious to their passage even as she and Rani—how to describe it—flowed, wafted, *breathed* into one body and out, then into another and out again. It felt like walking through cobwebs.

As the river of humanity flowed through Varanasi, they passed from crowded dwellings into an area of high, gated walls. One gate was open, and gathered outside it were sturdy-looking horses hitched to little wagons that porters were loading with boxes and bales. Inside there were a few servants scurrying about with bundles in their arms in front of the largest house Mala had ever seen. *It's huge!*

Rani paused. *It is really rather modest. This is merely the courtesans' quarter. Soon we will pass through the nobles' quarter, and then past the old palace. There the mansions are the size of a whole village.*

The crowd streamed past as Mala sat on the tigress's back wondering at this strange shimmering shell or wall or whatever it was that separated them from the ordinary world.

Inside the gate, a plump woman in blue stood before the doors, giving orders. "Not there," she said to one man, who was just about to set his load in a wagon. "Put it on this one. And someone fetch my lady Addhakashi's litter from the storeroom."

Addhakashi! Rani's ears twitched. *Odd that her servants are packing the household. But it makes sense she would leave. Varanasi hasn't been as hospitable to its courtesans since Prasenajit became king...*

Mala barely listened to Rani. She was staring at the plump woman shouting at the servants. She was the same one who in Mala's vision had been holding Kirsa. This servant of the courtesan Addhakashi had rescued Kirsa, Mala was sure of it. "Rani, I must get off! My daughter is in there." She began to dismount, but found that her legs would not obey her.

No! Stay on me or you will be seen. The tigress started to move again while Mala looked back over her shoulder at the gated mansion until it was out of sight. *She's not there. But I will take you to her. Be patient.*

They wended through broad, curved streets shaded with enormous old trees. Some of the mansions inside were so tall that the roofs were visible over the whitewashed walls. On one roof a bevy of gaily dressed people was observing the masses moving by.

Rani looked up. *It must be a foreign merchant. A true Arya would not miss the Ashvamedha. It's the first in the living memory of you mortals.* She sniffed. *I hope it will be the last. It sickens me.*

At last, the river of people entered a huge park. It flooded out into the surrounding trees, but Rani, with Mala on her back, stayed with the main current until it emptied into a wide clearing surrounded by the thick interlaced branches and the aerial roots of what seemed to be a vast, single bodhi tree. Its branches were filled with chattering golden-furred monkeys with black faces and the voices of many birds. A memory tugged at Mala. Angirasa had said that in the Deer Park of the Kashi kings, the sacred grove in the city's heart, there was an ancient bodhi tree so enormous that no one could find its original trunk.

"Why are we here? How... how did all this happen?"

I'm as mystified as you. The tigress seemed curt. *You have no training, no knowledge of the inner pathways that the adept yogi uses to become invisible. But She has her reasons to bestow her favor on you once again.*

"She?"

The Devi. Durga. Kali. Lakshmi.

"Favor me?" A bitter taste filled Mala's mouth. It seemed that the goddess had withdrawn her favor several times when her divine presence would have helped.

Rani rumbled deep inside. *This displeases you?*

Mala turned this way and that, peering through the edges of this separate reality that she and the tigress were moving through, certain that the crowd around them, in them, with them, must hear, but no one paid the slightest heed. "Oh, no, no, no. I just..."

As to why... Rani paused. *You are here to see your daughter. She is with the Sakyan king.*

"Kirsa!" Mala whipped around and looked toward a low rise where a colorful array of nobles had formed a semicircle around a flat red brick altar. She was taken aback with awe. Angirasa had told her of this ancient altar of the Kashi kings. Built using the sacred laws of geometry, he said, which only the Brahmins understood. If one looked at it from above, one would see the shape of Garuda, king of the eagles, wide as five men were tall from wing to wing, and the length of a man from the tip of Garuda's head to the fan of his tail.

She shook herself. Her eyes swept the glittering assembly, searching for her daughter. What had Angirasa said the Sakyan colors were? She couldn't remember. Nowhere did she see Kirsa's face. She wanted to run up to the altar and push aside the four Brahmins clad in immaculate white who stood in front of it, their heads shaved except for the topknot of long hair at the crown, tied with elaborate ribbons that flashed with gems. Her eyes landed on the fourth priest, who stood at the head of the eagle, hair gathered his topknot in a single strip of plain white cloth.

Mala's heart stopped. He was tall and slender, and there was something familiar about him. His face was turned so she couldn't be sure. As she peered through the rippling curtain, one of the other priests began a long, beautiful chant.

"*Om!* Surya, ruler of the day! Varuna, ruler of the night! Indra, who commands his Maruts to battle demons and all powers of evil! Hear us as we proclaim the heroic deeds of this stallion, who was born of the gods and who will return to you this day!"

He finished with "Svaha!" and threw powder at a fire that burned to the north of the altar within the semicircle of the nobles watching from under their white parasols. Multicolored flames shot up. Then the priest took up a brand from that fire and walked to a stack of wood on the south side of the altar.

Typical, Rani rumbled. *Do these men even mention Ratri, goddess of night, or Ushas, who brings the dawn? The Aryas have never properly worshipped the Devi...*

"*Om!* All honor to Agni, whose mouth eats the sacrifice and sends the food to the gods in their heavens on the smoke." The priest touched the brand to the wood. Flames leaped up. "Svaha!" he called out.

Then the priest handed the brand to the tall, slender Brahmin, who took it and began a chant. "As Indra did when the world was young, as the heroes Yudisthira and our king's divine ancestor, Prince Rama, did in the days of our forefathers, we gather to consecrate the reign of the new world emperor, the new Chakravartin, King Prasenajit." He stepped closer and held the burning brand over the stack of wood piled on the center of the red brick altar, continuing to chant, but Mala was no longer listening.

She could not take her eyes off the tall, handsome man clad in blue and gold who stood behind the altar. He gave off such an aura of arrogance and confidence that Mala wondered for a moment if he were King Prasenajit. She shook her head to clear it. Now she remembered. Blue and gold. Sakyan colors. It could only be the Sakyan king. For a moment, no one else existed, only he. He scanned the crowd as if looking for someone or something, and his eyes seemed to penetrate the shimmering wall around Mala.

Then his gaze moved on, and Mala was released from its spell. Now the beautiful woman standing next to him caught her attention. She gaped.

"It's her!" She had spoken aloud. "The courtesan Addhakashi..." The walls of her separate reality began to thin.

Careful. Rani swiveled her great head and looked at Mala out of the corner of one blue eye. *I can't protect you if you—*

"Kirsa!" Three children stood near him under the shade of parasols: two boys, and between them a little girl, her daughter, dressed in a cream-colored antariya with colored flowers. Mala slid from Rani's back.

What are you doing? The tigress was angry. *Get back on!*

But Mala couldn't help herself. She stepped forward through rippling light, and then the sweaty crowd surrounded her.

The heat and smell and sound nearly knocked her over. The air was thick with the mingled odors of human and animal sweat, of sandalwood smoke, of something else. Fear. The smell of fear, of what looked like hundreds of animals—lowing water buffalo and quaking hare; silent, fierce-eyed falcon and clucking hen—all tied to stakes near the altar, lowing and bleating and bellowing. She turned frantically to try to get back on Rani's back, but the tigress and the magical tunnel had disappeared.

In spite of the heat, a chill came over her as faces turned to her. They would think she was a demoness or a witch to have appeared so suddenly.

But no one seemed to think it was anything out of the ordinary.

A man in clean but threadbare clothes gave a sniff and sneered at her. "Watch where you're going." Someone shoved at her from behind. "You're blocking my view." Mala turned to the speaker, a woman with kohl-lined eyes and intricate braids studded with beads and ribbons falling over her bare shoulders and breasts.

"Forgive me," Mala began, staring at this strange-looking creature, but others jostled and pushed and she nearly fell. The press of bodies—she had never seen such a variety of colors and shapes—held her and everyone else up. Some were threadbare, like the man who sniffed, but some wore jewels and multicolored antariyas patterned with flowers and strange symbols. Some of the young women wore flimsy, opaque shawls draped around their shoulders; old women were wrapped more modestly with the long ends of their antariyas thrown over their shoulders, covering their breasts. Mala had always been tall, and she looked down on many of those surrounding her. She would have hunched low so as not to attract attention, but she didn't want her view of Kirsa blocked. Nevertheless, she lost sight of her daughter

239

when a small procession led by a tall, slender man, just past his prime, moved in front of the altar, followed by four women.

He was dressed in blinding white linen that fell in elaborate pleats from his slim waist. A narrow golden circlet studded with flashing gems of all colors rested on his head, and his hair fell loose, in contrast to the Sakyan king and others who wore the warrior's braid.

Three of the red-garbed women accompanying him looked around at the gathered nobles with bold airs. The fourth, short and plain despite her more gaudy attire—her antariya was laced with gold thread, and necklaces and jewel-encrusted bangles loaded her neck and arms—looked down at the ground.

"There's King Prasenajit and his queens." "Three beauties and that squat creature." "She's the chief queen, though."

Prasenajit and his wives moved aside enough that Kirsa became visible once again. The two boys had moved protectively closer to her. All three were holding hands. Mala wanted to fly to Kirsa. She couldn't believe her own eyes. Her daughter was standing with the king of the Sakyas, Angirasa's people. It was where she had sometimes dreamed Kirsa would be, but now she wanted to go to her, snatch her away.

Just then, an animal bleated in terror louder than the others. From the line of offerings to Indra staked at the side of the altar, two men selected a white goat. They untied its halter and led it up the rise to the altar.

The sacrifice had begun.

A cloud of wood-smoke wafted toward them, Mala's eyes began to smart. The priest turned and signaled a man who held a long, sharp knife. It was Valmiki.

The goat buckled and fell as the knife slashed its throat. The victim's blood splattered Valmiki and three other white-robed priests standing nearby. Some even reached the silk-clad, bejeweled nobles who sheltered under the shade of white parasols. One or two of them stepped back. The rest stood motionless.

Mala tried frantically to keep Kirsa in view. Through the shifting crowd by the altar, she would glimpse the Sakyan king and at his side, the courtesan Addhakashi, but sometimes she lost sight of Kirsa entirely.

Then at the moment it seemed people could not pack together more tightly, from behind Mala came pressure like a wave rising on whispers of awe.

"The stallion!" "Ah, perfect." "Black as night." Then somehow the crowd was separating, creating a path straight to the altar.

A Brahmin walked past holding the horse's halter, then came the horse, followed by a troop of ten Kosalan soldiers in red and black with red gems glinting on their scabbards and helmets.

When the stallion and its attendants reached the altar, the four presiding priests, led by Valmiki, stepped forward to offer the blessings.

"We circle three times with the offering," one priest said, and they led the horse around the altar.

When they stopped, Valmiki held a bucket of water for the horse to drink. It lapped at it thirstily. The priests all bowed their heads and murmured prayers. The animal began to sway then thudded to the ground. Poisoned, Mala realized. The water was poisoned. A Brahmin wrapped a blanket over the stallion's head and covered its nostrils and mouth until it breathed no more.

What had Rohit said? According to ancient custom, the stallion had been kept from breeding with any mare for the whole year, to make its semen pure and strong. What the sacrificial stallion must do, so must do the sacrificing king. Also according to ancient custom, for the whole year King Prasenajit had slept every night between the legs of his chief queen, but he never entered her. He hoarded his potency to show the discipline and restraint of a Chakravartin, a monarch fit to rule the world, like the kings of old. He might abstain from his poor, plain queen, but Mala wondered whether he'd satisfied himself on any of the beauties accompanying her.

Valmiki's beautiful, deep voice floated over the heads of the assembled watchers, chanting a prayer. They chanted the response.

As the horse lay before the altar, the queen stepped forward with two of the younger queens, who grasped her elbows when she stumbled. When they reached the horse's side, the chief queen stopped and swayed. The young women smirked.

As the Brahmins raised a cloth screen around the queen and the horse, the two younger queens began to chant and leer at them. Mala was dumbfounded as the priests returned their lewd looks. But then, Indra, to whom this sacrifice was dedicated, was known for his lust.

Then the queen's voice came faintly from behind the screen, chanting her part. A priest hissed at her to speak louder. Her voice rose above the cloth curtain, trembling, begging for a mate. The other royal women continued to circle the sacred space, asking for the queen to be satisfied.

"*Om!* May the manfully potent stallion bestow the seed within you," Valmiki called out.

The royal wives chanted in response. "*Of this stallion's cock the praises let me sing. The potent swift steed of many victories, may he lend fragrance to my mouth and my womb. May he give length of days to our lives!*"

Servant girls poured pitchers of water over the chanting women. When they finished spluttering, they continued:

"*O thou water, be to us quickening like the holy semen of this horse and bring to us fresh power, that our king may give us children and there may be known to us great joy. Water! What fluent benediction is thine! Let us partake of it here, like the loving, divine goddess-mothers.*

"*Thee we approach in the name of the Celestial Being, to whose dwelling thou dost speeding go. Give us, O water, of thy strength!*"

No sound came from behind the screen. Suddenly Mala understood what the queen must do. She wanted to gag.

Another Brahmin began his chant.

"*O first among wives! O pious queen, learned in the sacred knowledge of the Vedas and endowed with devotion! Give thyself to this stallion!*"

"*Svaha!*" Valmiki called.

"*Svaha!*" the crowd answered.

An excited hubbub ensued as flutes and drums played and the three young queens danced around the partition, exhorting the queen to mate with the horse with lewdness that shocked Mala. Others around her, however, shouted encouragement in equally coarse terms while three of the priests, still holding the cloth that screened the queen and the horse, laughed and shouted the praise of Indra's potency and their king's, and most of all the stallion's. Valmiki stood to the side, expressionless, his chin raised, until at last he cried out:

"It is done!" Silence fell.

The priests dropped the cloth and two of them knelt alongside the queen, who sat up. She looked dazed, and her face was streaked with tears, but as the Brahmins helped her stand, she composed her face and stepped

THE TIGRESS AND THE YOGI

away from the motionless stallion with trembling dignity until she stood next to King Prasenajit. He did not acknowledge her presence with even a glance.

Valmiki called out again. "Gods, receive the horse! Let this ax split its ribs and sever its limbs." At that, the priests began to butcher the horse. With cries of *"Svaha!"* and *"Vasat!"* they threw several pieces into a vessel over the western fire to render the marrow, saving the haunches for the end of the rite. "Let not your dear soul burn as you fly to the gods. Let no cut do lasting harm to your divine body, which shall ascend to heaven. Let not the smoke darken your spirit, nor the cauldron split asunder as you cook."

Then Valmiki beckoned to Prasenajit. "O first among kings of the earth! Purge thy sins!"

The Brahmin held the king's head over the smoke, and he inhaled and exhaled three times, coughing violently.

"O Indra! Ruler of the gods! Our king is purged of sin and worthy to rule the earth as you rule the heavens!"

And then the true slaughter began. It took hours. Some animals went without a sound, some bellowed as their throats were slit and their blood drained. To the smell of sweat and fear the nauseating stench of entrails and blood were added.

Now Kirsa was in view, her face stricken and full of terror and disgust, but the two boys remained close to her, and Mala was glad of it. Now Kirsa was hidden by the movement of priests and servers offering the sacrifice.

Every time her face became visible, Mala wanted to wave her arms and shout, but every voice was stilled. Immense as the crowd was, there was no human sound save the priests' chanting. Everyone was mesmerized by the ancient ceremony unfolding before them.

Several large fires burned on the dais, each with a cauldron hanging over it. A dozen priests had joined the four Brahmins who had performed the ritual, butchering the animals and throwing meat into the cauldrons to cook.

The sun's disk was far in the western sky when the crowd surged forward, ready to receive the offerings as the priests divided up the cooked sacrificial animals. It carried Mala closer and closer to the dais and Kirsa. Then she stumbled and dropped to her knees, and would have been crushed, but a hand grasped her arm and pulled her up.

"Careful. You'll be trampled."

Her eyes swept past the man who helped her. She craned her neck toward the dais, searching for Kirsa's face. But the king and his wives, Valmiki, and all the nobles who had formed a semicircle around the altar were moving away, surrounded by guards.

"Kirsa," Mala whispered.

The man tightened his grip on her arm. She could not break free to run after Kirsa. For the first time, she looked at him. His broad face and black unbound hair streaked with grey were familiar, but she couldn't place him.

"Come," the man said. "I must talk with you."

She looked at him again, and recognition dawned. The attire of a holy wanderer; the face and physique of a warrior. It was the man who had rescued the dog, long ago, back in the village of Gauri. "I must go after her... she... she's my daughter..."

His eyes widened. "You must come with me now," he said, insistent.

"Where?" she whispered.

"To the cremation grounds."

She shuddered, remembering the night of the attack. "Who... who are you?"

He looked at her with wonder and pity. "I can't tell you here."

"Who are you?" she cried.

"Shhh." He glanced over his shoulder, but no one was paying attention. "My name is Harischandra. Do not speak it," he whispered in her ear. "I am the chandala now. I can tell you what happened."

"No, I must go to my daughter." But when she looked back to where the Sakyan king had stood, there was no sign of Kirsa. Mala felt utterly bereft.

"She is safe," Harischandra said, as if he knew her thoughts. "I can help you."

Gone. Kirsa was gone. Mala shook her arm free of his, trying not to cry. "Then let's go."

They began heading out of the Deer Park. Dusk was falling. The priests had finished offering the last of the dismembered stallion to the fire. The eerie chanting of the ancient hymns died away. Mala found it odd that there was no exultation at the completion of such a grand offering. Indra's thousands of eyes did not gaze benevolently down from a clear sky. Instead, smoke from Agni's altar and the damp air of Ganga's waters mixed in a dense fog that blanketed everything. It swirled in acrid wisps around the trees like ghosts of sacrificial victims. Instead of joyful chanting and laughter, an uneasy silence prevailed.

Mala and Harischandra joined the subdued worshippers, who with bowed heads and sidelong glances were threading their way through the forest toward the river.

PASSING IN THE NIGHT

WHEN KING SUDDHODANA'S PARTY RETURNED to the mansion, Kirsa wanted to run up to the roof and hide. She could not have endured the killing of all those animals without Siddhartha and Chandaka, who had held her hands tight during the awful ceremony and helped her dry her tears after they left.

"We must get the stink from the smoke of all those burning animals off of you." Lakshmi took her in hand right away and led her to the bathing tank, where Ratna had already begun her own bath. "I don't care what the priests say. It's vile to kill all those animals."

"Are you excited, little sister?" Ratna asked, whose shining eyes clearly indicated that she was, took a wooden ladle and in a rush poured water over Kirsa's hair, getting soap in her eyes. "Everything is ready to go! We're leaving tonight."

Kirsa rubbed her stinging eyes, wondering how Ratna could be so cheerful after watching all those poor beasts be put to death. She shuddered. "How can you be excited? It was horrible!"

"Oh, poor thing. Here." Ratna moistened the towel with water and wiped away the soap. "Hurry now. Let's get out."

"Why must we go tonight?" Kirsa asked as Ratna rubbed the dry towel over her.

"We must go before King Prasenajit knows we're leaving. He'll be celebrating the end of the Ashvamedha with a grand feast and won't notice our friends have been so rude as to avoid his banquet—or at least, for a little bit. That's why we have to leave the city as fast as we can."

"Ratna! Kirsa! We're ready to leave," Lakshmi called from the corridor.

When they were dressed in fresh clothes, they scurried out to the courtyard, where two trains of ponies were loaded and ready. One would take King Suddhodana and his entourage to Kapilavastu, while another would take Amrapali to the capital of a clan allied to King Bimbisara.

Amrapali was kneeling in the courtyard, hugging Chandaka to her breast and weeping. Kirsa didn't understand why Amrapali couldn't come with them or Chandaka go with her. Still, even though it was sad that they would be separated, she was relieved and glad her first real friend would be coming to Kapilavastu. And in spite of the fact that Ma was somewhere out there, not knowing where Kirsa was, the prospect of this journey with Prince Siddhartha thrilled her.

Now it was evening, and Sakyan soldiers were helping them into the hastily loaded wagons.

"Come, Kirsa," Lakshmi said, holding the curtain of Addha's vehicle aside. "In you go."

"I get to ride a horse," Chandaka called as he pushed his mother away, oblivious, it seemed, to her swollen eyes and sad face. "Prince Siddhartha and I will be at the front of the caravan, with the king!"

Amrapali, her face ravaged by tears, was frozen to the spot in front of her own wagon. Addha went to her and put her arm around her. "Try not to worry. Chandaka will be the playmate of the future Sakyan king. Think what it means. We'll send word to you as soon as we've arrived. And I'm sure it won't be long before we can exchange visits."

"Lakshmi," Kirsa said as she climbed into Addha's wagon, "did you tell Matsya where we are going, so he can tell my mother when he finds her?"

"Tsk, child," Lakshmi said. "Don't worry about that now. Think of the palace you will live in!"

Kirsa frowned. "You will be living there, too, won't you?"

"No, Addha is to have her own grand mansion. Perhaps it will be even grander than the one we once lived in here in Varanasi."

Before Kirsa could consider this news, hooves thudded on the street outside.

"The kings!" a guard called.

"Look at this fog," Bimbisara said, dismounting. "Prasenajit's priests are not happy about it. The people were all muttering that it's a bad sign."

"That's good for us all around. No one will be so sure that Indra blesses the Kosalan's claim to be a world emperor. And it gives us an excuse not to be at the banquet. Prasenajit will think we couldn't find the palace for the mist." Suddhodana gave a sly grin.

Addha and Amrapali embraced, weeping, then Addha joined Kirsa in the curtained vehicle. The drovers and guards gave hushed commands that were further muffled by the smoky fog, and soon the caravan was passing through the Shining City's dark and quiet streets. At first, Kirsa peeked through the curtain at the stragglers heading back from the sacrificial grounds, hoping that by chance she would see Matsya and his wife, or maybe even her mother. The events of the long day had exhausted her, though, and at last her eyelids began to droop. She lay back on the cushions next to Addha, lulled by the creaking wheels. Soon, she dozed and dreamed.

They were in the middle of a vast lake. Kirsa was holding onto Siddhartha's waist as they floated on a swan's back through dark water. Pink water lilies glowed with the lights of tiny oil lamps that floated atop the lily pads.

"We shall be together forever," Siddhartha said.

From somewhere came a harsh cry. "Ho, who goes there?"

"Watch out," someone else shouted. "You'll run them over."

Kirsa roused as the voices wrested her from the lovely dream. The wagon came to a halt. She yawned and looked around through half-open eyes. She was curled next to Addha, whose breath was soft and even. Across from them, snoring Lakshmi's head drooped over her chest.

Outside the wagon, a voice muffled by fog answered. "We are sorry, my lords. We were headed out of the Deer Park toward Mother Ganga and got lost in this fog."

The chandala. Was she still dreaming? Kirsa smiled sleepily and rubbed her eyes. "Harischandra…" she murmured. She wanted to greet him, but then she remembered she shouldn't say his name out loud. Still, the guards shouldn't talk to Harischandra like that. He was a king, even if it was a secret. She pushed herself up but as she shifted, the courtesan pulled her closer.

"What is it, little Kirsa?" Addha murmured, kissing her brow.

"It's Harischandra."

248

"Oh, foolish child. You were imagining things. Hush now." Addha pulled a silken coverlet over the two of them.

"No, it is him..." She wanted so to see the kind king, but her eyes wouldn't stay open. Besides, what had she been dreaming? Oh, yes. Siddhartha and the swan. She snuggled against Addha.

"Out of the way, now," the guard said.

The murmur of voices outside the wagon ended, and the creaking of wheels began again, and soon Kirsa was afloat on the swan's back.

INTERLUDE

KALI

S OMEONE, A BEING, AN AWARENESS, observed Mala from within.
This Consciousness, within her yet separate, observed her mind.
Time became a sluggish river in which Mala could dart like a fish while everyone and everything else slowed as if moving through thick oil.

It was the universal Mind that Asita had spoken of, and it watched from behind her eyes yet from outside her physical self. It flooded her senses, her mind, her consciousness.

Even so, it could not quite quench the longing for her daughter that still sometimes seared Mala so badly that she wanted to die.

For now, though, the Consciousness would distract her. Until the embers of longing inevitably flared again.

Almost a year had passed since the Ashvamedha.

Before he left his hermitage, Asita had told her that Kirsa had escaped her captors, had gone to live in a palace, a prince's playmate. Mala lived in a ruined temple, with outlaws for companions. What did she have to give her daughter?

Kirsa was better off in the Sakyan king's palace.

Or so Mala tried to convince herself.

She had struggled with what Asita had tried to teach her of the techniques yogis used to join with the Mind. It was so hard, such a long road to follow to be free from suffering.

Then the Consciousness he had described began to come unbidden, without the hard work, the endless hours of sitting alert and focused. She tried to summon it at will with what she remembered from Asita's lessons, seated in the lotus pose, following her breath. But she could not make the heightened awareness come. Not yet.

Yet lately she had sometimes awakened with the sense that she was both observer and observed. The observer, the Being, Consciousness, the dark goddess Kali—whatever it was, she had come to call the Watcher.

The Watcher had been with her since she awoke that morning.

Behind an enormous banyan's tangled grey-white trunks, she and Rohit waited for a victim. The other men waited on the other side of the trade road, hidden in the thick undergrowth.

Tiny insects buzzed in her ears. The banyan's limbs and aerial roots were transparent, luminous, revealing the sap flowing through it. Like prana, the sacred energy that flowed through her body. A damp cool rose from the forest floor, while bright hot sunlight lit the white flowers on a vine trailing from a branch. It reminded her of the shrine she built to the Devi when she was a girl, not far from her parents' hut; the cool, dark place where she hid the day they were murdered.

There had been no hiding place for them. Even now, grief's knife cut deep. Mala smothered a sob.

Next to her, Rohit appeared not to hear, not to move, not to breathe, not even to blink, trapped in that sluggish river of time through which she swam so swiftly.

In this heightened state, Mala was at once exultant and terrified. Exultant because on raids it gave her an edge. Everything was Now. Everything was more *real,* though only to her, it seemed, and not to her outlaw companions or to her victims.

The heightened state always ended, though. That was what she feared. She sometimes doubted existence itself. It was almost as if everything was a dream only she dreamed. One day, she feared, she would stop dreaming, and everything—the forest, the thick undergrowth that hid her and Rohit on this side of the road and the rest of the men on the other—everything and everyone would disappear. And then, when she woke, she would be alone in suffocating black nothingness. Forever.

She shook herself. Nonsense. Think of what you're doing, Mala, she told herself. Soon a small caravan will come by, and there will be booty.

At that thought, a victim materialized in her mind's eye—or perhaps it was in the Watcher's eye. A lone merchant, somewhere around the bend in the road. Of course the others would not have seen him yet; it was her heightened awareness that told her he approached.

She closed her eyes to better see. The merchant's voluminous robe was rich but hung oddly on him, as if he weren't used to such attire. He rode a fine-looking horse and held the halter of an ox that trudged behind him with a lowered head. The ox carried only two bales of goods. The bales bounced with each step as if they held very little. Perhaps they contained gold or gems, but wouldn't it have been easier for the merchant to put such goods in a wooden chest and carry it on his horse's back? And if he had such valuable cargo, surely he would have a guard. Strange.

She must let Rohit know someone approached. She opened her eyes, reached out to touch his arm.

Very slowly, as if moving through cold, thick oil, Rohit turned. He and the others knew that her senses told her things they didn't perceive. Their raids had become more successful since this perceptive power, this Consciousness had begun to show in her.

Rumors of the gang's successes—her successes—had spread along the trade road. The dozen or so men who had joined in the last few months might look at her askance, but none complained of the rich prizes her power brought. Only Rohit was wary. "You don't control the power, it controls you," he warned. "You don't know where it will lead."

The merchant was very close now.

Mala slid her hand into the leather sack she carried that was filled with carefully selected smooth stones. Her fingers closed around one.

Stay a moment.

That voice. The Devi. Mala's eyes were open, but everything went dim. "Mala!" her sweet mother shrieked in terror. She was a child, back in the shelter of her shrine near her parents' hut. Her beloved father gave an agonized scream. "Oh, Devi," Mala whispered in anguish, "you protected me. Why did you not protect them?"

The dimness fell away. In all her glory, the black goddess Kali stood before Mala, hair wild and tangled about her face, eyes bloodshot and the whites vivid against her dark skin, teeth sharp and pointed and dripping with blood. Around the goddess's neck hung the skull garland; severed arms hung from the belt around her waist. In her many hands she carried bloody weapons.

Pray to me, Mala! Take your revenge! Kali's voice filled her mind.

The Devi hadn't helped her then. But Kali would help her now. Instead of the helplessness that had overwhelmed Mala the day of her parents' murder, power infused her. She stepped out of the shadows and hurled the rock.

"Ma-a-la!"

It was not her dead mother's voice but Rohit's.

She was a few feet from the horse. Its rider sprawled on the pale dirt, face to the sky, eyes open and staring and mouth agape. Dark red spread from his skull, crushed by the stone she had thrown. His robes had fallen open, revealing a Kosalan soldier's red and black uniform. At his waist was a short sword.

He was no merchant, but a decoy.

"Ma-a-la! Wa-atch ou-u-ut!"

Then three warriors emerged from the trees, swords drawn, but slowly, so slowly, held back by time's magic. The muscles of their faces contorted bit by bit into fierce grimaces.

It was a trap.

Strike, Mala, strike!

She stooped and seized the Kosalan's blade.

Black Kali danced around her, in one of her arms a severed head. With studied calm, Mala faced the three warriors. In their own time, they were running, but in hers, they had progressed only one step toward her. Rohit, in mid leap, seemed to float, his short sword drawn, his muscles straining.

The sword glinted in Mala's hand. Wildness filled her and yet she felt fully in control. One, two, three powerful strokes beheaded her attackers. She laughed at the blood spurting from the bodies as they toppled, headless, to the ground.

Kali laughed. *Well done, my dear,* the goddess said.

"*Om,* Dark One, I salute you!" Mala lifted her blade, but Kali had already disappeared.

Back at camp that night, there were a few grumbles that the bales held nothing of value, but the swords and knives taken from the dead Kosalas were forged from the finest Maghadan metal, and the men were happy enough with them and the four fine horses they had taken. The ox they had already slaughtered; its meat sizzled on a long spit over the fire.

A jug of fermented kadamba juice circled from man to man. When Anu passed the jug to Mala, he kept his eyes down. The others stared but looked away as soon as she turned to them. Already uneasy with her powers of perception, they had become frightened, even awed.

Only Rohit tried to catch her eye, but she avoided his glance. She didn't want to go with him into the forest and find a private place to make love. The power and elation she had felt earlier was gone, replaced by disgust. Profound shame filled Mala. She didn't know herself.

She wondered if Kirsa would recognize the blood-soaked woman who stood on the dusty road.

An overwhelming urge to rid herself of the bloody pollution made her rise to her feet. Ganga would wash her clean. She turned from the fire and the men's questioning eyes and headed toward the path to the river. As she reached the forest's concealing shadows, Rohit's footsteps rustled behind her.

"Mala..."

She paused. He knew how to comfort her when her grief and loss became overwhelming. She turned and reached for him.

He hesitated before extending his hand. His face was twisted with pity.

Who was he to pity her? There was revulsion, too, in his eyes. Red anger flickered around her. "Leave me alone," she hissed, and whirled to run down the path.

At the river she searched for Kirsa's face on the dark surface lit faintly by the stars, but it was Kali that appeared, her tangled hair floating atop the eddies and currents.

A good day, Mala. You served me well.

Mala closed her eyes to shut out the goddess's image, but only that terrifying face appeared in her mind's eye. "I want to see Kirsa," she murmured. "My daughter, my darling."

But you must avenge your daughter, Mala. Render all praise to me, and your power will grow. Vengeance will be yours.

Mala swallowed. "I cannot," she whispered. "She would hate what I have done today."

Today was nothing. I danced on Shiva's corpse, and all bow before me!

Praise me! The Kosalan king pays his priests but not his soldiers. Discontent grows in the Kosalan ranks. Soon, its warriors will bring weapons and horses to you willingly. Soon you will lead an army.

Mala gazed at the image floating on the water's surface. "I?" Her breath burned in her chest. "Lead an army?"

Your army! An legion of outlaws...

Mala's breath ignited a flame in her heart.

Soon you will avenge the hurts done to your mother, your father, your lover, Kirsa...

"I will avenge her, O Kali..." She reached a hand out to the water.

You will cut off your victims' fingers, as the Beggar King cut off Kirsa's. You will string them in a garland around your neck, and because of this bloody necklace, you will be known as Angulimala, Gruesome Garland...

"*Om,* Kali!" Mala bowed to the floating image.

"No." Someone else spoke. Someone she'd never heard before. "No, revenge is not the answer. Get up, Mala. Seek an enlightened teacher. You walk on the knife's edge. Without guidance you will fall. It will slice you in two."

Mala sat up and bent over the riverbank. Only stars glinted on the surface. She waited, utterly still, for that calm voice to come again, but it did not. She peered into the swirling water. Kali's faint image returned.

You will be known as Angulimala, and men will tremble at your name...

"Angulimala," Mala whispered. Then she straightened. "Yes, men will tremble!" The current hissed and swirled against the bank.

"I am Angulimala," Mala cried.

PART IV

THE SUMMER PALACE

THE SUMMER PALACE

KIRSA FROZE LIKE A FRIGHTENED hare at the quick crunch-crunch of heavy feet on gravel. Siddhartha squeezed her good hand and put a finger to his lips to indicate quiet. Just in front of them, Chandaka peered through the dusty leaves of the hedge at the path circling the pool, whose waters shimmered under a crescent moon.

A sentry, the yellow sash and bright blue of his uniform muted to grey by the night, stood at the intersection of a well-tended walk that led from the manicured private gardens of the royal family to the equally lush and well-tended larger grounds.

In the three years since Kirsa had arrived at Vishramvan Palace, she had not lost her wonder at the queen's gardens. In daylight, the famous lotus pool, almost a small lake, sparkled silver or sapphire depending on the sky's color, but at the moment its wide, dark waters reflected the moon and stars. The faintest outline of King Himalaya's distant, snowy peaks seemed to float above the night horizon, but Kirsa was so frightened she couldn't appreciate their mysterious beauty.

She drew a shaky breath. This was positively the last time she would go along on one of these midnight escapades. Lately, Chandaka's pranks had escalated from putting frogs in Princess Sundari's bed to more elaborate schemes. These included sneaking out at night to play among the pools and fountains of the formal gardens. At first, he went alone, but soon he convinced Siddhartha to join him, and in turn Siddhartha urged Kirsa to come.

"I want you to see how beautiful the gardens are at night," he had said, eyes shining.

"It isn't safe. Anyone could be hiding out there," she had replied. Anything or anyone could be hiding out there. She still had nightmares about the men who attacked Ma and Bapu and King Ram jumping out of shadows.

"These gardens are the most well-guarded place anywhere along Ganga's river," he had said. "Trust me. You will be in no danger."

She did trust him. He said there was no danger. How could she say no?

The heavy footsteps stopped so close to where they crouched that Kirsa could have reached out and touched their owner's muscled legs. Her blood pounded in her ears. The hedge was not thick. Even though shadows hid them, the gold thread woven into the fine linen antariyas the boys wore would glisten between the twigs and leaves. She wanted to pull the end of her own plain, dark blue one over her head and disappear.

The man wheezed, trying to catch his breath. "Have—have you seen them?" he called to the sentry in a hoarse whisper.

"Halt! Who goes there?" the sentry responded.

"It's Sabal, you fool. The prince's bodyguard."

"Oh, Sabal." The sentry laughed.

"Shhhh! You idiot. Keep your voice down."

Chandaka clapped a hand over his mouth to stifle a laugh. Next to Kirsa, Siddhartha shook with suppressed merriment. Only she feared being caught. It shocked her sometimes, the way her prince, while remaining outwardly respectful and obedient, would become an eager participant in Chandaka's pranks. Now and then, the boys had been caught. The king blustered while the queen clenched her jaw and turned mottled red. Once, her majesty had threatened Chandaka with banishment, but Siddhartha interceded.

Kirsa imagined she would be banished, too; or worse, betrothed to some impoverished noble's son. She was nine already, an age where some girls were not just betrothed, but married off. If either happened, it only meant it would be harder for Ma to find her, though Kirsa had long ago lost any real hope she would see her mother again. "I'll never let that happen," Siddhartha had said.

This evening's escapade into the wild part of the palace park was more dangerous. Bandits and wild animals didn't roam the formal gardens, but who knew what lurked in the overgrown forest just beyond them? Kirsa almost hoped Sabal would catch them, which she couldn't help but think would happen in mere moments, but then she considered the punishment for her and Chandaka... oh, why couldn't they go back to the prince's chambers?

"What's going on?" the sentry said in a quieter tone.

There was a pause. "The prince has... has... escaped."

"What?" The sentry let out an explosive breath.

Kirsa closed her eyes, as if that would help keep her hidden. Partly their success in keeping their late-night explorations secret was due to Chandaka's innate sneakiness. Partly it was Siddhartha's uncanny knack for making the guards and servants look away at just the right moment, another of those almost magical things he did, like understanding the language of every slave in the palace.

His old nurse Vaddhesi, who had served the royal Gautamas for three generations, said divine powers ran in the family, the gift of their forebears, the sun god Surya, and the wise Gautama, one of the Seven Celestial Sages. "King Suddhodana's grandfather, the great philosopher king Jayasena, could see all his past lives," she had told Kirsa. "And of course his majesty's father, Sihanu, was a powerful wizard, but he made evil use of his gifts, which is why our lord Suddhodana had to usurp the throne to save the clan. And his majesty speaks to animals," she had added with pride. "When he first ascended the throne, he escaped a rival's ambush when an eagle landed on his shoulder and whispered in his ear where the traitor had deployed his assassins."

"But how did he get away?" The sentry now spoke in the same hoarse whisper as Sabal. "Where could he be? Shouldn't we rouse the palace?"

"No. For the love of the gods, no. You can't tell anyone! Imagine if their majesties find out." Sabal's voice shook.

Kirsa had seen the servants thrown down at her majesty's feet and lashed until their backs were bloody for nothing more than a dropped drinking cup. What the great Queen Prajapati would do if she knew that her beloved nephew and the two of his companions she liked least and he loved most ventured into the gardens at night, unseen and unprotected—well, Kirsa did not want to think about it.

As for what the king would do, she was even more afraid to imagine. He was indulgent with Chandaka to a point, but when roused, was as terrifying as a demon. Not a month ago he had executed a courier for bringing bad news about a Kosalan incursion into Sakyan territory.

"But what can the prince be thinking of, to run off like that?" The sentry walked over to Sabal, and now Kirsa was staring at two pairs of feet, biting her lip and trying not to breathe.

"It's that troublemaker Chandaka. The king should have sent him away long ago."

Chandaka flashed a white smile over his shoulder. He was proud of his mischievous reputation. He'd begun earning it almost the moment they arrived. They had only been at the palace a few days when he jumped into this very lotus pool to chase a black swan. Only after he jumped did he discover it was much deeper than the little pond at Addha's old mansion. He would have drowned if Siddhartha, who was younger and smaller but at least knew how to swim, hadn't jumped in after him.

In the time that had passed since that day, Chandaka had only grown more daring.

"The prince loves him better than any of those spoiled noble boys," the sentry said. "They can't send him away."

Siddhartha gripped her fingers tighter, and she had a sudden thought that he was not shaking from laughter but was as frightened as she. He could and did defy their majesties' anger to protect a stablehand or kitchen maid or a body servant who displeased one or the other over some small thing, but it wasn't easy. Defending Chandaka, who was so much more important to him, would be more difficult.

"Look, right now, there are only three of us who know he's gone: you, me, and the old nurse. Don't tell anyone else."

"You'll never find them alone. They could be hiding anywhere! Let me come along."

"All right. Let's circle the pool first." Their voices faded as they walked away along the stone retaining wall at the water's edge.

"That was close," Siddhartha whispered.

"Right under their noses, and they didn't see us!" Chandaka was exuberant. "I knew this was a good place to hide."

Even in the dark, she could detect the half smile on Siddhartha's face. Earlier, when the boys came to get Kirsa in her room near the servants' quarters, Chandaka had nearly exposed them by ducking into the kitchens to grab a small bundle. One of the maids was trysting with a cook's helper, and it was one of those times when the prince seemed to cast a spell to make the three of them invisible. That Sabal and the sentry didn't see them was due to that same spell, no doubt.

They waited in the hedge until their pursuers were vague shadows at the far end of the moonlit pool, then Chandaka jumped up and grabbed the bundle that had nearly got them caught earlier.

"What have you got there?" Siddhartha said.

Chandaka held it up. "Food for our journey. Naan. Cheese. Some dried mango."

"Where are we going? You still haven't said." Kirsa didn't want to spoil things, but by Chandaka's starlit grin, it could be a long way to some forbidden spot.

"You'll see." As Siddhartha and Kirsa stood and brushed themselves off, he strode away. "It's not far to that new path I found. Once we've started down it, no one will be able to find us."

"But we'll get lost," Kirsa began. Without a word, Siddhartha took her hand and hurried after Chandaka, who had stopped at a rock not far away, pointed into a dark, overgrown mass of shrubs, and disappeared.

When they reached the rock, they found the merest suggestion of a path. Siddhartha gave her an encouraging look, let go her hand, and parted the bushes so she could enter. She took a breath and plunged in, raising her arms to protect her face from leaves and twigs. She almost tripped over Chandaka. When Siddhartha bumped her from behind, all three sprawled on a moist layer of leaves covering the trail. "When you walk in the forest, careful of leeches," she remembered Ma saying. "They can move as fast as you when they sense your warmth."

She scrambled to her feet. Chandaka laughed as he stood up. Kirsa rubbed her eyes. His skin had a strange glow. In fact, there was an aura around all three of them. Even though the foliage of the tall trees above them blocked any sight of moon or stars, a faint glimmer that came from nowhere and everywhere gave off just enough light to see. She held out her arms in wonder, but before she could say anything, Chandaka swung the bundle over his shoulder and headed into the underbrush.

"Come on," he said.

Kirsa followed him, Siddhartha followed her. Aside from the crickets, no animal made a sound; not even a nightjar croaked in the underbrush, and the cracking twigs and rustling leaves their passage caused seemed all the louder to her. Branches slapped her face and a bug crawled around her neck and down her back. She tried to wiggle and brush it away, wondering whether being lost in the wild part of the palace's vast park would be worse than being found. There was a line beyond which Queen Prajapati's gardeners could not tame the ancient forest that protected the northern side of the palace and the Sakyan capital. It formed a wall no army could penetrate, and in that way provided safety from human enemies.

The older retainers like the nurse Vaddhesi told tales of the tigers and wild boars that sometimes wandered out of the forest and into the gardens. Vaddhesi also spoke of nymphs, demigods, and demons that haunted the place. Kirsa didn't dare look to either side into the thick vegetation, for fear she would see a raksha's two red eyes peering back at her.

Ahead of her, Chandaka slowed to clamber over a large log that had fallen across the trail. As Kirsa prepared to follow him, something slithered over her sandaled foot. She shrieked. An unfamiliar bird or perhaps a monkey let out a wild cry that made her jump.

"What is it?" Siddhartha whispered.

"It was... I don't know... a snake crawled over my foot," she whispered back.

"Come on, you two," Chandaka said from the other side.

Siddhartha helped her scramble over. "Ow," she said when a sharp twig poked her palm. Her antariya caught on a dead branch and ripped. She thanked the Devi she'd worn a plain, old one. The boys must have ruined their fine ones by now. At last they came upon a slight break in the undergrowth, a little clearing where the path divided. They stopped and gazed up the length of slender trunks whose branches were so high above they were lost in the dark, and the eerie glow didn't penetrate. They stared and craned their necks, turning this way and that.

"How old do you think these trees must be?" Siddhartha said at last. "I'll bet they were here long before the Arya clans came to this land." He put his hands on his hips. "I'll bet no other Sakyan has ever been here. No other Sakyan." His small chest swelled with pride. "So, which way, Chandaka?"

Chandaka had been standing silent, his brow wrinkled and his lips pressed together. "Um..."

266

Kirsa was disoriented from staring up for so long. All the narrow little trails looked the same. "Chandaka…? Wh—which is the way back?" He didn't answer. Her skin prickled. He didn't know where they were. All of a sudden the forest seemed to press in on them.

He frowned at her. "Don't be scared." He spoke too loud. "Uh, that way. That goes to the gardens."

"Are you sure?" she said timidly. "Then maybe we should go back. Siddhartha must be in his room before dawn."

"What are you worried about?" he said. "Plenty of time. Besides, I wanted to show you this special place." He swiveled his head, still frowning.

"That way," Siddhartha said, pointing down one of the paths. As soon as he spoke, it seemed as if one of the paths filled with the same glow that surrounded the three of them. Kirsa gazed in wonder. What was this aura? "We should go that way."

Chandaka cleared his throat. "Right, I was just about to say that." Before Siddhartha could lead the way, he crashed through the shrubs ahead in the direction the prince had indicated. Siddhartha motioned her on and once again followed.

Soon Kirsa's breath came in ragged gasps. She hurried on in miserable fear that a green-skinned, red-eyed demon with blood dripping from its teeth would reach out from the dark and snatch her. The sensation of creepy crawling things in her unbound hair and under her clothes made her want to jump out of her own skin.

"How much farther?" No sooner had she spoken the words, they burst out of the narrow confines of the path. Here, there was no undergrowth. In the center she could make out a huge trunk of a tree with vast spreading branches that extended out over her head, almost low enough that if she jumped up high as she could, she could touch one.

"Ah!" Chandaka let out a soft whoop and ran to the tree trunk.

"Shhh!" Kirsa said, looking around. The narrow trail hemmed in by dense shrubbery seemed suddenly preferable to this open area, where she felt very exposed.

"Look," Chandaka said as he grasped a low branch and put his foot in an indentation on the trunk and began to climb.

Siddhartha ran after him, and there was nothing for Kirsa to do but follow.

"It's a tree house!" Siddhartha said, looking up. There was a platform of some kind, something made by human hands, or perhaps divine ones. She looked around. Someone had built it. Someone who might come back.

Chandaka leaned down from the platform. "Hand me the food and come up," he said. "It's a grand tree house. Like a palace, almost, with so many rooms. Well, not rooms, exactly. But come up. You'll see!"

When she and Siddhartha hoisted themselves onto the platform that circled the trunk, Kirsa's eyes widened. The persistent eerie glow revealed old boards, some rotted or broken, so she took care as she stepped. No one had been here for a long time. No one was likely to come. It was odd, but though she had a sense that spirits frequented this place, she felt safe.

Above, branches hung low like a sort of roof that would not need much thatching to withstand the monsoon rains. In her mind's eye rose unbidden the image of bright golden cloth studded with pearls and semiprecious stones draped over the tree limbs to separate the platform into chambers, and enormous silken pillows scattered around low tables laden with platters of rice and fruit, and oil lamps hanging from branches here and there. For a moment, it all seemed real. She blinked, and the image was gone, but the sense that this had once been a true palace in the trees remained.

They sat leaning against the trunk and ate the food Chandaka brought. When they finished, they rested for a while in companionable silence, the only sound the unseen crickets chirping.

"I feel some god meant this place to be ours," Siddhartha said. "It will be our secret palace, our safe place. Whenever one of us is in trouble, we will come here, and the other two will know where to find us. We will swear never to bring anyone else."

"I swear," Chandaka said.

Kirsa said nothing. She was thinking there was someone she would like to bring here. The boys watched her, waiting. "Could... could I bring my ma, if I find her?"

Chandaka and Siddhartha glanced at each other.

"Yes," Siddhartha said. "When you find your ma, she can come."

ANGULIMALA

I T SEEMED A LIFETIME SINCE the Ashvamedha.

In those early days, Mala and Rohit's little band took only what they needed, ambushing foolish travelers who should have known better than to walk the trade road with little protection. They were satisfied to capture a single merchant and his mule carrying bales of Varanasi cloth and a few cooking vessels. Whatever the goods, which sometimes included a bag of silver coins or jewelry set with semiprecious stones, they left the victims penniless but unharmed.

Mala had never experienced anything like this outlaw life. Its freedom gave her solace and lessened the bone-deep ache for her lover and child, which not even Rohit's passionate caresses had erased. He and his men did not need her to care for them the way she had cared for Angirasa and Kirsa. They demanded nothing, were grateful that she repaired the temple's thatching and caught fish for their meals; though Ketu insisted on cooking. She was empty, but her emptiness felt light and new, as if she was floating down a river whose waters and shores held unexpected wonders.

The goddess came to her in a dream. *Put aside your longing for Kirsa. She is a prince's playmate, a prince who is destined for great things. Worship me. With blood.*

Mala found a grove and an ancient stone linga which she kept secret from the men and where she offered hares or birds. Then on a raid Rohit captured a bow and began to teach her to shoot. They disappeared for days into the forest, making love and hunting. Her arrows flew to their mark like the rocks she hurled. When they came back, she offered deer on her secret shrine. Her emptiness began to fill with purpose.

The dark goddess came again. *The Sixteen Kingdoms quarrel among themselves and make each other weak. Dare to take what you wish. Take your vengeance.*

They sought bigger prizes, overcame small caravans with one or two guards. Their successes drew others to their band, ordinary thieves and murderous-looking renegades that Rohit didn't trust. Rohit swaggered as if he were the reason for their victories, though all could see that Mala always threw her stone first and always hit her mark. Tension arose between her and Rohit. It added spice to their lovemaking.

Kali visited Mala's dreams more often. *Remember the cruelty visited on you, on Kirsa. Take your vengeance,* the goddess said. *Remember the cruelty visited on you and your daughter by those who thought themselves above you.*

The Beggar King had cut off Kirsa's fingers. The searing memory came unbidden and often, until one day it came to her how she should take her vengeance. She would cut off the fingers of her victims and wear a garland of them as Kali wore a garland of skulls.

One day it began. She sliced off a nobleman's beringed finger and tied it into her sash. She made no explanation or excuse.

That night Kali came. *Angulimala, they will call you,* she said. *The one who wears a gruesome garland. A garland that is the sign that I protect you. You will be like a queen and rule the outlaws.*

It was not long before she was leading the gang. She and Rohit stopped being lovers then started again.

It was a lifetime since the Ashvamedha, yet only three years had passed. Three years since the last time she saw Kirsa.

But Mala had grown strong. There was no point to looking back at that moment. There was nothing she could have done. She couldn't have seized Kirsa and fled Varanasi. So she swallowed her grief and began her outlaw life.

And now, as Kali had promised, she ruled an army.

People up and down the trade road called her many things. She was Angulimala, Gruesome Garland, for the necklace of her high-caste victims' fingers around her neck. She was the outlaw queen who commanded an army. She was Mata-ji, who out of boundless love shared the spoils of her raids with the poorest and the untouchables. They knew she had suffered at society's edges, too. And some called her Black Kali and feared her dark rage. She reveled in all her names.

Angulimala's heavy sword came down on the prone man's neck, and the head rolled away from his body. Of the other guards, two were dead. The third lay groaning in the dust, clutching at his entrails, which spilled between his fingers.

The bearers and other servants had scattered into the forest that lined either side of the road as soon as the five outlaws appeared, dropping the two curtained litters so their occupants tumbled out. Without their drovers, the oxen loaded with the household goods of a wealthy Brahmin of the Surasena clan stood mute in the hot sun.

"Mercy." The round little Brahmin dropped to his knees and pressed his palms together, looking up at her. His topknot was askew from the fall and the sun glinted off his shaved forehead. His thick, luxurious cotton robe, so white it hurt to look at it, was darkened here and there with sweat. Angulimala sniffed. Or perhaps urine.

"Have mercy, M-Mata-ji," he said. The word must curdle in his mouth. Most Brahmins considered the honorific "Mata-ji" a perverted sacrilege and damned her as a scourge and a demon, not a mother goddess.

"Take it all," his wife added, weeping and falling to her knees next to her husband. She wiped perspiration off her hands with the end her silk antariya, forest green with a subtle pattern of dark orange flowers. It was modestly wrapped, covering her breasts as befitted a fine Brahmin lady. She began to pull at the emerald rings that adorned her fingers. "Give these to the poor, the hungry... O fierce Kali, honor us by accepting our gifts..."

The woman's hands shook so much she couldn't get them off. Angulimala's three new recruits laughed. They were deserters from the Kosalan forces, drawn like so many others to serve the outlaw queen who ruled the trade road.

"I accept your *gifts*. In Kali's name." Angulimala smiled down on them. "But what's this?" she said, slow and gentle. "You seem to be having trouble removing those lovely rings."

The Brahmin's wife raised her head. Her mouth dropped open. She was like a hare caught in a snake's stare. Then she renewed her frantic effort to pull the jewelry off.

The new men would want to see her live up to the name Gruesome Garland and to take her victims' fingers. She could hardly disappoint them.

"You don't have to do this, Mala," Rohit said.

She glowered at him. He still dared to challenge her, still dared to use her old name. He was a mosquito in her ear. Always buzzing about the days when she was simply Mala. She did not like to be reminded of that beaten-down creature. She had long ago left her behind.

"No, you don't have to do this, my queen," said Daruk, one of the new recruits. He stood over the man he'd disemboweled and sheathed his bloody sword. A warrior of the conquered Pancala clan, Daruk had been forced to serve as a charioteer to some Kosalan Kshatriya, an insult to his illustrious lineage. Angulimala was making good use of his desire to avenge that insult. "Allow me the pleasure to do it for you." He bowed over his joined palms.

She laughed and turned to watch, imagining other pleasures Daruk could provide. Not a handsome man, but well built, tall, light-eyed, sun-bronzed, with a mouth set in a perpetual cruel smile.

As Daruk pulled a knife from his sash, from the west came a low rumble.

Hoofbeats. Soldiers were riding hard through shimmering heat, half hidden in a cloud of dust.

Not waiting to make out the colors of their uniforms, Angulimala and her four men leaped onto their horses. Kosalas or Sakyas or Maghadas or one of the allies of the three great powers, the riders far outnumbered the bandits. The forest was their best chance; never mind the oxen and the Brahmin lady's emerald rings.

"Retreat," she called, signaling them to follow her, but at that very moment, a whole troop of foot soldiers in blue and gold burst from the forest. The front line drew their bows. Angulimala wheeled her horse around. They might outrun them if they headed the other way.

From the east, more cavalry raced toward them. Perhaps sixty Sakyas surrounded the five outlaws.

Angulimala defeated most of the foes she met on the road. Kali protected her. If she did not feel the power of the goddess within her, she would slip into the forest without a fight and not consider it a dishonor. This time there had been no opportunity to slip away. Her horse neighed and reared, sensing her fear. The Sakyas fell back but blocked any path of escape.

The red aura rose around her. The Sakyas knew where she would be. Someone in her camp had betrayed her. At any moment death would come from a Sakyan spear. She was not ready to die. "*Om,* Kali," she muttered under her breath, "keep me alive to find my betrayer and I will offer him at your altar!"

She shortened her mount's reins, causing him to paw the air again. Rohit and the others wheeled their horses and flicked their whips, and the animals bucked. The foot soldiers fell back a little more, but the horsemen remained firm. She glared at them and saw fear in their eyes, but the faces were expressionless.

She shifted in her saddle. Curious. The Sakyas had every good reason to want her dead, but no one had yet sent an arrow to her heart or tried to pull her off her horse.

Trust me.

She felt Kali's strength coursing through her. The dark goddess had a purpose. There would be a way out of this.

Her horse shook its neck and stamped the ground. Angulimala straightened, flinging her long tangled and matted hair behind her shoulders so she sat bare-breasted, her only clothing a rich red cloth twisted and knotted around her groin that left her long legs naked to the hip. No Sakyan warrior looked her in the face, but she was well aware of her effect on men. Her strength and power intoxicated them. She could feel their lust and fear.

None met her eyes, but she felt their stares on the infamous garland that adorned her neck, a thin leather strip with severed fingers knotted on it, with a few shreds of blackened flesh still stuck to them. The thick hoop at her nostril glowed yellow in the sun; the rubies set in the golden cuffs on her upper arms sparkled. The oil on her skin accented the contours of the muscles on her limbs.

They look on you and despair at their desire, Kali said.

Angulimala smiled. Her eyes swept over the Sakyas, but still none met her gaze.

Then of one accord, her captors drew back, opening a path. All heads lowered in bows; the foot soldiers knelt. Murmurs rose as an enormous black warhorse pranced past. "Your Majesty." "Majesty." "Hail to King Suddhodana."

Angulimala sat straighter, threw her shoulders back further. Then she saw him.

The man who came unbidden to her dreams.

She'd seen him in the flesh only once, at the Ashvamedha. Even from where he stood on the dais with all the other nobles, his power had been palpable. So strong was his aura that on that day, for a moment, no one else had existed, not even the daughter she had been seeking and who was very near him.

Now, as he rode up to her, light flashed. A jolt struck deep in her groin. Everyone else disappeared, and only they two remained. And when his eyes met hers, she wanted in every atom of her being to make that jolt strike him, too.

ॐ

The Sakyas so outnumbered Angulimala's little band that they let them keep their weapons as they all headed west on the trade road. As the sun was setting they came to a track that led off into the forest and followed it to an encampment where perhaps another thirty warriors clustered around cook fires. The smell of roasting deer filled the smoky air.

Angulimala's men were tense and pale. "Do not fear," she said under her breath, turning on her horse. "Kali has a plan for us."

"Please, be our guests this evening." Suddhodana smiled. Try as she might, Angulimala could not look away from the tall, broad-shouldered king. "Sukesa," he shouted. A middle-aged man with a potbelly stepped forward. He was nothing like the well-muscled warriors all around them, but they stepped aside and gave him respectful and friendly salutes. "Feed them. Give them a good spot around your fire."

"Yes, m'lord."

Her men would remain under guard. As she wondered what her fate would be, the king dismounted and signaled them to do the same. "Your queen and I have business to discuss," he said to her men. "Come, Angulimala."

She hated being ordered like that, but there was no resisting that voice. Suddhodana led her through the camp, occasionally calling out to someone,

274

making a joke, asking about a wife or child, or issuing a brief order. As she followed, Sakyan warriors bowed to the king and stared at her.

It had been a long time since she was not in charge of things, and she didn't like the feeling. Her senses hummed with tension, and not just because she was a captive.

Kirsa. Asita had said that Kirsa would live in the Sakyan king's palace. She believed him, yet for these past three years, she had hungered for word of her daughter.

She must satisfy her hunger, but she must do it very carefully. If she revealed that she was Kirsa's mother, it could ruin everything for her daughter. The king would cast her out. Angulimala's heart beat fast. The thing she most wanted; the thing she most dreaded. The child would not recognize the bloodthirsty outlaw her mother had become.

In the tent, an oil lamp hung from a pole and another sat on the low table where two youthful pages were setting out a feast. Suddhodana waved them out without a word, and they backed away, letting down the tent flap as they exited.

She was alone with the Sakyan king.

They settled on cushions, and he took rice and venison from a great silver platter and put it in a wooden bowl. He signaled her to take food as well and began eating with good appetite. She hesitated.

"Are you afraid I'll poison you? You can see I'm eating." He leaned toward her and held out a piece of meat. "Here." His hand shook just slightly.

Ah. So he felt the same. She smiled slowly and opened her mouth, leaning in to accept his offering. A little shock as her lips brushed his fingers. Their eyes met, then mouths, then they seized each other and did not let go for a long time.

Later, they lay on a huge bed in Suddhodana's tent. Angulimala didn't know it was possible for a man to couple so many times in one night. They joined like the essence of the spirit Purusha and his lover Prakriti, elemental Nature herself; like the god Shiva and his Shakti. Nothing had prepared her for this.

He gave a long sigh. From this, she knew it was the same for him.

The single oil lamp hanging from the tent pole burned low, throwing dancing shadows over the twisted bed linens.

"You're very quiet," he said.

She must ask. She struggled to frame a question that would open a conversation about his son, some line of questioning that might possibly lead to Kirsa but would not reveal their relationship. For almost as much as she feared ruining Kirsa's life, she feared the power this man would hold over her if he knew.

She took a breath. "I was thinking about who betrayed me to you." Far from what she wanted to ask. Think, she must think.

"No one betrayed you. My eagle saw you. He told me."

"You speak to animals?" So it was true that the Sakyan royal line had powers.

"Only to the eagles. The one who found you for me was an orphaned eaglet that I found as a youth and raised at Vishramvan Palace. He is my best friend. I might say my only friend. The court is full of intrigue, and I had many enemies."

"Intrigue," Angulimala said slowly. Dangerous for Kirsa. "You have a son. Prince Siddhartha. There are tales about him. A prophecy. He will rule the world or become a great sage." She paused.

Suddhodana almost glowed. "He will do both! He is extraordinary—the court loves him, the kingdom loves him!"

A hopeful sign. "So he is not a lonely child, as you were?"

"No. That is, he has many companions among the nobles' children." He put his hands behind his head. "But does he have true friends? That is the question."

"Does he?" She held her breath.

"I would say only two."

"Two?"

"Yes. Two children that karma brought to my kingdom. A boy of about eleven, Chandaka. He is the Maghadan king's illegitimate son. King Bimbisara's legitimate son would readily poison Chandaka if he knew of his half brother. So I brought him to my court for his protection."

"A hostage?"

"No!" Suddhodana was offended. "Of course not. Bimbisara and I are allies, sworn brothers. No one knows who Chandaka really is, except me and my wife, and a courtesan."

"And Siddhartha's other friend?" She couldn't keep a little tremor out of her voice.

276

"Ah, yes, Kirsa. The granddaughter of my sister and my royal priest. A tragic tale. She is an orphan. Too long to tell now. Soon it will be dawn," Suddhodana said, leaning over her. "And we have much to discuss before then. You and I, we should be allies."

"Allies?" King Bimbisara was his ally, and Suddhodana protected the Maghadan king's son.

"Yes. I have a plan that would benefit us both."

He spoke of his idea, that she and her army would attack Kosalan travelers while letting Sakyan caravans pass. The Sakyas would grow in strength, share their wealth with Angulimala and her men.

She listened and did not speak. This time, her silence did not come from cowardice, as when her parents died, or craven failure to protect Kirsa when the Beggar King took her. This time, it would protect her child's position at court. Even more, it would prevent Suddhodana from knowing the power he held over Angulimala. He was the kind of man who would use that power for his own ends. Best if they were on equal footing, at least for the time being.

THE KING'S COMMAND

H IS ARMY IS CAMPED ALONG *the banks of Yamuna's river, in the Chedi kingdom,* the eagle said. *King Suddhodana faces not only Chedi forces, but Kosalan as well. You promised your aid. Now you must come.*

Angulimala shifted atop her horse and eyed Suddhodana's eagle, who was perched on the thick branch of a dead tree. She had learned to understand the bird's regular messages about targets she and her army might attack on the road, rich caravans of the Kosalas or their allies.

So far, the arrangement had proven profitable for both the Sakyan king and Angulimala and her army, but she did not like to be told what she must or must not do. Especially by Suddhodana. She did not like the feeling that she was in over her head with the Sakyan king. Lust was clouding her judgment.

Now that they had taken their pleasure from each other for some months, she'd become accustomed to their long nights of sex. Perhaps it was because weeks might pass between meetings, so that when they saw each other they came together like animals, both determined to win the battle, both desiring to be vanquished.

Still, he had never said she *must* attack the caravans of Kosala and its allies. Only suggested that a particularly rich one was returning from the lands beyond Gandhara, or that Sakyan merchants would profit if another clan's rice never made its destination. Her army reveled in the loot they collected. There was plenty, enough to keep for themselves and to make gifts to the poorest of the poor, who worshipped her and sheltered her outlaws in the rare times that they ran into trouble.

To face a trained fighting force, though, was something different. Angulimala had not had the strategic training true Kshatriyas received. Many of her men had, however, and had once been soldiers in the very Kosalan army that was now camped on Yamuna's banks. Talk from her troops reached her ears. They were full of desire to take part in real fighting, not the lopsided skirmishes with the mercenaries wealthy merchants hired. No matter how well-trained and numerous such opponents, the outlaws overwhelmed them and rarely lost a man. This would be like a reward to them.

The eagle stretched its wings and shook itself, then resettled. *His majesty awaits your word. When shall I tell him you will arrive in the Chedi kingdom, Angulimala?*

In good time. Angulimala raised the small waterskin strung from her woven belt, loosened the spout with great deliberation, took a measured swallow, and closed it again. *Tell his majesty I will be there in good time.*

The eagle's fierce amber eyes, so like Suddhodana's, stared, unblinking. It was almost as if the king himself were looking through them. Good. He would see Angulimala was in no hurry. The muscle in his jaw would tighten, his pupils would widen with anger at her effrontery.

He would not command her.

Except after the battle, in his tent, on that famously huge bed he took on campaign. "Just for us two, Angulimala," he said, as if anyone could believe he didn't have slave girls or courtesans or his enemies' wives and daughters on their backs there. No, he would wait for her. Then she might let him think she had obeyed his command, until she straddled him and he came into her with a roar great enough to shake the earth.

Tell his majesty I will not fail him.

The eagle swiveled its head. *He will reward you richly.*

I know. Angulimala smiled at the bird. His fierce eyes blinked once, twice, and then he took off, flapping until he caught an upward draft and soared.

Soon, my love, Suddhodana, she thought, and headed back to her encampment.

ॐ

The vultures started tearing at the Chedi and Kosalan dead before the arrows had stopped flying and the clang of swords ceased. A few Sakyas and outlaws stayed behind while their fellows chased the retreating enemy, picking their way through the bodies strewn on the field, dispatching the wounded. Angulimala's men killed not only the enemy but also their own who were too grievously injured to last much longer, while slaves carried injured Sakyas to large tents in the rear.

"After long suffering, they mostly die," said Captain Sukesa. He leaned across his horse and handed Angulimala his waterskin.

She accepted with a grateful nod. There was an oozing cut on her side where an enemy had slashed at her and would have done more damage but for the thick woven belt that held her own waterskin, which was lost in the fighting. "Thank you, Sukesa." She took one swallow. It wasn't enough, but they'd both been fighting hard. He would be thirsty, too. She handed it back.

He shook his head. "Finish it."

She raised her eyebrows. He nodded for her to go ahead, and she lifted the skin to her lips again and took several long, grateful pulls while wondering why the Sakyas wouldn't give their men a merciful death.

"They mostly die, but some live," Captain Sukesa said. Suddhodana had attached the officer to Angulimala. At first she'd been suspicious. She didn't want anyone tagging along while she fought, but during the battle he'd proven very useful, shouting to her over the uproar what the next likely tactic of the enemy and the Sakyas would be, and how to deploy her men to take the best advantage of it.

"Our surgeons have studied at the great schools in Taxila," he continued, "where the best physicians in the world come to exchange knowledge. They've brought more than one soldier back from Yama's kingdom."

"Outlaws prefer a quicker end," she said, wiping her mouth.

"I'm surprised," Sukesa said.

"Surprised? Why?"

"I wouldn't think they'd be eager to stand at the throne of the Lord of the Dead and face Yama's judgment." His lips curved in a half smile.

Angulimala gave a derisive laugh. "My men fear neither mortal nor god, not even Yama Dharmaraja."

"I see. It's only Mata-ji they fear."

Angulimala stiffened, but Sukesa was grinning. She could like this Sakyan, given time. "And well they should."

They rode back away from the field, past dejected groups of prisoners. There were Kosalan soldiers in their black and red colors and Chedi in their bright orange. Along with the troops were frightened-looking inhabitants of a few nearby villages. The women huddled with their children, their eyes red with weeping. A very young woman with a baby clutched to her breast caught Angulimala's eye and gave her a mute, pleading look filled with despair and terror. Angulimala looked away. The poor thing might survive the victors' revels. She was pretty enough to have a future, however wretched, as a slave, but a baby was too young, nothing but a burden and a nuisance to get to market where the mother would be sold. It was surprising it was still alive.

They reached the center of command and dismounted, handing the reins to slaves who would feed, water, and brush them. The massed soldiers parted as Angulimala and Sukesa made their way to the king.

"The poets will sing about this fight," Suddhodana cried to his troops from the howdah atop his white elephant. The beast raised its trunk and trumpeted as the king swung down. He landed like a dancer coming down from a graceful leap, remarkable given his size and the height of his royal mount. "When the Sakyas and the Bandit Queen's forces were outnumbered three to one, and we evened the odds in the first wave."

The soldiers of both armies cheered, then began to laugh as the king's son Nanda began to scramble out of the howdah. He was just a boy, not old enough to fight, and it was a long way down for him. His feet lost their purchase and he hung from the harness, his hands white from the effort. Sukesa rushed to help.

"No, Captain," Suddhodana said. "He'll figure it out himself." The well-trained elephant offered its trunk, and Nanda managed to step onto it, but failed to wrap an arm around it before he swayed and fell. He landed in a heap but sprang up instantly, seeking his father's eyes. Suddhodana's face was impassive. Silence reigned. Then the king gave a laugh. It had a cruel edge. All Sakyan officers standing nearby joined in with nervous chuckles, except Sukesa, who clenched his jaw. Suddhodana glanced at the captain. "Never mind," he said to Nanda. "You'll do better next time."

Nanda flushed, but straightened his shoulders. He gazed up at the king, who already seemed to have forgotten him.

"All of you, Sakyas and Angulimala's followers, fought well today," Suddhodana called out. A few cheers went up. Sakyan warriors and outlaws eyed each other. "We've won much treasure from our enemies' war chests. Enough for at least double share for each man." At this, everyone cheered. "And we've captured many cattle and slaves from the surrounding Chedi villages. Already, our priests prepare the bulls for their knives. Indra will feast tonight and so will you all. You'll all drink your fill of good Sakyan rice wine!"

"Jai! Jai! Victory to King Suddhodana!" "Victory! Jai!"

Cheering followed the king as he sauntered away through the crowd. There was a moment when Angulimala could have approached little Prince Nanda. She wondered what he could tell her of how Kirsa fared in Vishramvan Palace. As she studied him, he became aware of her scrutiny and looked up at her. The little fool froze for a moment, his eyes wide, then scampered away.

Under a full moon, Angulimala threaded her way through the feasting armies. Her men and the Sakyas mostly stayed to their own fires, which was a good thing.

Firelight glowed on sweaty faces. "Mata-ji!" her men would call when she passed. The Sakyas, if they saluted at all, did so in silence. Raucous laughter from the camp whores covered the screams of unwilling female prisoners. When a heartbroken wail pierced the din, there was a momentary lull as the soldiers and their drunken harlots looked at each other with haunted eyes. Angulimala stopped in her tracks and recoiled, certain it was the young woman who'd been holding her baby. Then a whore gave a shriek of laughter, and the feasting resumed louder than ever.

As she left camp, the sight and sound and smell of celebrating victors began to fade. With great relief she took a deep breath. Sweet, damp river air replaced the nauseating miasma of roasting meat, rice wine, and unwashed humanity mixed with the stench of rotting bodies and overflowing latrines.

Angulimala found the path to the shrine where Suddhodana's page said she would, in a spot where the forest and river met. As she followed it, a dark presence enveloped her. When she came to the clearing, there was a shrine to the Great Mother, a place where the forest tribes worshipped She who came before all other goddesses, even Kali.

Suddhodana was standing in the clearing. It pleased her that she had made him wait. He had left his hair unbound, and it tumbled over his broad shoulders. His aura flickered around him like starlight. When he saw her, he strode to her. His Maghadan sword glinted as he drew it from the jeweled scabbard at his waist and put the tip at her throat.

"Twice now you have kept the king of the Sakyas waiting." He lowered the sword, grasped her hair and yanked her head back. "Whore." He forced his tongue down her throat. She leaned into him as if in surrender, let him kiss her harder. His teeth ground against her mouth. Then he thrust her away and raised the sword to her neck again.

This was no love play. She had gone too far. The pressure of the sword's tip hurt when she tried to swallow. No use. Her mouth had gone dry. His diamond aura sparked against her red one and sent a shiver along her spine.

"Did you think to make a fool of me in front of my army by making me wait on Yamuna's banks? You will pay." He growled at her. She forced herself not to tremble.

"My love," she began, reaching out to him, but the sword tip was at the notch of her collarbone. He forced her down to her knees in front of him. Shadow hid his expression. She could only guess at it, and that frightened her more than if she could have seen it. He put the sword aside and rested the tip on the ground. The wild thought that he would strike off her head terrified and exhilarated her.

He said nothing, but what he wanted was clear. She put her hands on his narrow hips and looked up at him like a meek supplicant, or so she hoped, then undid his sash and pulled off his silken antariya.

ॐ

She lay in the crook of Suddhodana's arm with one bare leg flung over his groin, an arm over his chest. Her head rested on his breast and his heart beat slow and steady beneath his ribs.

"One more time," she said.

He laughed. "My goddess, how many times must I prove my love?"

"Once more. Who knows when we'll see each other again?"

"I would obey your slightest command, Mata-ji," he said. Angulimala rubbed herself against him with a purr. "But I confess, divine seductress, I cannot. You've emptied me." He paused. "You are Shakti to my Shiva, the Divine Energy that rouses pure primordial Consciousness and creates the universe." His tone had become serious.

"Such talk," Angulimala said, discomfited by this sudden change. "One would think you're a rishi, not the ruler of a rich kingdom."

"There are times." He sighed. "You know what it is to command." He shifted, pillowed his head in the other arm. "It's lonely... though perhaps less lonely for me than for you."

"What do you mean?"

"I have my queen."

She traced a finger across his chest. "Queen Prajapati?" Angulimala knew he had a wife, of course, but he hardly spoke of her. "I thought you told me you don't share her bed."

"Oh, I don't. But in matters of state, she's the most intelligent person at my court. She provides me with wisdom and restraint. Two qualities that I am sadly lacking." He chuckled.

Angulimala let out an incredulous laugh. She had never seen him like this, self-mocking, almost humble.

"You may laugh, but I couldn't do without her," he said, matter-of-fact. "Whereas you have no consort."

"I have no need of one," she said sharply. Angulimala found herself strangely jealous of this queen. She shifted so she was half on top of him. "And I can give you what your wife cannot."

"Ah, no more! I've already said. Besides, it's nearly dawn."

"What does that matter?"

"Today I must return to Kapilavastu and prepare for the plowing festival."

"Let someone else drive the king's plow. Little Nanda, for instance. Or Prince Siddhartha."

"It's not a joking matter," he said in exasperation. "The king must break the first furrows in the rice fields. It's an ancient tradition."

Not so ancient as sacrificing to the Great Mother, she thought. But

284

there were things she would rather ask him. "What about the heir? When does he learn to drive the plow?"

"When I'm dead and he's king." His voice was sharp. "You're always so interested in my son. If he weren't just a boy of ten, I'd think you had designs on him."

"Should I not watch him with interest? After all, he was born with the thirty-two signs of a great man on him." Angulimala ran a finger along the king's collarbone. She wanted to ask about Kirsa. Usually, she was able to steer the conversation so she learned something about her daughter's life at the palace, but at the moment she was having trouble. "Is he as potent as his father?"

Suddhodana pushed her onto her back and rolled on top of her. "Too young to tell. He's not very interested in girls. Except that one I've told you about."

"Kisa? Was that her name?" He was hard again. She didn't want things to go too fast, for him to stop talking about her child.

"Kirsa." He leaned on his elbows and nuzzled her neck.

"Oh, yes." Angulimala sighed. He nibbled at her ear. "The child whose lineage is clouded, but you took her in anyway."

"Well, what was I to do when I saw her at the courtesan's mansion? It was plain from her eyes that the story Addha told about her was true. To have the amber eyes, one has to have the Gautama blood."

"But the court, how do they treat her?" Angulimala tried to sound casual. "I mean, if her mother is not known."

"We're a civilized clan. In these cases, when the father is a noble, the child takes his caste. Except of course, if it was begotten on a tanner or chandala or some other very low occupation."

"Of course." Angulimala fell silent.

Suddhodana stopped his nuzzling and caresses and stared into darkness for a moment. Then he looked down on her. "But to tell you the truth, I don't care what the priests say about karma determining one's station in life. If I had my way in this matter, I would allow an untouchable's child to be raised up to the warrior's caste, even to a Brahmin, if they were worthy." The shadows couldn't hide the angry glint in his amber eyes. "They're mortals, just like anyone else. It disgusts me how we treat them.

Bhela thinks I'm mad, but I think all people are the same. It is their deeds that determine whether or not they are noble."

Her heart opened. A tiny, absurd hope flitted in front of her. "But... you are king... it is up to you, isn't it? I mean, the laws are your commands. If you found out this Kirsa's mother was some... some..."

"No king can win every battle," he said before she could finish. "He must pick the ones that will do his people the most good. Don't you do the same?"

"Yes. I suppose I do. I will not fight when I feel I will lose." The hope flitted and died. Then he kissed her, very tenderly, not like he'd ever kissed her before. Tenderness stirred in her, too. He mounted her, and they moved together in a way that was new to their lovemaking, passionate but gentle, breathing sighs of pleasure in each other's ears instead of the cries and groans of insatiable desire.

After, as he drew back from her, Angulimala put her arms around his neck. "You're a good man," she said, and meant it.

He rolled off her and rested his head on his arm, watching her with lids that drooped with exhaustion. "The merciless Bandit Queen thinks I'm a good man." His low laugh had a touch of contempt to it that stabbed her to the heart. Then he closed his eyes, and almost at once was asleep.

Angulimala was wide awake. What a fool she was. She had almost found herself falling in love with him. She rose, wound her antariya around her legs and put her knife in her sash, then went to gather her men.

THE PLOWING FESTIVAL

T HE ORDINARY FOLK MASSED ALONGSIDE the flooded field where the race would take place. The nobility filled the royal viewing stands, with the higher ranks seated in the first rows on roomy, cushioned benches. Among the standing crowd, many wore bright turbans or scarves to protect themselves from the sun, while servants of the royal household held white parasols over their masters. Neither was very effective against the heat.

The warriors stood waiting behind their ceremonial plows of dark metal, which were plated with silver chased in elaborate designs. While the lowly farmers must make do with wooden implements all year long, these iron blades would be put away after the single day of the plowing festival.

Kirsa wiped the sweat from her brow and shaded her eyes with her hand, scanning the approaching procession for any sign of the prince. She was afraid he wouldn't come; the rite upset him so, though he had promised not to miss the race. The plowing festival was one of the most important festivals of the year. Sakyan rice was famous. Indeed, Suddhodana's name in the common tongue meant "pure rice," reflecting the importance of the grain to the clan. It was famed for its quality and provided the foundation of Sakyan wealth. No, it would not do for Siddhartha to miss the rite.

"Don't see him, eh?" Dev, Siddhartha's cousin, gave her a satisfied smirk. He was wedged next to her a dozen rows behind the Gautama family benches. "Your precious prince is in trouble this time," he said, poking Kirsa with a stubby finger. She gritted her teeth. Surely he bathed as often as any of the royal companions should. Though a bastard son of the king's brother, Devadatta was still considered a royal Gautama, yet somehow dirt remained under his fingernails. "And where is your darling Chandaka? Maybe the two of them snuck off to your secret spot—what do you call it? The summer palace?"

Kirsa pretended she didn't hear. She would never, ever say anything to anyone about the green bower that she and Siddhartha and Chandaka had found last year, and that they stole away to whenever they could. Most especially she would never say anything to loathsome Dev. How he had found out about it, well, that was a mystery.

To distract him, she pointedly wrinkled her nose. He always smelled like the stable. His weird eyes, one dark brown and one the Gautama amber, flickered then narrowed. He needed no words to understand her meaning. The other companions liked to whisper just loud enough for him to hear that his unpleasant odor was because he had three fathers. They would snicker behind their hands that the twin horse gods and the king's brother Dhotodana had gotten dark, stocky Devadatta on his mother, a household servant of the lowest caste. No one said it to his face, however. They didn't like to fight him. Next to Siddhartha, he was the best at any of the martial arts of any boy his age, and better than some who were older.

Kirsa edged away from him until she was almost on top of the girl next to her, the daughter of a minor noble, who was half-fainting from excitement and the heat of the sun.

"Oh, Kirsa, wherever is the prince?" the girl said.

No sooner had she spoken when cheers erupted from the people lining the road to the royal rice fields. The king and the Brahmin Bhela came into view and sauntered past the stands. Retainers and pages followed, but Siddhartha was not among them.

"The king looks angry," Kirsa's neighbor continued. "Do you think they'll start without our beautiful Siddhartha?"

Kirsa bristled. This silly creature who had never exchanged a word with the prince dared to call him beautiful. She swallowed the pang of jealousy as her grandfather Bhela mounted the dais next to the field.

The crowd's impatient murmurs died. The Brahmin's face, always stern, could not be said to show particular displeasure that Siddhartha, who should have stood next to him for the blessing, was nowhere to be found.

"They're going to go on without him," the noble's daughter said with a shocked look.

"Who does that prince think he is?" someone muttered nearby.

Dev snickered. Kirsa clutched an end of her green antariya in her sweaty hands.

Everyone had waited too long in the hot sun for the rite to start, and heir or no heir, it must begin. So the king's priest raised his hands and began a chant to bless the twenty plows that stood at the field's edge decorated with the colors and crests of the noble families who sponsored them. A proud brown buffalo in a silver harness would pull each one save for the king's. Suddhodana took the reins of his white bullock's golden harness from a servant. Its horns sported silk ribbons of Sakyan blue and bright yellow.

As the chant faded away, the conch sounded. Whips cracked, and the water buffalo and white bullock lowed and bellowed as the race, if it could be called such, began. A roar of laughter went up as the warriors, mighty men in the martial arts but lacking any ordinary farmer's skill with a plow, struggled to guide their unwieldy implements through the soft mud. It was comical but also dangerous. The beasts could trample a man if he should lose his footing and fall in the slippery mud underneath the shallow water. The first time Kirsa witnessed the festival celebrating the rice-planting season, a man had been dragged underneath an animal and drowned, even though the puddles that covered the paddy were scarcely a few fingers deep.

"What a sight," Dev said with a harsh laugh. "I could drive better than any of them."

"If you were a farmer," the noble's daughter said, and she laughed. "You do smell like one!"

Several noble youths and girls seated nearby tittered. Dev's swarthy face flushed even darker. Kirsa put him out of her mind and turned to the warriors' curses and splashing. There was a hushed gasp when one almost slipped under the heavy hooves of a water buffalo, but another man pulled him out of danger. The two of them, their colorful livery smeared with clay, supported each other while the others worked their way past. The king alone seemed capable of managing his plow, even if he was as mud-splattered as any of them.

The whips cracked again and again as the beasts strained forward. The plow blades and the beasts' hooves had to churn the submerged field.

The rice would not take if the soaked earth, heavy with silt brought down from the god Himalaya's high kingdom by the monsoon rains, was not broken apart.

When real farmers performed this task, they moved with ease through the shallow water. The warriors didn't know what they were doing and they beat the animals until their ribs showed under bloody froth. More than anything, Siddhartha hated to see dumb beasts treated with such cruelty. He told Kirsa once that it was because in a previous existence he had been a bullock who had been beaten nearly to death by his master. Kirsa's grandfather Bhela disapproved of the way he talked about his former lives, saying a boy of ten couldn't possibly know such things, but she wanted to believe her prince.

Still, whether or not he had once been born as a bull, as the heir to the Sakyan throne Siddhartha must one day do his duty and drive the royal plow, so that the sweet, full grains would thrive. And he should have been at the festival that day, or he could lose favor in the people's eyes. Not everyone at court loved him, and there were others eager for a chance at the throne.

Heads turned as Chandaka appeared out of nowhere at the royal stands. As he shouldered his way through the rows of seated onlookers, they drew away from his muddy, wet clothing. He stopped briefly, squinting into the sun with an anxious expression not at all like his typical cocky grin until he caught sight of Kirsa and clambered the rest of the way, ignoring the angry stares of those he passed. When he squeezed between her and Dev, he made no attempt to exchange the usual cutting remark with Siddhartha's cousin but turned to Kirsa with a face that was pale under his sun-darkened skin. He smelled of the river and the rich mud that stuck to his antariya and legs.

"He's here," he said.

"Where?" Dev and Kirsa spoke at the same time.

"There." A few heads turned as Chandaka pointed, then more and more followed, until all onlookers were staring at the middle of the field. There was a little rise on which a venerable old rose apple tree grew. Farmers took their rest under it as they worked the paddies, and wandering saints sometimes stopped there and told stories to the peasants and their children gathered at their feet.

Today it was not any farmer or sage who sat there, but Siddhartha. Had he been sitting there all along? His legs were crossed in the lotus position, his hands resting on his knees, his head bowed. He was quite still, as if he had been meditating for a while.

"Look," someone said. "The shade is deep under that tree, but the prince—he—he—"

"He shines! It's the light of the gods!" People were gasping and pointing. Their faces filled with wonder; they murmured to each other and nodded.

Kirsa and Chandaka exchanged a look. They'd become used to it, the strange glow that sometimes surrounded him when they visited their summer palace, but never had they seen it outside the wild, mysterious heart of the royal park.

"It's a sign from Indra. He's blessing Prince Siddhartha and the rice!"

Whether or not the gods were blessing the Sakyas, Kirsa knew in every nerve that the lowing animals' suffering filled Siddhartha's heart with pain. The warriors and the king hadn't yet seen him. Muscles straining, they slogged on, whipping the animals who sank to their knees in the mud and could hardly move forward.

The king, who was somewhat ahead of the rest, reached the rose apple tree. When he caught sight of his son he halted. One by one, the other contestants halted, too.

"Siddhartha!" The king's harsh shout wafted across the water to the onlookers. The crowd quieted. All went silent.

The prince didn't move.

"Siddhartha!" Suddhodana repeated with palpable anger.

"Now he'll catch it," Dev said into Kirsa's ear, then clapped his hands once and let out a harsh laugh that insulted the hush. Several people turned to him and glared. Dev pressed his lips shut in a sullen frown.

Siddhartha raised his chin. It was impossible to make out his face at this distance. He and the king faced each other. Siddhartha spoke but no one could hear, and Suddhodana bowed his head and gave an inaudible answer.

Murmurs rose. "Is the king bowing to his son?" "It can't be." "What does it mean?"

Kirsa held her breath. What did it mean?

Then the prince stood. He put his palms together and bowed over them to his father. They exchanged some more words.

Then Suddhodana called out to the crowd. "Farmers, come forth."

Slowly, hesitantly, a few separated themselves from the onlookers and waded to the plows. Then others followed, until all the reins except for those of the king's plow had been taken from the warriors by laborers who knew what they were about.

A cheer went up when Suddhodana handed the golden reins to Siddhartha. He looked so small next to the grown men and the enormous beasts. When he gave whistles through his teeth like the farmers always did, the white bullock moved forward, without straining but strong and slow, and the farmers followed, guiding their water buffalo with ease and calling encouragement to Siddhartha.

"Well done, little lord!" "That's it; he'll do the work for you, if you let him." "Our prince knows how to take care of the clan's rice."

It was no longer a race, with suffering beasts straining under the warriors' blows, but more like a joyous parade. With each step, the animals lifted their legs high though the mud hampered them, and they tossed their heads and snorted as if to say "See how strong we are. We will make this wet clay into fertile earth for Sakyan rice."

When all the plowing teams had reached the end of their furrows, the priests heaped garlands of yellow, orange, and red marigolds meant for the victor over the white bullock's neck. Suddhodana, who had just reached the finish line, placed his hand on Siddhartha's shoulder and whispered in his ear. Then the king and the prince removed all the garlands save one and walked down the line, placing one on each brown water buffalo's neck.

The onlookers went wild. Everyone from the highest Brahmin to the lowest Shudra swarmed into the wet field. They splashed to the finish line without regard to their clothing, whether it was fine silk or threadbare cotton, which was all soon splattered with damp earth.

Even Dev had been swept up by the uproar and ran off without a backward glance, leaving Kirsa and Chandaka seated on the high bench under the hot sun. They watched the distant commotion in silence.

Then Chandaka shook his head. "I've spent almost every waking minute with him for four years now, but this... it's like nothing I've seen..." He turned to Kirsa. "Who is he?" he asked with uncharacteristic seriousness.

"He's Siddhartha," she replied, but who or what Siddhartha was, she did not know.

A FORMER LIFE

I N THE EXCITEMENT FOLLOWING THE plowing festival, rumors flew. Some said that as Prince Siddhartha meditated under the rose apple tree, he reached samadhi, the deepest state of concentration; a feat beyond the abilities of any ordinary ten-year-old. Others claimed to have seen Indra descend from his celestial city on his seven-headed horse to bow before him. No, no, said yet others. They claimed that Shiva sat with Siddhartha the whole morning, marveling at the young prince's mastery of the Lord of Yoga's disciplines. Then the Great God rode his bull Nandi alongside Siddhartha as the boy guided the king's plow.

Whatever the truth, between Bhela's questioning and interviews with the wisest sages from the Nigrodha Grove about the incident, Siddhartha had no time for Kirsa and Chandaka. Weeks passed before the three of them had a furtive, hurried moment to plan an escape to the summer palace.

The night they went, they had no trouble eluding the prince's guards and body servants. Siddhartha had removed the gold circlet and neckpiece, the marks of his rank, and all of them wore dark antariyas. They reached the secret path without incident and traveled it in silence. When they climbed up the tree's wide trunk to their green bower, they were awkward with each other. Chandaka, as usual, had wheedled a delicious feast out of one of the cooks. To Kirsa's surprise, he had also brought an oil lamp, which he lighted with a flint and hung from a limb.

"At last," Siddhartha said with a too-broad smile, "some light for our summer palace. We need it."

Not when you're with us, Kirsa thought. Maybe Chandaka had brought the lamp to reduce the glow Siddhartha gave off and make things seem somehow more ordinary.

Without speaking, they settled in a circle and opened little packets of folded leaves that held rice studded with dates and pieces of lamb. They gobbled them down, then stuffed delicate honey-soaked cakes into their mouths. It all might have been delicious if Kirsa had slowed down long enough to taste it. Every meal at Vishramvan Palace was like a grand feast at tables laden heavy with delicacies. It was getting harder and harder to remember the days when having an onion to flavor her rice made it as fine as food for the gods, days with Ma and Bapu. Their faces were fading. She let out a sigh and put aside the last little cake without finishing it.

At the same moment, Chandaka wiped his mouth with the back of his hand and said, "I'm ready for a nap."

Siddhartha burst out, "I've missed you! I can hardly say how much."

They all looked at each other, waiting for someone to say something, then Kirsa and Chandaka spoke at once.

"We missed you, too," Kirsa began.

"You haven't seen your new horse yet!" Chandaka chimed in. "He's a beauty."

The expression on Siddhartha's face quieted them.

"I want to tell you what happened," he said, glancing at each of them as he crossed his legs in the lotus pose he favored, one foot on each thigh.

Kirsa hugged her knees to her chest. She had overheard the king and queen and Grandfather Bhela talking about it. "We must have a firmer hand with him," Bhela had said. "The sages in the grove give him dangerous ideas. Remember the prophecy, your majesty. Do you want him to succeed you or to become a rootless saint with a begging bowl and walking stick?" The king had pounded on the table. "He will be both the wisest king and the wisest sage. Everyone saw what happened under the rose apple tree. Something divine surrounded him. But he took the reins of the water buffalo as a king would. I tell you, he will be both."

Kirsa hugged her knees tighter. She wanted to hear what Siddhartha had to say, but Chandaka shrugged.

"Is there something to tell?" he asked with forced lightness. He unwound the blue turban he'd lately taken to wearing, the style of some of the older courtiers, letting loose thick, straight hair that fell over his shoulders and one unruly short shock that dropped over his brow. He wadded the cloth into a cushion of sorts for his head.

"Chandaka," Siddhartha said. "If I can't tell you two, none of it matters."

"I'm sorry," Chandaka replied. He settled back on the rough planks, arranged his makeshift pillow under his head, and stared up into the leaves. "Go on. Tell us." It was plain that he wasn't sorry. He was a little scared, and so was Kirsa, that this would change their friendship. But then it occurred to her: it had changed already.

Siddhartha looked at his hands, which rested one on top of the other in his lap. "You know I didn't want to go to the festival," he said, speaking to Kirsa. "I've never liked it, but the whole kingdom counts on me to be there. Even that didn't matter as much as that I had promised you I would not miss it, and I meant to keep my word. Still, the whole night before, I couldn't sleep. Something drew me to the field, and when the third watch was almost over, I slipped out."

"You got Sabal in trouble," Chandaka said.

Siddhartha winced. "I know. He got a whipping. I couldn't prevent that, but at least after the festival, I made Father give him a gold purse and make him my guard again. And I apologized. For myself and for Father."

"Kings should never apologize," Chandaka said, yawning.

"Why shouldn't they?" Siddhartha said, but Chandaka didn't answer.

"You will, Siddhartha, when you are king," Kirsa said.

"Who knows what I'll do," Siddhartha said unhappily. "Anyway, that's a long way off. Let me finish." Kirsa nodded. "I walked to the royal rice field and settled myself under the tree and repeated the mantra Sveta taught me."

"Good old Sveta," Chandaka said, yawning again. "He's not bad for a holy man," he murmured. "Knows some good stories... what mantra did he teach you...?" He let out a long sigh and closed his eyes.

"I can't say it to anyone else. It's not like a chant or hymn from the Vedas that the Brahmins would teach us. It's just for me." Chandaka didn't reply, so Siddhartha continued. "I sat under the rose apple tree and quieted my mind. Then it was like time stopped, only it hadn't, because the sun came up, so maybe it was more like it slowed down. I saw incredible little living things, tinier than a grain of sand swarming in the air around me, and the air itself was made up of little particles of... of... I don't know what, but the particles were dancing, dancing, Kirsa!"

He seized her maimed hand and pulled it toward him. "Dancing…"

Kirsa's heart beat fast. She waited for Chandaka to laugh or mock, but he was still, his eyes closed, his chest rising and falling with even breaths.

Siddhartha smiled. "I hoped he'd fall asleep. I don't think he wants to know."

"But I do," Kirsa said, glad it would be their secret. She wanted it all to herself. They drew closer to each other and leaned against the tree trunk that rose through the center of the old wooden platform. The lamp hanging from the low bough cast leafy shadows on Siddhartha's face. "Please go on."

"I could see every animal, even insects, and I understood the purpose of every one, down to the very smallest, so small we can't see them. But they're everywhere, everywhere! They live in us and on us… Oh, it was a wonder, but it scared me."

"Little animals? Like bugs?" The idea made Kirsa squirm.

"Yes. No. I don't know. Creatures." He shook his head. "It's odd. Do you remember that teacher who came to the sacred grove? The one they call Mahavira, the Great Hero?"

Kirsa nodded. "But I wasn't with you. I was with the rishiki Saibya that day." As much as she liked to be with Siddhartha, sometimes listening to rishis and sages bored her. She often went to help Saibya, a woman wise in the healing arts, who lived in the grove and treated those too poor to afford physicians.

"That's right," he said. "Saibya says you have the healing gift."

It was a great compliment. Even the best doctors in Kapilavastu respected the rishiki. "Did she really?" Kirsa was warm all over. "But you know Saibya was once a student of Mahavira Jain. She came to doubt him."

Siddhartha picked up a shriveled leaf and twirled it by its stem. "When I heard him teach, I doubted, too. He said his followers must wear masks across their nose and mouth so as not to inhale an insect by accident and kill it. I remember Father laughed at him and said all he had to do was keep his mouth shut and no bug could get in." He paused. "But then, sitting under the rose apple tree before the plowing festival, I laughed, too, but not like Father. I saw that Mahavira's followers couldn't possibly keep from swallowing bugs because even right now, we're breathing in thousands and thousands of tiny creatures, and that every one of them is necessary for this world to exist.

"I don't know how much longer I sat there, full of wonder, until I became aware that my father's plow approached. All the sloshing and noise made a frog jump out of the paddy right next to me. Then a snake slithered up and swallowed the frog, and next a hawk swooped down and grabbed the snake and flew away with it in its beak, and high up in the sky an eagle saw the hawk and dove down and grabbed it in his talons. And all of a sudden, I could see this endless chain of the eaters and the eaten, and that this is what causes suffering for every creature, that they must eat and that they will be eaten, on and on forever the wheel of existence turns. It made me want to weep.

"All of a sudden, everything went dark. There was nothing. Nothing but dark. No sky, no paddy, no frogs or snakes or eagles or air or anything.

"And for an instant, it seemed like… oh, dear Kirsa, I don't know if this will make sense to you… it seemed like that quiet darkness was the only real thing… have you ever felt that… that everything is a dream?"

The hairs on Kirsa's neck rose. Once, as a small child, she had gone with Ma to bathe in Ganga's waters. Afterwards they lay on the bank, looking up at a gathering thunderhead, and suddenly, for one instant, the blue sky behind the towering cloud seemed to open. Beyond it was nothing but darkness that would swallow her up. "Yes," she whispered, "I… I… think I know."

"I knew you would understand," Siddhartha said. "But the moment passed."

Kirsa nodded. That day long ago, Ma had said something, taken her hand, and the darkness was gone.

"And there was Father," he continued, "shouting at me, and I looked at him, and said, 'Why are we here? Why do we make the earth and the animals and each other suffer?' And Father said, 'The gods alone know.'

"But I don't believe him. The gods don't know, either."

Kirsa sat, dumbfounded and frightened. She didn't want to think about these things. She wanted to hear something magical, but not so frightening as a vision of nothingness.

"What was that story again?" she said.

"What story?" he said.

"When you were a bull. In a past life."

"It's no story. It's true. Besides, you know it already."

"Tell it to me again."

"Once, a kind farmer was given a young bull in payment of a debt."

"That bull was you."

"See, you do know it."

"Go on," she said, looping a finger in the golden hoop earring hidden in his curls and giving it a slight tug.

"Ow, I give. I'll tell it." Kirsa leaned her head on his shoulder and he continued. "I grew to be stronger than any bullock in the land. My fame spread. A wily merchant made a bet with my kind master that I couldn't pull a hundred wagons loaded with stones. I told my master I could do it, but when they hitched me to the wagons, instead of trusting me to accomplish the task he became afraid and beat me cruelly to urge me on. I wouldn't move. So he lost the bet."

"And he didn't have a thousand gold pieces to pay the merchant. He begged your forgiveness and promised never to beat you again, and you gave it, and told him to bet twice as much that you could pull the hundred wagons."

"And then I did. Why am I bothering to tell you anything?"

"To please me," Kirsa said.

"To please you, yes. The best reason." He took her hand and she let out a contented sigh. "Of course, I pulled the wagons all the way to the capital city, where the king was building a palace. My kind master won the two thousand gold pieces and sacks of money from the grateful king, an unheard-of fortune. He used it to buy land that once belonged to other poor farmers who had been cheated by wicked landlords and merchants, and he gave it back to them."

"He was a good man."

"He was you," Siddhartha said with a sly smile.

"What? I never was a man!"

"You've been everything, from a worm to an elephant." Kirsa stared at him. "So have I. We have been together in all our lives," he said in a voice full of passion. "I have been your mother and father, and you have been mine. Do you believe me, Kirsa? Do you?" His eyes searched hers.

She wanted to believe. From the bottom of her heart, she wanted to, yet something made her hesitate. She looked away, and the moment was lost.

THE HERMITAGE

ALONE IN THE LONG, NARROW hut her men laughingly called the palace, Angulimala reclined on a pile of cushions, smoking. Earlier in the day, she had gone to an old shrine not far from the outlaws' encampment and made an offering, but it hadn't done any good. Wherever she looked, there was Kirsa's face.

The bhang was strong, but oblivion would not come. She inhaled again. The pungent smoke burned her throat, but her senses were as clear as during a fight. The smell of the pipe filled her nostrils. What was usually a faint rustle of insects in the thatch was so loud that she looked up, expecting the roof to have been eaten away. One of her guards murmured something to the other, and their laughter rolled like a wave from the doorway at the other end of the house. Their profiles were dark against the wavering orange light of the campfires. The single oil lamp cast shadows that seemed to sharpen rather than soften the outline of her charpoy and a low table against one wall.

A whisper in her ear. "Ma…"

"Kirsa," Angulimala cried out, then clamped her mouth shut.

There was a brief silence. One of the guards poked his head through the faraway door. Had the house gotten longer? She shook her head.

"Mata-ji? Did you want something?"

She couldn't see his face. Maybe he could see the way she was sprawled on these cushions and wanted to fuck her. She considered waving him to her. No, no! She didn't want him. She wanted Suddhodana, and no one else. "Go away! I'm praying."

"Yes, Mata-ji."

The thought of the king had roused her. She had no illusions that she loved him or he loved her. Their coupling was elemental; nothing to do with what she had felt for Angirasa. She could have a half dozen of her soldiers at once, and it wouldn't compare. When would blessed oblivion come? She took another long pull of the pipe. It had gone out. She threw it aside.

It had been difficult, taken a long time, but she'd mastered the ability to bury her thoughts of her daughter in a dark corner of her mind. Or she had thought so. That corner held other memories of her former lives that she did not like to revisit: the happy childhood she'd had until her parents were murdered, the miserable time as the potter's slave, the peaceful years with Angirasa and Kirsa. The sages and priests didn't know what they were talking about when they spoke of death and rebirth. The truth of it was that life might strike so hard that afterwards you were not the same person. You had died and were reborn. You did and felt things you would never have dreamed of before.

A few days ago, she and Daruk had gone out alone and had attacked a family, plain folk, not rich Brahmins or nobles but an ordinary farmer, his wife, and their daughter, who looked about ten, the age Kirsa would be now. What possessed them to attack innocents? Angulimala still wasn't sure. Daruk raised his sword to strike the child. Angulimala was paralyzed, wanted to scream "Halt!" but couldn't. The mother flung herself in front of the sword. The blow fell on her, covering the child with blood. The girl stared in disbelieving anguish at her dying mother. "Ma," she had said in a faint voice. Bizarrely, a desire to comfort the child seized Angulimala. As she knelt to put her arms around her, the girl looked at her with utter horror.

That look had enraged her. As quickly as she had wanted to comfort the girl, she wanted to kill her. She slashed the girl's throat.

Nausea brought bile to her throat as she remembered it. She had lost count of how many she'd murdered. She only killed the high-caste ones. Most rich bastards deserved it.

Not the child.

Ever since, Kirsa's six-year-old face seemed to watch her from every corner. What did the girl look like now? She would be eleven, twelve soon.

She would perhaps have had her first blood and be ready for a betrothal, even a marriage.

Mala pawed around for the pipe, stuffed some more of the bhang into it, and lit it from the lamp's flame. She sucked at it so hard she started coughing.

Footsteps sounded on the wooden stairs at the longhouse door. "You can't go in. She is praying," the guard said.

"I go in when I please."

Rohit? No. He did not come in when he pleased. It had been years since they'd slept together. She was about to shout out to send him away, but hesitated. "Let him pass," she called out. It was someone to take her mind off Kirsa, off what had happened.

"Well?" she said. As soon as he sat down next to her, she wanted him gone. What had she been thinking? They would have sex? The idea was repulsive.

One glance in his eyes said that wasn't what he was thinking either. How insulting. She swayed a little where she sat, blinked her eyes. Everything tilted a little. No, she didn't care whether he wanted her or not. A memory of the first day she and Rohit made love and he had called out her name. It made her sad for a moment, then she remembered how they lay in a passionate tangle in that little coracle and it drifted out on the river and their thrusting rocked it so hard it swamped.

Her laugh came out as a snort. He looked at the pipe and frowned. With a little snicker she held it out to him. He shook his head.

"Mala," he said. She tightened her jaw. The next time he called her that, she'd strike his head from his neck. "A Naga tribesman came with a message from Asita."

"So?" Asita. It had been so long since she'd seen him. An age. A dark age. The Age of Kali... when the dharma was forgotten... wasn't that what Asita had said? Or was it Angirasa? The thought of Kirsa's father made her sad again; no, angry with Rohit for making her think of him.

"The old yogi is at his hermitage," Rohit said. "The rains are approaching, and he's preparing his retreat. He wants to see us."

"Why?" She didn't want to see him. Why would he want to see her?

"Why not? He's our friend."

Angulimala couldn't stop swaying. She stared into the lamp's flame to steady herself. Asita had been her friend. He had helped her accept that Kirsa was better off without her mother. He and that fellow Harischandra who built Angirasa's pyre, they'd persuaded her that life in the Sakyan kingdom, the playmate of a prince, would be better for her daughter. For the first time, she wondered: Why had they tried so hard to convince her?

Her throat tightened. Tears sprang to her eyes. They had deceived her. What happened to the farmer's family wasn't her fault. It was theirs. And Daruk's. Such a thing would have been utterly unthinkable if she and Kirsa were together.

But they were not together. She had become Angulimala.

Maybe she was unfit for anything else. Maybe it was her karma, something from a past life that must flower in this one. It was meant to be, that she would become the Bandit Queen.

"We could go to the hermitage then stay a few nights at the old temple in the Forest of Bliss…"

"Oh, no. Rohit, no." She groaned and tossed the pipe down. He picked it up and knocked the burning herb onto the dirt floor, scattering little red sparks. Ridiculous to go back to the temple and the old camp where they had once been lovers. It was another lifetime. She took a deep breath. "Impossible. I promised Suddhodana we would attack that Kosalan caravan. It could be here any day."

"You used to tell the men the outlaw life was a free one. Now you do whatever your lover says." Rohit narrowed his eyes.

She looked away. Her lover. The thought of Suddhodana made her groin ache. Despite this raw lust, now and then she felt she was tiring of him and wondered if he was tiring of her.

This was troubling. He was her link to her daughter. She had learned much about his ambitions to make his son a world emperor, a Chakravartin; much that was disturbing about the Sakyan court, which had dangers from which she could not protect Kirsa.

But Kirsa was one of Prince Siddhartha's dearest companions. That was protection in itself. The boy was rumored to be exceptional. Even though he wasn't yet twelve years old, he already promised to become something great, perhaps a philosopher king like the Arya monarchs of former ages. At first, that had been enough, but lately, the desire to see Kirsa had become so strong…

302

Angulimala had murdered a child. She wouldn't be able to look Kirsa in the eye. Her daughter would see who she was, what she had done, and turn away in horror, just like the farmer's child.

She shuddered and put a hand to her breaking heart.

Rohit seemed not to notice her distress. "Is what he pays you worth it?"

"You take your share," Angulimala said bitterly. Red pulsed around her.

When they struck their bargain over a year before, Suddhodana promised he would pay her outlaws as if they were his own soldiers if they would stop attacking Sakyan caravans. Rohit had made a grand fuss about it, saying they should not be beholden to any ruler along Ganga's river.

"Tell me, do *you* think it's worth it?" she said. She was looking down a very long tunnel at Rohit. Hadn't he been sitting right next to her?

"Mala," Rohit began.

"Angulimala," she said, looking around for her sword. She had thrown it somewhere when she returned from the Devi's shrine... there it was, on the dirt floor over there... so far away. The red pulsed stronger, but her limbs were too heavy to move.

"Come, just for a day or two."

Go see Asita. Go to the old camp in the Forest of Bliss. She was the Bandit Queen, the leader of an army of hundreds of cutthroats. She had no time for sentimentality. What would her other men think?

This was ridiculous. It didn't matter what the men thought. She was Mata-ji. She could do what she wanted.

And perhaps Asita would help her. Maybe it was meant to be. "*Om, Kali...*" Then an overwhelming urge to weep seized her. Or not her, but this creature who was sitting next to Rohit in the longhouse, this creature that was her but that somehow she was now watching from somewhere outside herself. Sobs shook that one.

Rohit put his arm around that one, who let him, unable to control her wailing. Mala felt sorry for her, that creature, that Angulimala, that tender Rohit comforted.

"Mata-ji—" One of the guards appeared out of the darkness, sword drawn.

He must wonder... he would tell the others. But it didn't matter what he saw or heard. Or any of them. The one Mala watched buried her face in Rohit's shoulder.

"Go, go," Rohit commanded. He waved them away while that one cried until Mala's stomach hurt—no, it wasn't her stomach—yes, it was, it was Angulimala's stomach. Who was the watcher? Who was watched? Who was she? The sobs slowed and then ceased.

"Are you all right?" Rohit's brow was knitted with concern.

"Tomorrow. We'll go tomorrow. Now leave me."

Oblivion descended at last.

ॐ

When the two of them readied the horses early the next morning, she offered no explanations to her army. She hardly had one for herself. What had happened the night before seemed far away, unreal.

She dressed as if heading to battle, her sword and knife at her side, bow and quiver hung over the horse's withers. Around her loins she wore a thick, soft deerskin and she wound a length of white silk around her breasts. Her long, matted hair she tied back with a leather strap and a rope of white pearls, then she donned the infamous garland of bones.

"You look every inch the Bandit Queen," Rohit said so no one else could hear, "but I doubt it will impress Asita."

Angulimala pretended to ignore him, but his remark irritated her. She wasn't sure why she was taking such care to look the part of a bloodthirsty outlaw for the old yogi. Was she afraid of him? No, no. And yet.

"Send Rahu if the caravan is sighted," she growled to her chief lieutenant, a scarred outlaw everyone called Marut for his booming voice. It was as loud as the thunder of any of Indra's storm warriors and could be heard over a battle's cacophony.

"I obey, Mata-ji," Marut said. His broad forehead was wrinkled, as if he were puzzled. It made her angry. Who was he to question her? She didn't answer to anyone.

They took forest trails, avoiding the trade road, which would have been the quickest way. It was quiet, except for monkeys above in the trees and the songs of birds, and the occasional bark of a deer. Last night's disturbing events had left her heart bruised and tender, but in the dappled sunlight and cheerful forest sounds it seemed like they'd happened to someone else. It hadn't really been her who was crying. It had been the bhang. She started to almost enjoy the journey. It gave her time to consider her next step with

Suddhodana, how she could maneuver him in such a way that she would be able to see Kirsa. She winced. Of course, she must not let Kirsa see her. That much was painfully true. *But om, Kali, a glimpse, just a glimpse.* No, Black Kali would not understand. *Om, Devi, protectress of children, a glimpse, please, a glimpse.* Surely the Great Mother would understand her longing to see her daughter.

She must be very careful, though, not to ruin everything for the child.

They arrived at the hermitage late in the afternoon. The old yogi was sitting under the large banyan tree that formed the heart of the hermitage. The journey had softened something in her, and to her surprise, the sight of Asita gladdened her.

"Ah, Mala! Rohit!" She flinched a little when he called the name. He must know very well what everyone called her now. Her regalia hadn't fooled him. The girl and woman she once was still lurked inside her.

"Have you come to thatch my roof, like you used to? There's no need," Asita said. Angulimala had her second surprise as a dark-haired, slight girl of about fourteen appeared out of the platform in the tree that was the yogi's shelter. "This is Lila. She's already done a creditable job of tying the grasses. She's a good cook, too." He laughed.

Rohit raised an eyebrow. "A divine nymph for our rishi Asita?" he whispered.

Angulimala grunted. She knew better. Asita preferred men. Despite her resistance to coming, she couldn't help but smile at the familiar barking laugh. "Namaste, old man," she said. Joining her palms, she bowed to him and the girl.

Lila, who was rather pretty, bowed without saying anything. When she looked up again, their eyes met. There was a dark aura around her, and a look of one who had seen too much at an early age. Angulimala had a sudden clammy intuition that Lila knew what had happened to that farmer and his family. She didn't want Asita to know, but then, Asita knew everything. Still, he had welcomed her warmly. Before she quite knew what had happened, tears flooded her eyes. She pretended to brush away an insect to hide them.

"Namaste," Rohit said. "You look well, Asita-ji."

"I'm well taken care of." He looked fondly at Lila. "This poor child's father, an impoverished Brahmin widower, couldn't care for her. He didn't want to trust her to any of his fellow priests—ha, some of them are lewd devils—so he gave her to a merchant I know, a good man, not the sort to take advantage of a situation like that. The merchant knew that I had taken care of Ratna, and thought I could do the same for this sweet thing. I don't think she'll be a courtesan, though."

Angulimala had to agree. No patron would want those disconcerting eyes on him.

Then came another surprise. A gangly fellow, past youth but somehow not yet a man, walked out of the forest with an armful of firewood. The sacred thread of a Brahmin was looped over his left shoulder; his head looked as if it had once been shaven, but now hair of uneven length fell to his shoulders, not matted and tangled like Asita's but combed and clean.

"Just in time," Asita said, smiling with pride. "This is my student Nalaka. A very gifted one, too."

Nalaka halted. He appraised Angulimala with narrowed eyes, then raised his chin and gave her a look filled with disgust and contempt. He set his load down carefully and stacked it without bothering to offer her a bow and namaste.

A surge of anger and jealousy ran through Angulimala's veins. Twice in the past she had asked Asita for the teachings that would free her from suffering. Who was this haughty Nalaka, and how was it that this arrogant fellow deserved to sit at the yogi's feet and learn, and she had not?

"You turned me down, Mala," Asita said.

Mala jumped. He read her mind. Yes, that was one of his powers.

Because I'm Angulimala now, she thought, glaring at him. The Bandit Queen. Who has the blood of a child on my hands.

She shuddered.

"Mala?" Rohit said. "Are you all right?"

She was not all right. She was chilled and shaky as if with fever.

Asita was watching her. He knew, he knew. "Go to the river, Mala. Mother Ganga will wash it all away. You remember the path."

She nodded and without a word or glance stumbled away. She felt four pairs of eyes on her back, and one pair that burned into her.

GANGA'S WATERS

F OR HOURS SHE STAYED BY the river, but no matter how many times she plunged into the water, rose and raised her hands to the westering sun and called to the Devi, she did not feel cleansed. Not as she had as a girl. So many times she'd gone to Ganga after helping her father at the tanning pits, like the day she ran away from the tiger and her white cub and knocked Asita down. Always, even while the potter's slave, Ganga's arms had given her comfort. Evenings after she worked alongside Angirasa at the cremation grounds, washing away the ashes in the goddess's waters had given her intense pleasure. It seemed that the times she and Kirsa would bathe together, and Matsya and Matsyani would come by in their boat, and they would all talk and laugh and tell stories, had happened to another person.

She could not control the great sobs that grief tore from her. She wept for all that she'd lost. Wept that she could not feel clean. Wept, her very bones juddering within her, until the tears came no more. Her cheeks were stiff with their salt, her eyes dry and swollen.

Slowly, she dressed herself in her deerskin, wrapped the pearls in the white silk, picked up the necklace of her victims' fingers and hesitated. Then she threw it into the water. The dried-out bones floated for a moment before slipping under the surface.

Yes, Mala, let Mother Ganga carry them away. Today marks the end of grasping.

She started. It was not Kali's rough voice, but the Devi's, tender and gentle, like the voice that had soothed her when she was a girl.

Raise your sword to destroy ignorance, not to maim and kill.

"*Om,* Durga..." She looked around, expecting to see the warrior goddess riding her tiger, but there was no one, just a Presence. What could this mean? The Presence was warm, kind. Loving. Yes, loving. She cast about for the short sword with the jeweled scabbard she'd taken from a fallen warrior. It lay among some rocks at the river's edge, drops of water sparkling on its gilded hilt. It was a thing of beauty, but she must throw it into the river, too. It disappeared into the current.

Now you are ready to seek release.

She felt lighter, freer. Ready to seek moksha.

The surges of power she had so often felt those last few years were nothing compared to the warmth coursing through her now. Filled with bliss, she made her way back as the sun sank behind the trees. Dusk had settled at the hermitage when she arrived. There was no sign of Rohit or the horses. Lila, Nalaka, and Asita were seated cross-legged around a small fire. She felt a rush of tenderness toward them.

"She is evil," Nalaka was saying. "Even in Taxila they speak of Angulimala's atrocities. You should send her back to her vicious outlaws."

She halted. All warmth deserted her.

He is a fool, like all men. Only one who does not understand could say you are evil.

Kali's voice. Harsh, demanding, but full of power. Searing heat spread through her. The feeling of freedom vanished—or had she banished it?

She wanted that bliss back. "No!" she cried out. The others turned. She stepped out of the shadows. She ran to the yogi, against her will, yet compelled to do so. When she reached him, she stood uncertain.

You don't need him...

She threw herself down at his side and touched her forehead to his foot. She did need him. She needed him terribly, to help her forgive those who had wronged her and to forgive herself for those she had wronged so terribly. To help her feel clean again. To help her free herself from the suffering that had always flowed through her veins, but that until now she hadn't understood was as much a part of her as the flesh that covered her bones. Everyone suffered, she realized. It was what made mortals different from the gods. One needed to suffer in order to learn how to be free.

"Asita," she said with a tremulous voice. "Give me teachings."

The only sound was the crackling of fire. She raised her head.

Asita was smiling at her. "Sit. Eat," he said, as if he'd expected her to humble herself and beg. To him, this was nothing unexpected or out of the ordinary. He nodded at Lila, who picked up a wooden bowl filled with cold rice.

With shaking hands, she accepted the bowl from Lila and began to pick at it with her fingers, but Nalaka was glaring at her. His palpable hostility left her with no appetite. She was ashamed and embarrassed that she had shown such weakness in front of the skinny Brahmin, and at the same time angry with herself for being ashamed. She wanted to weep at the same time she wanted to snap his neck and slice off his fingers.

No. She couldn't think like that. She turned her thoughts from him. "Rohit," she began.

"Gone, as you can see," Asita said. "Open your eyes, girl."

She flushed. "Yes, but I meant, where has he gone?"

Asita shrugged. "Maybe to seek a guru of his own."

She wondered if he would have gone back to the outlaw camp. There was not much to hold him there. Rohit had only stayed for her, and she had repaid his loyalty with cruelty. "But he's always admired you," she said, filled with regret and wishing he were here. "I should go after him, bring him back." Even as she said it, she knew her true motive was selfish. She wanted Nalaka to see that someone loved her.

"He's on horseback. You'd never catch up. Besides, he isn't the one asking for teachings."

She raised her head. Her heart skipped a beat.

You have no need of the old fool's teachings. The harsh voice filled her mind.

A memory flashed before her: an attack on a caravan when the army was no more than a ragged troop. The screaming horses and the bloodied guards. The haughty Kosalan Brahmin she'd dragged from his litter, the fingers she'd chopped from his hand before disemboweling him. The dark joy when she left the man's wife alive. "What misdeed did I commit in a former life to outlive my husband?" the woman had wailed. "Kill me, kill me. My children will cast out their widowed mother."

"Throw yourself on his pyre, woman," she had said. The men she had begun to gather around her cackled and cheered.

Asita's fire crackled. She inhaled the smoke and came back to herself. Somewhere in the forest an animal screamed and a tiger's deep growl resounded. She stared into the flames. What had she become? There were so many such deeds. Her skin crawled and burned as if biting insects swarmed over her. She wanted to jump out of it, be someone else. She didn't dare think what penances might be required of her to cleanse her karma. Red danced at the edges of her vision. *But I do need Asita's wisdom, O Devi, I do,* she thought.

At the end of the meal, Asita said, "Before, you merely asked for teachings. This time you demand them. You are ready. You will join Nalaka as my pupil, Mala."

This time, when Asita spoke the name she was born with, she didn't wince.

"Namaste, Angulimala," Nalaka said with a snicker.

Instead of the joy she knew she should feel now that the old yogi had agreed to show her the path of yoga, she felt fear. She would not know as much as Nalaka. She would have to learn from him, too. But why should she? She had wisdom to share, too. Few had been through what she had experienced: seeing her own parents murdered, the gentlest man she'd ever known strung up like a dead deer's carcass, her child mutilated and stolen from her.

Then Mala knew that to follow yoga's path, she would have to relive all of that, to feel all those hideous wounds inflicted again, to face the terror and anguish, and yes, the horrors of what Angulimala had done.

She raised her eyes to meet Nalaka's. I'll show you what evil is, she thought. "Namaste," she replied, forcing herself to give him a bow over her joined palms. "Please call me Mala. Garland, it means in the sacred language, as I'm sure you know. It's the name my parents gave me."

Nalaka's gaze flickered slightly. "And who were your parents?" he asked with an edge in his voice.

He would know she had no great lineage to recite as was the custom when a student sought teachings from a guru. He was only trying to humiliate her. But Asita was no Brahmin with an ashram full of rich brahmacharins from exalted families. He knew where she came from, and he had accepted her as his pupil. Let Nalaka turn up his nose. She would show him.

"My father Talu was a tanner who lived near the village of Gauri," she said with pride.

Nalaka drew back with repugnance. Ah, he thought she was polluted. She wanted to reach over and touch him, see how he would react.

Asita was watching him carefully. Nalaka glanced at the old yogi, then looked away, frowning and biting his lip.

Guard against arrogance, her instinct said. "He was the best at his trade for miles around," Mala continued with as much gentleness as she could muster. "My mother, Sujata, was of the merchant caste, but when she refused to marry the man her father chose, her intended husband raped her. Her family disowned her, considered her no better than a whore. My father took her in, loved her, made her happy. She always told me that true nobility has nothing to do with birth." She spoke as if teaching a child. "That is my lineage. And yours?"

Nalaka flushed at this and looked sidelong at Asita, whose intent gaze clearly flustered him. "My father Bhrigu was the son of Mahendra," he mumbled. "The son of Parama," he went on, giving a string of names that Mala paid no attention to.

Nalaka wasn't as far ahead of her as she had thought. She began to relax and turned to the bowl of rice. "Eat every mouthful of grain with full awareness of what went into the food in front of you," Angirasa had always told Kirsa. "The farmer who raised it, the farmer's wife who gathered it in, the tree that gave the fuel to cook it, and divine Agni, the god of fire, for the heat of his tapas, which cooks it for you."

"This is delicious, Lila," she said. "Thank you."

"No time to waste," Asita said, looking at them both. "We begin your lessons now, Mala. Let me tell you how defilements are the stuff of awakening, and how without impurity, there can be no purification." He paused.

Nalaka looked discomfited.

Mala smiled. "Please, go on, Asita. I want to know more."

311

RIVALS

"WHAT CONNECTS ENTITY TO NONENTITY, Nalaka?" Asita asked. The yogi reclined on a pile of mildewed rags, supported by one arm, the other elbow resting on a raised knee. At ease, it would seem, but Mala knew that where the old man was concerned, appearances could deceive.

Raindrops dripped on the thatching, a steady plop-plop. The thunderous downpours had ended. This was one of the last showers of the second half of the monsoon season. It was a huge relief to come to its end. Asita's shelter, always cramped for the four of them, had become unbearable. There had been only a few days between the two great rains, not even a week to dry out and prepare for the onset of the winds from the mountains and the cold storms they brought. Five months of steady rain. Mala felt like moss was growing on her skin.

Asita said that to live in such close proximity was an excellent way to learn control of the senses and emotions. "Like Lord Shiva at his cave, we must let nothing break our concentration when we meditate or practice the poses. When we are not meditating or posed in one of the asanas, we must treat each other with patience and kindness, no matter what we feel." He issued the reminder to Nalaka frequently. It gave Mala great satisfaction that the Brahmin had more difficulty with this practice than she did, especially on those nights when Asita snored louder than usual.

"Eh, Nalaka?"

Mala held her breath, wondering what the old man would do this time. Nalaka sat with his legs crossed and his hands on his knees, staring over the hermitage into the dense wall of green on the other side of the clearing. He was mooning after Lila, who as soon as the rains began to lighten that morning had disappeared into the forest. The crowded shelter had served to inflame the Brahmin's desires for the girl, which had not been so obvious when Mala first arrived and they were all sleeping under the stars. The night before, she had once again awakened to his tossing and turning, a frequent occurrence during the past months, and lay still and quiet on the hard planks as Nalaka half rose from his narrow pallet to stare down at Lila in her sleep, giving off waves of frustrated desire. When he could bear it no more, he descended from the shelter into the pattering rain to rid himself of his lust and returned soaked. No wonder his pallet's straw was moldy. It amused Mala that after such nights, Asita would always give the teaching on the paradoxes of sex and love.

"Nalaka!" Asita reached for his walking staff and brought it down on Nalaka's shoulder with a crack. The Brahmin yelped, as crushed by Asita's wrath as he was bruised by his staff. "What is the greatest sin?" Asita growled at him. "Eh? Eh?"

Nalaka lowered his head and stared at his hands resting in his lap. "Inattention," he mumbled.

"What? What?" Asita barked at him.

"Inattention! Inattention is the greatest sin," Nalaka shouted back. Mala was taken aback to see that tears had sprung to his eyes. "'Impatience the worst crime, and imprecision the worst evil. So say the Brahmins as they build the fire altar...'" He hung his head with weary resignation. "So said my *father*..."

The grief in his voice when he said "father" struck Mala. So much pain. There was a tale there. She brushed away a twinge of empathy. Why feel sorry for one raised with the advantages of the priestly caste, the gods-on-earth?

"Three points on which even orthodox Brahmins like your father, Bhrigu, and your former guru, Valmiki, and I would agree."

Valmiki, Mala thought. Another who needed none of her sympathy.

"A good Brahmin—and there are good ones, like your father, Nalaka—focuses his full attention on the sacrifice he leads." The yogi sat up and crossed his legs, resting his hands on his thighs. "For he knows even the slightest break in concentration can ruin the sacrifice. He is patient when making the offering, be it bull or goat, so that the knife cuts clean and the animal does not suffer. And he is always precise: when he builds his fire altar in the shape of the eagle, just as our Arya ancestors have done for generations, according to exacting geometric principles; when he casts his horoscopes and divines the location of the stars with celestial mathematics; when he chants the sacred hymns exactly as he heard them from his guru, who heard them from his, and on and on back to divine Vac, who first spoke the Vedas."

In a rare moment of unspoken accord, Mala and Nalaka looked at each other and blinked. Neither of them had ever heard Asita speak of the priestly caste with such respect.

"Ha, yes, I see that look." Asita waved his finger. "What is the old man saying? That those dusty old Vedic rituals have something to offer? Well, yes, they do! It's an advantage, Nalaka, to have had that Brahmanical training. Even if one sees how hollow and meaningless the rites have become, the discipline of learning and performing them is useful." He paused. "I see your thoughts. You are thinking, Didn't old Asita teach us Lord Shiva's words: 'The enlightened person has no need of ritual'? But how many of us are enlightened? Eh? Eh? Certainly not you two!" He laughed again. "All right then," Asita said. "Back to philosophy. Now, Nalaka, what connects entity to nonentity?"

Nalaka cleared his throat and lowered his eyes, as if he was trying to think of an answer. Of late, this had been happening to the young Brahmin a lot. So much for Brahmanical discipline and training. From Lila, Mala had heard that before her arrival, Nalaka had come with the discipline for austerities but not for memorization. Asita's tutelage had shown him how to make use of such discipline to develop his mind, which with immense hard work had reached extraordinary levels. This had so impressed the old yogi that he sent Nalaka to Taxila for two years, where his pupil had dazzled great scholars and sages from many lands with his prodigious memory.

Nalaka licked his lips and began to recite a verse that Asita had taught them. A great sage of his lineage had composed it.

"The Primal Mind was alone and afraid.
'Of what am I afraid?' it asked.
'There is no one but me.'
Then it knew. 'I am afraid of my solitude.'

314

Desire not to be alone rose in the Primal Mind and searched for something to grasp.

And then, there was another, one to be desired.

Desire is the bond which binds entity to nonentity..."

Nalaka paused and looked to Asita for approval.

"Hmmph." Asita glowered at him. "You say the words, but you don't understand."

"Of course I do," Nalaka began. "The First One became two, Knowledge and Energy, the Great God Shiva and the mother of all goddesses Shakti, the male and female principles that couple eternally and create the ground—"

"Words, empty words to you." Asita knitted his white eyebrows. "Then what breaks the bond?"

For Mala, it was such an easy question, not worth a second thought, but once again Nalaka seemed stumped. His eyes kept wandering to the forest's edge. Mala sat with perfect stillness, one palm face up on top of the other in her lap, careful not to show her amusement.

"Ah, what's happened to you?" said Asita. "Why do I bother with you? Mala, what breaks the bond?"

As she prepared to answer, the clouds parted and the sun bathed the clearing in gold before a purple cloud covered it again. Shafts of light reappeared and disappeared. Mala forgot everything for a moment, enchanted by the brilliance of raindrops as the sun caught them and the play of sun and cloud.

"Some say that the conquest of desire is the fullest satisfaction and the road to highest bliss. Others say that only complete sexual consummation is truly desireless and therefore closest to Atman."

"And what do you say, eh, girl?"

"I don't know," Mala said truthfully. What she did know was that since she'd arrived here, her groin no longer ached for Suddhodana. In fact, it ached for no one. Certainly not her fellow student, whose lanky frame held no attractions. It was more than just not feeling desire. She had never felt so complete in herself, so *right* about what she was doing here, right now, her only responsibilities to do the light chores required of her at this simple hermitage, and to learn.

To learn! To take a meditative seat in emulation of the Great God and turn the third eye within. It was glorious. Sometimes she even forgot about

Kirsa, though there were days when the desire to see her daughter was so strong she couldn't sit still and roamed the forest with her bow, looking for a deer to bring back. Yet those times passed, and the strong sense of being freer than she had ever been always returned.

"Well, you'd better think about it," Asita snapped at her. She was startled. He rarely criticized her, and sometimes heaped the praise he once gave to Nalaka on her. "I don't know if you'll ever be ready." Ready? For what? She glanced at Nalaka. In his eyes she saw equal puzzlement. He shrugged his shoulders. The yogi threw his staff in their general direction. "Begone, the both of you."

They scrambled from the shelter without speaking to each other. The sun came out again, and a breeze scattered drops of water from the leaves and branches above, but the rain had stopped. Nalaka gazed with longing at the spot where Lila had disappeared earlier, then turned to the path that led to the river, let out a long sigh, and walked off with his head lowered.

Mala shook her head. Lila cared nothing for him. There was someone else. Mala had seen him one day right before the rains started, when she was returning from a hunting expedition with a brace of hares and heard the moans. A slender, well proportioned Naga youth with a tangled mop of dark hair and skin brown as wet earth had the girl pinned to a tree. The young man had his naked back to Mala as he thrust against Lila. For an instant, Mala thought it might be rape. Then the girl wrapped her legs around her lover's waist and embraced him, raising her face in rapture, her eyes closed and mouth wide.

Nalaka would be shocked if he knew. The girl had Arya blood and a Brahmin lineage but had given herself to a casteless tribesman. Mala had a suspicion Lila was pregnant. There was no sign she had had her courses for the four months they had been confined to the shelter.

She sighed. She should discuss it with Asita. What would they do with a baby here at the hermitage?

Lila did not return that evening. Nor the next, or the next.

Days turned into weeks with no sign of her. Mala almost felt sorry for Nalaka, who was convinced she'd been eaten by a tiger and grieved for her. He refused to believe Mala when she told him about the Naga youth until

Asita said it was true. "Lila is destined to be a priestess of the Nagas," he intoned. "She will learn their ancient rite and offer men to the Mother, may the gods forgive her."

Several months passed as their lessons continued. From the beginning, Mala had quickly grasped the meditative techniques Lord Shiva had devised in the misty past and Asita taught in the present. She could enter such deep concentration that Asita had to forcibly drag her from her meditations. "It's not good to do it for so long so early in your training," he said.

She also mastered the yogic power to understand all languages of man or beast. It was surprisingly easy. "The Devi gave you the gift for it," Asita said, "on the day you met the tigress. You didn't build on it until now."

Mala was proud of her successes and took pleasure in Nalaka's venomous jealousy at her swift access to deep meditative states. She in turn envied Nalaka's knowledge of the nadis, the thousands of nerves and their paths through the body.

One day, Asita decided to go to Varanasi to engage in debate with other sages. "The young these days think they're so wise. Think they know everything. The fools need someone to show them what real knowledge is."

"Wonderful!" Nalaka exclaimed. "It's been too long, Asita-ji." Then he turned to Mala. "Oh, how sad though. You'll have to stay here. *Angulimala.*" Nalaka snickered. She stiffened. He knew it was like a slap to hear him say that outlaw name. "King Prasenajit has put a price on her head. We wouldn't want to risk having someone recognize her. I'll go get my staff."

Asita nodded. "He's right." Mala gritted her teeth. "You must stay, my girl. You haven't yet fixed the nadis in your mind," Asita said. "This will be a good time to practice."

In order to fully command another being's body, animal or human or celestial, she must master this knowledge, and her failed attempts frustrated her. She gave Asita a sullen look. How was she to do this on her own while the yogi was away? How could he leave her floundering?

"Your grasp of the subject is nearly perfect, Nalaka," Asita said. Nalaka lifted his chin and shot a proud look in Mala's direction. "You will stay and drill her on the nerve channels between the heart and the mind," the yogi continued. "I will be away until tomorrow."

"I... what?" Nalaka gaped.

Mala was equally dismayed. She'd rather be alone than be there with Nalaka.

Asita walked across the clearing without a second glance. As he headed into the forest, he called out. "You've got a lot to learn from each other!" Then he disappeared.

Nalaka's mouth worked, but he was too angry to speak. He spat at her feet and glared, then stomped over to the cook fire's cold ashes. "We might as well have something to eat, now the old man is gone. I'm starving. Get some wood."

"But there's hardly any rice left. What will Asita eat tomorrow?"

"The old fool will get alms in the city."

Nalaka's disrespect shocked Mala. While Asita did not demand that they touch their foreheads to his feet or that they obey him without question, he was still their guru.

"What are you waiting for? I am senior to you. You have to do what I say when our guru isn't here." He crossed his arms."I think," he said, a slow smile spreading across his face. "I think maybe we should do what Asita says. Maybe I should show you the nadis."

"Show me?" Mala was uneasy.

"Yes. That's the trick. You will remember knowledge imparted directly to your mind."

That smile made her skin crawl. To let him so deep into the layers of consciousness she was just beginning to understand herself was dangerous. She would have few defenses against his superior knowledge once their consciousness joined. He could make her feel and do anything. He could destroy her.

But she had power, too. She would show him what it meant to be Mala, to be Angulimala. She would show him suffering and pain that he'd never dreamed of. They stared into each other's eyes. Foolish Brahmin. He didn't know what was coming.

"Well, Nalaka," she said at last. "Teach me."

Their eyes locked and then—

Shock. Her smell, Mala's smell, disgusts her—no, disgusts Nalaka. She must bathe more often. She laughs at this, then plunges into his senses, his mind, his memories.

White-peaked Dhavalagiri. He hates it. Hates the mountain goddess's

318

wild beauty. Hates his poor, rough Koli clan. Hates his strict Brahmin father, his foolish, fussing mother.

Mala sees flashes of his life. He fights everyone, everything. Fights his dharma.

This Mala understands. She fought hers, too.

Memories whirl past.

Anguish. His idolized older brother runs away to war, is killed in his first battle. Nalaka's parents grieve their lost son. Don't see that their remaining son grieves, too. He has lost father and mother, like Mala lost hers.

Passion. Kissing the woman-girl Atimaya, the Koli chief's beautiful daughter. Her body under his. "Run away with me," she says, but her passion frightens Nalaka. "Atimaya is not a suitable match," his mother says, and sends him away.

Humiliation. Studying at Valmiki's famous ashram. The other students mock his manners, his stutters over the prayers. Rage swells. He fights everyone. "You're too stupid to learn the rites," says Valmiki's prize pupil, Kapur. Later, Nalaka breaks his nose. Mala wants to cheer.

More flashes. Desperation when Valmiki casts him out of the ashram. A time of wandering, blurry, disjointed. On Varanasi's streets, urchins filch food from his alms bowl. Can't even beg. Starving. Mala knows hunger, too.

Karma brings him to Asita. For the first time, Nalaka doesn't want to fight. Yoga gives him the tools to master his anger. The hymns a Brahmin chants failed to move him; in solitary meditation, his heart and mind soar. "You are the best student I've ever had," Asita tells him, and he swells with pride.

Mala sees what Nalaka must learn.

She lets him step into her mind.

"Come," she says, "and see my pain."

She will spare him nothing.

She is loved and happy. The world shuns her as untouchable, but the Devi speaks to her.

Her parents' murder; love shattered and lost. Anguish; only a child, she can't help. She can't even speak for them. She hates herself. She deserves to be a slave.

The Devi appears again. Hope amidst hunger and misery, until she gathers her courage and escapes. A lover. What joy—a child! Then Angirasa murdered; Kirsa stolen. Where was the Devi? Hate turns to rage that blooms red. Fierce Kali gives her refuge. She offers bloody sacrifices to the dark goddess.

She kills a child. For no reason.

"Let me go," Nalaka cries. "Release me, Mala!"

You see? She wants to say to him, but her insides churn. Is it Kali she serves, or her own dark rage, her own madness?

"Let me go!"

She dives into Nalaka's mind, Nalaka's emotions.

And sees that he feels something new. Something extraordinary. He feels her pain; for the first time in his life he suffers for another.

And it humbles him.

"Let me go!"

His lesson was over. Mala tried to release him gently. Nalaka tore himself away, sprawled on the ground, weeping and clawing at the dirt. She took his hand with more tenderness than she had felt for a long time.

He raised his face. "I had no idea..."

"Nor did I. You suffered, too."

It was over; it had begun. They were brother and sister now. Spiritual siblings. Asita's children.

Gratitude to Asita rushed through her. He had shown them the road to peace.

She closed her eyes. She could see Kali dancing against her lids.

O Mala, the madness is over. You need not offer me blood or vengeance, but love and compassion for others.

She wanted to weep, to cry out, "But the darkness will always be there!" Could she keep it at bay? Such crimes she had committed. Was she any kind of a mother at all?

"Mala," Nalaka said, squeezing her hand gently. "All will be well."

"Yes," she replied, opening her eyes and smiling at him. But she was not so sure.

PART V

THE CAVE IN THE SNOWS

THE SNAKE GOD

"**D**ID I EVER TELL YOU that once I was king here?" Siddhartha asked, waving his arm to take in the tree house. They were leaning against the familiar, rough trunk. His aura was very dim that night, as if he'd been dusted with faint starlight. The shadows were too deep to see much.

"I'm nearly twelve years old. Not a child that you have to tell stories." Kirsa was sorry as soon as she said it, but she was chilled and cross, and in truth had been leery of these stories since the time he'd told her that in a previous life, Dev was her husband.

She shivered and pulled the woolen shawl closer. It was too cold to come to their hideaway. That winter had been as bad as anything she had known in the six years since she came to Kapilavastu. It had snowed several times; huge, swirling white flakes they tried to catch on their tongues. Often in the morning there was frost.

Siddhartha took off his cloak and covered them with it, then put his arm around her. "You're not twelve yet. And besides, they are not stories." He looked down at her. In the dark, his eyes were impossible to read. She couldn't tell from his voice if he was hurt.

She drew her knees up, trying to cover her frozen feet with her antariya. "I could be twelve. No one knows my birthday."

"I do. It's the same day as mine. And that's not for another month."

"How do you know the exact day I was born?" If he could explain how he knew, maybe she would believe again. At least it would change the subject from his birthday. The king and queen would hold a great feast, with princesses from every friendly kingdom, not to mention Brahmin and Kshatriya girls and the daughters of rich and influential merchants and guildsmen. The court had been buzzing about betrothals and alliances for weeks now.

He cocked his head. "You've never asked that before."

He often said they would be together. She wanted him to convince her. "I am now."

"Well, it's like all time exists at once, and I'm not me anymore. Does that make sense?"

"Not one bit."

They both smiled, then looked over to where Chandaka was sleeping on his side under a woolen cloak, his cheek resting on one hand. His breathing was steady and slow. They turned to each other again, and Siddhartha kissed her. They had done this only a few awkward times before. The cold made his lips seem even more warm and soft than those first stolen kisses.

After a few heady moments, he put a light hand on her neck. She flinched a little at his cold fingers. Her heart fluttered. Then to her shock, he touched his tongue to her lips.

"What are you doing?" she said, pushing him away.

"Oh, no." He drew away with a sigh. "Didn't you like it?"

In truth, she wasn't certain what she felt. "I don't know. I was surprised."

"Chandaka says that's how Ratna kissed him."

"Ratna kissed Chandaka?" Her exclamation broke the forest's hush.

A bird or animal rustled in the leaves above. "Shhh!" He put a finger to his lips. "I shouldn't have said anything."

"Well, you did, so now you have to say everything."

"All right." He paused. "They went to bed together," he said in a rushed whisper.

With astonishment and a bit of admiration and a little pang of something else, she wasn't sure what, Kirsa looked at the dark lump that was Chandaka asleep under his cloak, and the first question that popped into her mind was how had he afforded it? Ratna had become the most sought-after young courtesan in Kapilavastu. Her patrons were all very wealthy.

"She did it for free," Siddhartha whispered, with that uncanny way of knowing what she was going to ask before she asked it.

This was too much. "But what did Addha say?"

"Chandaka says she doesn't know." His forehead wrinkled. "I really shouldn't have told. He said you would be angry if you knew. Promise you won't say anything."

"I promise," she said, already thinking of asking Ratna about it. Why hadn't Chandaka told her? They were best friends. "And I'm not angry, except that he didn't tell me, too."

She and Siddhartha were both quiet a while. It wasn't surprising, what happened between Ratna and Chandaka. He was a couple years older and went often to visit their old friends at Addha's mansion. He had far more freedom to roam the city than Siddhartha, who was born here and would rule in Kapilavastu but was only allowed out for sacrifices and to visit the sacred grove, and then only with at least a dozen bodyguards.

Without speaking, they lay down on the planks, curling together under the wool cloak. They often lay like this, but this time she began to think of what Chandaka and Ratna must have done. Siddhartha had tried to kiss her like a man kisses a woman... no! She didn't dare think further. They were just children. "But go on," she said, putting it from her mind. "About all time existing at once."

"I will try." He turned on his side to face her. The faint glow surrounded him. His breath was warm and sweet. "It happens when I meditate for a long time. Little bubbles rise in my mind. I'll look into them and see other lives, other worlds. Then it's as if I'm not 'I' but... but... it's like something behind my eyes watches what I think of as 'me' drop away, and it sees everything, and somehow I remember it, even though 'I' am not really there. Sometimes I—that is, this watcher that's behind my eyes—can choose what to see, but sometimes the me that's right here now is there, too, and gets scared and can't."

Kirsa had trouble following. "So you could choose to see when I was born?" It was a disconcerting idea. Kirsa had gone with the rishiki Saibya several times when the wise woman was delivering babies. She recoiled from the thought that this watcher or this 'I' Siddhartha was babbling about was somehow there at the moment she appeared between her mother's legs.

"Maybe I could, but as I said, it's scary. Things go out of control. One time I looked in one of those bubbles and everything dropped away, and I was in a forest with these huge, huge animals, terrifying, taller than the tallest tree. Another time I was riding inside an enormous metal bird that was so far up in the sky, it must have been above even Indra's heavenly city."

Kirsa held her tongue. Giant animals, well, that was possible, but a metal bird?

"It sounds impossible, I know," he said. "I don't understand it—yet. Those worlds are very far away from now, from this life. Not just in time, but in space. One of the times Asita came to visit the grove, he gave a teaching about how time and space are the warp and weft on the loom of the universe. Ever since, I've seen that we're woven into this particular place and time, and if you know that, you can pull the threads or gather the fabric up somehow and move to another time and place on the loom."

Kirsa sighed. Siddhartha was fond of that skinny old yogi. Asita frightened her a little, with his barking laugh and bright blue eyes. She had slipped away, miserable about her stupidity, the day he gave that teaching about looms of space, to visit Saibya and help her tend her garden. It was that day the rishiki had said Kirsa had a healing gift. Saibya's presence had comforted her many times when palace life was cruel. Kirsa would go to her when all those princesses came for Siddhartha's twelfth birthday celebration.

"Do you see?" he asked. She didn't, but let him continue. "I think those worlds are maybe too far away on the loom. I can't control the threads... but things that happened here, between Himalaya's kingdom and Ganga's river, I can sometimes tug a strand and... and see things."

"But did you see me born? Is that how you know my birthday?"

"Not exactly, no. When I'm Siddhartha, in this life, I'm too caught in the here and now, too tightly woven into this moment's place in the fabric of time and space. But I can sense where a strand leads, back or forward, here or there. So I feel a truth."

"And that's how you know we'll be together."

"Yes. Even if I can't see it. At least, not yet."

She wished she could be so certain, but she still wasn't sure how he could be. Once, another sage visiting the grove said that everything that happened was set at the beginning of time and could not be changed, and that had made Siddhartha furious. With great fervor he had challenged the rishi, who'd said that murderer or saint, you couldn't change who you were or your destiny. Yet wasn't that what Siddhartha was saying right now? It was all so confusing.

"But some things from my past lives," he said, "I can see. It's like the fabric of the universe can fold, and I can see those parts of it, like they were happening right now. Like when I was king of the Nagas and this was one of my palaces."

At last, the story. "Tell me," she said, drawing yet closer to him. It didn't matter that she didn't understand these philosophies he so loved to think about.

"Nowadays," he began, "the Nagas walk the earth as men and sacrifice to the Great Mother, but once they were snake gods with great powers, and mortals sacrificed to them. Their good king Campeya was my father. He built a palace under the Campa River, where he lived when it was hot, and this tree house for the rains."

A thrill went up her spine as Kirsa began to lose herself in the world Siddhartha created with his words, just the way she always had. "I was a snake, too, wasn't I?"

"Yes, and we were married and much in love."

Kirsa's heart gave a funny little jump. "Ah." If only Queen Prajapati and Grandmother Pamita and Grandfather Bhela would allow them to marry in this life, but they wouldn't. No one treated her as if she were a real Gautama, though she had the unmistakable eyes. It gave her a curious empathy with Dev, this rejection, though she disliked him as much as ever. It was because of their lineages. He at least saw his mother daily even if he ignored the sad, somewhat faded concubine who spent her time dressing the hair of younger and more desirable women. No one knew Kirsa's Ma. It troubled her that Ma's face had faded in her mind, it had been so long since she'd seen her.

"All the same, though I had you and was a rich and powerful prince, I was unhappy, because even if I could take the form of a human I was still a snake god, not a mortal man, and only a mortal man can reach moksha."

Grandfather Bhela said that a person had to be born a man to attain it. She wished she could ask Bapu. She felt certain he would say something different. Because if what Grandfather said was true, Siddhartha could free himself from the round of birth and death. So could Chandaka, so could all his companions, even Dev, and she couldn't, which made her sad. "Siddhartha," she said suddenly, "do you believe girls can reach moksha?"

He hesitated a moment. "Not every girl. But not every boy, either. It's very hard. "

Too hard for her, she was certain. A tear slipped from each eye.

"When my father Campeya died, and I became king," he continued, and she let herself be carried away in the story, "I wanted very much to become truly human so I could free my soul from rebirth. I vowed to never hurt another being and never to use my divine powers to help myself, only to help other people. When I had a son who could become king after me, I would renounce my royal dharma and riches and go to a hermitage to meditate. One day, a Brahmin saw me bathing in the sun. He was a wicked man and cast a spell on me to make me his slave. To make sure the spell worked, he tortured me. Since I had taken that vow, I couldn't use my much greater powers against him."

"Didn't any of your people come to help you?"

"You did. My beautiful wife, the snake queen."

"How can a snake be beautiful?" she teased.

"To another snake she would be, silly. In our palace under the river, we had a magic mirror. Each of us could see the other one in it when we were apart. When the Brahmin kidnapped me and put me under his spell, you saw in the mirror that he was traveling around as a snake charmer and making me dance. He was getting very rich, because everyone wanted to see the fearsome king of the snakes as a slave, dancing to a charmer's flute. You took on the form of a beautiful woman—you know that in the days when the gods walked the earth, the snake people could take human form." Kirsa nodded. "And then you set out to rescue me, when a very handsome and rich young nobleman, a bit of a wastrel and scoundrel, saw you and fell in love."

"Really?" Kirsa was charmed. "Will I meet this handsome scoundrel in this life?"

Siddhartha paused. "You already have."

For a moment she was puzzled. Then she knew. "Not Chandaka!"

"Yes," Siddhartha said. His expression was unreadable. "This nobleman said he was so rich he could give you anything you wanted if you would marry him."

"How funny," Kirsa said. "Chandaka has nothing but the coins your father gives him."

"And all his food and clothing and weapons and a fine room in the palace. He could save those coins, but he gambles them away. It's his karma from that life, bearing fruit in this one."

She ignored Siddhartha's disapproving tone and smiled to herself. It was ridiculous to think of anything romantic between her best friend Chandaka and her, but still, there was a certain satisfaction to this. From the lowest kitchen maid to Bhela's haughty daughter, the palace girls who vied for Chandaka's attention would be jealous if they knew. "Did I marry him?"

"No. Would you have wanted to?" His voice was tense.

"Of course not. I was the Naga king's wife." The tale was now as real to her as the other tales he had told. "Was he angry that I wouldn't?"

"No." Siddhartha sounded relieved. "He admired your fidelity. He said he could see you were troubled, and he asked if he could help."

"He was very kind."

"I suppose he was." Siddhartha frowned a little. "So you told him everything. You both set off to find the Brahmin and me, and with a sincere heart he offered the Brahmin his whole fortune to free me, which was very good for his karma. The Brahmin let me go, and I rewarded the reformed scoundrel with bags of gold, but not too long after another gambler cheated him out of it all."

They smothered laughter. "That's Chandaka. If you know who that gambler is in this life, you could tell him so he can win it back." Siddhartha went quiet. "You do know who it is," she began, and then somehow she did, too. "It's Dev." Siddhartha nodded. Karma was strange. "But Dev hates gambling and gamblers."

Siddhartha shrugged. "Karma works in strange ways."

"But what happened to the Brahmin?"

"The Brahmin who kidnapped me and made me do his bidding was afraid I would take revenge," Siddhartha said with audible relief, "but I told him about my vow never to harm anyone. He was so grateful, his heart changed from wicked to good right then. In a future life, he would become a very great sage who lived a blameless life and won the love of a nymph, who gave him a beautiful, wise daughter. Do you know who that is?"

"Who?" Kirsa was mystified.

"Ratna."

"Truly?"

"Truly."

"And we're all connected... it makes me dizzy... And what happened to us?"

"We ruled the Nagas well and wisely and long. That life was a happy one for us."

"There are unhappy ones?"

He didn't say anything but just pulled her closer, and they curled together the way they always did, like tiger cubs, and fell asleep.

"WHEN YOU ARE READY."

"**H**E SAID IT AGAIN THIS morning." Nalaka broke the silence of their walk back to the hermitage. He was behind Mala, carrying the deer's carcass. It was thanks to her that he had transformed from a squeamish, inept hunter into a lean, tough, and skilled one. Now he liked to carry the kills he made, careless of the blood dripping over his shoulders. "I asked him when you and I were to go on our solitary retreats, and he said, 'You're not ready yet.'"

"That is strange," she said. "Because lately, he's been leaving us on our own for longer and longer to go and give teachings elsewhere. Doesn't it seem to you that's a sign he thinks we are?" In the dry season, Asita would often leave them at the hermitage while he wandered along the trade road, giving teachings wherever he chanced to rest.

Several times over the past couple years this included the Sakyan kingdom, and he had brought the news that Kirsa was well and happy. "A lovely, slender girl," he said after the last visit. "Well matched with Siddhartha."

Well matched with Siddhartha. Kirsa would be almost twelve years old now. Not too young to be at least betrothed, if not married. Noble families frequently married their children very young. The idea of her daughter marrying the prince took Mala's breath away. It eased her heart in one sense but made it ache all the more in another. But when she asked Asita if this was truly possible, he'd frowned. "A hindrance. She'd be a hindrance." Mala hadn't known what he meant by that and hadn't dared ask further.

"It's confusing," Nalaka said. "At the very same time he said we're not ready, he told me that we don't need any teacher but our own awareness."

"He said the same to me." Mala wondered what she would do without the old yogi to help her in the moments of anguish over what she'd been and done and the pain of Kirsa's absence. "He'll say things like, 'Your guru is your practice, my girl.' Sometimes I think he means that I'm ready." But truthfully, I don't know, she almost added, looking over her shoulder.

Blood dripped down Nalaka's chest and there was a smear across one cheek. He'd come a long way, she thought as she continued down the shaded path dappled only here and there with sunlight, from the first time he'd succeeded in shooting a stag. She'd made him gut it. He'd almost fainted with revulsion.

"Many rishis and yogis go on retreat when they are far less accomplished than we," said Nalaka. "You would be surprised at some of the sages I met in Taxila. They would claim to have spent a year in a cave or in the forest but were charlatans, or really had no learning at all, or sought only to use powers that they had gained through their yoga practice for questionable purposes. The last were the worst. So I don't understand why he doesn't think we're ready. Maybe there's something more to it."

"What do you mean?" Mala stopped at a fallen log and sat down. She took off the strip of white cotton she used as a headband to wipe the sweat from her brow. It was soaked. The forest provided shade but little other relief from the hot, sticky air.

Two monsoon seasons she had spent at Asita's hermitage. The third couldn't get here soon enough. The heat for the last few months had been terrible, hotter than raking the ashes at the cremation grounds in the hottest season. The cremation grounds. A memory of Angirasa and Kirsa washing the ashes away in Ganga's river pierced her. She would never learn to detach from her daughter, as Asita said she must.

He didn't know. He had never had a child. She ran the wet cotton over her sweaty neck. She should find a rishiki, one who had given birth and then renounced the life of an ordinary mother. Such a woman would understand. Mala winced inwardly. At least in part. Such a woman might not understand that Mala had been a bloodthirsty bandit.

"He's always hinting he's got a special plan for us," Nalaka said. "Then again, maybe he's become too accustomed to all this good deer meat we bring back and doesn't want to let us go." The old man would not kill any being himself, even an insect if he could help it, but when a supplicant came for his blessing or his two students offered the flesh of an animal, he accepted readily. "We holy seekers live on alms," he would say, letting out a barking laugh, "and can't refuse what's given as dana."

Mala was glad Nalaka had become such an accomplished hunter. She had lost some of her satisfaction in it, as she knew the primal instinct for survival that filled the prey's mind. Most beasts were less articulate than eagles or tigers or elephants, or even snakes, who after all had once been able to take human form, but she could still understand and feel what they felt. When she took an animal's life, she always thanked it for its sacrifice. *Om, you have given your life for others, the greatest of gifts. May you be reborn as a human who understands the oneness of all things,* was her prayer for them. *Then you may find liberation from the wheel of existence.*

Mala stood up with a grunt. "Yes, he does seem to enjoy a well-cooked hare or smoked deer meat," she said. "But he'd only need one of us to supply him with that. I'm the obvious choice, being a far superior hunter." Nalaka snorted with mock derision. "So by Indra's thousand eyes," she continued, "why would he want to keep you around?"

"Ha." Nalaka lifted his chin and grinned. "He's got to have one pupil who has mastered yoga's powers."

"And that would be you?" she snapped.

His grin faded. "Of course not... I'm sorry. I was teasing. I'm in awe of you, Mala. Truly. You overcame so many obstacles so quickly—"

"Stop," she exhaled, shutting her eyes for a moment. "It's all right." In barely two years she had come a very long way on yoga's transformative path, so simple yet so difficult. Move into stillness. Send your intelligence into every last nerve and sinew, into all your flesh and bone; let it suffuse your blood. See the body's very atoms and know they are the same stuff from which the stars are made.

She knew how to turn all her intelligence inward, knew the feeling of boundaries slipping away, and had felt in her deepest core the oneness that was yoga's goal. She hungered to feel it over and over, to lose her little self in the overarching Self, in Atman.

Asita said that this hunger was greedy, grasping, the very opposite of the detachment a yogi seeks, and she must conquer it or the ability to rest at will in profound samadhi would elude her, despite her extraordinary abilities. "You and Nalaka have special gifts," he told her. "Many aspirants spend a lifetime to come the distance you two have traveled in such a short time, especially you."

Her grasping hadn't kept her from acquiring many of the powers of an accomplished yogi. She could read minds, see objects hidden from ordinary sight, become invisible, control hunger and thirst, and had almost mastered the ability to transport herself long distances in the blink of an eye. It was very difficult for her, however, to gain sight of the past and future, and impossible for her to see her past lives. Nalaka had more facility with those skills, while from the start, she had been better than Nalaka at understanding the languages of birds and animals, and the old man said she would understand all human languages as well when she returned to the world.

When that would be, she couldn't imagine. Everyone would still see her as Angulimala and not Mala, who wanted only to be left in peace. She rubbed her temples. Sometimes she doubted if she could ever wash away the stains of her outlaw's life.

"Mala? Is something wrong?"

"No. I'm all right."

"Your face... you look so... I thought you might be angry and seeing the aura." Nalaka asked in a timid tone.

She turned and started walking. As Angulimala, she had reveled in the power she felt when the red light danced at the edges of her vision. Now she feared it. "No... don't worry. I'm fine. Really. And what you said, that my obstacles are far greater than yours, that's not true, you know." She stopped again and looked around.

Nalaka shrugged with the deer on his shoulders. Mala smiled at him.

"I remember when you couldn't even carry a haunch, you were so weak."

"And when I was so fastidious," he chuckled. "I'm much better about such things now."

"The next thing we know, you'll go back to Varanasi and become like Angirasa and Harischandra, and be Varanasi's chandala, smeared with ashes like Lord Shiva." Early in their friendship, he had described his strange encounter with the wandering king and his presence at Angirasa's death.

334

Nalaka gave a noncommittal grunt. "One day, perhaps. I don't know if I have the courage to rake the ashes."

"Courage?" Mala stopped and faced him. "No, I had love."

There was no need to say more. By now, Nalaka knew almost everything about Angirasa and Kirsa.

"To love takes courage." Nalaka looked pensive. "But let's make haste. This gift of the forest"—he shrugged again—"is beginning to smell, and the flies are flocking."

"But we still don't know. When will we be ready?" Mala asked.

"And for what," Nalaka said.

ॐ

When the rains started, Nalaka had expected a rigorous set of lessons and practices as well as more of Asita's entertaining stories of the celestials as they sheltered under the tight thatching he and Mala had done during the dry season. He had acquired a taste for the bawdy tales of Lord Shiva's amorous adventures that the yogi had always relished telling as a counterpoint to strict austerities, but as the monsoon continued, the guru seemed distracted. Days of tending to a few chores were followed by silent sitting and staring into the sheets of rain.

Nalaka began to reflect about his friendship with Mala. He would miss her when it came time to find a solitary hermitage.

That first disastrous sharing of their minds had nearly killed him. Nalaka would never forget how it had shattered him to see and feel her parents' murder, the loss of her daughter, and some of the worst of her outlaw life.

When they spoke of it after, Mala confessed she had wanted to crush Nalaka as much as he wanted to crush her. She told him she saw him as a spoiled boy who needed a brutal dose of her reality, but when she experienced his life, she emerged with an understanding of a different kind of suffering. Though he had not been through the horrors she had, his pain was as real and deep as hers.

Mala's life was a revelation to him. Prior to knowing her, he hadn't ever considered the limits placed on any woman. Even now he marveled at the enormous effort it had taken Mala to throw off the limits of her sex and caste. This alone had shocked him and forced him to think about a woman's

335

life in a way he had never done before. Mala had loved and been loved, and where that loving lived in her heart was a wound that still bled from the losses she'd suffered. When Nalaka entered her consciousness he recognized the dark hole, the aching absence, though his came from a different source.

It was a gift to him that she had felt his suffering more profoundly than he had ever allowed himself to do. Their mind-sharing transformed him. He came to see that he could never have true compassion for anyone if he did not accept his own pain.

After that, they became more than friends, even more than brother and sister. Never lovers, though. Asita taught that a yogi should not despise the body and its pleasures, but that restraint of the senses increased one's tapas, most especially during such rigorous training as they were undergoing. Besides, neither had the slightest sexual interest in the other. One day, Nalaka had blushingly confided to Mala that he remained a virgin. She had roared with laughter. "And how old are you? Twenty-seven? Twenty-eight? Well, don't worry. I've had enough sex for both of us." And that was that.

Their apprenticeship with Asita created a deep bond, but other things also drew them together. As an outcaste, Mala had never had friends among Gauri's children. "It's not too late to have a happy childhood," he told her, and when they were not practicing or listening to Asita's teachings, he showed her how to play. They made up games, imagined themselves gods, built a perch high up in a sal tree where Mala learned to talk to monkeys and Nalaka gazed into the misty past or future, trying to divine their karmas. They both recovered a sense of wonder that their suffering had stolen.

They didn't talk much about their former lives, a snippet here or there. Each had seen much of the other's, so it wasn't really necessary.

The rains seemed to make Mala reflective as well. Nalaka respected this. Asita taught them how to create mental limits to their abilities to look into the minds of others and keep others with the same skill from looking into their thoughts. "So you can live like normal people when you wish," he said. Days might pass when they didn't say a word to each other.

Then colder storms came and lashed them for some weeks. The first time it snowed, the falling white flakes mesmerized Mala. They melted almost as soon as they touched the ground, but some accumulated on leaves and branches.

"It's beautiful," Mala said. "How deep does it get in the mountains?"

Nalaka laughed. "Deeper than a man is tall!"

"One day you will see for yourself, Mala," Asita said. "You will go to Dhavalagiri for your hermitage."

"What?" Nalaka said. Somehow he had imagined he would be sent there.

"Would you really want to go to your home?" Asita said with a little cackle.

Nalaka smiled somewhat ruefully and shook his head. It was not hard for him to practice the detachment from family that Asita said was essential for true liberation. "Where will you send me?"

"The desert outside Taxila," he replied.

"When?" Nalaka and Mala asked at the same time. He sensed she was as enthralled and terrified at the thought of living in a cold, white world as he was to live in the stark, beautiful western desert.

"When you're ready," Asita answered, and said no more.

THE SWAN

"TULSI." KIRSA PINCHED A LEAF off one of the tender young plants and crushed it between her fingers. The fragrance of Vishnu's sacred herb filled her nostrils. "I love this smell best of all, Saibya-ji."

Kirsa had come to the grove to avoid watching all the beautiful girls, some as old as sixteen, some as young as ten or eleven, but all with arms loaded with bangles and eyes shaded with powdered lapis and lined with kohl. They would preen and parade for Siddhartha, but he had already told her he would have none of them. "You're the perfect age. Almost thirteen. We are well matched in so many ways. Besides, the ruby and diamond necklace was always yours, in a way. It came with you to Kapilavastu. I will put it around your neck after the race."

Yet no matter what he said, she feared he wouldn't be able to resist the wishes of the king and queen and would choose another. She wouldn't be able to bear it. So she stayed away.

"It is one of the Preserver's great gifts. Its uses?" The rishiki was kneeling next to her on the moist earth. Saibya plucked a spray and held it to her nose.

"Steeped in hot water, it makes a drink that relieves pain," Kirsa said, trying to focus on the subject at hand. "Scattering its dried leaves in the granary will keep insects away. Eaten regularly it adds years to one's life."

"But that was too easy, my dear. Even a child knows the tulsi plant." Saibya rocked to her feet and brushed off her hands. "Now, over to the ashoka tree." Kirsa and Saibya picked up their baskets full of herbs and strolled over to the tree, which was dotted with flowers the colors of the rising sun. "Tell me of its purposes."

"We make an extract from the bark to ease a woman's bleeding during her courses, a potion from its dried flowers to cure the bloody flux and to purify the blood."

"And?"

"And a paste made from the bark mixed with oil is good for the complexion."

"And?"

"And—and the paste is good for scorpion bites, too." Scorpions made her think of Dev, who could sting with a look or word. Not a week ago she'd overheard one of the queen's maids saying Prajapati wanted to betroth her to Devadatta, an idea which she was sure he found as dreadful as she.

"Kirsa?" Saibya was studying her.

"Um, we use the leaves and bark for headache."

"Very good. Did you bring an offering for the tree's nymph?"

"Yes." Glad to get Dev out of her mind, Kirsa bent to put her basket down and from under the newly plucked leaves pulled out a marigold garland. "Siddhartha's mother held on to the branch of an ashoka tree when she gave birth to him," she said, putting the garland around the base of the trunk. "Some say that he was born with his eyes open and took seven steps."

"And that he came out from under Queen Maya's rib, and that flowers rained from heaven, and the gods all appeared and bowed to him. The only thing I can believe is that flowers rained down on Maya, because she was shaking the branch of that tree and the ashoka blossoms fell around her." Saibya gave her a sharp glance. "What does Siddhartha say about all of that?"

"He says that signs and miracles and rishis flying through the air aren't as important as what we see with our own eyes. Is that what you think?"

The rishiki nodded. "He's a wise boy. But consider, the converse is also true. Even if I haven't seen something, that doesn't mean it doesn't exist. In the end, I think that there are no mysteries, really, only things we have not yet observed carefully enough to understand."

Kirsa smiled to hear Saibya, who possessed miraculous healing powers, say such a thing. Kirsa had been with her at the bedside of one who was near death and impossible to save, but Saibya effected a cure.

"But I think our lesson is done for the day. Someone's come for you."

"What? Oh." A little page was scurrying down the path that led from the grove through the great park to the palace.

"Kirsa, didi!" the boy called out. It was Raju, a very young page sent from the Malla clan's kingdom to serve at the Sakyan court. Kirsa had dried his homesick tears more than once and was quite fond of him. "The queen sent for you. The race is about to begin."

Kirsa's heart fell. It seemed she had been wrong to think no one would miss her. Maybe, she thought, some other girl had caught Siddhartha's eye, and Prajapati wanted Kirsa to see it.

"Run ahead, Raju, and tell her majesty I come."

The soft silk swished against Kirsa's legs as she hurried down the breezy passageway and out into the gardens. She had to wrap the antariya tightly, which forced her to take small, rapid steps. Queen Prajapati must know that the clothes Princess Sundari gave her were too small. A length of cloth suitable for her daughter, who was only nine while Kirsa was tall for her thirteen years, would be too narrow, no matter how long. "Why do you wear that old blue thing, Kirsa?" the queen had said yesterday, arching an eyebrow. "Didn't Sundari give you a new yellow antariya? It's very pretty. Why don't you wear it? Show some gratitude to her highness."

The yellow silk was covered with elaborate flowers of seed pearls and little chips of precious stones stitched with colorful thread, and was indeed pretty—or had been, before Sundari wiped fingers covered in curry sauce on it. The turmeric stains didn't wash out. Kirsa managed to cover them, but she had to let her knobby knees show. She was just glad it was long enough to toss an end over her shoulder and cover the small mounds of her growing breasts.

She hadn't had time to bind up her dark, thick hair, and the sun beat down on the waves that flowed heavy down her back, making her neck wet with sweat. The potential brides would no doubt have ropes of pearls braided into their tresses. She put a hand to her head. She had nothing. There was a hibiscus bush, covered with deep pink blooms. She stopped to pluck one and tucked it in her hair. As she hurried on, the pair of swans that wintered in Vishramvan Palace's park came gliding past, followed by four cygnets. They should have flown away to Brahma's sacred lake in Himalaya's kingdom to make their nest by now, but perhaps the severe cold had kept them here.

Kirsa put her palms together and bowed to the graceful birds, then began to walk along the pool's edge toward the practice fields. The swans eyed her. Sacred they might be, but they were dangerous when they felt threatened. A few months ago when the fluffy beige cygnets hatched, a gardener passed too close to the nest and the male beat him with its enormous wings. She quickened her pace and soon left the pool behind.

At the practice field, the viewing stand had been festooned with alternating strips of bright blue and yellow cloth. The shade they cast didn't dim the rich colors the watchers wore. The stiff breeze that blew from Himalaya's distant snowy peaks made the white pennants woven with the sun god's golden swastikas swirl and snap.

All heads were turned to the far end of the track as the gaily painted, undersized chariots approached. The rapid beat of ponies' hooves and the rumbling and cracking of wooden wheels grew louder. The charioteers, each dressed in the livery of the archer's family, shouted at their teams or cracked short whips. The young archers held onto their vehicles' sides, struggling to stay upright.

Kirsa shielded her eyes with her hand. Though some of the competitors were older and more experienced, Siddhartha and Chandaka were in the lead. Captain Sukesa always said that Siddhartha seemed to float rather than stand on the chariot so that it never swayed or tipped, and Chandaka had as steady a charioteer's hand as he had ever seen in one so young.

The archers let go of the sides to nock their arrows and struggled to keep their balance. The target was a regulation-size mock chariot with two life-size wooden soldiers draped in Kosalan black and red standing in it. It was fixed rather than moving, but the shot was still a difficult one. It was an exercise to prepare them for the chaos of real war. In a speeding chariot, an archer had to calculate a trajectory and shoot up into the sky, not straight at the target, because of the danger of hitting one of the other racers.

Dev was driving the chariot close behind Chandaka and Siddhartha for Prince Nanda, who swayed as he tried to nock an arrow in his bow. Everyone knew that Dev felt it beneath him to serve as his cousin Nanda's charioteer. He was one of the finest archers of all Siddhartha's companions, almost as good as Siddhartha, who was the best and who said Dev deserved a chariot and charioteer of his own.

Nanda was Prajapati and Suddhodana's legitimate son, though, while Devadatta was a bastard by the king's brother Dhotodana. Unlike Siddhartha and Chandaka, they seemed to work against each other. Just as Nanda drew his bow, Dev, his face a grim mask, flicked his whip, urging his team forward. The ponies jerked ahead, causing Nanda to stagger, grip the chariot's side, and shout at Dev, who bared his teeth and lashed again.

At that moment, Siddhartha loosed his arrow and it rose in a great arc. The crowd looked up as one, following its arc, and a great "Ah!" rose when it plummeted down and struck a wooden Kosalan high in the left breast, its feathered end angled up at the sky.

The competitors loosed a half dozen other arrows. Only two even struck the fixed chariot; no other hit a wooden warrior. Kirsa followed Nanda's arrow until it thudded into the grassy earth a few feet away from the target. Chandaka drove past the finish line followed by Dev, and soon all the teams had slowed to a stop. Charioteers and archers dismounted and stable boys hurried forward to unhitch the vehicles and lead the sweating ponies away.

The competitors milled about, laughing and clapping each other on the back, all except Nanda, who slumped his shoulders and kept his eyes on the ground, and Dev, who looked more grim and furious than ever. Kirsa waited in agony. Now was the time Siddhartha would choose.

When the congratulations were over, Siddhartha searched the stands with a furrowed brow. Her heart dropped to her feet. He knew she hadn't planned to come, that she was going to the grove. Who was he looking for? A sea of slender arms covered with golden bracelets waved at him, and soon most of the hopeful girls had left their benches and flowed onto the field, surrounding him like a flock of many-colored chattering parakeets. He edged away, still scanning the crowd, until Chandaka poked him and pointed in Kirsa's direction.

When their eyes met, his face broke into a wide smile. She almost fainted with relief and happiness. She shouldn't smile back. If the queen saw... but how could she help herself? His father and the queen would never let them marry, but in this one moment everyone would see which girl Prince Siddhartha wanted. She had never felt anything like the surge of confidence that pulsed through her. She tossed her hair back from her shoulder and smoothed the yellow silk. It might be stained and small, but it matched the golden flecks in her amber eyes and flattered her warm brown skin, not so dark as Ma's was, but still darker than most Sakyas.

"Son!"

"Siddhartha!" The king and queen called to him simultaneously.

He ignored them. He slung his quiver and bow over his shoulder and pushed his way through the pack of prospective brides, whose chattering died as he hurried toward Kirsa. Whispers ran through the crowd. "Do you see?" "He disobeys his father!" "The queen looks furious."

"Did you see my arrow?" He reached her, breathless.

Kirsa couldn't speak for joy and fear but smiled and nodded, shaking with nervous happiness. He often said he didn't care about these contests, but he was always pleased when he won, as if it was a surprise. Out of the corner of her eye she saw the king and queen approaching, Suddhodana's mouth set, the queen's face livid. "Their majesties," she managed to whisper.

He walked up to the king and queen and bowed over his joined palms. "I choose Kirsa."

The king's eyes blazed. He furrowed his brow in a deep frown. He cleared his throat and opened his mouth, but Queen Prajapati put a hand on his arm. Her jaw worked, but she said nothing. Kirsa quailed before them.

Ignoring their majesties' fury, Siddhartha reached into his sash for a little sack. "Hold still." He pulled out the glittering garland of rubies and diamonds, the necklace Harischandra had brought Addhakashi and that the courtesan had returned—somewhat reluctantly—to the Sakyan king, from whom Kirsa's father had stolen it. Her prince hung it around Kirsa's neck. The gems felt cold and sharp. She wondered what Bapu would think to see it around his daughter's neck. Her throat tightened.

The deed was done. Now was the moment for the king and queen to acknowledge the prince's choice, but they said nothing. Whispers rose from the gathered nobles. Everyone's eyes were on her, as hard and cold as the necklace's gems. She wanted to disappear. The only thing she could think to do was bow over her joined palms.

When she looked up, the king's blazing eyes had cooled somewhat. He lifted his chin, looked from his son to her and back again and gave a slight shake of his head. "What is to be done?"

The queen's face had grown harder. "We will discuss it later." Then their majesties began to walk back toward the palace. Siddhartha took Kirsa's hand. She clutched at it as they fell in behind the courtiers and invited guests. Queen Prajapati glanced over her shoulder, and though their glance met only for a moment, Kirsa held her breath. Then she straightened her shoulders and lifted her chin, but Prajapati had already turned away.

Kirsa and Siddhartha walked in silence while all around, excited young people joked and laughed and talked of the race and the finer points of this archer or that, or how well Chandaka drove, or whether Dev could have won if he'd given his team their head and not used the whip.

Chandaka, who had been the center of a bevy of cooing females, elbowed up to Siddhartha's side. "If you don't want any of them, there are a few I'd gladly take," he said behind his hand but loud enough for everyone to hear. "See that Licchavi girl?" He looked over his shoulder. "Breasts like great cushions!"

Good-natured and lascivious laughter erupted, including from the blushing young Licchavi. Kirsa went hot and bit her lip. She was more comfortable with the modest style of attire that Saibya favored. She could not do as others girls her age did and go naked above the waist, covered only by an opaque shawl of fine Varanasi muslin, a fashion that Addha and Ratna had brought to Kapilavastu. The Licchavi's shawl was so transparent she might as well not have been wearing anything. Kirsa glanced sidelong at these fashionable beauties all around her, the flashing jewels at nostril or navel, ringed fingers and toes, elaborately coiled hair shiny with fragrant oil. She touched the necklace and realized it must look silly with her stained yellow silk. The short spurt of confidence she'd felt earlier fled.

The noisy crowd had reached the path that circled the round lotus pool. Queen Prajapati led the older guests on, waving a hand and smiling as she responded to some admiring remark by one of the visiting nobles. "We enlarged a natural spring," she was saying, "and lined it with rock from Rohini's river, which supplies my gardens with water in the summer." She continued with some technical discussion of the engineering required, to the clear amazement of her listener, who perhaps didn't know that Queen Prajapati was the cleverest woman in the Sixteen Kingdoms. That made her all the more intimidating to Kirsa.

The royal party moved on while the young people stopped to watch the Licchavi girl walk up to the water, swaying her hips. "Oh, how adorable," she said as she knelt, pointing to a fluffy little cygnet paddling alone around the lily pads.

"You shouldn't get so close." Dev walked up, sweaty and surly. He pointed toward the adult swans that were leading the rest of their offspring away in a rapid glide, unaware that one of the brood was so close to a human. "They can be vicious when protecting their young."

"Nonsense," said the Licchavi. "Surely they know I'm no danger to this little thing. Look, it's swimming right up to me." She posed herself on a flat rock that angled out over the water and smoothed her emerald green antariya. She looked over her shoulder at Siddhartha and Chandaka and fluttered her eyelashes, then looked back at the cygnet and reached a hand toward it. The rock tilted, and she slid into the water with a splash and a shriek.

Titters rose as the Licchavi managed to stand. Kirsa suppressed the urge to join the laughter at the foolish girl, telling herself the poor thing might be hurt. The water came up to the girl's round breasts, which were perfectly visible now under the soaked muslin. She tried to raise her arms in a comical attempt to free them from a tangle of lily pads, and the muddy bottom and lily roots hindered her attempts to move back to the rocks. The cygnet gave soft, rapid croaks and hisses and swam around in little circles.

On the far side of the pool, the swans became aware of the noise and saw their stray cygnet. The male began to half-glide, half-fly toward the girl, its loud hiss audible even from a distance. Chandaka rushed to the water's edge as Siddhartha dropped his quiver and bow and followed. The pool had always seemed so wide to Kirsa, almost like a lake, but the swan covered it in a flash and was upon the Licchavi and her two would-be rescuers, wings beating and jabbing at them with its beak. Chandaka was lying flat on his stomach on the rock, ducking then holding out his arm and calling to the girl to grab his hand, but she just shrieked louder. She tried to cover her face with her arms, on which the swan's beak had already made bloody gashes. Siddhartha lowered himself into the water and moved toward her, an arm raised to cover his head against the beating wings.

By now, the royal party had realized something was wrong. An archer and spearman from the guard came running but stood perplexed as to how to help without injuring one of the boys or the terrified girl.

Then at Kirsa's ear there was a *fffft*, and an arrow flew between Siddhartha and Chandaka and struck the swan's wing. She turned in alarm to see Dev lower Siddhartha's bow with a proud smile on his lips. "No one else dared," he murmured to himself.

The bird hissed and croaked in panic as it floundered. Red blood stained its white feathers, and its wings beat more as it attempted to turn around. Chandaka managed to grab the Licchavi and pull her out of the water, soaked, covered with mud and blood and torn lily roots and weeping hysterically. Siddhartha swam toward the bleeding swan, which had managed to head into deeper water, the cygnet paddling at its side. The male flapped and hissed but its struggles were becoming more and more feeble. The prince treaded water until the poor creature's neck drooped and it looked about to drown. At this point, Siddhartha swam in close, and wrapping an arm around the bird, swam back to the pool's edge.

"Devadatta!" King Suddhodana's shout made Kirsa's bones vibrate. "You could have killed Siddhartha!" Suddhodana was white with rage as he strode up to Dev, who was holding the bow Siddhartha had dropped when he went to help the Licchavi. He seized Dev's arm. "What were you thinking? I will have you whipped."

No one made a sound, except the mother swan and her cygnets on the pool's far side, who honked and whistled in distress.

Dev was white, too, and trembling, but he raised his chin and looked the king in the eye. "I was—was sure of my aim, Uncle."

"You've killed Brahma's sacred swan, Devadatta." Grandfather Bhela had pushed through the crowd and drawn himself up to his full height, which was equal to the king's. "This is a great stain on your karma." Dev paled a little more.

"Dev! You saved that poor girl," Siddhartha called out. He sat on a rock by the water, the enormous swan in his lap, its blood ruby red on snowy white feathers. Its chest rose and fell with its rapid breaths.

The Licchavi's hysterical sobs had calmed, though she was still shaking. She was leaning on Chandaka, who had his arm around her and was saying something in low, soothing tones. She looked up at him with wide, damp eyes, a trembling smile on her lips.

The king and Bhela exchanged a look.

"It's not Dev's fault," Siddhartha insisted, and Kirsa felt he was right. "He did it to save a life. And it's just an ordinary swan, not the true mount of Brahma or his wife Sarasvati. And Bhela-ji, the swan isn't dead. If Kirsa and I save it, won't that lessen the stain?"

DEVADATTA

F OR TWO DAYS KIRSA AND Siddhartha nursed the swan. It gave Kirsa
more joy than the gift of the ruby and diamond necklace, which in
any case the queen had ordered returned to the royal treasury after
the birthday celebration "for safekeeping."

Or so she said.

Kirsa didn't care about the necklace. She wanted this to go on forever,
tending sick and injured beings with Siddhartha. His hands were as gentle
and healing as Saibya's. By the third day the swan returned to the lotus
pool, not yet able to use its wing but well enough to glide about with its
mate and offspring.

Then Kirsa could no longer ignore the rising flood of court gossip and
politics that she barely understood, and her bliss washed away.

Suddhodana had sent Dev to the Nigrodha Grove to serve the sages
and meditate on his shocking deed. The court whispered that the king was
foolishly hoping Dev's absence would make everyone forget the matter,
but the Council of Brahmins would have none of that. They declared that
Devadatta must make the appropriate sacrifices and penances to deflect the
god Brahma's anger, and they needed three days to prepare to debate just
which penances and offerings at the eagle altar those would be. The joke
that passed through the palace and city was that three days were needed for
the priests to study which rituals might provide them with the largest fees.

As usual, the king grumbled about costly Vedic sacrifices draining
the royal treasury at a time when the Kosalas threatened Sakyan borders,
while the queen insisted they must listen to the Brahmins. "Time to start

worshipping Shiva, who doesn't demand ritual observances," he was overheard muttering. "No, the Lord of Yoga only demands perfect self-knowledge," the queen had retorted, "which you do not possess." The courtier who had eavesdropped on this conversation whispered it in strictest confidence to a member of the Council of Brahmins, and there was no stopping its spread. Their majesties' respective factions magnified the conjugal squabble into a raging controversy. Meanwhile, Siddhartha's steady if not vigorous defense of Dev's actions mystified everyone, including Kirsa and Chandaka.

"He saved a life," Siddhartha had dared say to Bhela. "And Kirsa and I saved the swan. We dedicate our merit for doing so to Dev"—this was not Kirsa's idea—"and there is no imbalance in the cosmic order. Sacrifice might not be needed."

The Council of Brahmins convened on the fourth day. Even to Kirsa, the matter seemed about something more than Dev shooting the swan, but she didn't understand what. She had decided she would find Chandaka, who hadn't bothered to hide his contempt about the whole swan affair, and go to the tree house, but he was flirting with the kitchen maids and ignored her. She could have gone to the grove, but something drew her to the council. She arrived late and stood at the western portal of the great hall. The panels of the high roof had been drawn back, and a draft cooled her warm forehead and blew a loose strand of hair that tickled her cheek.

Sun poured through the wide opening. Gold and jewels flashed as courtiers shifted on the bright cushions laid out in neat rows over the flagstones. The white-robed Brahmins sat in a circle in front of the king's dais, from which the king and queen watched the proceedings, seated cross-legged on low, wide mahogany thrones. Prajapati was intent. Suddhodana slumped against his throne's carved back. Siddhartha sat at their feet, looking miserable.

After all the uproar that preceded the council's meeting, there was no real argument, no lively debate. All the priests agreed that Dev must be punished. The disagreements centered on obscure points of Vedic practice. Bhela, who as the king's priest was the moderator, sat quiet and immobile, his face a mask.

The court's disappointment at the lack of spectacle was palpable and the king was bored. So he sent the page Raju to the grove to fetch one or two sages to add some spice, as well as to order Dev, who should have presented himself by now, to appear. That he had not showed shocking disrespect for the Council of Brahmins.

No sooner had Raju run off than things turned more interesting.

The old Brahmin Vikram seized the arm of a priest of middling rank who had dared to yawn. The senile Vikram, whose days as a prodigious scholar were long past, burst into an unintelligible harangue. Most ignored him until the old man let out a thundering shout.

"I know how we should punish young Devadatta, you simpering fool." He sprayed spittle over his captive's face. "It's high time we bring back the glorious ancient rite of human sacrifice!" This remark silenced everyone. Eyes bulging, he raved on about the former glory of Vedic ritual that was now in the hands of a generation of half-witted Brahmins who didn't know the hymns any better than they knew their own asses. "And you dare yawn as if the gods didn't see you. The Sakyas have become degenerates!"

Vikram continued to rant, still grasping the other Brahmin, who turned to Bhela with a pleading expression.

"O learned Vikram," Grandfather Bhela intoned in his deep, vibrant voice that commanded everyone's attention like the sounding of a gong.

Vikram stopped and looked around as if he'd just awakened. He released his captive and scratched at his thin topknot. "Times have changed, times have changed." Then he sighed and shook his head. "What was I saying?"

"We bow to your wisdom," Bhela continued in soothing tones. "Now let others speak."

Near Kirsa, a young Brahmin whispered to a fresh-faced warrior. "Human sacrifice. The most interesting idea this whole day. A pity no one takes the old man seriously."

"What?" The warrior feigned surprise. "I'm shocked, simply shocked, my friend. You of all people know the Aryas gave up such barbaric practices too many generations ago to count."

"Yes, but if you're going to revive the custom, that surly, misbegotten Dev is as good a victim to offer as anyone." They both smirked.

Kirsa was appalled. They were joking about offering the life of a youth of twelve, hardly more than a boy, on the sacrificial altar. Saibya sometimes said the Sakyas had let their liberality get out of hand.

There was a slap of sandaled feet behind her. The page Raju rushed up. "Kirsa, didi, what should I do? No one would come!"

At that moment, Suddhodana caught sight of the boy. "Come, child," he said. Brahmins and courtiers all turned and stared. Raju looked like he would faint. "Come, come."

"It will be all right," Kirsa said, though she was none too sure, given Suddhodana's infamous temper. With a gentle hand she urged Raju on. He stumbled up to the dais and fell to his knees, bowing to the ground.

"Speak, my boy," Suddhodana said with clear impatience despite his smile.

Raju sat back on his heels. "The sages were all at their meditations, my lord, and Sa—Saibya-ji had just received a message," he said, hanging his head and twisting his hands. "She—she was called to the Houses of Healing. A fever has broken out among the sick…"

"This is what you get, my lord," the queen said, "for touching your forehead to the feet of these radicals. They have no respect for tradition, for the Vedas—"

"Now, now, my dear." Suddhodana smiled again. "It is a long tradition among us Sakyas that no sage should be disturbed at his meditations."

"Saibya is not meditating," the queen said. Two red blotches appeared on her cheeks. "It does not offend you, my lord, that she ignores your summons to treat outcastes?"

The king and queen stared at one another.

"Aunt," Siddhartha said. "Saibya-ji is doing *your* bidding. She has gone to the Houses of Healing, which you so generously support."

Her beloved nephew's words did not have their usual softening effect on the queen, but they emboldened Raju. "Saibya-ji said th-that she thought it no sin to shoot a swan," he said in a rush.

"What effrontery," the queen began. Raju ducked as if anticipating a blow, but just then Siddhartha's jaw fell open.

"Look," he said, pointing at the doorway. The king's eyes widened, Bhela's unreadable mask turned into a scowl, and the queen put a hand to her mouth. The assembly fell silent. Two sages in white dhotis walked up to the western doorway. One was the magician Kshanta. When she recognized the other, Kirsa let out a gasp.

Dev had cut off his thick warrior's braid and shaved his skull clean. He wore the white dhoti of a wandering mendicant as if born to it and carried a sturdy staff. He had a sling over his shoulder in which he had tied his begging bowl, the only other possession allowed a holy seeker. Dev's staff clacked on the flagstones as he strode across the great hall. Kshanta waited at Kirsa's side, giving her a lascivious grin.

Kirsa edged away. No female, no matter how young or old, was safe around this man. A rishi of very poor reputation, he claimed to cure women of barrenness with his spells, but everyone said his success in these cures had less to do with magic and more to do with seducing naïve and unhappy wives. He had been at the grove for a few months and was one of the reasons Saibya said the Sakyas were too liberal.

When Dev reached the dais, he planted his bare feet wide and thrust out his chest. Everyone waited for him to bow, but he did not. The king was grim, the queen furious. His boldness stunned Kirsa. Not only that, but he exuded a new charisma, not as great as Suddhodana's but equal to Siddhartha's. Where their auras were radiant, however, Dev seemed to darken the light pouring through the open roof. It was as though a shadow clung to him.

No one said a word. At last, he broke the silence. "Uncle." His voice caught a little. He cleared his throat. "My king. After I—I shot the swan, you sent me to the grove to meditate while old men who—who..." He seemed to shrink a little but then recovered. "Old men who possess much knowledge of the Vedas but no wisdom prepared to decide my fate."

The assembly erupted in shouts, but he raised his staff and brought it down on the stone floor with a crack that silenced the hall. He gave a quick look over his shoulder at Kshanta, nodded. The Brahmins stared at Dev, aghast.

"I went there in all humility," he said.

"Humility, indeed," the young Brahmin near Kirsa muttered, inducing a little titter from his neighbors. Kshanta swiveled his head, looking around with a fierce glare. The titters died instantly. The magician fixed narrowed eyes on the Brahmin, who paled a little. Kirsa's hackles rose. She tried to catch Siddhartha's eye, but with mouth agape he stared at Dev.

"As I sat alone, examining my heart, I was at first troubled." Dev's voice trembled but carried over the hall and up through the roof to the listening sky. "I—I prayed for guidance. Neither Brahma nor any other celestial sent a sign."

"That is because you need us priests, who understand how to speak to the gods," Bhela said. "They hear only when prayers are sent to them on the sacrificial fire's smoke."

"But I sought guidance from the wise sages and yogis that you, O king, in your generosity and in your quest for truth, have assembled in the Nigrodha Grove." Dev eyed Bhela, who scowled, but Suddhodana looked pleased. "It came to me, as I sat alone, that I must not endanger the clan. I must find out for myself what the gods wanted." He paused and swallowed, glancing over his shoulder again. Kshanta nodded once more. "I have come to bid farewell."

Everyone looked astonished. "What arrogance!" Bhela exploded.

"Come now, Bhela, he's just a boy," Suddhodana said. "You are very young, Devadatta. What will my brother—your father—say when he comes back with his troops from defending our borders and finds his son gone?"

"My father," Dev's mouth twisted, "will hardly miss me. Nor will you, Uncle, or anyone at this court."

For all Kirsa's dislike of Dev, pity stabbed at her. Oh, a few troublemakers at court would miss him, not for himself but as a pawn. A bastard he might be, but also by blood a possible pretender to the throne. Suddhodana's expression said that despite his words, he wouldn't be sorry if Dev left. One less Gautama to challenge his rule when the time came.

Siddhartha unfolded his legs and stood up, eye to eye with Dev. "I envy you, cousin," he said.

Kirsa's heart skipped a beat. Suddhodana looked as if he'd been struck. Prajapati exchanged an alarmed glance with Bhela.

"It was prophesied that you would become the greatest sage to have ever lived. Cousin." A smile touched Dev's lips, but his eyes were hard. "Would you dare take this path?"

Suddhodana jumped up. "It was prophesied that he would rule," he said.

Dev was very pale. A third time he glanced back at Kshanta. The look between them gave off such dark energy that everyone involuntarily shrank away from the magician. "I will achieve what you do not dare," Dev said, turning back to Siddhartha. Then he addressed the assembly. "And perhaps it is I who will be the greatest sage. Or the greatest king. Or both!"

The king was livid. "Your insolence has gone too far," he said, hoarse with fury.

The whole assembly was frozen. The royal guards looked ready to seize

Dev at the king's command. "Begone!" Suddhodana managed to shout at last.

The assembly held its breath. Dev turned and looked at Kshanta, nostrils quivering and jaw clenched. His amber eye blazed and a little glint of red glowed at the center of his dark one. At some unseen signal from Kshanta, he brought down the staff once, twice, a third time.

There was a searing flash of light. Kirsa squeezed her eyes shut. When she opened them, everyone around her was rubbing their eyes.

"I can't see." "Nor I." "I'm blind! I'm blind." Panicky cries rose around her.

"Look," the young Brahmin said. "They're gone!"

Dev and the magician had disappeared.

"I AM READY."

T HE MONSOON ENDED, AND THE cool, dry weather lingered. Asita set off to give teachings along Ganga's banks, leaving Mala and Nalaka on their own. To prepare for their solitary times, they decided they would challenge themselves at "retreats" nearby in the forest, where they would go alone to deepen their practices, returning to the hermitage after a few days to compare their experiences and learn from each other.

Mala had found a clearing with an ancient stone pillar sunk into the earth at an angle, the linga of the god the Nagas called Rudra, who Asita insisted was none other than Lord Shiva, the Great God, in the guise in which the Aryas first met him. Nearby was a worn flat rock with a faint depression in its center, the yoni of the Mother, whom the Aryas worshipped as the Devi. Both stones had the familiar dark stains, dirt or moss or the vestiges of the human blood spilled over them long ago. It was one of those old shrines to the Great Goddess she often came upon, but this one felt different. The place roused no sense of the benevolent, guiding presence she felt as a girl. It exuded a dark power even greater than Black Kali's that had infused her as Angulimala. As soon as she set foot in it, her hackles rose and the red aura played around her vision.

Here she would face her demons.

The first few times she visited this spot, the voices of ancient sacrificial victims had called across the centuries in extinct tongues, and the ghosts of those she murdered hissed and whistled meaningless syllables in her ears. More terrified than she had ever been, she tried to concentrate on her breath, to still her shaking limbs, to block the incomprehensible words. Each time she tried to take a seat in the evil place, it took every ounce of her willpower to stay through the eerie chorus, barely able to follow Asita's instructions: "Whenever you meditate, you must resist the desire to rise from your seat once, twice, and a third time. That will deepen its effects."

She always jumped up after the third time and scurried back to the hermitage without waiting for whatever deepened realizations might come. There she would anxiously wait for Nalaka's return. He would arrive a day or two after, his face almost shining with calm strength. He didn't ask what happened, but he seemed to know she was having trouble. Jealous of his progress, she couldn't bring herself to seek his help.

One morning, Nalaka left for his retreat and Mala said she would leave soon for hers; she had some chores to do around the hermitage. Nalaka lifted an eyebrow. He must know how she dreaded going to the old shrine.

When he was out of sight, she sat on the log by the ashes of their morning cook fire and didn't move for a long time, trying to summon the courage and determination to go and spend at least one night at her retreat.

She arrived in the clearing around noon. Beams of sunlight surrounded the linga and yoni with gold. The forest was unusually still. Mala settled herself under a young sal tree and crossed her legs in the lotus pose. As usual, the voices started as soon as she began her breathing exercises, but this time, instead of trying to push the noise away, she took a deep, ragged breath and listened. As her hoarse breathing quieted, she began to understand the spirits' strange babbling. Their many voices coalesced into one whose singsong rhythms rang in her head.

For the evil you have done, your shame,
No crime of Brahmin or Kshatriya is to blame.
Your deeds are yours alone.
For each being, no matter how black her karma
Can choose to live according to the dharma.
Once done, a deed cannot be undone.
To right your wrongs comes not from austerities or penance
Save if they bring to your heart compassion and forgiveness.
Your redemption is yours alone.

Pale figures swam through her rising red aura. It soon darkened to purple and turned noon into night. There was a snake that became a brown-skinned Naga with matted hair and his throat slit. *Ages past I murdered a man of my tribe,* the snake-man cried, *and for this my people gave me to the Mother.*

A parade of lighter-skinned conquering Aryas, also with their throats slit, drifted past Mala. One fluttered closer and she resisted the urge to brush it away, knowing it would have no effect. *With horses and chariots and steel swords my brother warriors and I drove the ancient tribes from these forests,* he called to her. *They had no weapons to fight us but stealth and sacrifice. They captured us one by one and offered us to their goddess.*

One after another, a half-naked villager, a merchant in rich robes, a fat Brahmin, their heads nearly severed from their necks, and many more, women and children, too, passed in front of her, some with a tale of a wrong they had done the Nagas, others wailing that they had done nothing. Guilty or innocent, they had been tied to the linga and their throats slit so their blood flowed over the pillar into the stone.

As the spirits told their tales of bloody vengeance or cruel injustice, the purple aura pulsed stronger. A maiden attired in the robes of a highborn Arya rose from the earth. In front of Mala's eyes the rich robes fell away. Blurred figures materialized into men who threw the maiden on her back and raped her. It was no use trying to stop it; it had all happened long ago.

No, Mala, the girl said. *This is yet to come.*

Mala uncrossed her legs and tried to scramble backward, away from the horror. *How... how did you know my name?*

The girl didn't answer. Then Mala was rooted to the spot as a woman appeared in the vision, tall and muscular, with tangled, long hair and a necklace of blackened fingers. The woman turned a face painted red and white to her, the dark goddess Kali's face—no, no, it was Angulimala, it was she...

The woman grinned. A mist—no, pungent smoke from a sacrificial fire—passed in front of Mala. When it cleared, the girl was strung from a tree, and the woman—Angulimala—Mala—no, it could not be her! She had left that life—slit her victim from crotch to gullet so the intestines cascaded out of the girl's body. The stench made her gag.

No! Mala got to her hands and knees and tried to crawl away.

Conquer your anger and hatred, the girl said, *or my blood will be on your hands.*

My hands? How? Mala didn't want to look at the girl, but something forced her to. *Tell me how to stop it!*

Conquer your anger and hatred…

Out of purple shadow shot with bolts of sunlight flew all the ghosts, circling round and about Mala, all their faces becoming her face, and all chanting, *Redemption is yours alone… conquer your anger and hatred…*

She squeezed her eyes shut, but the purple pulsed on her eyelids. She moaned and curled up on the hard ground, clapping her hands over her ears, but she couldn't stop the noise. The earth opened under her. She was falling, falling into the hell realms. Yama's dogs chased her, howling, and she flapped her arms and legs as if it would help her fly away, but dogs and demons surrounded her, laughing, laughing, revealing white teeth dripping with blood.

"Asita!" she cried. "Asita, help me!"

Nothingness.

"Mala." A hand shook Mala's shoulder. "Mala."

She rolled onto her back and opened her eyes, looking up into a canopy of leaves. Morning sun dappled the clearing. The forest was alive with birds and animals and insects. A whole day had passed.

"Drink this." Lila. It was Lila. She leaned over Mala and handed her a waterskin. Her eyes that saw everything gazed at her with concern. The girl of the hermitage had grown to a lovely young woman. Her slim body was naked to the waist and necklaces of seeds and semiprecious stones and golden beads fell between her high, small breasts. Her long dark hair was oiled and braided with the same sorts of stones and beads.

"Is it the Divine One?" Mala started at the male voice and sat up. The speaker knelt a few feet away, slightly behind Lila, holding the hand of a small child with creamy brown skin. As soon as Mala saw him, he prostrated himself and pulled the boy down with him. It was the young Naga that she had seen with Lila right before the girl left the hermitage, and no doubt the child was their son. It was not so strange to see him as to realize that he was speaking in the Naga tongue, and that Mala understood him perfectly.

"It is Mala, from Asita's hermitage," Lila murmured in reply. "You spent the night in this haunted place?" she asked, her brow furrowed and her lips curved in a strange smile. Mala nodded. "Its ghosts frighten the bravest souls. Not even I, the Great Mother's dedicated servant, would dare do so."

"Angulimala," Lila's lover said in a shaking voice, raising his head a little. Mala shuddered at the name. "It's the queen of the outlaws, Kali incarnate! O Dark One, our priestess means no disrespect..."

So Asita had been right. He had said Lila would become a priestess to the Nagas.

Another tribesman, his tangled, dark hair streaked with grey, spoke. "It is a sign, Priestess. She is to aid us in the sacrifice."

At this, Mala became aware that there were perhaps a dozen Nagas around the edges of the clearing, and that in its center, bathed in the morning light, a man was sitting with his back to the linga, hands tied behind him, and that he was staring at Mala. He wore the white robes of a Brahmin, but they were dirty and stained. His topknot was undone and fell to his shoulders. It took her a moment to realize that the familiar high cheekbones and wide forehead of the Arya race belonged to none other than Valmiki, whose light brown eyes looked at her with drugged incomprehension.

"Valmiki," she said in a soft voice. "Valmiki." She shivered with the pleasure of seeing him bound like this.

"I meant no harm..." His voice faded and head lolled. "No harm..."

"You know this one?" Lila asked.

Mala nodded. "He was my village's landlord. Why do you hold him captive?"

"Valmiki was leading the soma sacrifice in Gauri," Lila said. Mala remembered those sacrifices that she was forbidden to attend and the last one when the Devi warned her to escape. She also remembered that the Nagas knew best where the soma plant grew and often brought baskets of leaves for Valmiki. "He sent a messenger asking us to bring some," Lila continued, confirming Mala's memory. "The woman we sent never came back. Our hunters found her two days later, tied and beaten and near death. Before she died, she told them that after she had delivered the basket of leaves, Prakash followed her and attacked her."

"Prakash?" Mala shook her head. "That wicked man."

"When we returned to the village to seek justice, Prakash was not there, but his master remained to collect rents." Lila glanced at the Brahmin. "So we took him."

"I didn't know," Valmiki said again. "Please..."

"The villagers made no attempt to stop us," Lila continued. Mala wondered at this. The old ways were truly dying if that were true. To allow a Brahmin to be taken like a common criminal showed unheard-of disregard of the laws of dharma.

The Naga with grey-streaked hair spoke. "The Mother demands vengeance. Prakash is Valmiki's servant. The master must pay."

Mala shouldn't have cared what happened to this man, but the voices from last night whispered in her ear. *Conquer your anger and hatred...*

And what had Asita said? Lila would offer human sacrifices, may the gods help her? "Lila," she began, "you will lead this rite?"

Lila nodded, her face full of defensive pride. "The old priestess died last month. She taught me the Mother's worship. She grants special boons when we offer the blood of criminals." Her mouth set in a bitter line. "My own father was a Brahmin, but when he died, one of his fellow priests... he did things to me... Valmiki will atone for his sins, too."

"This one is a god-man among the Aryas," the Naga with grey-streaked hair said, pointing at Valmiki. "Our young priestess is wise. He serves the sun god, and so she tells us to offer him in the light of the sun, as the Arya priests offer beasts to the Thunderer at the eagle altar. This is her first sacrifice since the old woman died."

"I gave him soma," Lila said, lifting her chin. "He will not suffer overmuch."

The figures Mala had seen last night fluttered in and out of her sight. *You can stop this... conquer your anger and hatred... your redemption is yours alone...*

"Lila!" Mala jumped to her feet. She did not intend to shout. The Nagas stiffened. Valmiki managed to raise his head and open his eyes wider. "Think of what Asita did for you, and he was born a Brahmin." Mala knew what it meant to have blood on her hands. She didn't know what Lila's future would bring after this day, but if she could find a way to make the young priestess reconsider, at least this once, she might stop the girl. "Doesn't that matter?"

Lila stood and faced Mala. "That priest, my father's friend, he... I will never forgive," she said bitterly.

"I've suffered, too, at the hands of this very Brahmin. He did nothing when my parents were murdered."

Valmiki, who was much more alert, furrowed his brow. "Your parents?" he said.

"My father was Talu, the tanner of Gauri. My mother was Sujata. Prakash murdered her, just like he murdered my lover, Angirasa."

Valmiki leaned his head on the linga and looked up. He closed his eyes against the sun. "You... you are the girl they called Mala... that day Asita came to Gauri..."

"Yes," Mala said.

"But Angirasa... your lover? He stole my wife... but I know nothing of this, nothing. I thought he died long ago, killed himself after he murdered my Moti, my dark pearl... Moti... my Moti..." Valmiki started to weep.

"He didn't murder her. It was Prakash," Mala said with sudden certainty that what Angirasa had suspected was true.

Valmiki closed his eyes and rolled his head from side to side. "I knew he was violent sometimes. I didn't know he was evil. I will make amends for what he has done, but not if I'm dead..."

"You are afraid to meet Yama Dharmaraja. To stand at the Lord of the Dead's throne and answer for your deeds," Lila said.

Her vehemence surprised Mala. The quiet girl Lila had been at the hermitage was in danger of becoming someone like Angulimala, someone who sought vengeance. It was not the way. *Conquer your anger and hatred.* "Your tribesman is right. Perhaps the goddess had a purpose in bringing me here. She brought me to keep you from killing a Brahmin. That stain will follow you forever, Lila."

There was a hush as Lila and Mala faced each other. In the young woman's eyes that saw everything, there was loneliness, uncertainty, deep hurt from an old wound. A frightened girl looked out of the beautiful priestess's eyes. Lila had spiritual gifts, too, not the same ones, perhaps, that Mala and Nalaka had, but gifts that would help her guide her adopted tribe.

"I've felt as you have," Mala said. "I took vengeance. I don't know if I can ever wash the stain from my karma."

"The Mother demands a sacrifice," Lila said.

"Your father was a Brahmin. He taught you about Rita, the cosmic order?"

"The law. From which dharma springs." Lila nodded.

"The law demands justice to maintain balance in the universe," Mala continued, hardly knowing where her words were coming from but feeling elated, light, her eyes open to the ancient wisdom that had always been around her but was until now unseen. "That balance... it's like an equation..."

The priestess looked at her, mystified. "What are you talking about?"

"The same sacred geometry that measures time and space, from the laws numbers obey to divide night and day, and hours and moons, and years, the numeric truths that guide the Brahmins when they build the eagle altar," Mala said in a rush. What had Angirasa said? She stopped and rubbed her temples. "I see the divine scales... Rita means good keeps evil from tipping the scales. To right a wrong, you must not commit another wrong, or the universe falls out of balance..."

"Balance? This is the Kali Yuga, the age of the dark goddess! Those who follow the dharma are rare. What difference if we sacrifice one man, when armies—your own outlaw army—murder innocent women and children? It's the way of things."

"That's wrong!" The light filled Mala, made her dizzy. "Every little act makes a difference." Lila's brow furrowed. "A man who is a soldier in an army will do wrongs that he would never do on his own." She gulped, thinking of how easy it was to get the men under her command to commit horrors. "People lose themselves in a crowd and commit the worst sins... and in a sense, they can be forgiven. Or at least understood. But you can stop a horror. It's your choice alone. You are the tribe's priestess—"

"And the Mother demands blood," Lila said.

"Perhaps she does. But Valmiki's blood? How, for the evil your father's friend did you?" Mala stopped again, her head still spinning, still searching for the right words. "It's wrong. If you must take vengeance, go find Prakash and tie him to the linga!" The very thought of such vengeance on her old nemesis made Mala shiver. She wanted to see him suffer. "Slit his throat and let his blood run, but do not sacrifice Valmiki."

As soon as she spoke the words, she knew they were wrong. What mortal had the right to extract that price from a criminal? What god? The universe itself had its way, the way of karma.

"Our priestess is right. The Mother demands sacrifice," the grey-haired Naga said. He held up a knife of sharpened bone.

No, Mala thought with blinding clarity, not even the Mother had the right.

There was silence in the clearing.

Lila walked over to the linga and took the knife from the old tribesman. She looked down at Valmiki, whose lips were trembling in a low prayer. "*Om, bhur bhuvah svaha, om,* the earth, the air, the heavens." The most sacred mantra that Angirasa had taught her, the one every Brahmin repeated at sunrise and at sunset. "We meditate on the divine light of the sun," he chanted in a hoarse, shaking voice.

Lila lifted the knife high and raised her face to the sun, her eyes closed. Golden light poured over her. The world held its breath.

"May it illuminate our minds," she finished the prayer. *"Om."*

The knife plunged down. Mala looked away, waiting for Valmiki's death shriek. But there was nothing. When she turned back, Lila had cut the hemp rope binding the Brahmin's hands.

"May Rita be preserved." Lila's lip curled. "Go, Valmiki."

He had slipped down onto the dirt and was having trouble righting himself so that he could stand. Mala went to him and grasped his arm, pulling him up. He blanched. He was sweaty and smelled faintly of urine and fear. She let go, and he staggered, so she reached under his armpit to support him.

"I… where… which way do I go?" He looked confused, frightened, weak. To her own astonishment, compassion flooded Mala's heart.

"I will take you to Asita's hermitage," she said to him in a soothing voice, and turning to Lila bowed her head slightly. "May you always serve your tribe with the wisdom you have shown this day."

Over joined palms, Lila gave her a silent bow. Her little boy toddled up and took his mother's hand. Mala had forgotten about him and his father, who had hardly moved from where they had prostrated before her. The boy stared up at her without fear. Mala's throat constricted. If this child could do that, maybe Kirsa could look at her without revulsion.

The Nagas watched in silence as Mala led Valmiki away from the ancient shrine. The elation and light that filled Mala earlier suffused everything. She had conquered her anger. She had conquered her hate. She had conquered her fear. She had saved a man who wronged her parents. The inner radiance was burning away the black stains from her karma.

Close to the hermitage, they came to the trade road. The creak of oxcarts and the shouts of drovers grew louder. Instinctively, Mala drew back into the dense undergrowth.

"We must part here." Valmiki drew away and looked toward the road.

"But Asita—"

"Send him my greetings and tell him he was right about many things."

"What things?" Mala began.

Without replying to her question, the Brahmin nodded toward the road. "The caravan we hear is heading east. They will take me to Varanasi."

Mala stiffened and reached for the knife at her side. "You won't tell them you saw Angulimala..." The light suffusing everything suddenly dimmed. How quickly old patterns returned.

"I did not see Angulimala," he said quietly. "I saw Mala, who saved me. I owe you my life."

She relaxed, dropped her hand from the knife's hilt, and bowed her head. "In a way, I owe you mine," she began, but Valmiki had turned away from her and was crashing through the undergrowth toward the road.

She wanted to call and run after him, but a light touch on her shoulder restrained her. Mala whirled. "Nalaka?" No one was there.

No. Let him go. It was the Devi's voice, gentle and yet powerful, just as on the day she prevented a much younger Mala from revealing herself to her parents' murderers. *One day Valmiki will repay you.*

"He owes me nothing... I only did what was right, what dharma demands," Mala said, swiveling around, hoping the goddess would appear. She dropped to her knees and bowed her head in prayer. *Om, Devi...*

You are ready.

The voice faded. Mala was alone.

ॐ

When Mala reached the hermitage, the old yogi was seated at the foot of the banyan. His bright blue eyes looked at her without surprise.

"I am ready," she said.

"I know." His familiar rough laugh grated against the elation that had traveled with her from the shrine.

"You know what happened," she began.

"Yes. Let's cook some rice. I have much to say, and then you must go. It is a long way to the cave in the snows."

"Nalaka—"

"Be silent, my girl! Your task is yours; Nalaka has his own. Though you dwell on the flanks of the great mountain Dhavalagiri and he in the desert near Taxila, distance will not separate you. You know each other's minds and how to link them."

Mala sweated over the small cook fire that she built in the shade of the banyan, trying to suppress her impatience and annoyance with the old yogi. Smoke rose through the leaves and a few fell from the tree into the metal pot of ghee, fried fragrant seeds, rice and water.

Her annoyance lifted as Asita described the sacred cave on Dhavalagiri. "There are two skulls placed outside it."

"Skulls? What are they doing there?"

"That's a tale. They belong to Siddhartha's grandparents, the Sakyan princess and her Koli husband, Anjana. But that's a tale for another time. Maybe their ghosts will tell you."

"There are ghosts?"

"Oh, yes. You'll meet them soon enough. Ha!" Asita's bark took Mala back to her childhood when she'd first heard that strange laugh on the path to her parents' hut. Her throat tightened. Perhaps she wasn't quite ready to leave this cheerful forest hermitage. "But there's something I must tell you. Siddhartha has chosen Kirsa as his bride."

"Ah!" Mala reeled. This was what she had hoped and feared.

"Suddhodana and his queen aren't pleased. No dowry, no important alliance by marriage." Asita cackled. "But they can hardly object to them being cousins. They're cousins themselves! They can't say too much, though. Your girl's got Gautama blood," he said, wagging his finger, "and the prince loves her. She'll be a princess yet."

Mala picked another fallen leaf out with her knife and tried to listen with calm attention as the rice bubbled. Her mind raced. Kirsa would marry Prince Siddhartha. Her gentle daughter a princess, perhaps one day a queen. Mala wanted to stay close, to see all this happen. It was hard to imagine how it would change the child. But she was no longer a child. Maybe she had changed already, become haughty like the imperious Queen Prajapati.

Her daughter was happy. She didn't need to worry. No, of course she worried, but oh, the cave in the snows! Skull guardians. Bracing air and wind and endless blue sky. Freedom. No more suffering.

"Watch you don't burn the rice," Asita said, peering into the pot.

Mala shook herself. "Aren't... isn't Kirsa young to be married? She's hardly thirteen."

"In another year or two. The king will try to keep the possibility open for other clans to hope for an alliance by marriage while he convinces them to make treaties with him against the Kosalas. He and the queen will no doubt also try to use the delay to convince Siddhartha he needs a true princess for a wife. But he loves Kirsa more than anything. It would take a divine enchantress to wrest his heart from the girl. Now I want to tell you about your pupil," he said. Mala looked at him in surprise. "A girl approaching thirteen. Kirsa's age." Asita's eyes sparkled. "Named for her grandmother, Yasodhara, but they call her Dhara. Almost the same mix of Koli and Sakya in Dhara as in the prince, but more mountain blood in her. Not as much risk of Gautama madness. She's got more warrior spirit than Siddhartha, too. She could rule the Sakyas."

The idea took Mala's breath away. A woman who would rule a whole clan, perhaps many clans, and Mala would be her guru. Then she frowned. "Suddhodana wants his son to fulfill both halves of the prophecy."

"Bah. The boy can't rule the world and at the same time conquer his passions and be a great sage. Once one has tasted a king's power, detachment from the senses becomes almost impossible—Suddhodana knows that all too well, eh, my girl?" Mala couldn't help flushing. "Ha! Yes. Temptations are too great. But that Gautama madness keeps Suddhodana from seeing the irony of wanting Siddhartha to rule the world yet keeping him from any real experience of it. Nalaka will have to deal with all that, when the time comes."

"Nalaka will teach Siddhartha?" A guilty pang surprised her. He would be there with her daughter while she would not.

"You couldn't be the prince's tutor," Asita said, as if he'd read her thought. "Even if you no longer command an outlaw army." Mala looked away from his bright blue eyes. "But Dhara will be like a daughter for you. She has all the fire of her namesake, but being raised in the Koli clan's mountain village, she has no refinement or education, aside from her father's training in martial arts. And she knows something of the Mother's ancient rituals," he added softly. "The Devi is strong there."

The Mother. The Devi. The mountain Dhavalagiri was one of her forms. They were infinite. She was more than bloody, dark Kali, who had ruled Angulimala. She was Durga, fighting against evil; Parvati, who matched Shiva himself in yoga; the giver of wealth, Lakshmi; wise Sarasvati; all goddesses. Mala would know all of them. Her hurt and fears ebbed, and elation surged again.

"You're burning the rice," Asita said, matter-of-fact.

"Oh!" Mala descended to earth and lifted the pot's handle, singing her fingers. The rice was stuck together and scorched to the bottom.

Asita raised a white eyebrow. "You may want to invoke Annapurna."

Mala gave him a rueful smile. Dhavalagiri's sister, the goddess of cooking, might have things to teach her. She scraped the rice out as best she could and put it in wooden bowls, the burned grains mixed in with the sticky white ones. Asita ate with gusto, but excitement tempered Mala's hunger. It made her feel like a traitor to her own sweet child that she hadn't seen for six years, but the truth was that the warrior girl drew her.

Then she had an uncomfortable thought. "You don't want me teaching Dhara strategy and tactics, do you? It seems like that's what she should be learning, not yoga, and I... I want to forget all that... forget being Angulimala... the horrors I committed..."

"You can't pretend what you did as Angulimala didn't happen." Asita's sharp tone stopped the tears of self-pity threatening Mala. "If you try, it will become a dark shadow that follows you. At first, you might be able to ignore it, but the more you do that, the more power you give it. Then you will try to run from it, but you can never escape. You can only dispel the shadow by entering its darkness, accepting what you've done, taking the lessons you've learned from it and using them for good."

Mala felt like a child who had suddenly entered an adult world.

"My girl." Asita's voice had never sounded so warm and soothing. "Right now, Dhara needs yoga. It sharpens intelligence, concentration, agility, and stamina. All useful in battle, you know yourself. Indeed, some say it is dharma for a warrior to use those qualities in a just war."

This troubled Mala. "All warriors should learn yoga, then. With the powers I've learned from you—to disappear, to enter another's mind, or to draw on supernatural strength—they would be invincible. There wouldn't be any need for war."

"Ah!" The yogi held up a hand to silence her. "Did I say powers? No.

Qualities, that's what's needed, qualities that most people could develop—intelligence or agility or complete awareness of mind and body—though only some make the effort. And among those, few develop the powers you and Nalaka possess. Siddhartha and Dhara will. But those powers are seductive. You must be wary of them and teach her to be so as well. Use natural courage and skill enhanced with discipline and effort. You have those qualities in abundance, Mala."

The unexpected praise brought tears to her eyes and made her tongue-tied. She sat quiet for a long time while Asita told her more about Dhavalagiri and the Kolis. After a time, he paused and waved at someone behind her. Mala turned, eager to see Nalaka.

It was not he, but the white tigress, Rani. She padded into the clearing.

"Here is your vehicle, the tigress Durga herself rides. It's time to go."

"Go?" Thrilled as she was to see Rani, the leave-taking had come too suddenly. Mala stood hesitant and confused.

"Farewell. Now begone!" Asita barked.

"But Asita…" A flood of questions overwhelmed Mala.

Come, Rani said. *The mountain goddess waits.*

CAVE IN THE SNOWS

A SUDDEN WHIRLWIND SWIRLED AROUND Mala and lifted her onto the great cat. A tunnel like the one they traveled together to the Horse Sacrifice opened before them. She had so many questions. "Asita! How will I meet Dhara? Will she come to the cave?" He sat utterly still. "What practices should I do? How will I feed myself?" He made no sign he heard.

"What if I need you?" she cried over her shoulder. "And, what did you mean, if all goes as planned?" Then she was riding the tigress through strange, diffused light. "Asita!" she called, but they were already in another world.

We will head north, Rani said. *Through the swamps of the Terai to the foothills of Himalaya's kingdom—*

"Wait!" Mala clutched the soft fur that shimmered silver in the peculiar atmosphere. An idea was taking shape.

What it is? Rani's ears twitched.

"We must go west," she replied. "To the Sakyan kingdom."

To see Kirsa. Just once before she began her retreat. Who knows how it might change her.

As Rani carried Mala through the strange, in-between world, they flowed like water through dense stands of trees and the solid wood of thick trunks, and crossed streams and swamps without getting wet. Though it was afternoon, in the shimmering light everything seemed bathed in moonglow.

"What will I look like to Kirsa in this alternate reality? Will she be able to see me?"

Rani let out an angry chuff. *You should have thought of that before. I thought it was a bad idea to see your daughter at all. Asita said nothing about taking you to Kapilavastu. But I ignored my better judgment. Furthermore, what makes you think* this *is the alternate world? Perhaps the world you thought was* real *is the illusion.*

Without stopping, Rani swiveled her head to give Mala a disapproving glance with one eyebrow cocked, exactly like Asita would do. Mala's heart swelled with bittersweet affection for them both.

The tigress continued on through the thick forest that formed the border between the lands of the Sakyas and Mallas.

Mala thought it best to avoid the subject of her daughter. "Interesting, what you say about what's real and what's illusion. Asita says everything is an illusion, a dream we dream. There could be infinite worlds, couldn't there? They're just what we imagine them to be."

Mala felt she was just beginning to understand what Asita meant. She marveled at the sea of millions of dancing atoms, pinpricks of light that ebbed and flowed in the shapes of trees or birds or flowering vines that hung like curtains, everything fluid and nothing fixed, no boundaries or firm objects, even she and Rani not separate beings but seemingly one.

Indeed, Rani replied. *Some sages say that what we call reality is just a shared hallucination.*

An exquisite shiver ran up Mala's spine. "How does one share a hallucination?"

That you will have to ask the sages. In truth, such questions do not trouble me. All that matters is what my own senses tell me.

Mala smiled. There was no need to reply.

Kirsa tore off a piece of stale naan and tossed it far out into the lotus pool. The swans glided toward it.

"I'm sick of everyone talking about Dev. He's gone and good riddance." Chandaka walked up and flopped down next to Siddhartha and Kirsa. An elegant green and gold antariya was wrapped in elaborate folds around his waist in the fashion currently so popular with courtiers, and he smelled of expensive sandalwood. Ever since he slept with Ratna, he had become quite a dandy.

Across the bobbing lotus pads, the palace's pale walls reflected the setting sun's red, while from behind a nearby clump of fragrant rosebushes came the flirtatious laughter of a palace maid and Siddhartha's guard Sabal. The swans dipped their necks into the water that reflected purple and pink clouds and retrieved the bread.

"No one said anything about Devadatta." Kirsa tore another piece of bread and threw it. "We can't think of anything except to wonder what the charioteer Chandaka will wear next. Who are you trying to impress tonight?" She gave him a prim smile.

He flushed just a little. "No one. But I'll wager you weren't thinking about my attire. You were thinking about him."

"You lose. I wasn't," Kirsa said, which wasn't exactly true. She was thinking about Siddhartha thinking about Dev.

"Then I'll wager he is," Chandaka said, nodding his head in Siddhartha's direction.

The prince had been staring at the swans gliding toward the reeds that sheltered them at night. The injured swan was getting better by the day. "Am not," he snapped.

Chandaka raised an eyebrow as if to say "See?" Kirsa bit her lip. In the days since his dark cousin's extraordinary exit, Siddhartha had been moody, even rude.

No one said anything for a while. The sun disappeared and darkness fell with surprising suddenness. Lights winked on in the palace and danced on the rippling water.

Chandaka jumped up. "I suppose we should take our seats at dinner. The queen will be angry if we're late."

Kirsa hoped Siddhartha would look up so they could share a smile. Chandaka had never been one to worry about being on time until the last few days. The voluptuous Licchavi girl had remained at the palace under Saibya's expert care, ostensibly to heal from the shock of the swan's attack. She would be leaving tomorrow, and at tonight's intimate family feast they would celebrate her full recovery, which seemed to have more to do with Chandaka's caresses and kisses than any of the rishiki's herbal draughts.

Siddhartha, however, remained lost in his own thoughts. Kirsa sighed and rose. She had never liked royal family dinners, but after Siddhartha placed the ruby and diamond garland around her neck, they were pure torture. For his sake, she put on a proud face, but it was all she could do not to squirm under the queen's cold eye.

Siddhartha stood up and brushed himself off. "You should go in, Chandaka. I think your Licchavi is expecting a betrothal this evening." Chandaka started to laugh, but the prince kept a straight face. "At least, that's what I heard Aunt Prajapati say."

Chandaka's laughter died. He looked from Siddhartha to the palace's lights and back at the prince. "Wait. Stop. You're serious. The queen said we were to be betrothed?"

"Why, yes. She thinks it would be a good match. You do like the girl, don't you?" Siddhartha opened his eyes wide in feigned innocence.

Chandaka's face collapsed into a stricken expression. "Yes. No! Not like that! Ah, no, betrothed?" Kirsa and Siddhartha burst out laughing. "It's not funny. I'll be sent away."

"Nonsense." Siddhartha chuckled. "The bride goes to her husband's home. Oh, we will so enjoy seeing you married. And a father!"

Kirsa frowned. Chandaka was right. It wasn't funny. "The bride does not go to her husband's hearth if he doesn't have one. He goes to his wife's family..."

"It's just what the queen wants. To get rid of me."

Siddhartha's laughter died. "No, Aunt Prajapati wouldn't..." They looked at each other. "I see... oh, dear... we won't go in, then! We'll go to the tree house." He straightened his shoulders. "No one's ever found our hiding place. We'll be safe. We can stay there until she's gone."

The idea made Kirsa very uneasy. "We shouldn't go," she said.

"Shhh!" Siddhartha looked toward the rosebushes, where Sabal had been dallying with the maid whose coos and giggles floated toward them along with the flowers' fragrance.

"We will get into trouble." Kirsa looked over her shoulder. Her neck hairs prickled as if someone was watching her.

"Trouble's nothing new for Chandaka," Siddhartha said, trying to grin but looking as nervous as she felt.

Chandaka shook his head, his brow furrowed with worry. There wasn't a trace of his typical, mischievous carelessness. "Kirsa's right," he whispered. "We would be in real trouble."

"But if we stay, you'll—you'll have to go with—marry her and—and go away. Oh, I couldn't bear it if you left Kapilavastu!" Siddhartha said.

"Shhh," Kirsa said.

"We must go," Siddhartha said with low urgency.

Chandaka nodded. "You're right."

Kirsa's unease about heading for the tree house was growing stronger, even knowing what it might mean if they stayed. She must stop them. "But what about Sabal?"

From behind the rosebushes there was a series of ecstatic cries. "Ai!" "Oh!" "Ahhh!"

"There's your answer," Chandaka hissed. "Now run!" At the same instant, the boys each seized one of Kirsa's hands, and they took off for the hidden path.

As usual, Chandaka took up the lead and Siddhartha followed Kirsa. They crashed through the thick growth that separated the park's wilds from the manicured gardens, heedless of the twigs and branches that tore at their skin and clothes. Once past the green wall, they stumbled along the path in silence. The night closed in, and the mysterious glow that usually surrounded Siddhartha in the forest to light their way did not arise. The boys didn't engage in their usual banter. Kirsa had gooseflesh in spite of the close, warm night, and struggled, breathless and shaking with fear and peculiar excitement, to keep up.

They had just about reached the clearing when Siddhartha grabbed Kirsa's arm. "Stop!" he hissed.

Kirsa and Chandaka halted. A nightjar croaked, then suddenly stopped, as if something had smothered it. "Wha—what is it?" she said.

"I heard something. Behind us."

Kirsa didn't dare turn around. It was dangerous, whatever it was. Maybe if she didn't look, it would go away.

"Look." Siddhartha shook her arm, insistent. He pointed a trembling finger. Something flickered white through the trees. "I think it's a ghost."

"Or a—a demon," Chandaka said, his hot breath in her ear. The white thing loomed behind the trees. Kirsa wanted to run, but her limbs felt as heavy as the boulders lining the queen's great lotus pool. Siddhartha's sweaty hand squeezed her arm.

Nearer and nearer it came. Kirsa was hypnotized. It was not as big as a horse, but big enough that something—someone—rode on its back. She stared into the shadows, terrified yet drawn toward what was approaching. She took a step.

Siddhartha seized her arm. "Kirsa, no."

The white thing was almost upon them. "It's... it's a... a tiger! Run!" Chandaka cried. "Run!"

Lulled by Rani's steady lope and mesmerized by the dancing lights, Mala became lost in the twilit world. An hour had passed, or an eternity. Shadows flitted across her inner eye. Then one of the shadows became a girl who was running down a narrow path under towering trees. The girl glanced over her shoulder. The glint of amber eyes took Mala's breath away.

"Kirsa? Kirsa!" Mala shouted, but no sound came out. Two youths emerged from the shadows; each seized one of the girl's hands, and all three raced to a giant banyan whose leaves gave off a faint sparkle as if strewn with tiny diamonds. It bent its branches toward them and the taller youth clambered onto a thick bough then reached down to grasp the girl's—it was Kirsa! It was!—to grasp Kirsa's arm and pull her up. The second one turned to face Mala. He had Suddhodana's face, only younger, his amber eyes. Had they traveled back in time? It could be, but no, no, it wasn't Suddhodana. It was he, Mala realized with a shock, the extraordinary boy, Prince Siddhartha. Their eyes locked. Mala's heart lurched. A powerful urge to bow, to touch her forehead to his feet, to confess everything to him made her knees turn to water. What was this? Then he, too, disappeared into the sheltering branches.

Rani growled.

The dancing atoms winked and disappeared. Had Mala dreamed she'd seen the children? They were so real.

It was night under the high, leafy canopy. The trees around them were solid; everything was fixed, real, no longer the fluid dance of particles. They were in a kind of clearing. In front of them was the banyan. Mala blinked. It had been no dream.

The tigress stopped. Her ears flicked back and forth. *She is there.*

Mala slipped off Rani's back and strode to the tree. She grasped a low branch and swung herself up toward a kind of platform that was built around the thick trunk. There was a gap between the trunk and the platform. She stepped to a higher branch and placed her hands on the old planks. She hesitated.

Kirsa was up there. What would her daughter do when she saw her?

It was not too late to jump down, mount Rani, flee this mysterious forest. Mala pulled herself up.

As she hoisted herself onto the platform, dim light bathed everything. Three young faces looked at her: a youth with dark eyes and a shock of dark hair falling over his brow; Prince Siddhartha, the young image of his father, his amber eyes glowing green-gold, like those of Rani's orange and black mother that Mala met so many years ago; and Kirsa, sweet Kirsa, long hair framing her oval face, golden eyes, grown lovelier than Mala could have imagined.

The moment she'd yearned for was upon her. "My child, my child." From a vast inner distance, Mala watched herself half croon, half weep, stretch out a hand to her daughter.

Kirsa froze. Her eyes sought Mala's. At the moment their eyes met, Kirsa cried out and fainted.

"My child!" Mala let out an anguished cry. The shock had been too much, but Mala could make it all better, if only she could touch her daughter, brush the hair from her cheek, kiss her brow. She heaved herself up, desperate to wake Kirsa, to hold her in her arms, to tell her everything would be all right now that they were together.

Then the dark-eyed youth thrust himself between her and Kirsa, drawing a knife from his sash.

In an instant, red pulsed at the edge of Mala's vision. She could snap this puppy's neck if she chose. "Out of my way," she said. She would brush him aside like a fly. The youth got into a defensive crouch. Someone had trained the boy well, and he was not such a boy, but almost a young man, perhaps fourteen or fifteen. Her fighting instincts crackled through every nerve. He would be no match for her. She whipped out her own knife.

"No!" Siddhartha said. "Chandaka is only trying to protect her. You want her to be protected…" Mala, poised to strike, halted with arm suspended. The boy emanated power. If he asked her, she would bow to him. Did he even know? "We are her friends, don't you see?"

"By the gods," dark-eyed Chandaka said. "Siddhartha—watch out—

she's dangerous…" His voice shook and he licked his lips, but he was brave enough. "Stand back, or I'll… I'll…"

"Put down your knife, Chandaka," Siddhartha said. "Don't you know who she is?"

"It's Angulimala! The outlaw queen!"

Mala drew back and her arm dropped as if he'd struck her. The knife fell from her slack fingers.

"It's Kirsa's mother," the prince said, putting a hand on Chandaka's arm.

A groan escaped Mala. Kirsa would know what she had been. But Kirsa was still unconscious, thank the Devi. *Om.* The old prayer came back, the one her own mother taught her: *Om, I bow to the Glorious Mother, Devi Ma who protects all children, She who does not fear, I honor You. Om…*

"Don't—don't be afraid. We won't hurt you," the prince said. Mala let out a short laugh. Not hurt her? She was the infamous Angulimala.

Then she began to shake all over under his gaze. It burned with a pure fire that would consume her if she didn't look away. "You needn't fear us. We will tell no one you're here."

Mala feared no soldiers that might be guarding the prince and spring from the shadows, for her senses told her there were none. But his eyes saw everything; they lit dark places in her heart that she couldn't face.

Then Siddhartha's eyes flickered. "She—she's safe with us, you know." He nodded over his shoulder at Kirsa's still form.

He was afraid of her. Mala exhaled in relief. Her trembling stopped. He had no idea the effect he'd had on her. He was putting on a brave face, but he was afraid of Angulimala. He was still just a boy, a boy who had no idea of his own power.

Chandaka edged toward the knife, and the red pulsed faintly again. With one swift and elegant move, Mala stooped to pick it up and put the point under his chin. Chandaka tried to swallow. His eyes were wide.

She lowered the knife and threw it aside. It skittered off the platform. Oh, how much she had not changed. She bowed her head then turned toward Kirsa, who lay with her lips parted. Under the modestly wrapped antariya, a dark color that looked grey under the mysterious glow, her daughter's chest rose and fell with shallow, even breaths. Mala ached to go to her. One touch, just one touch. It would bring such joy. The feeling that she was unworthy of such happiness kept her rooted where she stood.

"I swear to you, no harm will ever come to Kirsa," Siddhartha said. "I—I love her."

At this, Chandaka glanced from Kirsa to Mala. Then he crossed his arms and looked away into the leafy boughs surrounding them.

Ah. The handsome, foolish youth loved Kirsa, too. It took Mala by surprise. Tears blurred her vision. She put her hands over her eyes and lights whirled. She staggered and leaned against the trunk, almost fainting as a vision seized her.

… Brilliant, clear day. An archery contest. Chandaka and Siddhartha, now two fine young men, compete with a half dozen others. Chandaka's arrow hits the wooden target draped in red and black, then Siddhartha steps up. His arrow splits Chandaka's. They both look at Kirsa, who is lovelier than Mala dreamed she would ever be, and she clasps her hands together, her eyes shining. The two of them love Kirsa, cherish her in a way that Mala had never known.

Oh, it's bittersweet. Mala wants her to be happy. And yet, the only person who ever truly loved Mala was her daughter.

Jealousy stabs her. Mala wants Kirsa's love all for herself.

Then twilight. In a scented garden, a fountain burbles. The prince and another young woman stand in a passionate embrace. Mala can't see the girl's face but can tell by her lithe young body and the silky hair flowing straight down her naked back that it's not Kirsa. Her daughter sits alone at the edge of a lotus pool as darkness falls. She cries, holding the diamond and ruby necklace. Mala can't bear it.

But she can prevent that. Yes, there is another future.

Lights tumble and whirl. She and Kirsa at the mountain cave together, just the two of them, surrounded by dazzling light and clear air infused with the sharp tang of gnarled cedars and the cries of eagles soaring overhead. Pilgrims seek Mala's counsel and Kirsa's healing skills.

Then so many images flood Mala's consciousness that she can hardly absorb them. A vast army swarms over Kapilavastu, arrows and spears raining death and destruction on its beleaguered defenders. With sudden horror, Mala realizes it's Angulimala's army, her outlaws, who set temples in flames and seize women and children. But where is Angulimala?

A lithe, young warrior—a woman, the woman the prince kissed—

wheels on a horse and raises her sword, and the few Sakyans rally behind her and charge.

Darkness. Then Mala awakes on a riverbank among a huge crowd listening with rapt attention to a man in a saffron robe. She tries to push her way to the front but can't. Darkness again. Now she hides along a lonely, dusty road, waiting for the yellow-robed man, her knife ready to slash his throat. There he is, but when his amber eyes search hers out, the knife falls from her hand…

The lights stopped whirling. Mala lowered her hands from her face. She looked from Siddhartha to Kirsa. Somehow, what Mala would choose to do here and now—to leave Kirsa with the prince or to take her to the mountain—would mean not just suffering or happiness for her daughter, but war or peace for thousands.

"I must seek my own salvation first," she said aloud.

"What did you say?" Chandaka looked at her, puzzled, but Siddhartha nodded his head.

There was a low growl from under the tree house. The two boys moved toward Kirsa.

"Don't be afraid," Mala said, wiping her eyes. "Rani won't climb the tree and eat you."

Their faces softened with relief, but they remained vigilant.

Mala's throat was tight with tears. "I must go. I must heal myself first, just as Asita said."

The prince nodded. "For some, the only way to truth and peace is a solitary one."

He was young to know this. It seemed to pain him very deeply. Mala had nothing to offer him by way of consolation. It pained her, too. "I am going alone to a sacred cave, to make my hermitage and seek peace." There. She'd said it. She was going alone. She'd leave Kirsa here. Mala's heart shattered.

"You must go, then, if that's your path," Siddhartha said. His voice sounded old and tired. In the midst of her own grief, Mala knew he was as sad as she, as if he understood a terrible choice he would make one day. "Then… then you can come back to those you love. It may hurt them that you've gone without them, but it would hurt them more if you stay."

He was talking to himself as much as he was talking to her. "Until then, Kirsa will be safe here," he said.

"And happy?" she whispered.

"And happy."

ॐ

A peacock screamed as Mala dismounted from Rani's back. For a moment, she was a girl of twelve. She was on her way back from bathing in Ganga's waters, and she had thought the bird's cry was a warning. Now, looking back, it seemed to have been the call that set her on this journey. That day she'd met a tigress carrying her white cub and an old yogi. She hadn't dreamed, hadn't dared to dream of such wonders as making treasured friends of the cub and the old sage, but that's what had happened.

She shaded her eyes against the sun and searched the boughs of a tall tree for the familiar bird. Its iridescent blue breast caught the sunlight; its long tail swept down from the branch.

Rani sat back on her haunches and chuffed at it. The peacock screamed again and rose from the branch with more ease than Mala would have thought possible, and flapped away. She smiled. No matter how burdened by its own beauty, it could still fly.

Rani twitched her ears. *You won't see any of those at the cave.*

Ever since they crossed the swamps of the Terai and started to climb the foothills of Himalaya's kingdom, the plants and animals were all unfamiliar and new. No, there would be no peacocks at her solitary retreat.

"But I will see eagles."

That and more wonders, even though our journey together is ended.

It was magical. They had begun wandering two moons ago, when Mala tore herself away from Kirsa. She left half her heart with her daughter, who didn't even know she'd been there.

Wise Rani said that nothing heals a soul like travel, and so they began their glorious journey. Safe in the twilight world, they made their way through the fifteen lowland kingdoms. The talk of war was everywhere. So were increasing numbers of sages and rishis, some saints, some charlatans, who challenged the power of the Brahmins and who ignited the hopes and dreams of the ordinary folk for a more just world. She and Rani wandered from rich Rajagriha, the Maghadan capital in the east, to the Gandharan clan's capital, Taxila, on the edge of the western desert, each city a gateway to fabulous worlds beyond. She could have journeyed for months, years, and still would have wanted to know and see more, but they only had two months before the lowland monsoon would become mountain blizzards. Rani said Mala must make her way through the lands of the sixteenth clan, the Kolis, who lived on Dhavalagiri's lower slopes, and come at last to the sacred cave near the mountain goddess's peak.

You must go by yourself from here on. Rani sniffed the wind. *For now, it is your path alone.*

"I know. Oh, Rani, how I'll miss you!" Mala threw her arms around the tigress's neck and buried her face in the silver fur.

Nonsense. I foresee you will achieve remarkable things as you make your way on yoga's path.

"I'm afraid, Rani." Mala tried to swallow a sob, but it escaped, and she broke down. "I'll be so alone." Her tears soaked Rani's thick fur.

This is what you were meant for, my friend. And it is not goodbye. I have an urge to explore the high forests, perhaps as far as Mount Kailash where Lord Shiva dwells, and will come to see you now and then. Rani nodded toward the river. *There is the path to Dhavalagiri. It follows the waters sacred to Rohini, the moon god's wife. Take it to the gates of the Koli village.*

Mala released Rani and stood, gazing at the swift, shallow stream. It sparkled in the sunlight, and its voice as it rushed downward was like laughter or the calls of nymphs and sprites. "It will run deeper when the rains begin, won't it?" She turned to Rani.

The tigress was gone.

Under a westering sun, Mala made her way up the road, which was so rocky and pitted it hardly deserved the name. Rani had said that traders sometimes took this road as a little-used way through the high passes to the Middle Kingdom. If so, it must be on foot. Ponies or mules would have a hard time, and to take a cart was unthinkable.

The road leveled off by a deep pool at the base of a roaring waterfall where Mala decided to stop and refresh herself. As a girl, she'd bathed in Ganga's turbid green river that cleansed sins but also hid secrets. She marveled at Rohini's waters, which were clear and bright. There were no dark, opaque depths, but everything was visible and magnified, all the way to the boulders at the bottom. It was so inviting. No one would find her in this remote place. Mala didn't see any danger in taking a dip. She pulled her knife out of her sash and dropped it next to the small sack that held her hermit's bowl and a change of clothing, stripped off her antariya, and leaped in.

She came up gasping and spluttering. It was freezing cold even though it was late summer. Her limbs went numb, and it was difficult to move. She struggled to the pool's rocky bank as fast as she could and pulled herself out, teeth chattering. It was a good thing her clothes were dry. She donned the antariya, then made her way to a boulder bathed in sunlight and settled herself against the sun-warmed rock. With the heat radiating at her back, she fell asleep.

ॐ

"... a Maghadan blade, I'm sure of it, Father."

A girlish voice penetrated the deep silence of Mala's sleep. It was Kirsa talking to Angirasa, but what did Kirsa know of Maghadan blades? No, that couldn't be. Someone must be near, even though she was still so far from the village. She tried to rouse, but she was too tired. It must be just a dream. She shifted her head and prepared to dive back into dark slumber when someone else spoke.

"Indeed. You know weapons as well as any young Koli warrior, daughter." A man's voice. And she hadn't dreamed it. She struggled to open her eyes.

"Whoever carries such a blade is dangerous. We should bind her while she sleeps."

Mala snapped fully awake, eyes wide open. Her hand flew to her the knife in her sash. Which wasn't there. Of course. She had left it by the waterfall. Fool. Already she was making mistakes. Did they know who she was? Nalaka had said the Kolis rarely left their mountains. They might have heard of her, but they wouldn't know her by sight.

A sun-bronzed man with his hair pulled back in the braid of an Arya warrior was crouched a good arm's length away, weighing Mala's fine Maghadan knife in one hand.

"Look! She's awake." A slight girl with dark, silky hair and warm brown skin knelt on one knee next to the man, pointing at Mala.

"Indeed." The man watched Mala with dark, almond-shaped eyes. She lifted her chin. A smile played at his lips.

For an instant, red flickered around Mala. Whatever amused him, he would find out what it was to mock her. His gaze traveled over her in such a way that her loins quickened, and a muscle in his jaw twitched. Ah. Subtle lightning passed between them. She gazed back at a round, handsome face with high cheekbones, letting her eyes travel over him the way his had explored her.

"No one else around, Chief Dandapani," someone called. A horse nickered. Two men rode up and dismounted. "She seems to be alone."

"Alone?" The girl's eyes, the same almond shape as her father's and dark but with golden glints, went wide. "A woman made this trip alone?" She was clearly impressed. "Are you human or divine?" she asked. "You must be divine, or the Devi gave you powers. It's very dangerous to travel these mountains alone. Especially for a woman."

Mala exchanged a glance with Dandapani. She was certain he knew who she was, even if his men did not. She was also certain he would say nothing. "If I were divine," she said to Dhara, "I would have burnt you to ashes with my third eye."

"Your third eye? Are you a yogi, then?"

"I am. My teacher Asita has sent me to live at the cave on Dhavalagiri."

The girl jumped up. "Father! A woman yogi!" She took a step toward Mala but her father held out an arm and restrained her. "I remember Asita! He was a funny old man."

"Daughter, what does the dharma command us to do?"

"Oh. Yes." The girl put her palms together and bowed. "Please, yogi-ji, please come and sit by our fire and tell us stories."

Dandapani looked at his daughter with a lowered brow. "Dhara," he said.

Dhara. It was she. Now Mala saw the aura. This was the girl Asita had said she was to teach. A wild, undisciplined creature, he had said, with almost the same bloodlines as the extraordinary Siddhartha, the same gifts, the same potential but a different destiny.

Dhara stared at Mala, lips parted in excited wonder, every sense alert. "If it would please you, we would like you to sit by our fire and enjoy a meal with us. That is, as many meals as you like, yogi-ji—"

"I am called Mala."

"Namaste, Mala-ji." Dhara bowed over her joined palms.

Easy to see she was undisciplined and wild, but easy, too, to see the possibilities in the young, lithe form, the eager intelligence. Mala returned the bow.

"Namaste, Dhara."

AFTERWORD

The historical fantasy genre gives writers license to make setting, characters, and plot in their novels resemble actual places, persons, or events as much or as little as they choose. Unlike writers of historical fiction, we are not constrained by facts. We can change timelines, names, or the sex of a main character. Or we may change a real place into a fantasy realm that closely resembles it, as Guy Gavriel Kay transforms China's Tang dynasty into the land of Kitai in *Under Heaven*. Or we may bring magical elements into a real setting, as Helene Wecker brings mythical creatures to late 19th century New York City in *The Golem and the Jinni*.

I've used that license to re-imagine the Buddha's story. Traditionally, Buddhists tell it this way:

Some 2500 years ago in northern India, a sage prophesies that the young Sakyan prince, Siddhartha, will either rule the world or become a homeless seeker of truth. He lives surrounded by luxury and beauty until one day, his charioteer takes him for a drive outside the palace walls that have sheltered him from harsh reality. For the first time he sees a sick man, an old man, and a corpse. He realizes that everyone suffers and dies, even wealthy princes. He takes no more pleasure in his royal life. His spiritual crisis comes to a head and he flees home and family to become a wandering sage. After six years of intense searching, he attains enlightenment and becomes a buddha, an awakened one, and travels through the kingdoms between the Ganges and the Himalayas teaching the path to freedom from suffering.

I conceived my books as a trilogy that would center on women from the legends that surround Siddhartha: a beautiful courtesan who becomes a follower, the aunt who raised him after his mother's death, and a young cousin whose grief is healed by his teachings.

But writers don't always get to choose what they write. A character who appeared on the page almost as soon as I began was not found in any Buddhist tales or Indian myths I had read. She was an outcaste girl who meets the goddess in the form of a tigress, an experience that awakens her hunger for spiritual knowledge forbidden to her caste. I felt compelled to write a story where her spiritual striving would lead her to the Buddha, who rejected the rigid class structure of his time. His followers represented all levels of society: from the lowest polluted ash-covered keeper of the cremation grounds to the highest disenchanted Brahmin who no longer found meaning in ancient sacrificial rituals. The outcaste girl became the protagonist of the first novel in the Sadhana trilogy, *The Tigress and the Yogi*.

Her name came to me as I sat was toying with a string of beads that monks use while chanting to count their prayers. It's known as a mala, which means garland in Sanskrit. I liked the symbol. So my outcaste girl became Mala and her adventures poured onto the page. She suffers hideous wrongs but overcomes them to find happiness with a lover and child. Then her daughter is stolen from her. And then...

Mala's next step eluded me. I searched the Terigatha, a fascinating collection of poems by women who were the Buddha's earliest followers (translated by Susan Murcott in a wonderful book, *The First Buddhist Women*), but none of their stories fit Mala as I'd come to know her. I was stuck.

Then two other stories captured my attention.

The first comes from the *Angulimala Sutta*, the discourse that tells the story of a ruthless bandit redeemed by the Buddha's teachings. There are always at least a half dozen versions of any story from India's mythological past and this story has several of its own, but the basic elements are these: a jealous guru demands his young Brahmin student bring a finger from a thousand people as a gift to his teacher. The youth is appalled, but dharma requires him to obey his spiritual mentor. He becomes an outlaw and collects his gruesome trophies on a string around his neck so as not to lose them, thus earning the name Angulimala, meaning "Gruesome Garland." When he has only one finger left to fulfill his guru's command, his path crosses the Buddha's. He tries to make the Buddha his final victim but fails, and the Awakened One shows him the path to peace.*

I came across the second story as I sought late-night refuge from writer's block in channel surfing. I landed on a movie set in contemporary India. *The Bandit Queen* purports to tell the true story of Phoolan Devi, a rebellious low-caste girl who struggles against oppression, abuse and sexual assault. She runs away to join an outlaw band and becomes its leader, seeking bloody vengeance against those who have wronged her. Because many regard her as a heroine, she eludes capture. Ultimately she surrenders to the law on condition that she will not be prosecuted for her crimes.

A controversial figure, Phoolan Devi went on to become a member of Parliament. She disputed the film's accuracy and published an autobiography to set the record straight. Whether or not the film tells an accurate version of events, it was riveting. (And the fact that Phoolan Devi was a member of the lowly Mallah caste and author Mala Sen wrote a biography of her just seemed to strengthen the link to my heroine, Mala.)

The two stories snapped together in my mind. Mala would become the outlaw Angulimala, and rather than obeying a guru's command, she would take revenge on an unjust society. This would lead her to the Buddha. Would it also redeem her? This remains to be seen.

In *The Tigress and the Yogi,* karma brings Mala and a very young Siddhartha together in a foreshadowing of the encounter between Angulimala and the Buddha later in the Sadhana trilogy.

The trilogy's second book focuses on Dhara, the warrior girl who becomes Siddhartha's wife, and her friend Sakhi, who stands by Dhara when Siddhartha embarks on his quest. The third book ties together the stories of Mala, her daughter Kirsa, Dhara, Sakhi and many other characters, legendary or completely imagined, with Siddhartha's return as the Buddha.

For more traditional versions of Buddha's story as well as to get a feel for his times and extraordinary teachings, see Karen Armstrong's *Buddha,* Iqbal Singh's *Gautama Buddha,* and Edward J. Thomas's *The Life of Buddha as Legend and History.* I would also highly recommend Stephen Batchelor's *Confession of a Buddhist Atheist* not only for his insights into the

* For a complete discussion of the legend's various forms, see Richard F. Gombrich's essay "Who was Angulimala?" in his book *How Buddhism Began.*

earliest Buddhist literature but also for its account of his own remarkable spiritual journey.

For more books about India's fascinating mythologies and religions, please visit my website, shelleyschanfield.com.

ACKNOWLEDGMENTS

I would like to thank everyone I've ever known, in this life or any other, but especially the following:

My patient spouse, Lloyd Stoolman; and my children, Joshua and Jessie Stoolman; and my beloved aunt Doris Harris.

My teachers Laura Kasischke, Barbara Shoup, Dave Waskin, and Tom Zimmerman, whose encouragement when I'd just started to write meant more than I can say; and Jane Ratcliffe, whose workshops never failed to inspire me.

Editors: Jane Ratcliffe, who understood exactly what I wanted to achieve and whose spot-on critiques kept me on track; Meghan Pinson for stellar copyediting and her colleague Rhonda Erb for precise proofreading.

My beta readers, whose thoughtful reading helped me more than I can say: my sister Jane Riches and my nephew Casey Simpson; friends Linda Longo, Kay Mahan, Kate Maple, Kate Mendeloff, Sue Rosen, Stephanie Renée dos Santos, Shanti Thirumalai, and the late Ben Yates.

Writers Pat Tompkins, Karen Simpson, and Elisabeth Khan, who were there from the beginning.

Writers, friends, yogis, and family who contributed, knowingly or not: Elli Andrews, Deedra Climer Bass, Liz Brauer, Syd Bridges, Janet Cannon, David Chan, Theresa Crothers, Kim Fairley, Stephanie Feldstein, Robyn Ford, Fritz Freiheit, Dan Gilbert, Aura Glaser, Lois Godel, Donelly Haddon, Ellen Halter, Skipper Hammond, Karen Hildebrandt, Yma Johnson, Jan Joyce, Ray Juracek, Linda Kurtz, Fartumo Kusow, Rachel Lash Maitra, Les McGraw, Patrick McHugh, Beth Neal, Meadow Rose Snyder O'Brien, Kaye Posselt, AJ Schanfield, Taryn Scherer, Christy Shannon, Susan Shore, Kate Stone, Dave Wanty, and Karen Wolff. If I've forgotten anyone, please forgive me and know I'm profoundly grateful to everyone who helped along the way.

And in memory of: my parents, Maurice and Norma Schanfield; parents-in-law, Alfreda and Leo Stoolman; my sister, Serene Schanfield; and my brother-in-law, Ron Stoolman.

COMING SOON:

CREATION HYMN

BOOK TWO OF THE SADHANA TRILOGY

A NOVEL

SHELLEY SCHANFIELD

CHAPTER 1:
DHARA

THIS WAS NOT THE FIRST time a wandering truth-seeker had followed the lonely path to the sacred cave to find wisdom or to die.

But this was the first time the wanderer was a woman.

Few visitors of any kind came through the village nestled below the white peak, and the wild-looking yogi mesmerized Dhara from the moment the scouting party found her. Though she was only twelve, Dhara's father, Dandapani, had allowed her to ride along on her pony as he and a few warriors patrolled along the river's shallows. They had come upon the mysterious woman at the waterfall, asleep by the pool. Though she had a sword and a bow, she said she had come to this remote place to make a solitary retreat at the cave and practice the Lord of Yoga's disciplines. She called herself Mala, a simple yogi who only sought peace.

All Arya clans obeyed the dharma that required them to offer hospitality to a truth-seeker, though among the Kolis there were those who suspected she was no wisdom-seeking yogi at all. They speculated that she was the infamous outlaw queen Angulimala, hunted in the lowland kingdoms whose roads she had mercilessly harried with her renegade army. If this was so, they had no quarrel with her. What happened along Ganga's river was no concern of theirs. Others whispered she was a demoness, for no mortal woman could have made the dangerous journey alone. Dhara didn't care.

That evening, the clan gathered around a great bonfire on the field by the river, just outside the village gates, to listen to the yogi's teachings.

"You may ask the wanderer one question, daughter, as custom allows," Dandapani said.

He crouched on his haunches next to her. Firelight gleamed on his broad forehead and his dark hair, which was drawn back in a long warrior's braid. His dark eyes crinkled above his clean-shaven cheeks. Dhara was certain there was no other warrior in all the Sixteen Clans so handsome, so brave as her father Dandapani.

"One question, my child," he said, "then we must let Mala-ji rest for her long climb tomorrow."

"I'm not a child. I'm nearly thirteen," Dhara retorted. There was some low laughter from the others gathered round the fire.

"So you are." Dandapani gave a thoughtful nod and picked up a thick stick to stir the embers. He tossed another split log onto the glowing coals. Erupting flames lit the gathered clan's faces, which were still ruddy from a whole summer of hunting in the high forests and tending the barley fields that terraced the steep slopes.

The yogi Mala sat on the other side of the open fire, her long, bare legs crossed so that a foot rested on each thigh, her palms down on her knees. She wore a deerskin around her hips. Though the night air was cold, her only cloak was a tangled mass of coarse hair that fell over her shoulders, barely covering her high breasts.

A woman yogi! A woman seeking the highest knowledge, which once gained would make others strive to learn wisdom at her feet. Not just some clever Brahmin wife from the village priest's instructive stories, who received all her learning from a wise husband but had no real mind of her own. In her excitement, Dhara was having trouble collecting her thoughts to form a question.

"Mala-ji," Dhara began, but her words fled when the woman turned hooded eyes to her. "Er—tell—would you tell us of how our ancestors came to this land?" Stupid question. Stupid.

Sakhi, who had been huddling close to Dhara in the cold night air, poked her in the ribs and shook her head, her lips compressed in disapproval. It was a wasted opportunity, as both girls knew the answer full well, having heard the tale from Sakhi's father a hundred times. The priest always told it the same way, how the sixteen Arya clans came with their horses and chariots to the land between Himalaya's kingdom and Ganga's waters. With the aid of their dazzling sky gods, they conquered the dark forest tribes, who had worshipped the ancient Mother and watered her earth with offerings of human blood.

The yogi stared into the flames, as if preparing to speak. Maybe it wasn't such a stupid question. Maybe Mala knew a new way to tell the story. There was quiet around the fire as the clan waited for her to begin.

"Ah. Yes. How the Sixteen Clans came to the land of the rose apple tree. Those who master yoga's powers can see the riders' dust, hear the chariot wheels rumbling as if it were today," Mala answered. A log fell with a crack and sent snapping sparks up to join the millions of stars glittering in the cold, dark sky.

Mala stared into the flames so long Dhara wondered what she saw there. At last she couldn't contain her eagerness for the yogi to continue. "Did they look into the flames to see it? Like you're doing now."

Everyone tensed. One did not disturb a truth-seeker or interrupt their meditations. That was the dharma, the law.

Sakhi gave her another poke in the ribs. "One question," she hissed. "As custom allows."

Dhara glared at Sakhi. So timid. So obedient. So annoying. Yet they were sisters of the heart, like twins born on the same day to different families, and never stayed angry at each other for long.

Mala seemed not to care about the interruption. "Those who can truly see know that time exists all at once and forever, the warp and woof of space," she said, her voice ringing over the surrounding cedars and hemlocks and up to the heavens. "It is the loom of the universe."

Dhara didn't know what the words meant, but they conjured something above and beyond the gods Sakhi's father spoke of, something that made Dhara shiver. The yogi's voice vibrated in her very bones. "I don't understand."

"It's good to admit you don't understand," Mala said, impassive and solid as a mountain.

The yogi's quiet approval silenced Dhara more effectively than any of her mother's tirades ever had. Once again words deserted her, and she awaited their return in agony, gazing at this marvelous creature.

Mala could be one of those dark-skinned worshippers of the Great Mother, those forest tribes conquered by the light-skinned Arya clans. The shaman's wife made Sakhi and Dhara shiver with horror and delight when she told tales of these mysterious people who hung their victims from a sacred tree and slit them, crotch to gullet. Conducting such a rite would be an easy task for someone with muscles like those that rippled under the yogi Mala's dark, oiled skin. She was not beautiful, at least not like Dhara's mother, who had a divine nymph as an ancestress, but Mala could be the warrior goddess herself, who fought the demon for the sky gods, or King Himalaya's blue-skinned daughter, who won the heart of the god Shiva, the Lord of Yoga.

"How many generations past did your ancestors settle the forests and plains? A hundred? A thousand? I will tell you what my guru Asita told me—"

"Asita?" Dhara burst out again. "But Asita lived in the sacred cave when I was little. How do you know him?"

"Dhara." Her father tried to frown. "Forgive her, Mala-ji. Asita was a great favorite among us Kolis."

"He spoke highly of his time with your clan." Mala raised her chin, and her lips curved. "Yes, Asita told me, and his guru Saungi told him, and Parasari told Saungi, and Manduka told Parasari." Mala continued the customary recitation of her guru's long lineage back to the Seven Celestial Sages in a singsong voice, with hardly a pause for breath. When she finished, the Kolis sighed and shifted, anticipating a good story from one with such a formidable memory.

"Nothing could stop the fierce Arya warriors as they swarmed over Himalaya's shoulders with their chariots and horses," she began in a soft voice, "though the forest dwellers sacrificed many victims to their ancient Mother. But She did nothing while the invaders felled vast tracts of trees to create pastures for their cattle. Now, in these forests were sacred groves that sheltered many sages, whose spiritual ardor surpassed the burning tapas of the sky gods themselves. When the fire reached the venerable sage Kapila's hermitage and consumed it, his fury was aroused at the warriors' wanton violence. Kapila opened his third eye and with the fierce heat of his inner fire engulfed thousands in flames."

Dhara and Sakhi exchanged a look. This was not at all what Sakhi's father, Bhrigu, had told them. The Arya clans burnt to ashes? His stories were all about how the gods walked among mortals during the great wars of succession that followed the invasion, and Vishnu the Preserver himself took human form to help the rightful king and his four brothers win back their inheritance.

"The ashes of the Aryas threatened to suffocate all mankind," Mala continued. "The gods trembled. The end of humanity would mean the end of sacrifice, and how could they live without the offerings made on the fire altar?" She smiled slyly at Sakhi's father, the Brahmin Bhrigu, who stood draped in his priest's robe at the edge of the circle of firelight, watching with wary eyes. Dhara's father always said that the clan showed more respect to Bhrigu than to his gods. Mala's story clearly made him uncomfortable.

"Brahma the Creator sat in council with the other celestials. As they considered what they should do, Shiva, the Lord of Yoga, passed by on his way to his cave on Mount Kailash.

"'Auspicious One,' the Creator Brahma greeted him, 'the ashes of the Aryas will soon extinguish all life. If humanity perishes, no one will perform the rituals that feed us.'"

"'Death is inevitable, even for gods. What difference if it's now or in ten thousand years?' Shiva replied, adding, 'Besides, those who are enlightened have no need of rituals.'" Again, Mala smiled at the priest, who remained expressionless.

"The other gods did not reply." The yogi searched the faces turned to her in rapt attention. "Not for the first time, each one wondered silently if the three-eyed yogi was really one of them. Who could remember him from the days when the Aryas roamed the sea of grass north of the mountains?" She shook her finger. "None of the celestials could say when they had first seen him motionless in the lotus pose, his matted hair and naked body covered with ashes. Underneath the filth, the supreme yogi was divine and powerful, but he was also rude and unpredictable. He would be no help in this matter.

"As for Lord Shiva, he went to practice his disciplines in his mountain cave without another thought of suffocating ashes, until one day when the beautiful goddess Ganga distracted him. When they lay spent after frenzied lovemaking, the goddess traced her finger up and down his naked limbs."

Dhara and Sakhi looked at each other in the same instant, each knowing the other's thought, stifling smiles.

Mala fixed her eyes on Dhara. "'This existence has its pleasures, my Lord Shiva,' the goddess sighed. 'Perhaps I could save it.'

"'You could let your waters pour over the ashes and bring the Aryas back to life,' Shiva said, and kissed her mouth, her neck, her breasts, and nuzzled her warm, soft stomach.

"Ganga shook her head. 'Their force would be too great,' she said. 'The flood would sweep away everything.'"

The yogi paused and shut her eyes. No one moved. Dhara dared a whisper behind her hand. "But your father never said anything about Ganga and Shiva."

Sakhi nodded, eyes shining despite Bhrigu's disapproving stare, pressing her lips tight to stop her laughter. Dhara clasped Sakhi's warm hand in her cold one. The sister of her heart did show a rebellious spark now and then.

"Then something occurred to Shiva," Mala continued. "'Yet there is a way, fair-hipped Ganga,' Shiva said. 'If you release your waters over my head, I will break their fall.'

"So Ganga stood up in all her glory, and he knelt and buried his face in her flesh. Her love poured over his strong shoulders, then frothed and tumbled from the supreme yogi's Himalayan cave all the way to the eastern sea, and her life-giving river restored the ashes of the Sixteen Clans to life."

Mala fell silent and gazed up at the mountain goddess's looming, snow-covered peak, which emitted a dim glow in the moonless night. Dhara was enchanted. So this was how Great Mother Ganga's waters had come to flow to the sea. She had a sudden desire to know the tale by heart and to enthrall future listeners just as Mala was captivating her village.

The yogi kept her face lifted and eyes shut. Silence reigned. The villagers glanced at each other, shrugging in puzzlement. Everyone wanted her to go on.

"There is more to that story," someone called out. "Kapila made a prophecy. About a Sakyan child." This prophecy about their rivals, the Sakya clan, was known but not given much credence in the village, although Dhara sometimes wondered about it. Her formidable grandmother had been a Sakyan princess.

The fire gave a sudden crack as a log split. Sparks flew upward and vanished. Dandapani rose from his crouch and tossed more wood onto the bed of red coals, glancing at Mala as he did so. Some strange current of energy passed between Dhara's mother and father and Mala. The wet wood hissed. Dhara's skin prickled again.

"Just so." Mala inclined her head. "I will finish the tale."

The yogi took a sip from the wooden bowl next to her. "Once revived, the Aryas showed the ancient sages more respect. The Sakya clan even offered Kapila a hermitage in their sacred grove and asked him for teachings. Irascible Kapila was bemused by the gesture. After all, he could easily lose his temper and reduce the whole tribe to cinders again. Still, the Sakyas' devotion to the dharma pleased him, and he stayed and taught many generations of their children.

"When it was time for him to leave, the aging Kapila made a prophecy. 'You Sakyas will become a great people. One day a scion of your royal house will become the age's greatest warrior and conquer the world, and your clan will endure for a hundred generations.'"

Mala had not said "prince." A scion could be a girl.

Dhara sucked in a breath. She wanted to jump out of her skin with excitement. "Behave like a princess," her mother would often scold. "The blood of the Sakyan clan's royal house runs in your veins." She held back. But could it be...? No. Yet, perhaps...

Dhara had dreams of glory. Her father had insisted she train with the boys as soon as she could hold a little wooden sword. Her mother disapproved, but her father said she must learn a warrior's ways so she could defend her birth clan against these very Sakyas, who were closely related to the Kolis but who behaved like enemies, stealing Koli women, challenging the borders, and claiming Koli lands by marriage. She glanced at him. Dandapani was staring intently at Mala, who looked straight at Dhara. The woman's haunted gaze pierced her to the marrow.

The yogi looked away and began to speak again. "Grateful for the prediction of such a rosy future, the Sakyas named their thriving city Kapilavastu in their beloved guru's honor. The old sage renounced every worldly possession and set off on the road to Varanasi, in search of death. He trudged a long way before he suddenly stopped. What if the prophesied prince didn't choose the warrior's path?"

Mala paused again. The fire had burned to embers. Dhara stared into the glowing red, letting the heat and smoke sting her eyes to tears as she breathed out. Prophesied prince. She cringed with angry embarrassment. She had dared imagine herself as a princess, leading a vast army and conquering powerful foes. She had even envisioned ruling the vanquished according to royal dharma so that even the gods would praise her justice, mercy, and devotion.

Prophesied prince. She should have known. She felt a fool, as if the whole village could see her secret dream. It was not something she had wanted even her heart's sister to know. She huddled closer to Sakhi, who gave her a quizzical look and squeezed her hand.

"What would happen if he chose the path of wisdom instead?" Mala continued, very softly. The trees bowed closer in another gust of wind, as if they, too, listened. "Kapila gazed at the threads of Time's loom, and saw that if the Sakyan prince renounced his royal heritage he would become the greatest sage of all time, a buddha, an awakened one, and show the way to conquer death itself. Conquer death! The old man trembled at the thought.

"But should the prince choose the way of a sage, the clan would have no strong king to lead them to greatness, and their enemies would wipe them from the face of the earth."

A world without the troublesome Sakyas was perfectly agreeable to many Kolis, despite the generations of intermarriage. A few sitting around the fire smiled and nodded with satisfaction, and the flames nodded with them in the night wind.

But an odd unease settled just below Dhara's heart, a place where she sensed the truth of Mala's tale but was afraid to look too closely. Then the thought struck her. What if there was a princess? A warrior princess who would lead the clan, while her prince bestowed his wisdom on his people?

"Kapila pondered whether to return to warn his spiritual children in Kapilavastu of this danger. After all, they had treated him well. On the other hand, he was old, hundreds of years old. What did it matter to him if a son of the Sakyas defeated death? He simply wanted to surrender to it. He wanted to die in the holy city Varanasi, Lord Shiva's dwelling place. For to die in the Great God's Shining City meant liberation from endless rebirths into this dream full of suffering that mortals call life."

There was a pause when the wind died, and the fire burned silently. It was so quiet that they could hear the distant splashing of the river in its rocky bed. The clan held its breath.

Then Mala continued. "A passing eagle heard Kapila's thoughts. 'I will take your message to them, Holy One,' the eagle said, dipping a wing in salute.

"Kapila shrugged. 'Bah. I doubt they'll listen,' he replied. Then he turned west toward Varanasi and continued on his way."

The villagers let out a collective sigh. They stood and bowed over joined palms and murmured their thanks to the yogi for such a fine tale, then they gathered up their sleepy children and dispersed to their homes. Dhara waited until almost everyone had gone, wishing desperately to speak to the yogi but not knowing what to say. Then her father took her hand and led her back to the chief's hall.

ॐ

In her room, Dhara lay wide awake and restless after the yogi's tale while Sakhi fell asleep under the skins piled over the bed. Princess Dhara. The vision would not go away.

Early in the morning, after a sleepless night, Dhara elbowed Sakhi awake and persuaded her to get dressed. They tiptoed through the sleeping hall and scurried to the top of the village's single, rutted road, where they hid in the bushes at the spot where the road split into two trails: one trail leading to the steep terraces, stubbled and brown after the harvest; the other disappearing into the thick pine forest, above which vast snowfields reflected the morning sun.

As they'd expected, Mala appeared. Sturdy staff in one hand and heavy sack slung over her other shoulder, she strode away from the village, upright in spite of her burden, her muscular arms and legs glistening with sweat even though fall chilled the air. She stopped.

Dhara followed the yogi's gaze to the forest's edge, a little higher on the path. Her father Dandapani was there, his best bow and a quiver full of arrows over his shoulder. How had Dhara not noticed him? She shrank against Sakhi, who was staring with wide eyes.

"You might need this," he said as he stepped down to Mala and unslung the weapon from his shoulder. They faced each other on the path so Dhara could see them in profile but not the expressions on their faces. He handed the bow and quiver to the yogi, put his palms together, and giving a slight bow, walked away.

Dhara ducked down until her father passed. Then she glanced back at Mala, who looked directly into the shrubbery where Dhara and Sakhi hid.

Once again, Mala's eyes pierced Dhara. The suffering in them took her breath away. She could not imagine what would cause such terrible grief. Behind the grief, a cruel fire glinted in those eyes. Dhara knew it would burn her if she got too close to it.

But oh, it might be worth the pain.

ABOUT THE AUTHOR

While pursuing a black belt in Tae Kwon Do with her son, Shelley Schanfield became fascinated with the Buddhist roots of the martial arts. By profession a librarian, she immersed herself in research about the time, place, and spiritual traditions, including yoga, that 2500 years ago produced Prince Siddhartha, who became the Buddha. The stories of the Buddha's first women followers inspired her to write The Tigress and the Yogi, the first novel in a trilogy focusing on their struggles.

Shelley lives in Ann Arbor, Michigan, with her husband and two cats. She hung up her black belt to practice Iyengar yoga. Both disciplines have enriched her world and the world of her novels.